MISSING THE MARK

By

Brook Lynn Dorcent

Cover by Morris Publishing

Unless otherwise indicated, all Scripture quotations are taken from the New International Version of the Bible.

ISBN-978-0-615-37636-3 for printed version
Library of Congress Cataloging-in-Publication Data
2010908317 for printed version

FOR INFORMATION CONTACT
Brook Lynn Dorcent
brooklynndorcent@gmail.com
www.brooklynndorcent.com

Books by Brook Lynn Dorcent

The Mark Series

Missing the Mark (Novel one)
Pressing Toward the Mark (Novel two)
Forgetting Those Things…(Novel three)

Devotional

Spirit Over Will

For Mom, Always in our Hearts

Brethren, I count not myself to have apprehended: but this one thing I do, forgetting those things which are behind and reaching forth unto those things which are before, I press toward the mark for the prize of the high calling in God in Christ Jesus. Philippians 3:13-14 KJV

Acknowledgements

To Tammy and my sister, Tiffany, thank you for reading the very rough and unfinished manuscript. Your first impressions were very meaningful and motivated me to continue this journey. Danielle, you are on another level. Thank you for your input, support and words of encouragement. Mother Sharon, thank you for your words of encouragement. They were a big help to me. Darlene, thank you for letting me know that the manuscript was a page-turner as you read it on the treadmill! Toshiba, thanks for leaving no stone unturned. Thank you for being a sounding board. I appreciate you. I look forward to your writing future. Donna, your last minute editing skills were invaluable. Your responses to the book were so alive. Thank you for sometimes forgetting the characters weren't real. I'm glad they stirred up emotion in you. I love you. Elyse, you're so good. Thanks for reading my book and all your savvy tech support. Love you. Carrol, God knows how to bring good people into our life. I am so blessed to have you in mine. Thank you for reading and editing my manuscript. Most of all, thank you for never allowing me to give up my pursuit. I love you! My childhood friends, Lisa and James, y'all know I love you! You were the first to listen to all my stories. To my sister, Nicole, you are my biggest fan. Thanks for believing in me. I love you with all my heart. I'm looking forward to reading what God has instilled in you. To my parents, I love you. Thank you for your love and support. My children, Mommy truly loves you. Thank you for overhearing the conversations of the book and taking interest. It meant the world to me. My husband, Jacques, thank you for listening to the entire storyline before I wrote one sentence. The excitement and interest in your eyes, said "Go for it!" Or, as you say, "Do it!" Well honey, I did. I love you. To my Pastor, Bishop Rosie S. O'neal, I'm usually speechless in your presence and in awe of the blessings upon your life. Thank you for your love, guidance and support. Thank you for telling me that my writings are too important to be hidden. Most of all, thank you for being a wonderful example of the INCREDIBLE. I love you. Last, but certainly not least, I saved the best for last, my God, my wonderful Lord and Savior, Jesus Christ. You are the ultimate author/writer. There is none greater. I am so blessed to walk in your footsteps in this capacity. It is an honor and gives me great joy to minister and serve your people in this way. Lord, I thank you and love you.

The Call

Life for Lily Rose almost couldn't get any better. She enjoyed a quiet romantic dinner with the love of her life. Michael Carraway, Christian, compassionate, focused, accomplished, and sexy; he was all she wanted and more.

The hardwood floors of his new empty condo served as both table and chair. Lily and Michael shared their day over sweet and sour chicken. However, the conversation didn't compare to the warm glow in his eyes, the curve of his smile, and the brush of his hand against her face. He leaned in and kissed her sweetly. Oh yeah, she loved this man.

In his eyes, she saw her future. She was wrapped in a form-fitting wedding gown. The sound of the organ accompanied her entrance into the grand church. He waited for her with the biggest grin she'd ever seen. *God, he was beautiful.*

Lily just knew she heard wedding bells. "Baby, your phone's ringing." Michael's snapping fingers lifted Lily out of the wedding trance.

She recognized the number on her cell phone. Her heart raced. "Hello, this is Lily Rose. Mr. Peter, yes, I'm doing well, and you? I was very impressed with your firm. It's just that I still haven't talked it over with my fian…"

She paused then, looked at the man she loved. Correcting herself, she explained, "I mean boyfriend. I promise I'll get back with you soon."

Curious, Michael raised his eyebrows. "Baby, what haven't you talked over with me?"

Trying to sound indifferent, Lily responded, "Michael I've been offered a position at Williams, Wright, and Wilson."

"Are you serious?" Michael blurted out. "Lily, that's one of the best law firms in the country." The grand smile on his face was quickly replaced with furrowed brows. "Hey, aren't they located in Georgia?" he asked.

"Yes. Atlanta."

"Are you considering moving away? We just got settled from graduate school."

7

Trying to convince him, she responded, "Of course not. But you gotta admit; it is a great offer."

Michael thought, *Then when was she going to tell me about it?* It didn't make sense. She wasn't considering it. Yet, she hadn't turned it down. He stood and stuffed his hands into the pockets of his slacks.

Lily could see that Michael was confused or annoyed; she wasn't sure which. Standing before him, the top of her forehead met his firm chest. "Michael, they will pay for me to take the Bar exam there. I've already passed it in New York and New Jersey. They've offered me a competitive salary along with a company house and car. This is a chance of a lifetime. I couldn't just say, 'Thanks, but no thanks.' If nothing else, I need to pray about it."

Michael threw the questions at her faster than she could comprehend them. "Why aren't we praying about it together? Why am I hearing about this from a phone call? Is there a chance you would accept and leave?"

Holding her head down, she stared at his socks and slowly replied, "No."

The more he listened to Lily, the more he doubted her. He knew he shouldn't say anymore. He needed time to think. "Goodnight, Lily."

Lily's eyes widened and her head snapped up. "Oh, am I dismissed Mr. Carraway? Isn't that typical, Michael. Why can't we talk about this?"

He stared into her deep brown eyes.

"Michael, I thought we were on our way to marriage, but you can't even communicate with me."

Sadness and disappointment flavored the air. Michael pointed out calmly as he stepped into his shoes, "We should have talked when you first got the offer. I don't know if I wanna be married to a woman that can't come to me with major decisions. I'll walk you to your car."

Picking up her shoes and purse by the door, Lily stepped into the hallway. "Michael, don't bother. I know the way to my car." Before Michael could catch the door, it slammed in his face.

The timing of the offer was awful. Michael didn't want to be selfish, but the truth was; he didn't want Lily to even consider accepting it. He pulled the two-carat diamond ring from his pocket. He had bought it over a month ago. It was important to him that Lily had a fantasy proposal. Now, he wished he had proposed long ago.

The leftover Chinese take-out across the checkerboard picnic blanket stared at him. *What just happened? How did we go from the perfect evening to finding out that my future wife may be leaving me?* The thought deeply troubled him. He silently prayed. *Lord, please help Lily and me make it to the altar.*

No Rest Tonight

Welcomed by the two-story extravagant building in Central Islip, Long Island, Lily was relieved to be home.

A handsome couple cuddled on the couch. Her parents were watching the weather report. A storm was brewing in Miami, Florida. Lily's Aunt Floreece lived there.

She rushed into her sanctuary and slammed the door. The sound alerted them to Lily's presence. Her father and pastor turned his salt and pepper head towards the sound. Jokingly, he said, "You working on breaking that door. You got some money to fix it?"

Her thoughts were with Michael. The look on Lily's face informed Mother Rose that Lily and Michael had had a disagreement. It must have been a serious one. Mother Rose knew exactly what the problem was. Michael found out about the job offer in Georgia. Rescuing Lily from her husband's crazy antics, Mother Rose asserted, "Desmond, leave the girl alone. Can't you see she's tired?"

Pastor Rose continued to tease Lily. Extending his eyebrows, he asked, "Tired from doing what? She ain't got no job. Last I heard she was having dinner at Michael's. I hope that was all she was having, just dinner."

Mother Rose laughed. After thirty years of marriage, her husband still made her laugh. Lily didn't have it in her to say anything. Normally, she would play along. Tonight, she didn't want to participate in the game. All she could say was, "Goodnight."

Lily slowly mounted the spiral staircase. At the top of it, she listened, "Hey, Michael, hold on. She just walked in." Her cousin Vaughn was in Lily's room and had answered the phone.

Lily asked, "Vaughn, what are you doing in here?" Vaughn lifted the new coat. Lily understood that she intended to borrow it.

Wrapped in a terrycloth robe, Vaughn sat on Lily's bed, waved her matching fuzzy slippers and listened to Michael. She could tell by the sound of his voice that Lily had a story. Vaughn wanted to hear every juicy detail.

Lily took the receiver from Vaughn. "Yeah, I made it home safely. Goodnight, Michael." That was it; she hung up before Michael could say another word. She knew it was childish, but it was her way of getting him back for dismissing her earlier.

Too mentally exhausted to strip off her soft leather jacket, Lily plopped down onto the red plush chair. Tension rising in her shoulders, she threw her head back and closed her eyes. "Vaughn, I just bought that coat, and *I* haven't worn it."

Vaughn waved her hand as she placed the coat neatly across the bed. "That ain't never stopped me before. You know I ain't sittin' here to talk about no coat. So tell a sister...what's wrong?"

"Michael and I had a fight." There, she said it. Now maybe Vaughn would back off. She knew she wouldn't.

Vaughn sat straight up and uncrossed her legs. "Girl, I can see that. Tell me something I don't know. Was it about the offer in Georgia?"

"Yep."

"Ok, so did you tell him you were holding out for his marriage proposal, and if he didn't give you one, you were going to accept the offer?"

"Before we could talk about it, he sent me on my way. He said he couldn't believe I would consider moving away. Then, he had the nerve to tell me he wasn't sure he wanted to marry somebody that can't communicate with him on important decisions."

Vaughn grunted. "Well, he didn't hold back none. If you ask me, you're the one holding back. Michael could have proposed a long time ago. Dang, you've been with the man eight years. If he doesn't know if he wants to marry you by now, then he'll never know. I mean come on already."

Vaughn stood and continued her argument. "Look at you. You graduated from Yale Law School at the top of your class. You've had numerous job offers. This one is the best yet. Here you are holding out on some man you've been with for eight years. Eight years! The least he could do is give you a ring to let you know he is committed to you. Don't get me wrong; I like

Michael." Vaughn's lips curved in a sexy smile. "Lily, any woman would be glad to have him, with his fine self."

Lily smiled and pointed at her cousin. "Hold up now; that's my man!"

"Is he, Lily? Is he *your* man? What is he waiting for? I feel like he's dangling you along, waving a carrot in your face. It ain't no diamond carat, either. Lily, if I were you, I would accept that offer. I think Michael made that decision for you, by not making you his wife."

Vaughn draped the coat over her arm and approached the door. She looked back at her cousin and smiled. "Honey, don't worry. If Michael loves you, I mean really loves you, there ain't no way he'll let you go anywhere." Vaughn curved her pretty pink lips. "Well, there is one place he'll let you go."

Lily perked up and eagerly asked, "Where?"

"Down the aisle to meet him, girl."

With smiles on their faces and doubt in their minds, they both hoped that were true.

Lily's evening went from feeling totally connected to Michael, to complete confusion. Staring out of the window, she prayed, "Lord, what am I supposed to do? I love Michael so much. I've been waiting for his proposal for so long. Yet, this job offer seems too good to be true."

Would she stay and demand Michael to marry her or leave and start the career that most people only dream of? When the sun smiled through the white lace curtains, she awoke. She was still seated in the red chair and still, no answer from the Lord.

Your Move

The green Acura Legend swerved in and out of the Manhattan traffic.

"Michael, I understand you're upset with Lily, but I wanna live. Will you slow down man?"

Michael maneuvered around an angry yellow cab as he proclaimed, "Kyle, I know you are not talking about my driving, when you drive like you're half crazy." He quickly changed lanes, got around a crawling truck, and almost nicked a bicycling messenger. Michael waved at the messenger as a sign of apology. He received a sign too - the finger.

Kyle lifted his brow. "Yeah, but I'm a pro. You can't drive to begin with. Man, don't start doing tricks now." Kyle braced himself, gripped his seat just in case Michael wouldn't take his advice.

Michael shook his head at his brother. Kyle, Michael's fraternal twin, rode into the city with Michael each morning. Kyle was just as handsome as his brother. The two had the same bronze skin tone, great bone structure, firm build, and six-foot height. Kyle, however, was the smooth talker and flashy dresser.

Michael picked up, "Man, can you believe she would even consider going to Georgia? Her answer should have been flat out, *No*. Now that I have this job, I can give her the life she deserves. It's time for us to be married, not considering separating."

Kyle studied his brother's face. He had an opinion but he wasn't sure Michael wanted to hear it. He listened to the radio and sang along. The song bought back a pleasant memory. The current lady in his life danced out of her clothes last night to that very tune. "Oh, I think I'm ready for you, baby!"

"Kyle, what did you say?"

Popping back into the moment, Kyle jumped. "Huh?"

"Kyle, listen to me. Am I being unreasonable?"

"Oh, well, yeah man, you are." Kyle was honest to a fault.

Michael punched through the yellow light just before it turned red. At that time, he wasn't able to embrace truth. Pointing toward himself, he raised his voice. "What? I'm being unreasonable?"

"And you're deaf, too. I said yep the first time."

"Kyle, can you be serious for a moment? We're talking about my future here."

"I hear you, man. What about Lily's future? Why do you think she worked so hard in school? I think she should think about it."

Breathing deeply, Michael conceded, "I know it's a great opportunity, but why didn't she come to me right away? I really don't like the way I found out about it."

Kyle shrugged and answered, "Maybe she was confused and didn't tell you right off the bat because she was afraid of your reaction." Kyle shifted his focus to the tall city buildings that protruded into crispy clouds. Winter was approaching.

Michael listened as he calculated zipping through the next light. He reconsidered and stopped. Pedestrians flooded the walkway, squeezing through while brushing his vehicle with their coats, briefcases and swinging arms. He realized, "Fear is no reason for Lily not to come to me." On green, he sped down the next two blocks, pulled over to the curb. "Get out of my car, Kyle." Michael's tone was stern.

"What?"

"We're here, 34th and 6th Avenue."

Kyle laughed. "Oh man, I thought you were kicking *me* out."

"Very funny."

Grabbing his bag from the back seat, Kyle exited the car. Just before closing the door, he warned, "Michael, if you really love Lily, have an open mind about this. Don't try to hold her back."

"Yeah, yeah man."

"Oh, Michael, if Sparrow Electronics goes to 51 ½, do you wanna sell some shares?"

"I don't know. Call me later, Mr. Stockbroker."

"Cool man. Pray the market is up today. Peace."

"Peace, bro."

Speeding up the block towards the parking garage, Michael thought Kyle made a good point. He certainly didn't want to stand in the way of Lily's dreams. He loved her. Then again, he thought, *Should I listen to Kyle? He rarely attends church these days. Does he even have a prayer life?*

The cherry on the sundae was that Kyle was seeing a stripper, whom he liked to call a professional exotic dancer. It was all the same to Michael. The woman took off her clothes in front of strangers for a living. *Oh no! Kyle is not someone I should be taking advice from, even if the advice sounds right to me.*

That day was the first time in twelve weeks that Michael had to drag himself into work. He dreaded entering the elaborate building. His office was on the forty-eight floor and as he stepped onto the elevator, Lily held his thoughts. With each rising floor, his heart sank deeper. "Snap out of it," he whispered to himself when he stepped off.

Sea-blue carpet, the open reception area, and Clara, the receptionist, welcomed him with their usual greeting. Clara licked her lips. *God, this man is fine.*

"Morning, Clara. Are you enjoying the fall weather?"

Clara grinned. She was cute. Her large brown eyes were her strong point. They matched her mocha plump face and short black curly hair. "This is my kind of weather. I slept with my windows up. The fresh breeze kept me glued to the sheets."

"I know the feeling." Michael forced a laughed and walked on.

Leaving the huge semi-circle reception desk, he headed down the hallway. More sea-blue, silver streaked carpet connected with his designer shoes when he stepped into his office, which felt more like home than his condo. The rich blue colors comforted him.

He neatly hung his jacket in the closet and inhaled the smell of fresh coffee. First things first, Michael retrieved his coffee from the small round glass table and made his way to the drawing board laced with fresh drawing paper. He rested the coffee mug, rolled up the sleeves of his burgundy monogrammed shirt and attempted to address the business at hand.

His first assignment was challenging. His team was responsible for designing the new mini-mall in the Metrotech area of downtown Brooklyn. Michael slowly sipped the steaming black

15

liquid, but that didn't relax his mind. He tried closing his eyes, hoping to get a clearer view. The picture was clear. The pretty picture was of Lily.

Coffee and concentration was not going to help him get through the day. He oscillated in his chair so the skyline of Manhattan met his vision as he wanly sighed. "Ms. Rose, I love you, but the ball is in your court. You hung up on me last night."

Coming Clean

It was eleven in the morning before Lily let herself come down for a small bite to eat. The voice of *Sheila Summer*, leading gospel artist, filled the kitchen. It was more like Mother Rose's voice. She sang louder than the woman on the CD.

Any other time, Lily would have joined in with her mother. Today, she wished for an empty house to mope around in. She sat down at the wooden country table still wearing her clothes from yesterday.

Lily looked at her smiling mother. The 54-year-old brown sugar woman could have easily passed for forty. Her skin was radiant. She didn't own one wrinkle. Lily hoped she would look that good at that age. Her mother often told her that the secret was to remain meek and humble. God beautifies from within; His reflection shows outwardly.

"Good morning, sleepy head. You want some bacon and eggs?"

Lily didn't feel like eating until she smelled the food. "Come on girl; don't act like you don't want some breakfast."

Lily's lips slightly curved. "I'll have some. I am a little hungry."

With a chuckle Mother Rose affirmed, "I know you are. I'll fix you a plate."

She knew it was only a matter of time before her mother would ask about Michael. She didn't feel like discussing the argument. *Did we have an argument?* She wasn't sure what transpired between her and Michael the night before. Hoping to remove the spotlight off herself, she asked, "Mom, did Dad leave already?"

"Um hum, there is an eleven o' clock meeting with the musicians. They are incorporating new worship music in the Sunday morning service." Thrilled that her husband was out of the house, Mother Rose happily served Lily a savory breakfast with a side of truth. "Lily, I thought you were going to turn that position down."

"Mom, I never said that."

"I know my child. Lily, you were excited to receive the offer, but I know good and well, you didn't want to take it. You wanna know what I believe?"

Lily knew, but she didn't want to hear it. "Sure, Mom, what?"

"Girl, don't take that sarcastic tone with me!" Mother Rose sat next to Lily and took a sip of her green tea. "You and little Miss Vaughn cooked up a scheme to con Michael into proposing. However, things didn't work out the way you planned."

Lily looked stunned as she laid her fork aside. "Mom, that is not true."

Mother Rose waved her arms. "Girl, come clean with me on this one."

Lily exhaled. She could never pull one over on her mother; no one could. "Alright Mom, I was shocked and honored to receive such an offer. I don't want to leave Michael. Vaughn suggested that I give him an ultimatum. Either he proposes, or I take the opportunity of a lifetime. But, I couldn't bring myself to actually give him the ultimatum. Mr. Peter called in the middle of our dinner, and Michael and I were completely caught off guard. He had no idea."

"Honey, you ain't tellin' me something I don't already know. What I *don't* know is why you didn't turn Mr. Peter down."

"Because Mom, I don't know if I want to. I'm afraid that maybe if Michael doesn't propose, I should accept. I gotta think about my life."

"Big decisions like this should be made under prayer and direct leadership of God, not if Plan A fails, then off to Plan B."

Lily wouldn't let those words soak in.

Mother Rose sighed. "Baby, I have to get to church. Eat your breakfast and get some rest. Then get you some good prayer in; meditate on it." She kissed Lily's forehead on her way out.

Lily played with the scrambled eggs, believing with her whole heart, if Michael truly loved her, he would propose. It was time. She wasn't going to wait any longer. Considering it all, it took Lily a while to recognize her mother yelling from the front door.

"Lily, pick up the kitchen phone!"

"Ma, who is it? If it's Michael, I don't want to talk to him."

Mother Rose's reply was a slammed door.

Reluctantly, Lily answered, "Hello?"

"Hey, girl."

"Oh, Vaughn, it's you."

Vaughn laughed as she strutted in Lily's maxi coat in mid-town Manhattan. She loved the slender A-line, as it showed off her curves.

"Oh, it's you? Is that how you talk to your favorite sister-cousin? Listen, I just called 'cause I wanna know, did you talk to Michael yet?"

"Mom just gave me the third degree. I'm not up to round two."

"Girl, please, women in your mother's day waited for a man. We can't do that now. The one thing you know, I know, is how to get a man."

Lily knew that was true. Vaughn got just about any man she set her sights on - single, married, divorced, old or young. Vaughn had honey in her veins. Lily reminded Vaughn, "No offense, but you don't keep a man very long. There was one that almost got you to the altar."

Vaughn warned, "Lily, let's not go there. The truth is most men bore me, but if I find one with good credit and a healthy bank account, he might keep my interest." She chuckled.

Lily agreed, "That may be true."

"Lily, listen and stop stressing. Michael loves you. I know you see it every time he looks at you."

Lily's heart began to warm. She did see it, but more importantly, she knew it. Michael loved everything about her; her sharp mind, her heart to serve God, and her soul. Caving in, Lily sighed and asked, "Alright, Vaughn, what do you suggest?"

Confidently, Vaughn declared, "If you had listened to me the first time and had given him the ultimatum, you wouldn't be in this situation."

"Vaughn, do you have a suggestion? If you don't, I'm hanging up."

Lily started to nibble on a piece of bacon that was left on the kitchen counter. "Hold your horses. Girl, go up to your room, find something hot and sexy to wear, do your hair and makeup, and then go talk to your man."

Sucking her teeth, she repeated, "That's it? Look for something hot and sexy, and go talk to my man?"

Vaughn shivered as she stood outside of the deli. "Girl, sometimes I think you can be a little naive." Vaughn thought for a second and rephrased, "I know you can be naïve. So let me break this down...when Michael sees you, he's gonna start to realize what he'll be losing. Make sure it's tight so it shows the curves. Let him know you ain't never gonna have a honeymoon, if he doesn't propose."

"Vaughn you're crazy," Lily laughed.

"Maybe so, but this will work. I know he wants you, in every way. He's a man and you're a beautiful woman."

The thought of teasing Michael sounded like fun. He had cautioned Lily not to tease him. He was a man after all, even if he was a Christian man. He told her that being around her sometimes made his blood steam. She thought that it was time to bring on the heat. "Alright girl, I'll give it a shot. Thanks for the tip."

Forgetting her surroundings, Vaughn shouted into the phone, "It's time to start planning a wedding!" A big burly man, missing his front teeth smiled and winked at her. He held the door to the deli opened, and expressed, "If you're gettin' married, you're breakin' my heart." Vaughn made a humorous face of fear as she trailed in.

Let the Games Begin

Lily felt very uncomfortable in the hot pink form-fitting suit she selected. Too much male attention was Vaughn's territory. She was glad she had a long coat for cover as the train doors welcomed her to 34th Street. When she stepped onto the platform in tall black sling backs, she worried that Michael might be in the field today.

Lily didn't know if she could pull it off. She had teased Michael only once in undergraduate school. When things almost went too far, she regretted it. She vowed to remain a virgin until marriage. She just didn't know when that marriage was going to take place.

She wanted to get on the returning train and go home. The sound of screeching metal tempted her. But she also wanted to see Michael. She hated when they argued, which was rare.

"Hello, may I help you?" Clara recognized Lily, although they never met. She looked just like her picture in Michael's office.

Lily recognized the pretty round faced receptionist. Michael had described her to Lily. She seemed sweet and sad at the same time. "Yes, I'm here to see Michael Carraway."

"Do you have an appointment?" *I know you don't and Michael's not here, ha!*

Lily shook her head and Clara informed her that Michael was not in and offered to take a message. When Lily stated her name, Clara smiled. One thing she could tell was a woman on the verge of patching up a fight with her man. Her face screamed; *I miss my man.* "Lily Rose? Wow, two beautiful flowers in one. Are you his girlfriend?"

Disappointed Michael was out; she answered unenthusiastically.

Clara introduced herself, and led Lily to Michael's office. Michael was soon on his way back. As they walked, Clara chatted, "Michael talks about you all the time."

Lily didn't doubt Michael made it clear that he was involved with someone special - another reason why she loved him. Any and everywhere they went together, he let it be known that she was his. And if he didn't say it verbally, it was the way he touched her gently that revealed his care and consideration for her. So why weren't they married yet? She could not peg the answer to the question that nagged at the seam of her womanhood.

Lily noted that the office suite was filled with attractive professional women and she wondered would she soon be taking on the role as a professional attorney.

Michael's exquisite office reflected elegance and precision. Lily forgot Clara was standing there as she walked around observing the space.

"Lily, can I hang up your coat for you?"

"Oh…sure. Clara, I'm sorry, I've never seen his office. I really like it."

Clara remarked, "It's definitely a reflection of Michael's character."

How would she know his character? Michael just started working here. Lily forced the jealous thoughts aside as she slipped out of her coat.

She's got the perfect body and here I am with these extra twenty pounds.

Lily noticed the expression on Clara's face. She wondered, *is the hot pink too loud?*

Clara took her coat and told Lily to maker herself comfortable.

Michael entered his office just as Clara was leaving. She was startled when she saw him on the other side of the door. "Oh, Michael…. Hi, Lily's here."

His voice rose as he looked passed Clara. "Lily?"

"I'll leave you two alone." Clara slipped away.

Whoa-Man! Good googly moogly! She looked good. The glow in his eyes caught Lily off guard. She stood with her hands pressed together. She hadn't worn that suit since undergrad. It was good back then, and now she looked even better with her few added pounds. The fabric fell upon her skin like raindrops into a puddle. He was enjoying the rippling effect it had upon her shapely figure.

Wanting a full view of her bottom, Michael wished she would turn around. He tilted his head and smiled. The front view of her legs was pretty good.

He stood by the door with Lily in the middle of the office. "Baby, I wasn't expecting you."

"I didn't call, but I know we need to talk."

"I tried that last night. You hung up on me, remember?"

"Michael, I'm sorry. Let's not forget you threw me out of your apartment. Which is something you often do when you…"

She didn't want to finish her statement. She didn't come to argue. A taste of honeymoon is what she wanted to give him. Instead, she put him on the defensive.

"When I what, Lily?"

Changing her tune, she walked to the small leather couch behind her. He got his wish. Her bottom was wonderfully shaped and drifting in all the right directions. Taking a seat on the couch, she patted for him to come join her.

Woman, why do you torture me? He struggled with the first step.

Lily noticed his hesitation. "What's wrong Michael?"

You look like a delectable dessert. Michael wanted to run. No, he wanted to lock the door of his office and peel her clothes off. *Good God, help a brotha.*

Cautiously, he approached her sweetness. He sat away from her. The distance soon became non-existent. Sliding slowly next to him, Lily interlaced her fingers with Michael's. Seduction was not one of her strong points. She realized she had not prepared what she would say. A legally trained professional, Lily could make a very convincing argument with or without words. With her free hand, she lifted his chin to her. "Michael, I couldn't sleep last night. When I finally fell asleep, I dreamed about you."

What is she saying? He couldn't focus. He was getting lost in her scent. All he saw were soft lips whispering empty words. "Michael, I want the reality." Lily's hand ran smoothly along the back of his neck. Her breath was warm against his skin. His blood began to boil.

She whispered in his ear, "Michael, I want to be your woman, wife and your lover." For every word she spoke, she added a kiss upon his neck, his ear, his cheek, and finally, his lips. Drawn by her touch, he turned to her. They kissed passionately, igniting fires deep within them.

Lily was seduced by her own plan of seduction, and Michael was lost in it. His hands went to work. She didn't know how her jacket had been removed, or when he had lost his shirt. Lily didn't care. His bare skin against hers was all she felt. It was all she wanted to feel.

"My skirt is too tight."

"What?"

"My skirt is too tight. Baby, help me get out of this skirt."

Michael felt like he was being awakened from a hypnotic trance. "What…"

"I said help me…"

"Baby, I heard you."

Lily stood before him in her bra, skirt and stocking feet. *She really wants to do this.*

"Lily, do you want to lose your virginity in my office? Anyone can walk in, at any time."

Reality set in, as the tears stung and fell from her eyes. "That's not why I came here. Michael, I know it's not what we've planned. I know you don't want me like this."

"What? I'm a second away from ripping that skirt off of you."

Standing in front of her, he comforted her with his embrace. "Baby, I want you like this, and in a whole lot of other ways, too. But this isn't legal. I'm sorry, I shouldn't have let things go this far."

Lily felt guilty that she set him up. She set them both up.

Should I knock? Clara thought to herself. Lily hadn't left yet. She wondered if Michael was the type of man that would get busy in the middle of the day. He had only been employed with the firm only a short while.

Let's see what kind of man you are Michael. She smiled to herself as she swung the door open. Clara's eyes lit up and her smile broadened. *Uh oh! I see he's my kind of man.*

Michael almost fainted when he turned and saw Clara standing there. Lily's heart was beating so fast against Michael's chest; he thought she might be slipping into cardiac arrest. She buried her face into the soft chest hairs. Her nervous breath inhaled his cologne. If one could die from embarrassment, Lily was about to drop dead.

Michael was annoyed that Clara still held the door open. "Clara, excuse us. Whatever it is, give me a minute. I'll be right with you."

From the looks of things, you need more than a minute. Lily's shoes and jacket were scattered on one side of the room. His suit jacket, shirt and tie, were on the other. *Boy things must have gotten buck wild up in there.* Clara smiled mischievously. *If you wanted privacy, you should have locked the door.* "Michael, I'm sorry to interrupt your afternoon snack. Sharon asked me to drop off these plans and memo," Clara playfully apologized.

Lily trembled in his arms. Furious that Clara was having so much fun with the scenario, he snapped, "Just put them on my desk and leave!" She left the plans on his desk and his door wide open.

Michael turned when he didn't hear the door close. His voice rose ten octaves. "I can't believe she left the door open like that." He dashed for it like he was trying to catch a fly ball. He missed and stood face-to-face with Sharon, his boss. He shook his head. *Things can't get any worse.*

Sharon stepped into his office. "Michael, why are you half dressed?" She saw the back of the young lady with the messy hair. Lily hurriedly put on her jacket.

Sharon's question was answered. Michael, embarrassed, knew he was a black man that turned fire engine red. He humbly apologized, "Sharon, please forgive me." Walking her towards Lily, he introduced them, "Sharon, this is my girlfriend, Lily." Lily extended an unsteady hand.

A thunderous roar filled the room. It was Sharon's laughter. Michael stared at her as if she had two heads. When Sharon finally caught her breath, she spoke, "Lily, it's a pleasure to meet you, even under this uncomfortable circumstance."

Lily croaked, "It's a pleasure to meet you as well." Sharon explained, "Look, I'm no fool. I know what was going on in this office."

Michael interjected, "Sharon, we did not have sex in here." He didn't want a rumor to begin that he was having sex in his office. However, Clara probably had sent out a massive email by now.

Sharon thought the situation was hilarious. She and her husband had had some pretty wild times in her office, which was twice the size of Michael's. However, they were in charge, and she didn't want the other executives following suit.

25

"Michael, she's more beautiful in person. I can see how you can lose sight of your surroundings. However, I can't allow you to get it on in here."

"I know. Trust me; it will never happen again."

Suddenly, he felt a draft. Still without a shirt, he reached for it. Sharon backed away to the door. "Nice meeting you, Lily. I have an appointment to get to. Michael, get back to me on those plans tomorrow."

Michael reassembled his shirt and tie. With raised eyebrows, he whistled, "Baby, you better go."

Lily answered, "You don't think I know that? Oh God, I am so embarrassed." Her face fell in her hands. "What was I thinking?"

"That's the problem; we weren't. Baby, I told you before, don't tease me. Don't you know what you do to me? Don't you know how I feel about you? I'm a disciplined man. You know that. Otherwise, you would not be a virgin."

Lily stepped into her shoes and collected her coat. "Michael, what I do to you, you do the same to me. I was feeling things in this room that I never felt before. For the record, I wasn't going to stop."

She wasn't going to stop? That didn't sound like his steadfast and unmovable Lily. After all, she was a flesh and blood woman deeply in love. He was going to have to marry her and soon.

She smiled, remembering the moment. "I guess my skirt saved us." They both laughed aloud.

Michael's eyes washed over her. "Yeah baby, it *is* something else. Girl, you better get out of here before I change my mind."

He followed Lily as she walked to the door. Brushing his lips against hers, he whispered, "I'll drive out to your house tonight so we can really talk. Ain't nothing gonna happen in your daddy's house."

She flashed her pearly whites in agreement. "I know that's right."

Speechless

The Chrysler 300M glided down the Southern State Parkway toward the Belt Parkway. Mother Rose thought traffic was a bit heavy for high noon. She wished she had insisted Lily attend the daily worship and prayer service. Lily was acting out of character. *Listening to Vaughn for guidance?* She prayed aloud, "Oh Lord, please help my girls."

The "Son" was shining on Victory Ministries, a multi-million dollar church in Brooklyn. With prayer and careful consideration Mother Rose and her husband, the pastor, decided to build in the area. However, because of the drugs, prostitution and violence there, some of their members questioned their decision. Mother and Pastor Rose considered their reasoning as upscale. It was no secret to them that Christ was the lily in the valley. It was quite elementary to them; Christ wasn't leaving the area and neither were they.

The lobby of the sanctuary was outstanding to say the least. Covered in cream marbled floors, it was inviting. Mother Rose hurried to the elevator toward the prayer wing on the east side of the building. In these quarters were two large prayer rooms. Corporate prayer was held in the sanctuary twice a week. But, it was in the daily prayer rooms where she witnessed much healing and deliverance.

A fragile hand tapped her on the shoulder as she reached for the doorknob of the prayer room. A silver haired lady smiled at her. Mother Rose pecked the elderly lady on the cheek. "Mother Daniels, how are you?"

Mother Daniels spoke slowly while extending a yellow sticky note to Mother Rose. "I brought you this message since I was on my way down to the prayer room. I knew 'zactly where you'd be." Mother Rose read it. *Call Flo, URGENT.* She thanked Mother Daniels and exhaled. "I guess I better call her right back."

"Alright baby, I'm gonna get me some prayer and meditation in," Mother Daniels said. "I'll see you later."

Rushing to her office in the west wing, Mother Rose quickly dialed. Flo answered on the first ring. She barely had the phone pressed to her ear when she heard her sister's hello. "Flo, what's wrong?"

"Vie, I need to come stay with y'all a couple weeks."

"Why, what's wrong?"

Flo rolled her eyes. *Why couldn't she just say come? Why the fifty questions?* She knew why. Flo's life was a constant mess. She was on her second husband, Roosta. Flo was determined to make it work. She had to. This was her second chance to prove she was good.

Flo had a six-year-old daughter now. She never forgave herself for leaving Vaughn and her son, Ollie.

Mother Rose impatiently demanded, "Come on Flo; tell me what's wrong!"

Flo thought she might as well expose the drama. Her sister was the only one she could talk to. With no other choice, she divulged, "Alright, alright. I got into a fight with one of Roosta's women again."

"A fight? A physical fight?"

"You ever known me to have any other kind?" That was true. Flo was always fighting some man or woman.

"What happened?"

"Vie, you ain't gone believe this one. This chick came to my house. You hear me? My house! And, demanded I give Roosta a divorce, sayin' he's her man, and the reason he won't leave me is because I won't give him a divorce. I told that bitty to get the hell out my house!"

Flo was shouting and Mother Rose pulled the receiver from her ear. Flo continued, "She said she ain't goin' nowhere 'til I get on the phone and call a lawyer. Well, you know I slapped the crap out of her. Fo' I knew it, we were rollin' round on my kitchen floor."

Flo was right. She couldn't believe this one. Mother Rose just listened. "When Roosta got home that night, he saw the scratches on my face. And when I told him what happened, do you know what he said?"

I have not a clue. "What did he say?"

"He laughed and said, 'Keisha is a trip.'" Flo was heated. "Seven years of marriage, and he don't even care! He ain't got no

28

shame about his mess. If he had his way, he would have all three of us in the bed together."

Mother Rose knew Flo's analysis was accurate. Unfortunately, that was the problem. Roosta always got his way with Flo.

"Violet, can I come? I need to get away. Vie, please?"

"Of course, Flo. You know you are always welcome. How's my niece?"

"Lexi is fine."

Mother Rose knew the visit would be brief. Roosta would come to New York and sweet talk Flo back into the pit. It was the pitiful pattern they lived by.

"When are you coming?"

Without hesitation, she said, "Tonight."

Wow! She wasn't expecting that answer. "What time does your flight get in?"

Mother Rose got the rest of the particulars from her sister and hurried home. She was going to have to cook and get to the airport by five. She knew Vaughn would not be happy to see her mother. When she entered her kitchen, she looked toward the ceiling. "More drama. Please Lord, help bring peace between Vaughn and her mother."

A Taste of Home

"Does this house grow? Every time I see it, it looks larger and larger." Flo teased.

Floreece Jenkins was forty-five and she looked it. Years of living the street life had caught up with her. She was still pretty. However, the lines around her eyes and mouth were forming.

Mother Rose laughed. She missed Flo's sense of humor. "Stop it, girl. This house is the same size it has always been."

Flo turned around to wander the living room. "This furniture ain't the same. Look at yo' black sectional." She sashayed her way over to the sofa. "Whoa, let me take a load off." Flo fell down into the plush leather.

Mother Rose flipped a lever on the side.

"Whew! Girl, this is a reclining sectional? I can rest my butt and my feet." They laughed.

"Mom, Mom can I take a load off? Can I rest my feet?" Alexis, Flo's six year old, climbed onto her mother's lap. The caramel oval-faced little girl was excited to be on vacation when her classmates were in school.

"I knew I heard voices! Auntie Flo, Lexi!" Lily squealed as she pranced down the spiraled stairs.

Lily knelt and gave her plump little cousin a squeeze. "Ohhhhhhhh, Lexi I am happy to see you. Wow, don't you look pretty. I like your black and white dress."

Rubbing the little girl's hair, she added, "And look, black and white beads on your long braids to match. You've got style girl."

The precious little girl proudly nodded. "Yep, that's what Mommy tells me." She threw her little head back, and her beads clapped together. Laughter filled the room.

Flo cackled, "Lexi, you too much. Just like your Mama." Flo's voice became stern as she chastised Lily. "You ain't gave me my hug yet. You want me to tear your hind parts up, don't you?"

Lily smiled anticipating the embrace. Lily's aunt gave the best hugs. They were like being wrapped in warm cinnamon rolls. "Auntie Flo, I'm sorry." They enjoyed an affectionate embrace.

When Flo released her, Lily admired Flo's sassy short haircut. "I always loved your red hair. It looks good on you."

"Thanks, baby girl."

Pastor Desmond Rose arrived home from work just in time for the reunion. Is that Floreece?" With the mad rush of preparing for Flo's arrival, Mother Rose didn't have time to tell her husband of their house guests.

Flo turned towards the front door. "Des, man, look at you. Come on over here and give me some love."

Hugging Flo, Pastor Rose exclaimed, "My favorite sister-in-law!"

"That's right. I'm your only sister-in-law"

"That's why you're the favorite." He chuckled.

Kneeling, he said, "Look-a-here, Ms. Lexi. How are you?"

"I'm fine Uncle Desi." He lifted one of her long braids. "Give me these braids. You see I'm losing my hair. Let me have 'em."

She inquired innocently, "Uncle Desi, then what am I going to have?"

"You're young; they'll grow back. At my age, it just keeps falling out. See." He pointed to the small bald spot in the center of his head and continued to plead, "Come on Ms. Lexi. Help me out. You know you're my favorite niece."

Mother Rose put in, "Don't let Vaughn hear you say that."

"I know that's right," Flo agreed. "Where's my eldest daughter anyway?"

"I don't think she's home yet. Her car isn't outside," Pastor Rose answered.

Mother Rose extended her soft hand to assist her husband up.

The aroma wafted from the kitchen, into Flo's senses. "Girl, what have you cooked? It smells good."

"Beef stew and some home made biscuits."

Flo wanted to eat. She started moving in the direction of the scent.

"Shouldn't we wait for Vaughn?" Mother Rose suggested.

Flo turned not sure how to answer that one.

Lily decided she should give Vaughn a heads up that her mother was in town. "Why don't ya'll go ahead and eat," she said. I'll wait for Vaughn."

Flo nodded. She was nervous about seeing her daughter. She hoped Vaughn would give her a chance. If they couldn't have a mother-daughter relationship, maybe they could at least become friends.

Why is She Here?

Lily was checking her email when Vaughn finally walked into her room at eight that evening. Her speech was swift. "Girl, I got your message. Why did you want me to come straight to your room? I thought it had to be about what happened with you and Michael today. So tell a sister? What happened? Was it hot and heavy?"

"Vaughn, slow down. That's not why I left you a message."

Confused, she sat on Lily's bed and waited for it. The expression in Lily's eyes told her before Lily said, "Vaughn, your mother is here."

A shock wave sliced through her body. Vaughn always had mixed feelings concerning her mother. The little girl within wanted to climb onto her mother's lap. But she wasn't a little girl. No need for her mother in her life now. She spat out in disgust, "How many black eyes does she have?"

"What, Vaughn?"

"Lily, let's be real. The only time my mother rushes to New York is when Roosta has kicked her butt. She's running for cover."

Lily could feel her pain. Sympathetically, she pleaded, "Vaughn, be fair. That's still your mother."

"Lily, again, be real. How many black eyes?"

Keeping it real, she sighed and told the pitiful truth, "No black eyes. She's got scratches along the left side of her face."

Vaughn screeched. "Scratches? What is Roosta, a cat now?"

"Roosta didn't do it? Mom said she got into a fight with one of Roosta's women."

Vaughn sighed as she stared at her navy suede boots. "Then, it's like I said, Roosta did it." Vaughn started towards the door.

Lily called, "Where are you going? I waited up for you so we could eat together."

"I just lost my appetite. I'm going to bed."

This was going to be one long visit. Lily dined alone in anticipation of Michael's visit.

Selflessly

Refreshed from prayer, Lily rested on the couch. At eleven o' clock, Michael's headlights flashed through the picture window of the family room. To prevent the doorbell from ringing, she waited for him in the doorway.

Still dressed in his work clothes, Michael held Lily and whispered, "Baby, I'm sorry that I'm late. I forgot to tell you; I had dinner plans with my father." He stepped inside and peaked around. "Is everyone asleep?"

She whispered back, "Yes, and we don't have to whisper."

He smiled and extended a single long-stemmed red rose to her. Pressing his lips upon hers, he said, "I missed you."

Lily was swept off her feet. Michael never acted this way in her parent's home. She thought he was acting like this because he knew everyone was in bed. A smile worked its way from her heart to her lips. "Michael, I love you." She led him by his firm hand to the sofa.

Without hesitation, he urged her to tell him exactly what was in her heart. He wanted to know why she had not come to him when she first received the job offer.

A light flashed in her mind. Now she understood him. He had every right to be angry. She should have told him right away. "Michael, please forgive me. I'm sorry. I was confused. I'm not sure of your intentions."

"My intentions?" Now, he was confused.

"Michael, you have had this job for three months. Why haven't you proposed? I wasn't sure if you were going to. So if you weren't, I needed to start making other plans for my future."

He didn't know how to tell her that he had purchased a ring and that he was trying to come up with a fantasy proposal for her. Actions speak louder than words. He pulled the ring from his slacks.

She threw her hands over mouth as her eyes enlarged. "Oh my God! It's beautiful!" *He's going to do it now. Thank you, God.*

"Lily, I purchased this ring over a month ago. I was trying to come up with the perfect proposal, something you would always remember. I knew you were expecting it, so I tried to keep it quiet and hopefully surprise you."

Lily could see the love in Michael's eyes. *I feel so stupid, all my scheming and planning for nothing.* Her eyes filled with shameful tears.

His voice was cracking as he broke the news. "Lily, from what you've told me. This job offer is a chance of a lifetime. I can't let you turn it down."

"Michael, what are you saying? You're going to move to Atlanta?"

"No baby, you know I can't."

"Then what? Get married and live apart?"

He didn't realize he was still holding the ring. Lily was staring at it. "Lily, what happened in my office today proved to me I can't take another long distance relationship. I can't be apart from you."

Lily's head was spinning and her heart was racing. "Tell me Michael. What are you saying?" He sighed deeply. "I'm saying, I won't hold you back. One day you may hate me for it. I want you to go."

She felt a painful jab in her chest. She was almost at the point of collapse. Her voice was a hoarse whisper, "If I were your wife, you wouldn't say this to me. You wouldn't let me go."

He whispered back, "You're not my wife."

Those words stung in the very core of her being. Trembling, she stood. He stood. The emotions between them were powerful. They didn't know what to do.

Lily began pounding his chest. She was yelling, and she didn't care who heard. "Michael, you never loved me. You never loved me. Eight years I waited for you, eight years!" She wept loudly.

Shouts and sobs pulled Mother and Pastor Rose from their bed. The two looked like twins dressed in forest green flannel pajamas, a conservative gift from Lily. With her hand against her husband's chest, she prevented him from descending the stairs. "Desi, wait, that's Lily and Michael."

Pastor Rose exclaimed, "Oh let's sit on the stairs and listen! Sounds serious."

Mother Rose placed her hands on her hips. Lifting her eyebrow, she gave her husband the, I-can't-believe-you look. "Oh, Vie, you don't want to eavesdrop?"

She pushed him back and sat on the top step. Pastor Rose quickly joined her. Chuckling in her ear, he whispered, "You are one nosey woman."

"Me? Pastor Rose, keep calling me names and we won't finish what you were trying to start just a few minutes ago."

The, I-can't-believe-you look returned. "What I was trying to start? Woman, you are too much, with your fresh self."

Mother Rose tried to stifle her laugh. "Am I too fresh for ya?"

Pastor Rose loved his wife's face aglow in nightlight. "Never. As a matter of fact, I want to go back to our room and get fresh wit cha."

Mother Rose waved him off. "You hear that? I think Michael is crying, too."

Michael pulled Lily close to him. He *was* crying. "Baby, don't say that. Don't. I love you more than myself." He cried and held her for what seemed like an eternity. Still, it wasn't long enough.

Family Meeting

Mother and Pastor Rose held one another at the top of the stairs until Michael left. "Vie, Lily's still crying. Should we pretend that we didn't hear anything and just go back to bed?"

"No, I think you should go talk to Lily."

A door creaked. Flo stuck her scarf-wrapped head out of the guestroom. She complained, "I wish one of you would do something, so the rest of us can get some sleep."

Pastor Rose volunteered, "I'll go talk to her."

Watery eyes met Pastor Rose's concerned ones. "I wondered when and if y'all were coming down," Lily said.

36

Pastor Rose looked surprised. "You heard us?" Her voice was shaky, as she told him, "Of course, y'all have never been very good eavesdroppers. Eavesdroppers are supposed to be quiet."

Pastor Rose sat next to his daughter. While looking over his shoulder, Pastor Rose told her "That's cuz your mother talks too much." It was funny, but Lily couldn't laugh.

"I heard that," Mother Rose cried from the top step.

Lily yelled back, "Mom, just come down. I know you can hear us. And you, too, Auntie Flo!" Flo ran to grab her robe.

They looked like they were dressed for a sleepwear commercial, especially Flo. She wore pale pink satin pajamas with a matching robe. Lily studied her family. "We're missing one."

Vaughn called from the top of the stairs, "Here I am." She glided down wearing a flowing black velvet robe. It pleased Flo to see her daughter for the first time since her visit, although Vaughn never looked at her when she said, "Flo, how's Lexi?"

The coldness in Vaughn's voice hurt, and still, Flo responded pleasantly, "She's fine, asleep upstairs."

Mother Rose commented quickly, "Kids can sleep through anything." She wanted to keep the attention on Lily. Eventually, Flo and Vaughn would have it out. Mother Rose asked Lily what had happened.

Lily's tears continued to fall as she explained, "Michael said he wants me to go. If I pass up an offer this good, one day I would hate him for it."

Vaughn replied, "He makes a good point." Flo nodded. Vaughn didn't notice her mother agreeing with her.

Lily looked to her father for guidance. "If Michael truly loves me, he wouldn't say that. He would marry me. Do you know he already bought a ring?" She didn't wait for his answer as she gave her own, "Maybe he doesn't want to get married, and this is his way out."

Pastor Rose put a strong arm around his daughter. He said firmly, yet calmly, "Lily, that's not necessarily true. Maybe he loves you enough to let you go."

Vaughn rolled her eyes and grunted. "Eight years of waiting on a man and he loves you enough to let you go. Ain't that a kick in the head?"

Mother Rose gave Vaughn a look that said don't say another word. Vaughn took heed to the warning.

Flo wanted to know. "Lily, what are you going to do?"

Lily shrugged. "I'm going. What else? I see no reason not to."

Mother Rose looked concerned. She was ticked too. She had advised Lily earlier to pray about it. "Lily, is this the answer you received from God?"

"Mom, the way things have played out, I'm taking it as that's what God wants me to do."

Mother Rose sighed. "Lily, please give it more thought and really pray about it."

"I'm twenty-five years old. I've got to move on."

Her mind made up, she stood and climbed the stairs as her heart ached. She would never be the wife of Michael Carraway after all. The reality devastated her. At least, she still had her law degree. She intended to make good use of it.

Lily fell to her knees and rested her head on the bed. Sobbing into her pillow, she cried, "Oh God, I can't believe this. I waited so long."

Did I do the Right Thing?

Michael listened to the messages when he arrived to an empty home. The only one was from his analytical, extremely intelligent, non-Christian father.

Dr. Carraway attended church with his wife only on special occasions. After she died, he had no use for it. He let his boys continue going to church because they loved it and Pastor Rose so much. He actually couldn't understand God. How did he let his precious Belle die? She was young, beautiful and vibrant. He thought the death of his wife proved what he believed all along; there was no divine help.

Michael's father advised Michael at dinner that night; *Lily would regret rejecting an attractive offer. In life, you don't have anything but your own power and knowledge. Make a logical decision.*

That rang over again in Michael's ears.

Believing that was true did not take away the painful sting in his heart. He moved from the dim bedroom to the adjoining bathroom. Michael was missing a part of himself. It was evident as he faced the mirror and searched the unknown reflection. He gripped the sink in wonderment. *How would life be without Lily?* His mind floated back to when he realized she was the most wonderful person he had ever met.

Michael met 20-year-old Rebecca Stokes when he was only 17 years old. He called her Becky and convinced himself that she was the woman of his dreams. After his mother's death, his father spent more and more time at the hospital, and less time with him. Becky was a musical breath of air. Her melody seemed to soothe his soul.

Michael spent most afternoons at her little studio apartment. It was like hanging out at the candy store. He heard eating too much candy could give him a cavity, but for what he was enjoying, he welcomed a whole mouth full.

Becky told him one afternoon during a heavy petting session, "If we keep foolin' around, we gonna slip and have sex. You ready for that?"

Shocked at her directness, but too proud to show it, he announced, "I'm not afraid. I can be responsible."

She smiled, threw her long Latina tresses to the side and pointed mischievously at the condom on the little coffee table. "You know what to do with that?"

Even at 17, he felt ashamed she'd been the one to purchase the protection. "How much did you spend?" He had no clue about those things.

Cute, she really thought he was cute. Mature for his age, he helped her feminine needs. One, he was a virgin, so chances were he was safe. Two, she enjoyed the idea of teaching him the ropes. "I can afford it. Now do want me to teach you how..." She lowered her lashes and reached over.

His palms begin to sweat. He tried to remember the scriptures he learned in church about his body being a temple. But he couldn't, his body didn't want to be a temple at the moment. She slid her hand over his manhood. He yielded to whatever she demanded of him.

That was the first of many times that Becky taught him the ropes. Michael was certain what he felt for her was love. So when his father started hounding him about his grades, staying out too late, doing his chores and talking back, he moved out.

Kyle tried to warn him that he was making a mistake. But he couldn't tell Michael why it was a mistake. So Michael showed up with his bags at Becky's doorstep. Yet, she didn't answer. A man with sleep-red eyes stood in the doorway wearing only lose fitting navy sweat pants. "What you want?"

Buff, the man was a sure comparison to Arnold Schwarzenegger. His body and whisky breath terrified Michael. "Uh...is Becky home?"

"Beck, yo Beck! Some kid out here for you."

Becky stumbled to the door. A tiny little thing next to buff man, she ducked under his arm and lied, "Oh, this is the kid I told you about. I'm tutoring him."

Michael failed to hide his fearful devastation, his eyes filled with painful tears. "Who are you?" Michael whispered to him.

The guy jacked Michael up by his little white Polo shirt and flung spit into his face. "You bangin' my wife?"

Michael lied and violently shook his head until it hurt. He remembered that he wet his pants. "No...no sir...it's, it's just I've never seen you before."

Becky's husband let Michael down with barreled laugh. "Calm down, lil' man. I'm just playin' wit you. You want a cookie or somethin'?"

Becky jumped in, "Michael, this is my husband. Remember I told you he's in the military?" She slowly squinted, prompting him to play along.

Michael nodded yes - another lie. "Anyway," Becky continued, "we'll pick up next week. That's if you want to."

Michael knew he'd never want to see Becky again. Nevertheless, he'd miss and would never forget her.

Committing adultery at the age of 17 was the least of his problems. Michael's father wouldn't let him come home. Having no where else to turn, Michael ran crying to Pastor Rose. Finally Dr. Carraway agreed to let him come home, **if** he earned his keep. The arrangement; Michael cleaned the church a couple days a week after school. It was a great deal which afforded him the opportunity to get to know Lily.

She was everything Becky wasn't - smart, pure and honest. He cried and shared his heartache with Lily. Although she didn't understand, she listened and prayed with him. Most of all, she didn't judge him.

They soon began organizing church events together, youth programs, sporting events and amusement trips. They were a working team. He liked her a lot, but he couldn't tell if he was just a friend to her. A year later, after one of Lily's school debates, Michael walked her to her American Government class. She stopped in the stairwell and pointed out, "This is your last year of high school. I'm going to really miss you."

Michael nodded and realized her beauty. Her hair pulled back into a single ponytail enabled him to see just how striking her large brown eyes were. They searched his face and without any indication, she pressed her lips upon his. Sparks radiated in both of them as they dropped their school bags and dived into the kiss.

Their first kiss was also Lily's first. It didn't appear to be, for she showed him such passion. It was apparent to him at that very moment; Lily was passion. Whatever she did, she did it wholeheartedly and with purpose. That kiss had fulfilled her purpose. From it, he knew; Lily Rose not only liked him, she loved him. And he loved her.

No More Stopping

Ten days rolled by without any communication between Lily and Michael. She worked frantically preparing for her move to Georgia. Mr. Peter sent her the address of her new home. She mailed all her clothing, shoes, personal items, law books and laptop. He was kind enough to make sure someone was at her new home to receive the items.

A two-story, three-bedroom house with a large backyard and an in-ground pool was too much for Lily. The firm was being more than generous. Mr. Peter assumed her boyfriend of eight years would join her. They wanted to woo Lily with the best they had to offer.

Lily decided as soon as she was settled, she would find a smaller place. There was no need for that much space without anyone to share it with. Giving her room a quick glance over, she was basically ready to go. A few toiletries and some treasured family photos was all she needed.

She retrieved her college scrapbook from the almost empty closet. A picture of her and Michael at her graduation fell to the floor. She bent to pick it up. Lily observed herself in a cap and gown. Michael looked quite handsome in his navy suit. She remembered the words he whispered as he kissed her cheek. "Baby, as soon as I am done with graduate school, I am making you Mrs. Michael Carraway." The thought made tears fall onto the photo.

She raised her head at the sound of the creaking door. *Am I dreaming?* Through sniffling tears, she asked, "Michael, what are you doing here?"

He saw Lily kneeling and crying. He rushed toward her. "Are you alright?"

Lily was furious. She didn't want to see Michael. She refused his calls and ignored his emails. Now here he was, in her bedroom.

"Michael, why don't you leave me alone?"

He ignored the request and tried to help Lily to her bare feet. Lily shoved him away. "I don't need your help. Get off of me."

Uncaringly, Lily threw the scrapbook and graduation photo to the bed.

Michael picked it up and looked at it. The expression on Michael's face revealed he, too, remembered his own words. He sighed and placed the photo neatly on her night table. To resist the urge to hold her, he shoved his hands into his jacket.

Lily fell into a chair as she spat the words at him, "Didn't Vaughn tell you I was OK? I have a lot to do. Contrary to want you may think, I don't sit around here crying all day."

Truth is, I cry half the day.

Oh God, this is hard. Michael knew he made the best decision for Lily. It was a decision that was tearing them apart physically, mentally and emotionally. *Was my father right about this?*

Michael didn't want to be logical at this very moment when his precious Lily was hurting and he was the culprit.

He walked calmly and knelt before her. Taking her hands in his, he confessed, "Baby, this is very difficult for me. I don't want you to leave hurting like this."

He was choking up again. It angered him. He didn't want to cry anymore. He fiercely pulled her face to his, kissed her hungrily.

Likewise, she responded. He was out of breath when he released her. "I don't want you to go."

Lily looked into his eyes. She wanted to kiss him again. This time, she grabbed him. She kissed his lips, his cheeks, his eyes, his ears, his neck and back to his lips again.

Michael couldn't take the heat running through his veins. He threw his jacket to the floor. Lily pounced on him and they both fell to the floor.

He tried to speak but Lily kept kissing him. "Baby, stop."

She breathed deeply, "I don't want to stop. I'm tired of stopping."

Michael gently pushed Lily off of him. "Baby, if we do this, it won't change anything. I will not stand in your way."

Lily was crying as she told him, "Michael look at us. We love each other too much to separate again."

He sat up. "I know, I know. But in time, we will heal. Five years from now, things will look differently. If you don't go, you'll always wonder, what if."

Lily allowed herself to lie flat on the floor as salty tears dropped onto the plush white carpet. Her voice cracked as she demanded, "Michael leave. Don't call me anymore. Don't email me anymore. Right now, I don't want to be friends. Now get out!"

He stood, clutched his jacket and left. For ten minutes, he sat in his car, picturing Lily lying on the carpet crying. He could still feel Lily all over him and that's all he wanted, his precious Lily.

Roosta Comes to Town

Days later, Roosta finally came to collect Flo. That was a world record. Mother Rose was sure he would arrive a couple days after Flo. *That Keisha must be a trip.*

At five feet seven inches tall, Roosta wasn't an attractive man, not to Mother Rose anyway. He was white chocolate and had dreadlocks hanging to his waist. His large forehead protruded and was permanently creased with wrinkles.

Is he always upset, or is that just his face? She really didn't know. In spite of it, there was something appealing about him. In addition to being married to her sister, he had at least two other women at a time.

He walked into her home with an arm full of gifts. They were all for Alexis, his little girl. Flo always said he was good to their daughter. Flo didn't grasp that lie. *If a man ain't good to you, then he ain't good to your children.*

The family was playing a card game when Roosta bopped into the family room. The six-year-old yelled, "I win again!"

"What's my little girl winning?" Roosta adoringly asked.

Lexi jumped into her dad's arms, sending boxes flying through the air. "Dad, Dad, I kept asking Mom if you were coming. I knew you would."

He raised an eyebrow to Flo. "You did? And what did Mom say?" Holding her dad's face between her small hands, she answered, "She said you had business at home and she didn't know if you were coming." Lexi proudly announced, "But I knew you would."

Roosta smirked at his wife. "Hey, now, Flo, ain't you gonna greet your husband?" Casually dressed, he looked cool in his black pants, gray silk shirt and black suede jacket.

Mother Rose thought he might be cold; the top three buttons of his shirt were open, revealing a hairy chest. *Is he trying to impress Flo? Will she fall for it?*

Flo *was* happy to see him, and she knew that was outrageous. He was cruel to her, and yet, she missed him. "Hey Roosta," is all she said.

Lips poked out and arms folded across her chest, Mother Rose stood behind Roosta. She didn't like him. She felt he was a sorry excuse for a man. Vaughn and Lily continued to pass cards to one another, ignoring his presence.

In a stern voice, Pastor Rose spoke, "Lexi and Flo ain't the only people in this room. When you enter a room, you say hey to everyone."

"No disrespect man, no disrespect. I was just so happy to see my favorite two women here." He still carried Lexi in his arms. He walked over to shake Pastor Rose's hand. "Hey, what's up Pastor, Lily, Vaughn?"

Flatly, they responded, "Hey Roosta."

Roosta took Mother Rose's seat next to Flo. Mother Rose sat in the wicker chair by the entrance. If she knew Roosta, he was about to start some mess. She looked to the ceiling. She spoke from heart, "*Lord, here we go.*"

Roosta gave Flo his winning smile, "You look good, Flo." Flo didn't respond. She held her head down. *How can you say I look good with these scratches on my face?*

"Flo, you ready to stop playing games and come home? I need you." *That's a laugh.*

Lexi's attention was on all the presents as she tried to pile them up high. "Dad, are these all for me?"

"Yes, sweet-pea, you can open them."

Lily and Vaughn felt a fight coming on. So they went to help Lexi gather her presents. "Hey Lexi, let's take these up to my room and see what cha got," Lily suggested.

Excited, Lexi agreed, "Ok. Dad, will you be here when I get back?"

"Of course! In fact, I think we'll all be going home real soon." His temperament changed as soon as Lexi left. He demanded a response from Flo, "Woman, I asked you a question."

Flo rolled her eyes at Roosta. "I ain't going nowhere with you."

"Oh, yes you are. Damn it. You're my wife, and you are coming home. Get upstairs and start packing." He slammed his palm to the card table. "Now, Flo!"

Flo didn't flinch. That was enough. Pastor Rose wasn't going to keep silent. "Roosta, you heard the lady. She's not going anywhere. Flo is our guest, and *she* can stay as long as she likes. Banging on my furniture isn't going to change anything."

"No disrespect, Pastor. This is between a husband and a wife. Don't get involved with this."

Pastor Rose's voice was rising and getting deeper. "You're right. But y'all are in my home, so now, it's *my* business!" That was true. He told Flo about taking their business into the streets. He thought he would teach her a lesson when he got her back on his turf.

Mother Rose kept silent. However, she was laughing on the inside and it was starting to flow outwardly. Proud of her husband for standing up to Roosta, she clapped her hands. "Come on, come on. Dinner is ready. Let's go into the kitchen." She thought she would have a little fun. "Roosta, I assume you're staying for dinner? Will you be leaving us in the morning?"

He wanted to punch something, primarily Flo. "I'll leave, when my wife leaves," he answered with a phony smile.

Pastor Rose thought, *That's what you think buddy.*

I'll Kill You First

The lavender guestroom welcomed her with white and lavender lace window treatments and the deep purple carpet. Now it seemed cold to Flo as Roosta lay beside her. She gave him her back and hoped he'd go to sleep.

Roosta was fuming by the time he climbed into the king sized bed. *How dare you speak to me like that in front of your family?* "Ya know woman, you're walking a very thin line. I think you're overdue for a butt whipping. We are going home in the morning."

Flo rolled over on her side to face him. Roosta hadn't hit her in the last two years. She had him locked up the last time he did. She told him the next time he hit her, it would be the last time he did anything. She wasn't frightened when she threw her words at him, "Roosta, I told you, I ain't goin'. It ain't my home. You got your women coming up in there, demanding I divorce you. It's

47

your home! You have no respect for me. That's why those women don't respect me, either! I'm through Roosta."

Roosta rolled his eyes. *How many times do I have to hear the 'she was through speech?' You're not through, until I say you are.* He rolled over to face her. "Flo, you know the kind of man I am. I'm good to you and Lexi. You got a nice house, car and a big bank account. As long as I take care of home, I'm allowed to have as many toys to play with as I want to."

Flo couldn't believe her ears. "Toys? Women are toys to you, Roosta?"

"You're not, but Keisha ain't nothing. You and I have been married seven years now. Why can't you understand that?"

"Roosta, that ain't God's idea of marriage. One wife and a whole lot of toys..."

Roosta grabbed her face and pulled it two inches from his own. He shook her as he said, "You can't tell me nothin' about God. You know who saved you? I did. Remember where I found you, Flo? Remember?"

Flo didn't want to remember. *How stupid of me to allow you to be my savior?*

"I know you ain't forgot. I found you working in a drug house. Now, you wanna tell me about God." He pulled her wrists. "I'll tell you what God wants. He wants you to come home with me in the morning. Right now, He wants you to come over here and start acting like a wife."

She pulled away from him. "Woman, you owe me this. You're my wife. If you don't give it to me, I'll take it. I have every right." He held her down with the weight of his body. She felt powerless staring into the darkness, she prayed for deliverance. A flood of warm tears fell onto the pillow. She wasn't responsive, clearly rejected he insulted her, "See, Flo. You forgot how to be a woman. That's why I need women like Keisha. You saw her, ain't she fine?"

Flo felt like she would regurgitate. Roosta was licking her face.

"She is almost as fine as that little lady in the other room."

Who is he referring to? Trying to squirm from underneath him, she asked, "Who are you talking about?"

"Oh, you know. Vaughn! You think Vaughn knows how to be a real woman? Huh, Flo? Maybe I should find out?"

She lost control, remembering the days her stepfather raped her. Flo vowed she wouldn't let any man touch her girls. She hit him with a rushing mighty blow. The large diamond wedding ring cut Roosta across the head. The blood streaming down his head and into his eyes blinded Roosta.

Flo bounced out of bed as Roosta reached for her. Fuming, she swung her arms and yelled, "Not my baby! Not my baby! I'll kill you. I swear I'll kill you!"

"Stop it! Stop it!"

Pastor and Mother Rose ran into the bedroom and hit the light switch. Frightened, Pastor Rose's voice shook. "What in God's name is going on in here?"

Trembling, crying and screaming, Flo exploded, "He was talking about touching my Vaughn. I'll kill 'em. I'll kill 'em!"

Pastor Rose marched up to Roosta. "Not if I kill 'em first!"

Roosta held up both blood stained hands and begged, "Stop, stop please! I was just kidding. She took it the wrong way."

Mother Rose held her sister, raged, "That's nothing to joke about. From the looks of that blood running down your face, I bet you don't think it is funny now. Do ya?"

"Nah, nah, it's not funny." He held his head.

You Want Prayer?

Peace, could they get some peace in their home. Pastor Rose instructed his wife to let Flo sleep in their room. Roosta would take the sofa bed in the family room. Pastor Rose would take the guestroom.

Roosta asked, "Before you send me downstairs, can I have a first aid kit, or something?"

Pastor Rose retrieved the first aid kit and shoved it in Roosta's bloody hands. Trying to pretend he didn't have a headache, Roosta smiled at Pastor Rose and asked, "Ain't you gonna pray for me."

Not amused, Pastor Rose responded, "Look, clean up your head, and go downstairs. I need some sleep."

Roosta walked into the guest bathroom to clean and dress the wound, as he murmured, "Women are a trip. I can't believe she hit me."

Pastor Rose sat on the commode and folded his arms across his chest. He wasn't letting Roosta out of his sight.

"Sounds like you deserved it. If you would act like a man, instead of a scared little boy, she wouldn't have hit you. The only time my wife touches me is out of love."

"Really? I am not a scared little boy. I'm a man."

"That's interesting. Real men don't hit women. They don't cheat on their wives, and they don't make nasty jokes like the one you just made. Last time I checked, only punks did that."

Roosta's head was pounding, but he wouldn't show it. "Why don't you pray for my manhood?"

Pastor Rose coolly replied, "Go to bed. It's late."

"You call this late? It's only ten o'clock. You're gonna turn down a wounded man's prayer request? What kind of pastor are you?"

Pastor Rose stormed out of the guestroom mumbling, "You want prayer? You want prayer? I'll give you prayer." He knocked on his bedroom door and yelled, "Vie! Violet, hand me that blessed oil in the medicine cabinet."

Lily and Vaughn heard all the commotion in their bedrooms. Vaughn looked over and wondered how Lexi could sleep through all this. She wished she could. She had to go to work in the morning. Lily was reading the proposal for the job offer in Atlanta.

Mother Rose handed her husband a bottle of olive oil. "Desi, what's going on?"

"Roosta requested prayer."

"Is his head alright?"

"Vie, the wound is fine. His head, that's another story. You and Flo get down on your knees and start praying, right now!"

Pastor Rose jogged down the hall to Vaughn and Lily's rooms. He knocked on each door. "Girls?"

"Yes," they replied in unison. "Get down on your knees, and pray for Roosta, now!" They didn't even ask why. They would do it just to get some peace and quiet.

As he returned to the guestroom, he shouted, "I wanna hear y'all call on Jesus!"

Roosta thought it was hilarious. He had gotten under Pastor Rose's skin. That was something he could do to most people.

Roosta sat on the edge of the bed. Pastor Rose told him to stand. He was a couple inches taller than Roosta. He gently rubbed oil on Roosta's forehead, resting one hand on Roosta's heart, and one on his shoulder.

He wanted to lay hands on his head. However, he wasn't going to be cruel. He knew his head had to hurt because Flo knocked him a good one.

Muffling his laugh, he slipped into prayer mode. This was serious. *"Father, in the name of Jesus, we come before you seeking your Divine help. Rochester Jenkins has requested prayer. Lord, I don't believe he knows what he is asking. However, Father, I pray that you give him the mind of Christ. Touch his heart. Change his ways. Break the bonds that lead his soul into captivity."* Both men could hear the ladies fervently praying across and down the hall.

Pastor Rose continued, *"Lord, deliver Rochester from the hand of the enemy. Make him a new creature. He can be what you've created him to be. With you, all things are possible. Bless him now we pray. In the mighty and all powerful name, Lord, Jesus Christ, we declare it done. We love you Lord. AMEN! "*

Pastor Rose could feel the power of God. He walked out of the guestroom into the hallway waving his hands and shouting, 'Whew Jesus. Whew Jesus. Thank ya. Lord, we thank you."

Mother Rose was leaping in a long white nightgown and bare feet in praise to God.

Flo lay face down on the floor crying, "Oh Jesus, Oh Jesus. I'm sorry. I'm so sorry. Forgive me, Lord." Flo was ready to commit her life to Christ once again. This time, she hoped to stay in His divine will.

When Pastor Rose opened his eyes, he saw his girls embracing one another in the hallway. They were praising God together, "Thank you Jesus. Thank you Father."

Roosta had no idea what he asked for. He sat on the edge of the bed, tears falling onto his lap. His headache was gone, and so was his frustration for Flo. He decided to let her stay as long as she wanted. Maybe he would stay, too. He'd wait and see how things looked in the morning. During the night, he wept.

Don't Break Your Neck

Sunday morning was difficult for Lily. Intense sunrays rested on her bed, as a dark cloud suspended over her heart. She awoke and checked her email. She wanted to hear from Michael, although she requested him not to contact her. He had emailed her several times, asked her how she was doing. *How do you think I'm doing?*

The other emails were from Mr. Peter in Atlanta. He wanted to know if she needed anything. Realizing she didn't know what she needed, she picked up paper and pen and attempted to think it through. She wondered what Atlanta was like. Would working there help her forget Michael? Would she ever feel whole again? Unable to concentrate, she rested the list and read Michael's emails again. She sighed, deleted them and with a heavy heart, readied herself for church.

She walked into the sanctuary late, secretly hoping to see Michael's handsome face. Lily didn't see him, but he saw her. She was attractively dressed in a sophisticated burgundy suit. Her shoulder length shiny black hair was flowing in wavy curls.

Sounds of worship flooded the building. The music, shouts, and cries of hallelujah stirred up the Holy Spirit within her. In her sadness, she joined in and worshiped her heavenly father. Lily, a powerful and passionate worshipper needed a refreshing. She invited the music to wash over her, lifting her hands while closing her eyes. Michael watched and admired her.

Vaughn sat behind her mother, stepfather and sister in the fourth pew. Mother Rose sat on the first pew and Pastor Rose in the pulpit. Michael always sat on the second pew with Lily. That day, he sat in the balcony and Lily sat with Vaughn.

In between songs, Vaughn's smile sparkled. "Hey girl, I thought you weren't coming."

Lily flashed a bright smile also. "I can't hide forever. I missed church last Sunday."

She noticed Lily's wondering eyes. "Lily, I haven't seen him."

"Is it that obvious?"

Vaughn laughed. "Girl, you 'bout to break your neck."

"I guess he's not coming today."

Vaughn sincerely replied, "I'm sorry, but you look good. That boy don't know what he's missing."

As the worship team began singing another song, Vaughn jumped to her feet. "That's my song!" Pumping her arms, she enjoyed the song as her stylish red dress swayed. She halted when she saw Kyle enter the pew.

Cookies and Cream

Kyle had a wide smile on his face. On his arm was his new girlfriend, Sapphire, the professional exotic dancer. Vaughn had met Sapphire at Michael's condo. She didn't think Kyle could be serious about this woman.

Sapphire had golden skin. The flower bun in the center of her head accentuated high cheekbones. Her full bangs made her look younger than her thirty years. It was so obvious that her double D breasts were fake. Vaughn thought she tried to proportion her body to match her oversized butt. Vaughn had some junk in her trunk, but Sapphire's took the cake, pie and the cookies. Sapphire purposely stood next to Vaughn. Disregarding her presence, Vaughn continued to get her praise on. Sapphire knew that was not going to work. She thought, *Oh, you're gonna ignore me? We'll just see about that.*

Like old friends, Sapphire wrapped her arms around Vaughn and gave her a tight squeeze. "Hey girl," Sapphire taunted her using a high pitched voice.

Stunned, Vaughn bellowed, "Do I know you?"

"Of course, you know me. I'm Kyle's girlfriend." As if on cue, Sapphire let her floor length mahogany mink fall off her shoulders. Kyle's eyes smiled as some of the other brothers did. Her dress was silk, formfitting, sleeveless and red.

Kyle whispered in her ear and focused on her exposed cleavage as Sapphire giggled.

Vaughn rolled her eyes. The tension in her praise was noticeable. She stopped singing and bouncing.

Lily reached around Vaughn, shook Sapphire and Kyle's hands. However, that wasn't enough to end Kyle's charade. Lily pushed Vaughn aside and hugged Sapphire. Like the cream in a cookie, Lily was smooth. She placed herself in the middle of Vaughn and Sapphire and told her, "I'm glad you came to worship with us today."

Sapphire smiled. Lily thought she had perfect white teeth, better than her own. "I'm glad, too. Kyle and Michael are always talking about their great church. I wanted to come and check it out." Sapphire had never been a Christian. She had attended church on the holidays as a young child. Her memories were few and far between. Her previous boyfriend grew up in church and developed a bad taste for it. As a couple, they never went to church.

She couldn't explain it, but it felt good to be there. She liked the joyful and warm church atmosphere. She noted that at least five thousand or more people were in the building. The extremely large pulpit held a full-size band and the choir consisted of at least one hundred people. "Wow! Lily, this is a great church your father has."

Lily appreciated the comment. She politely informed Sapphire, "Oh no, this is the Lord's church. He has given my father the responsibility of watching over it."

Sapphire smiled, took her seat, placed a small peck on Kyle's ear and whispered, "Why when church people are given a compliment, they can't just say thank you? Everything belongs to the Lord." Kyle smiled, slipped his hand under his companion's dress and squeezed her thigh.

Sapphire pecked his cheek again, and this time she squeezed his knee. Lily noticed the gestures and thought, *These two are out of control.* Kyle hoped Vaughn had caught the gestures. He even told Sapphire to wear something bright. Vaughn always wore bright and fun colors. He had no idea they would both be in red.

The look on Vaughn's face told him it upset her. He wondered how she would react when he brought Sapphire to Lily's going away dinner after church. Giving Sapphire's thigh another squeeze, he smirked.

It's Too Late

On the way home from church, Roosta observed that the scratches on Flo's face were healing. It was the wounds within that remained raw. He tried to catch her eye with a smile. She noticed and looked away.

Roosta allowed Pastor Rose's words to ring over and over in his head. *God loves the man in need of a second chance.* If that were true, he wished Flo would give him a second chance. Then again, he was far from second chances with Flo. He had lost count after the second woman came to his used car lot and told him she was having his baby, for the third time.

At thirty-five, Roosta was a father of five. He had one child with Flo, three by a woman named Shay Lynn, and one by a woman whose name he couldn't remember. Now, Keisha claimed to be pregnant. He didn't really believe Keisha. She would do anything to keep him away from Flo and Lexi. However, if she was, it was probably his. How could he ask for another chance?

Since the night Flo whacked him a good one, God had yanked some mess out of him as well. He wanted a second chance. He wanted to be the husband Flo deserved. How would he accomplish that? Two weeks went by, and Flo still refused to come home. She wouldn't allow him to sleep with her in the guestroom.

After church, Flo quickly walked to the bathroom to change for the dinner party. Roosta followed her. "Roosta, can I have some privacy? I need to change."

I'm your husband. I've seen everything you got.

Flo read his thoughts. "Roosta, right now I don't feel like we are husband and wife. You have no right to be with me in this bathroom."

Flo had a cold look in her eyes. Roosta had never seen it before. Maybe it was too late. If it were, he would at least state his case and walk away. He knew he deserved a divorce.

"Flo, can we talk a minute?"

"I think we betta talk," she said.

Roosta held out his hand, escorting her to the bed. She declined and sat Indian style on the floor. So did he.

Roosta pleaded with his wife, "Flo, I'm sorry. I know that sorry don't mean nothing, but I am. I wanna change, I mean really change. I was never a drinking or smoking man. My problem is women. I love women. I know that's not right being that I have a wife. I need another chance. Desi has been praying and doing Bible study with me every day at church. It's been helping. I feel different on the inside. I'm so sorry."

He reached for her scratched face. She turned away. "Flo, come home with me. If I am going to change, I need you."

The ice in her eyes began to melt away. "Roosta, I don't know. You have never been faithful to me. Not even before we were married. I shouldn't have married you. I know God can do anything, but I find it hard to believe that you are about to change now."

He rubbed his hand across his face and felt the tender spot from Flo's smack. "I believe I can change. When we get home, I'm going to start going to church. I'm going to leave those women alone, all of them. I promise. But luv, I'm gonna need your help. I need my wife. Please come home with me."

"Roosta, I can't." Part of Flo wanted to go with Roosta. Part of her was afraid of him. She stood over her husband. He looked like a little boy in need of love. "I can't leave. I need to stay here and try to make peace with Vaughn. I don't know if Ollie will come around. I talked to him on the phone. I don't know if he'll even come today. But, if Vaughn and I are under the same roof, we might become friends."

Roosta's head fell forward and he stared at his socks. "What about Lexi? She needs to get back in school."

Flo agreed somberly, "I know. She can go back with you. You can take care of her."

Without meaning to, he raised his voice, "When will you be home? Lexi needs her mother. Vaughn's a grown woman."

She responded quietly, "A week or two, maybe more."

So You Wanna Play a Game?

After church, Vaughn jumped out of the silver Escalade, and rushed inside. Lexi imitated her big sister, and ran behind her. Mother Rose felt a breeze as Vaughn passed.

"Vaughn, are we playing a game? Why did we run to your room?"

Vaughn swiftly peeled off her dress. "Little girl, I am getting out of this dress. Can you believe that hoochie had the nerve to wear red, too? I know Kyle was behind that whole thing."

Lexi sat at Vaughn's vanity sniffing all the different fragrances. "What's a hoochie?"

She looked at her little sister. She couldn't believe she was venting to a six year old. "Oh, a hoochie? It's nothing. Forget I said it."

"Vaughn, can we play jump rope outside? It's a nice day and Auntie Vie bought me a new jump rope. Lily can play, too."

Lexi's words were buzzing tones in her ears. Vaughn frantically tossed the clothes back and forth in the closet. She needed something striking to wear for Lily's dinner party. Knowing Kyle, he would show up with that hoochie on his arm. Finally, her eye caught a slinky tan dress. The back of it was deeply scooped. *Perfect*, she thought to herself as she slipped into it.

Lexi was tugging at her dress. "How you gonna jump rope in that?"

Vaughn was confused as she pushed passed Lexi over to the black velvet jewelry box. She found a suitable necklace, a string of pearls that would sway down her bareback. "Huh?"

Lexi was annoyed with her big sister. She sucked her teeth. "I said, how are we gonna jump rope together? Your dress is so…tight."

Vaughn pleasantly smiled at herself in the full-length mirror. Kyle was going to pay for his antics in church today. She bent over to become eye level with Lexi. "Sweetie, I'm sorry, but we're having a dinner party for Lily today. I tell you what; Lily and I can turn the rope for you, and you can do all the jumping you want. OK?"

Lexi giggled. "OK, where's Lily?"

"She should be on her way soon." Satisfied with the body shaping dress, she commented, "Oh, Kyle, you are going to pay, mister."

I know

Mother and Pastor Rose changed into comfortable clothes and headed to the kitchen. Together, the two made the perfect culinary team. Most of the food was already prepared. Pastor Rose pulled the succulent turkey and prime rib from the fridge. Mother Rose put the sweet potato casserole dripping with walnuts and brown sugar into the oven.

"Desi, did you order the cake?"

Pastor Rose quietly responded, "Uh huh."

Mother Rose peeked up from the oven. "Uh huh? That uh huh means you are up to no good." She placed her hands on her full hips, and demanded, "What have you done?"

He took a step back, pretending to be appalled. "Me?"

"Man, you know you can't fool me. Spit it out."

Giving up the fight he would never win, he confessed, "I asked Michael to bring the cake."

Mother Rose gasped. "You did what? Oh, now you know Lily does not want him here."

He laughed as he prolonged the words, "I knowwwwwwww."

Mother Rose cracked up. "I like that idea. Maybe the two will cut out all this silliness. I would love to change this dinner into an engagement party."

Pastor Rose's graceful movement around the kitchen was a seasoned dance. He kissed his wife, stirred the large pot of string beans mixed with savory ham pieces, inhaled the steamy aroma and asked, "So we agree? Lily should marry Michael."

Mother Rose wrapped her arms around her husband's waist. "You look so sexy standing at this stove."

He smirked, "Cut it out woman. We've got a dinner party to prepare."

She kissed his cheek. "I knowwwwwwwwwww." They both laughed. Mother Rose continued, "Sweetness, I believe this offer *is* too good to be true. If those kids would pray about the situation, they'd know it too. I believe God has something else for Lily to do with her law degree."

Pastor Rose turned to face his wife. He kissed her forehead in agreement.

Lily entered the back door and found her parents cuddling. She often wished she and Michael would be that affectionate in their golden years. She shrugged her shoulders. *Oh well, that was a dream of the past.* Lily dropped her coat to the counter and quickly grabbed a plate.

Surprised, Mother Rose asked, "Lily, what are you doing?"

"Mom, I'm hungry."

Her mother raised an eyebrow.

"Don't look at me like that. I know you and Dad have tasted everything, so y'all are full already. But a sister is hungry." Lily packed her plate with macaroni and cheese, green salad and a biscuit.

Pastor Rose laughed as he conveniently reached into Lily's plate and took a bite of the homemade buttermilk biscuits. Mouth full, he yelled, "Now this is a good biscuit right here!" Pushing a bite size into his wife's mouth, she said, "Umm, Desi, you have out done yourself."

Pastor Rose sneaked a peek out the kitchen window. He told Michael to come through the back door. He wished he'd told him to enter through the front. *Man, Lily and her stomach.* He wondered how she stayed so small with her healthy appetite.

Saved by the bell, Pastor Rose asked Lily to answer the front door. Lily whined, "I'm not finished with my food."

Ignoring her, he added, "And take this tray of shrimp into the living room."

"Dad!" Lily stomped her foot like a ten year old. In her father's presence, she was always a little girl.

He waved her off and shoved the shrimp platter into her hands. "Oh, girl, get the door. This is your dinner party anyway."

Lily jogged to the door. Whoever it was, they were resting on the bell. When she opened the door, she saw why. Kyle had Sapphire's back pressed against it. *They're still at it.* Lily waited for Kyle to pry his lips from Sapphire's neck.

When Kyle lifted his eyes, he smiled. "Lily bug. What's up girl?"

"Kyle and Sapphire, please come in."

Sapphire threw her coat in Lily's direction. She caught it and wished she had let it hit the floor. *Why is she wearing a mink when it's sixty degrees outside?*

Sapphire looked around and nodded, impressed with the exquisite home. She liked the style, vaulted ceilings, hardwood floors, a bricked fireplace and a sizeable picture window. She beamed. "Lily, this is a lovely home." She paused and then continued, "Wait, don't tell me, this is the Lord's home, and He gave you the responsibility to watch over it."

Kyle raised his eyebrow and gave Sapphire a look that said, bad girl. She winked at him and gave him one that said, don't you know it. Lily looked between the two.

Their hormones are not going to make it through dinner.

_____

Let Me Show You Something

Vaughn called from the top of the stairs using her most smoky seductive voice, "Kyle, Sapphire I'm so glad you could make it." She glided down slowly. Tan strappy sandals crisscrossed her ankles revealing shapely legs.

Kyle's mouth dropped wide open. She had worn that same dress at their engagement party. It was a distraction for him then. He made Vaughn promise not to wear it again until after they were married. The dress was having the same effect on him now.

Vaughn sashayed towards Kyle. They stood breast to chest. Her scent aroused him, and his mouth curved into a sexy grin. She allowed her cheek to brush his. Feeling at home, she whispered, "You smell delicious."

Without effort, his voice deepened. "So do you."

The sound of his voice almost caused her to lose her balance when she turned on her heel toward Sapphire. Her bareback was in his full view. She stood with her hands on her waist. *This is what you get, bam!*

He swallowed hard, trying to keep control. Vaughn had Kyle's complete and undivided attention. He was frozen as he watched the pearls in the center of her back brush against her creamy skin. Forcing his hand into his pockets was the only way to control them. Sapphire loudly cleared her throat. Kyle didn't hear her.

Lily was amused at the look on Sapphire's face. She felt badly for the girl. Sapphire didn't stand a chance. *Why couldn't Kyle forgive Vaughn for her indiscretion and marry her?* It was obvious he was still very much in love with her. Then again, why did Vaughn have to cheat on the man? Kyle was a good man. Lily loved her cousin, even if she didn't understand her. If nothing else, she was going to enjoy the show between Kyle and Vaughn. It took her mind off Michael.

"Let's sit," Vaughn suggested, as she twisted her hips towards the sectional.

Kyle sat in the grandfather chair next to Vaughn. Sapphire sat in Kyle's lap. Lily's eyebrows lifted in disbelief. *Dang she's bold!*

Pastor Rose entered the living room with a cheese and cracker tray in hand. To his dismay, he found Sapphire wrapped neatly in Kyle's lap. Placing the tray before his guests, he reached for Kyle's hand. "It's good to see you, Kyle."

"It's good to see you too, Pastor Rose."

Pastor Rose folded his arms across his chest. "May I ask you a question?"

Kyle looked up at the distinguished gentlemen. He loved Pastor Rose, more than he loved his own father. "Sure."

"Do you have a license to be holding this young lady in your lap like that?" He firmly asked.

Kyle lowered his head in shame. Sapphire stood as she offered a freshly manicured hand to Pastor Rose. "Excuse me, Pastor. Kyle is just soooo irresistible. I can't seem to be apart from him."

Pastor Rose wasn't impressed. Actually, he felt sorry for her. "Young lady do you have a name?"

"Sapphire, Sapphire Jewels." He looked sideways. *That's a lie if I ever heard one.*

"Ms. Jewels, you are welcome in our home" He emphasized, pointing to the other chair, "Please take a seat in any one of these other chairs."

Vaughn chimed in, "Yes, no lap dancing tonight. OK, Sapphire?"

Pastor Rose shot Vaughn a look. "Vaughn, I could use your help in the kitchen."

Vaughn smirked and followed her uncle into the kitchen.

"Sapphire, did you enjoy the service?" Lily inquired, hoping it had an impact on her. Kyle should be trying to lead this woman to Christ, but Lily knew it was Sapphire that was leading him away. Kyle did not appear to be concerned about his spiritual growth. His sole reason for being in church was to get under Vaughn's skin. Considering her reaction, it worked. However, the conversation of church was now making him uncomfortable. So when the doorbell rang, he welcomed the interruption. "I'll get it, ladies."

The Prodigal Son Returns

Kyle stepped back. "Oh-my-God! Ollie, man it's good to see you. It's been so long." Ollie Sparrow could not conceal his surprise at seeing the man he thought would be married to his sister. The two exchanged another warm embrace and Kyle invited Ollie in.

Lily, ecstatic to see her cousin, ran to him. He lifted her off her feet with a bear hug. "Ollie! You came. Thank you so much. We've missed you."

"I've miss y'all, too."

When Flo heard her son's raspy voice, she rushed downstairs, loved him with blissful sobs, kissing his cheeks over and over again. It had been 10 years since she last saw him. During that time, he missed her wedding seven years ago and then Lexi's baby dedication service. He hadn't even met his little sister. "Ollie, my baby. My baby, Ollie. Oh God, thank you. Thank you Lord."

Flo's prayers had been answered; her 28-year-old baby was in her arms. Ollie couldn't understand it, but he held his mother as tears began to drift downward. Years of being separated from his family were getting to him.

Roosta came downstairs and gently pulled Flo away. Her body trembled as she held onto Roosta and cried, "Thank you, Lord. Thank you, Lord."

Mother and Pastor Rose and Vaughn hurried in after hearing the sobs; they found even Kyle and Sapphire cried. Vaughn and Ollie just stared at one another during that unreal moment. She was only 17 when she last saw her brother. Nine years later, she welcomed him with outstretched arms. He slowly walked into them and tightly held his sister. Vaughn cried until her makeup was ruined. Mother and Pastor Rose didn't wait for Vaughn to release Ollie, they just latched on. No one was sure how much time was spent hugging and crying.

When Flo got a hold of herself, she took Ollie by the hand and sat close to him on the sofa. There was awkward silence until Ollie recognized Sapphire. "Sassy, is that you?"

"Hi, Ollie, how are you?"

Kyle needed an answer. "How do you two know each other?"

The tone in Kyle's voice told Ollie that Kyle and Sapphire were more than just friends. *Is the future minister hanging out in strip clubs?* Ollie remembered Vaughn and Kyle played the cat and mouse game as kids. He gathered Sapphire didn't want anyone to know *their history.* So, he simply disclosed, "Sassy posed for a couple of paintings. She's a very good model."

The answer did not settle well with Kyle. That meant he'd seen Sapphire's jewels. Then again, a lot of other men had, too. She was a stripper. Ollie even called her by her stage name, "Sassy." The thought of other men looking at Sapphire never really bothered him, until now.

Ollie thought he'd better change the subject. "Flo, I assume this is your husband?"

Roosta stood to shake Ollie's hand. "Nice to meet you, Ollie."

With a firm hold on Roosta's hand, he said, "Nice to meet you. I hope you didn't do that to Flo's face?" Ollie pointed to Flo's healing scratches.

Roosta sighed ashamed that it was his fault. "Ollie, I ain't gone lie to ya, I didn't do it, but I'm the reason she has them." Ollie's protectiveness of Flo amazed her.

Ollie witnessed sorrow in the man's eyes. *Who am I to judge?* He never laid a hand on a woman, but he knew that he was far from perfect. "Look man, just be good to her. She's had a hard life." Ollie scanned the room for. "Hey, don't I have a little sister?"

Roosta informed Ollie, "Lexi is taking a nap upstairs."

"In that case, I'll meet her before I leave. If y'all excuse me, I need a cigarette."

Mother Rose helped Ollie find his way to the back of the house.

Girl, Don't Go Outside!

Ollie admired the transitioning sky as it transformed into a fiery red color. The mild October weather allowed him to enjoy his cigarette. Smoking for Ollie was a science. He took a long puff and slowly released the smoke. He bided his time, knowing she'd be along soon. She appeared after another long drag. "There you are. What excuse did you make?"

"I told Kyle I needed to check my schedule at work. I left my cell phone in the car."

He smiled, bringing his dimples to life. "Um hum." A work of art, he appreciated her beauty. The portrait he painted of her wrapped in red satin sheets still hung over his bed. "You look good in red. You always did." Ollie took another long puff, and made smoke rings.

Leaning on her shoulder against the house, her eyes washed over him. She loved his sexy lips, her belly jolted. The smell of the cigarette was enticing. He offered, reluctantly, she declined, "I quit three months ago."

"Really? Wow!"

He knew she was awestruck by his presence. Ollie burst out laughing.

Sapphire wrinkled her forehead. "What's so funny?"

"You are staring at me like I'm not real. Like I'm about to evaporate."

She laughed too. "I just can't believe Kyle's ex-fiancée, is my ex-boyfriend's sister."

Ollie tossed his cigarette. He inhaled Sapphire from head to toe. "Small world."

"Stop looking at me like that Ollie." Her demand was weak.

Ollie turned to face her. With skilled hands, he caressed her face. "Ah, come on girl, after all this time, you ain't over me, and I ain't over you."

Sapphire turned on her red heels. Ollie was right. If she spent one more second with him, she'd be packing her bags, moving in with him, paying his rent, all his bills, cooking his meals and cleaning his place. Oh no, she was tired of being his *Sugar Mama*.

He snatched her arm, pulled her close before she could escape. She didn't resist. They held one another's gaze. Ollie smoothly slipped one hand around her waist, whispered in her ear, "Where are you goin,' Sassy?"

"Back inside to my new boyfriend, the one with the J.O.B."

Ignoring her so-called frustration, his mouth found her neck, her spot. Soft in his arms, she moaned. He feasted, as her head reclined. Sapphire's brain shouted, run now! As always, her body betrayed her. His other hand magically disappeared inside her dress and found aroused breasts. Blinded by his expert massage, her heart raced, her skin was on fire and her eyes watered with desire. Sapphire buried her face into Ollie's neck. She sang his name through a muffled cry.

Vaughn gasped as she opened the kitchen door. "OH MY GODDDDDDDDD!"

Pastor and Mother Rose raced to the door. Ollie and Sapphire jumped apart.

I Wish You Would

The large sheet cake was getting heavier. Michael, glad to be approaching the back door of Lily's house, squinted in the darkness. *Who is Sapphire rubbing up against? It's not Kyle, because that guy is too slim.* Up close, he realized it was his old friend. "Ollie?"

"Mike? Man, it's good to see you." Ollie took the out, followed Michael inside, leaving Sapphire to trail behind them.

Vaughn blocked her entrance, stepped outside and closed the door. "Sassy, Sapphire whatever your name is, we ain't running no 'ho house."

Sapphire put her hands on her hips and rolled her neck. "Who you calling a 'ho?"

Vaughn matched her gesture. "That's what you're acting like. All over Kyle, and now all over my brother."

"You're just jealous 'cause Kyle is my man now."

"Oh, really?"

"Really."

"What is Ollie then? A paying customer?"

Sapphire reached her hand to the heavens. Flo stormed through the door and said, "I wish you would." Vaughn blinked, bemused to see her mother standing right beside her. Vaughn, like her mother, could handle herself. "Flo, I got this."

"I know that's right, cause ain't gone be no fightin' out here. Sapphire, what's the deal?"

Outnumbered, Sapphire sighed. "OK, Ollie and I lived together for three years. I just moved out six months ago. That's when I met Kyle. At first, Ollie told me to help him out, 'cause he was a struggling artist trying to get on his feet. I love Ollie and would do anything for him, but I'm tired of supporting him. The brotha needs a job."

Flo said, "I heard that, but what are you doing with Kyle?"

"I like Kyle. The problem with Kyle is; he's still stuck on you Vaughn. I'm just the rebound woman."

Vaughn felt sorry for Sapphire, she asked, "Sapphire, does Kyle know he's just the rebound man? You still want my brother."

68

Painful Goodbyes

Lily and Michael stole glances at each other all evening. As painful as it was for Michael knowing she would be leaving in the morning, it felt natural for him to be sitting with her at the table where they shared so many family meals.

He was in awe of the beautiful woman Lily had become. He even smiled without notice as he thought about their childhood. Lily and Michael were always the best of friends. Some things never change. But now he was losing his best friend. It was a relief to escape the thought as Pastor Rose entered with the cake.

Lily's eyes lit up like a Christmas tree. She exclaimed, "Oh! What kind of cake is it?" Michael clapped loudly, then, rubbed his hands together. He happily replied, "Your favorite, pineapple filling."

Kyle corrected him, "Man, that's your favorite, don't try to fool us." Everyone laughed.

Ollie lifted his glass, announced, "To Lily, the smartest female I know. And by you being offered a deal of a lifetime, proves it. All the best."

Mother Rose wanted to agree, but she couldn't shake the bad feeling in the pit of her stomach, she sighed. "Speech, Lily, the guest of honor must offer a speech."

Lily slid her chair back and it screeched against the hardwood floor. Standing, she attempted to speak without crying. "Well, if I would have known going to Atlanta would bring Ollie home, I would have left a long time ago."

The family laughed. She continued, "Seriously, Ollie, it's so good to see you. I hope when I leave you will still come around." Ollie nodded.

"Sapphire, thank you for coming. I hope you'll come to church again, soon." Sapphire smiled at the invitation. She enjoyed the service. Maybe she would attend again.

Michael admired his ex-girlfriend, the honoree of the evening in missionary mode; concerned about the salvation of Ollie and Sapphire. Her caring spirit drew him. Tightness enveloped his chest, but refused to shout, *Please don't go, Lily!* She had every right to pursue her dreams. He'd let go even if it killed him.

Lily directed her attention to Flo. "Auntie, Roosta, Lexi, I'm praying for your family. I believe a change has come over you all since you've been here. Lily smiled broadly at Vaughn. "Girl, what am I going to do without you? Who will be my fashion consultant now?"

"Girl, please, you never listen to me anyway." Rolling her eyes, Vaughn added, "Ms. Conservative."

The speech was getting harder for Lily as she was getting closer to Michael and then her parents. "Kyle, I hope to see you preaching soon."

Kyle looked at Sapphire whose attention was focused on Ollie. Ollie held her gaze. Kyle didn't know where he would soon be.

The mood at the table intensified as everyone held their breath, wondering what Lily would say to her love of eight years. She looked at Michael. In Lily's eyes, everyone and everything disappeared. Her quivering lips whispered, "Michael, I, Michael, I wanna thank you for the cake." She ran into the kitchen and out the door.

Michael stepped outside into the unusually warm night air. He found Lily seated on a wooden swing. Hands in his pockets, he slowly approached her. "May I join you?" Staring at him in the moonlight, she offered no response. He sat anyway and gazed at the stars.

Five minutes drifted by before he asked, "Lily, are you ready to go?" Flatly, she responded, "I've already accepted; I'm going."

The answer, in her eyes, revealed she wasn't ready. "Lily, that wasn't my question. Are you *ready* to go?"

"Michael, what difference does it make? First, you tell me you want me to go, and now the night before I am to leave, you ask me if I'm ready. I am sick and tired of your games."

A roller coaster of emotions drained them. He tried explaining himself, even though he was very unsure of the situation. As much as Michael valued his earthly father, he knew he should have consulted his heavenly father first. "Lily, the truth is I doubt this whole thing. Is there any way you could reconsider?" "It would be very unprofessional for me to reconsider. I've already given my word."

With a slight nod, he agreed and instantly released a gold necklace from his hand, revealing a mid-size ruby encircled in diamonds. "I brought you a gift to remember me by."

Pleased, she gasped. "Michael…you know; I will never forget you." Placing the gift around her neck, he replied, "Maybe not, but I want you to have it anyway."

Lily admired the forget-me-not as the diamonds sparkled in the moonlight. Michael slowly lifted Lily's face. His husky voice announced, "I am going to kiss you." They enjoyed a gentle kiss. The kiss ended their romantic relationship. In their hearts, they prayed it wouldn't be the last.

New Beginnings

Pastor Rose scratched his head as he circled the living room. He noticed two more large suitcases by the front door. Annoyed, he called, "Lily? Lily!"

She ran out of the kitchen wearing a beige business suit. Her hair piled in a neat bun on the back of her head. "Dad, what's up?"

"I thought you mailed all your stuff. I already put five bags in the car and here are two more."

Lily examined the luggage and frowned. "Those are not mine."

Baffled, he scratched his head again. "Then whose are these then?"

Vaughn bounced downstairs casually dressed wearing boot cut legged jeans, high heel ankle boots and a sweater. "Those are my bags," she easily announced.

"Yours?" They asked in unison.

Vaughn slipped into a butter-soft leather jacket and smiled. "Now, you know I ain't gone let my favorite cousin go to Atlanta all alone."

Pastor Rose shakily sat down. Mother Rose noticed her husband stagger as she descended the stairs. "Desi, you alright?" she asked, concerned as he reached for his wife. Mother Rose took his hand and looked at the girls. "What's going on?"

Vaughn did a little jig. "I'm going with Lily to Atlanta. I gave my notice two weeks ago and I'm ready to go."

Mother Rose's voice, soprano high, asked Lily, "Did you know about this?"

"I had no idea."

She sat next to her husband, feeling shaky too while looking distressingly at the girls. "You two are making major decisions with no thought to God. I don't have a good feeling about this."

Vaughn knelt before her concerned guardians. "Auntie, I thought it might put your mind at ease that Lily wouldn't be in Atlanta alone. We're young women. We don't have any kids, no husbands and no reason not to go. Lily has a house that is big enough for the both of us."

Mother Rose waved a warning finger at them. "Alright y'all want to have a youthful adventure, fine. Just make sure you keep a strong prayer life and find a church. Lily, you got that list of churches I gave you?"

Agitated for being treated like a school kid, she said, "Yes, Mom. We better get going; my flight's at eight."

Flo raced downstairs to wish Lily well. "Lily, wait up!" she hollered. "Come give your aunt a hug before you leave."

Lily enjoyed another cinnamon roll hug. "It was good to see you. Give Lexi a kiss for me."

Mother Rose unenthusiastically shared the news with Flo, "You better hug Vaughn goodbye. She is going with Lily."

Flo bent slightly forward. She felt as if she had been violently kicked in her womb. "Vaughn, you can't leave. I was planning to stay longer so we could spend more time together."

Vaughn looked her mother squarely in the eye. *Why is she trying so hard to be a mother now?* Years ago she dreamed of sharing time with her mother. Flo never made the time. She flatly explained, "I've already quit my job." With her back to Flo she told her, "I left a gift for Lexi on my bed. Please give it to her." She asked Lily, "Ready?"

Lily forlornly looked at Flo. "I guess we better get moving."

Free at Last

Upon arriving in Atlanta, Lily began feeling better about her decision. She looked forward to starting her career. Her heart ached for Michael, but she was living her lifelong dream as a corporate law attorney. And not just any law firm, but one of the most prestigious law firms in the country.

A black Lincoln Continental awaited her arrival for her first day at work. Exhilarated, she climbed in and smiled at Atlanta. In many ways, it reminded her of New York City - busy traffic and rushing masses of people all fighting to make the almighty dollar. In other ways, it troubled her.

Offered a deal of a lifetime, she didn't accept the offer for the money, but for the love of practicing law. Blessed with that choice, she wondered if corporate law was what she should be doing. She knew that so many people required legal services that couldn't pay for them.

Mr. Peter, a short stocky man with striking features, spent the morning introducing her to staff members, and touring the building's elaborate offices. The floors were lined in tasteful marble. Each door was made of fine mahogany wood. Paisley carpet sheltered the office floors. Crystal clear windows left uncovered drew the public into the legal world.

She felt everything the firm had to offer - power, money and strength. The firm employed over one hundred attorneys. It had four major conference rooms. Every office was covered in glass walls, except the conference rooms. Professional chefs prepared breakfast, lunch and dinner for all employees. The comfortable dining space was frequented. Two major lounge rooms complete with lazy-boy chairs and sofa beds blanketed the floors. Soothing waterfall sounds drone from the surround-sound system mounted within the ceilings. Lily knew she would enjoy working in an environment that understood the importance of resting.

The tour was long. She wished her shoes were broken in. Her feet hurt. Thankfully, Mr. Peter slowed his hurried presentation and informed Lily, "I purposely saved this gentleman last. He will be your mentor." He pointed to her left. "As you can see, your office is directly across from his."

Lily continued to walk slowly with Mr. Peter. *I know I'm fresh out of law school, but do I really need a mentor?* Mr. Peter answered her thoughts, "Lily, here at Williams, Wright and Wilson, we believe in rearing our young associates into partners. We have an image to uphold. You're in our care now. It's our responsibility that we teach you the Williams, Wright and Wilson way. Also, you are going to take on a tremendous amount of responsibility, studying for the Georgia bar and learning the basics of corporate law."

The words didn't even cause her to flinch. She maintained a 4.0 GPA in graduate school. She could handle Williams, Wright and Wilson. The confident look in Lily's eye pleased Mr. Peter. He hoped she would prove to be a productive asset.

Her mentor opened the door as if he heard their footsteps along the marbled hallway. Everyone was amazingly on point. "Lily, it gives me great pleasure to place you in the hands of Rick Parsons."

A smooth dark-chocolate hand gripped Lily's dainty one. Mr. Peter continued, "Rick, started like you 10 years ago. He was fresh out of law school. Although unlike you, he did not have to prepare and take the state bar exam." He proudly continued the introduction as if Rick were his son, "He's one of our newest partners, now. We couldn't provide you with a better mentor."

He is gorgeous. Lily's heart pumped blood faster to her brain than she could think. She continued to firmly grip Rick's hand as she admitted to him, "Mr. Parsons, it's a pleasure to meet you. I look forward to working with you." *My, My, My.* Rick reminded her of Michael. At least six feet in height and in visibly good shape; his chest bulged through his starched white shirt. He was indeed a fine chocolate brother. Lily thought she better get a grip and slowly lowered her lashes. This man was her mentor. How could she be looking at another man so soon? Especially, after an eight-year relationship with a man she was still deeply in love with.

Rick couldn't help but notice his beautiful protégé. Her eyes and smile illuminated the entire office. He gave her an inconspicuous glance over and wondered if any other woman could look that good in a black designer suit and matching pumps. Able to get a full view of her sweet face, he grinned. Her hair was pulled back, and wrapped neatly in a ball at the nape of her neck. It was clear to Rick that Lily dressed to professionally impress. *I would like an opportunity to get her in more casual attire.* He enjoyed her beauty from the neck up for now.

Mr. Peter observed the attraction between them, second guessing his decision of assigning Lily to Rick.

"Lily, I have the honor of inviting you to lunch today," Rick delightfully announced.

Lily quickly slipped back into professional mode. She felt the heat from Rick's eyes, burning a hole through her suit. The problem was she enjoyed the attention.

A graceful smile approached her lips. "That would be wonderful. Mr. Peters informed me today would be meetings, meetings and then more meetings." They all chuckled. With poise, she turned to Mr. Peters. "Will you be joining us?"

He briskly answered, "I wish I could." He really did wish he could. He knew instinctively that he should keep an eye on them. Rick was one of their best. Respectful and honorable, they never had any problems with him. Yet, he didn't like the look in Rick's eye as he observed Lily. Backing away to the door, Mr. Peter continued, "I'm already late for my next appointment. Lily, let's meet again in the morning."

Rick quickly slipped on his suit jacket. He was elated he would have Lily all to himself. Extending his arm towards the door, he invited, "Shall we, Ms. Rose?" The smile never leaving her lips, she thought, *Shall we what?*

Pull Yourself Together

Michael banged on the door of his brother's condo. Late for church, and concerned about his brother whom he hadn't seen in over two weeks, he waited for Kyle to answer. A family of four passed him in the hall. The father asked, "Everything alright?"

"Sorry about the noise."

"We don't care, but Mrs. Irene gonna call the cops on you, if you don't stop."

Michael smiled. "Thanks, I'll take my chances." Determined to break it down, if need be, Michael landed three more loud pounds on the door. "Kyle! Kyle! Come on Kyle, open the door, man!"

The locks unlatched, the door remained closed. Michael cautiously stepped in.

Kyle resembled an unshaven haggard wreck in white boxer briefs and a sleeveless t-shirt. Michael sat in the yellow leather chair next to his brother. *What is that aroma?* Michael quickly chose to sit on the loveseat. "Man, you stink!"

Kyle scratched himself. "Hello to you, too. Ain't you late for church?"

Michael pulled off his trench. "I think I'm just in time. You could use some church."

Kyle reached for his breakfast, a pint of butter pecan ice cream and packed an oversized spoonful in his mouth. "Man, I don't need church. Get out of here before you miss the word."

Michael understood what Kyle said despite the ice cream spewing out of his mouth, but he didn't know what to say to his brother. He knew he hurt over Vaughn, and his ego hurt over Sapphire, but his feelings were no excuse to throw his salvation away. He prayed in his heart, *God give me the right words.* "You still seeing Sapphire?"

"Nope." He drank melted ice cream from the container. "I don't want to see her, either."

Good, that woman is trouble. "I'm sorry I had to tell you what I saw at the dinner party. I just couldn't believe what they were doing outside, in broad daylight. You gotta pull yourself together."

"Michael, I just don't get how these women play me. Vaughn and I bought this place, and she moved in before we get married. I thought I knew Vaughn. We grew up together. I still can't believe that a couple months before our wedding I find her in bed, out cold and half naked. Plus an unused condom was next to the bed."

77

Michael rubbed his palm across his freshly shaven face. The situation baffled him and Lily. He asked Lily why Vaughn did it. Lily didn't know. Vaughn wasn't sure herself.

"I don't get it, either. Come to church with me. I thought Vaughn would make a good wife. I don't know why or how she could do that to you. As far as Sassy Sapphire is concerned, man, what do you expect? You barely know her! Come to church with me, afterward, I'm going to the youth center to play basketball with the teens. You gotta help a brotha out." He smiled trying to persuade his twin. "You know they gonna play hard."

Kyle smiled for the first time in two weeks. "I gotta shower and get dressed. You go to church and come back for me. 'Cause you right, without me, they gonna kick your butt."

It wasn't the answer Michael was hoping for, but it was a start.

Moving On

The hot steamy shower revived Kyle. He didn't realize how badly he needed a shower. He had been out of work for two weeks. He thought he showered twice during that time. Thinking back, he couldn't remember the last time he bathed. He shook his head, ashamed that he allowed women to distract him from life's basics. It was a good thing that Michael came by. He needed something to do, somewhere to go.

Church was the place he didn't want to be. Too much gossip traveled about what happened between him and Vaughn. The brothers joked that Vaughn was so fine that he couldn't satisfy her; hence, she got her groove on elsewhere. The sisters sympathized. They were overly sensitive, criticizing Vaughn, while throwing their *stuff* in his face.

At least with Sapphire, what you see is what you get. She sure did have a way of making him almost forget his emotional hang-ups.

The doorbell rang and Kyle trotted to answer it. *Michael is back too soon.* It was OK since he was ready for the physical exercise. The thought energized him. "Man, you ready to teach those little boys how to play some ball?" He frowned, stepped back, either Michael got a facelift and a boob job, or Sapphire was standing in his doorway.

Sucking his teeth, he attempted slamming the door in her face. She reached out, caught it seconds before it closed. "Kyle, wait, I wanna talk to you."

He wasn't going to let her play him again, especially with an old friend. "Girl, you are not too bright. You haven't figured it out by now? I don't want to talk to you."

Desperate to state her case, Sapphire tried to forget the night that her insides trembled from Ollie's perfect touch. She filed the thoughts deeply in her mind. In love with Ollie, and attracted to Kyle, she really didn't understand why Ollie held power over her. *I can't go back to Ollie. I deserve to be taken care of.* As she pushed passed him, she flipped her freshly done weave. She knew he let her in because he was stronger than her.

The condo was cozy. She liked the bricked walls and the tall windows. Kyle studied her. He wondered which striking ensemble waited under the mink today. Annoyed he was even thinking about her in those terms, he said, "You came to look at the apartment, or talk? Make it quick, I'm on my way out."

He wasn't going anywhere if she had her way. In her usual flair, her mink fell only to reveal a very low cut nylon black shirt. It barely covered her breast or her belly. She also wore tight blue jeans and extremely high heel black boots.

Kyle had a look of disdain on his face, because he was acquainted with the game. Vaughn played a similar number on him at Lily's dinner party. Problem. Sapphire *was* having an effect on him that he didn't want to deal with. He turned his back and walked to the window.

Disappointed that he did not respond to her the way he reacted to Vaughn, Sapphire frowned. She was just going to have to try another technique. *The damsel in distress.* She sat on the sofa and lowered her head as she told him, "I want you to know the entire story about me and Ollie." Kyle didn't turn. It appeared he wasn't even listening as he whistled. She continued, "We dated for three years. He tricked me into supporting him by using the struggling artist story. In the beginning, he painted and sold some of his work, but later he seemed to get lazy. It's true that I was a stripper when he met me. I worked part-time and I was a full-time dental student."

She rubbed her hand across her forehead, trying to rub away the memory. "Money got tight and, after a while, Ollie asked me to strip full time. That meant I had to quit school. I did it. I loved him, but he didn't do anything. Since we were living together, I suggested we get married. He didn't want to do that, either."

Kyle continued to watch the traffic below. The heavy raindrops splashed and slid down the window. He wished Vaughn were the woman in his living room explaining the past.

Receiving no encouragement from Kyle to continue, she let her voice crack. "Kyle, I'm a good woman; an ordinary woman. I do what I do to make a living, but I want the same things most women want, a husband, children, and a home." Still no reaction from him, she raised her voice. "Kyle, Ollie pushed up on me the other night! You know I had no idea he would be there. I ain't gonna lie to you, yes, there are still feelings."

Kyle turned for the first time and noticed her superficial tears. She had his attention and moved in for the kill. Sapphire walked close to him, touched his chest with the palm of her hand and fire flooded his veins. His eyes closed. *Sapphire, why do I still want you?*

She said, barely audible, "I know you still have feelings for Vaughn. We can't help what we feel, but we can move on. Kyle, can we do that? I need you, and you need me. Let me show you."

He opened his eyes drawn in by her simple, yet seductive, strip tease. With great desire and little resisternce, he went with her to the floor. Kyle knew Michael would be disappointed that he wouldn't make the game. In a spiritual snare, the only thing that mattered was the warmth and fullness of Sapphire's body. Kyle arrested all thoughts of Michael and Vaughn, and let his pain guide him to a place of ephemeral pleasure.

I See Clearly Now

Flo unwillingly returned home with her husband. Ready for sleep, she observed the king-size bed that no longer welcomed her. She still had no desire for him or their marriage after being home with him for two weeks.

They lived in peace. Roosta was becoming the husband she never had and always wanted. He was caring, helpful with Lexi, home directly after work and he prayed mornings and evenings. His sudden 180-degree turn couldn't turn away the memories of abuse and unfaithfulness. Praying for an answer from God, she didn't know if she still loved Roosta. She definitely didn't trust him.

He entered the bedroom freshly showered, and began to clumsily dress for bed. Flo watched his dreads fall around his firm youthful body as he stumbled into his underwear. How many times did she watch him do that and desire warmed her body? Strangely, she used to consider his awkwardness adorable. Flo grabbed her pillow, quickly walked toward the door.

Perplexed, Roosta asked, "Baby, where you going?"

"I will not sleep in this bed with you anymore. I'm going to the guestroom." Anger consumed her voice, and Roosta a man who wasn't afraid of anything, felt fear rising in his heart. "Flo, what are you talking about?"

He ran behind her in white boxer briefs and caught her arm in the middle of the hall. "Please, come back into the room so we can talk."

She huffed the words into his face, "I don't want to talk. I don't know what I want anymore."

Annoyed that he was doing everything he knew how to make their marriage work, he looked at the ceiling and sighed. His parents were not happily married. The best example he had so far was Mother and Pastor Rose. When he thought about it, he had become the same type of husband his father was.

In any event, he was trying. He even invited God into the picture. He felt clean and alive on the inside. He was ready for a new start. Flo wasn't giving in, not even a little.

He held her arm. "What do you want from me?" His voice, as well as his patience, was strained. He hadn't had sex in over two weeks. To some, that may not seem like much. To a man that never missed a day, it was extreme. Keisha entered his mind.

Flo noticed the blank stare on his face. "I don't know. Just because you said you're sorry doesn't erase the heartache," she answered sharply. "You can't just stick a knife in somebody's back and keep turning it and turning it. Sooner or later, they will die." She jerked her arm from his hold. "Roosta, I think I'm finally dying."

The next day, sitting in his small cluttered office, Roosta read the hundreds of emails he received while in New York. In two weeks, he still hadn't finished reading them all. *What was my partner doing while I was away? He certainly wasn't taking care of business.*

Roosta's father left him the used car business. He wasn't going to let it go under. There was a lot to be done as he prepared for venturing into selling new cars. He couldn't believe the timing of the trip to New York. Then again, it was the best thing that happened to him in his entire life.

Despite the drugs, the drama, the women and his babies' mamas, Jesus loved him totally. His love motivated him, even when Flo rejected him. Love was going to have to help him tie up all the loose ends in the office.

His eyeballs almost rolled onto his desk. There it was; the email he was waiting on. The very one that he clearly instructed his partner to address, and call him the minute it came in. After reading the reply, he missed the meeting and the opportunity. Roosta stormed out of his office, slammed the door, leaving shattering glass on floor.

He found his partner having a good time with Keisha. They stopped and felt the chill Roosta blew in. The 19-year-old girl slid off Paul's lap, exposing her hip-hugging, booty showing shorts. Roosta froze - Keisha said she was having *his* baby. Disgusted, he wondered, *Why did I even play around with a girl like Keisha?* Then he remembered, with Keisha, nothing was off limits. That was something he craved, until now.

He realized a life without limits had a price to pay. His anger turned to fear. *Oh God, what if she has HIV?* A chill went down his spine. Suddenly, the business deal, or lack thereof, seemed insignificant.

Paul and Keisha watched Roosta humbly back away. He slipped his hand inside his dress slacks, found his cell phone and dialed his new friend and confidant. A distinct voice answered, "Hello."

"Pastor Rose, it's Roosta."

All Work and Some Play

Where did the time go? It was February and Lily wasn't having any fun. She stared at the tons of paperwork on her expansive desk with great contempt. She effortlessly passed the bar exam. Yet, found that a corporate attorney's life was dull and tedious. She had Vaughn. The best legal secretary she could ask for. Rick was extremely professional and very helpful. She depended on them. And still, the work drowned her. The office phone rang. Resenting the frequent sound, she took a deep breath and answered, "Lily Rose."

A well-known voice responded, "Ms. Rose, do you have a minute for your mother?"

Calmer now, she relented, "It's good to hear your voice."

"You can hear it more often, if you called more often."

"Oh Mom," she whined.

"Don't oh Mom me, I miss my girls. How's Vaughn?"

Lily swirled in her chair and took in the cloudy sky. "You know Vaughn, vivacious as ever. She's got all the men's heads turning and loving every minute of it. I'm surprised no one has sued her for whip-lash."

Mother Rose cackled. "Oh good, you're alright. I see you haven't lost your sense of humor."

Her voice dropped as she admitted, "Mom, this is hard. There's so much to learn. This is more difficult than law school."

"You are going to get through this the same way you did law school."

"How?"

"With much prayer and supplication." *I should have known.* Her mother's answer to everything was much prayer and supplication.

"Lily, I have a church for you that needs your help."

Surprised, she asked, "Really? Which one? What kind of help?"

"Victory Assembly, in Atlanta. I just got off the phone with the First Lady, Mother Stevens. I told her about the career week you put together each year. They want you to organize one for them."

Lily rested her head against the leather chair. "Where am I going to find the time for that?"

"Girl, you've got to make time. God deserves your time, too. And before I go, how's your prayer life?"

She crossed her fingers and lied, "It's good."

Lily's prayer life was virtually nonexistent. She exhaled a quick prayer every night when she climbed into bed.

Mother Rose wasn't sure if she believed her. For now, she wouldn't push it. "Alright, baby, I gotta go. We have a women's meeting this evening. Oh, one more thing…"

"Yes, Mom?"

Mother Rose exclaimed, "Go home, it's seven-thirty already!"

"Go home, it's seven-thirty already." The words echoed from her lips and back to her ears.

"What did you say, Lily?" She looked up from her desk.

"Oh Rick, I was just on the phone with my mother. She told me, 'Go home, it's seven-thirty already.'"

Rick smiled as he stood in the doorway of her office. Leaning against the door with his arms folded across his firm chest, he loved the view. *Lily, you're beautiful even when you're tired.*

He agreed with Lily's mother, "She's right, your secretary left two hours ago."

Lily flashed him a flirtatious smile, sweetly asked, "If she's so right, then why are you still here?"

Rick playfully pointed to his chest. "Me?"

"Yes, you."

His voice deepened as he truthfully confessed, "I'm admiring you."

Her pulsed picked up. *He's flirting back.* She was at a loss for words. Apparently, Rick, too. They held one another's gaze.

Finally, he suggested, "Lily, you've worked enough. Have dinner with me?"

Staggered by the invitation, she blinked, then asked, "Dinner?"

He teased her. "You know the stuff you eat when it gets dark outside? Most people call that dinner."

Laughing softly, she said, "I know what dinner is."

"So you'll join me?"

"Of course, I'm hungry."

"Good, let's meet by the elevators in five minutes."

Is This A Date?

"Aunt Janice's Country Kitchen?" Lily didn't mean to say it aloud. Rick couldn't control his laughter. He seemed to laugh with his whole body. His head fell slightly backward.

"You're probably thinking I'm a cheap date, huh?"

"Date? Is this a date?"

He didn't answer her until they were snuggled into their booth. "Lily, that would depend?"

"Depend, on what?"

"If we both agree we're on a date."

She slowly looked him over and smiled. "Ohhhhh, I see, in that case, it's a date."

His eyes sparkled. She made it easy for him. "I like you, Lily. I brought you here because it's quiet at this time of night. I would like to get to know you better."

Lily glanced around the quaint little diner. The tables were draped in red and white tablecloths. Round red cushioned stools surrounded the front counter. The waitress approached them in a red and white checkered uniform.

"Welcome to Aunt Janice's Country Kitchen. What can I get cha?"

Rick was ready, he quickly ordered, "Joy, I'll have an omelet with cheddar cheese, onions, tomatoes, green peppers, a side of grits with extra butter and toast with jelly. Oh, and orange juice."

"And you Miss?" Joy lifted her chin up at Lily.

Lily didn't think Joy was living up to her name, but she liked what Rick was having. "That sounds good, I'll have the same."

The waitress rolled her eyes, gathered the menus and left them to their flirtations.

Lily found Joy's attitude amusing. She smiled and refocused on Rick. "Breakfast for dinner? I like that idea."

"I like to flip the script from time to time. The same old thing gets boring."

"Tell me about it."

He knew what she meant. "You need to get out of the office more. Lily, I was like you when I first started. All work and no play. Of course my wife didn't like that very much."

"Your wife! You're married? Is that why you said the same old thing is a bore? What's your game? Cuz I ain't up for no games," Lily rattled off.

Rick tried to hold in his amusement. He said slowly, "The sister in you comes out."

She started to slide out of the booth. Afraid that he'd scared her off, Rick grabbed her hand. "Please don't go. I'm not married. I'm a widower. I lost my wife and daughter three years ago in a fire. It was our vacation home. It was arson. I wasn't there and I…" He couldn't continue.

The pain in his eyes was real. *He's telling the truth.* "Rick, I didn't know. How old was your daughter?"

"She was five." His eyes began to fill with water. She hurt for him. "Lily, do you mind if we don't talk about this?"

"Sure, Rick, I'm sorry."

Joy interrupted, resting the plates in front of them, "That's two omelets, two sides of grits, toast and jelly on the side."

He admired his plate. "Joy, it looks wonderful."

"What you tellin' me for? I ain't cook it," she frankly replied.

Rick yelled to the cook, "It looks good, Jo."

Jo yelled back, "Enjoy, Rick."

Lily chuckled as Joy swayed away. She felt compelled to admit, "She's a peach."

Rick lowered his voice. "I think she has a crush on me."

"Yeah?" Lily peered over her shoulder. Joy's eyes were on Rick. She cheered him on, "Go for it. For the record, though, I think she's old enough to be your mother."

He smirked and started eagerly on his meal. Between bites, he asked, "Do you like it?"

"It's so good."

Her lips curved when she said, 'So good.' *I've got to taste those lips.*

"I was serious when I said I like you. I really haven't felt connected to anyone in a long time. In some ways, you remind me of my wife."

"Do I look like her?"

"No, but you are beautiful, dainty like she was. I bet you've got your legs crossed under the table right now. I saw you when you placed your napkin gently in your lap, like so." He mocked her and she found it amusing. *He's cute and funny.*

"I'm not one to beat around the bush," Rick explained.

She put her fork down and looked him directly in the eye. "So don't."

Yes! She is making this easy for me. "I'd like to spend time with you outside of the office. I know this is unprofessional. I am your mentor. Still, that doesn't prevent me from being very attracted to you. I will never be anything but professional in the office; outside, I won't make you any promises."

He laid his hand upon hers. Soft as velvet, he pulled her hand to his mouth while innocent anticipating eyes captured him. Using teeth and tongue, Rick considerately kissed her hand, inside and out. Heat enveloped her, leading her to press her knees together. She lowered her long eyelashes, pleaded, *Oh God, help me.*

Where Do I Go From Here?

At church, Pastor Rose tapped softly on Michael's open office door. The church was Michael's second home. Pastor Rose often teased him when they were building the new church that he would give Michael an office. He made good on his promise. Michael's office was small, yet functional. There was just enough room for a glass desk with a laptop computer, a table for the printer/fax machine, and two small chairs in front of his desk.

The tap pulled Michael away from the list of names he was compiling.

In his usual friendly voice, he asked, "May I come in?"

Michael was always amazed at Pastor Rose's humility. He certainly didn't have to ask. After all, Michael wasn't a minister or deacon, but still he had his own office. Michael quickly stood, invited him, "Please come in, Pastor."

With a wave of his hand, he said, "Sit, sit, Michael."

Both gentlemen sat.

Pastor Rose gingerly crossed his legs and informed him, "I got your letter. You could have come and told me you no longer wanted to work on career week."

Michael began to fiddle with the silver-cross pen in his hand. Avoiding Pastor Rose's eyes like a young child being chastised, he carefully admitted, "I guess...I have a difficult time turning you down."

Pastor Rose noted the pained look on Michael's face. Michael was grieving the loss of his relationship. "Son, I understand if it's too painful for you to do this without Lily. As a matter of fact, before I even received your letter, I was going to ask you if you were up to it."

Michael loved when he called him son. Pride and emotion exuded from the word when he used it. Looking up at Pastor Rose's gaze, he apologized, "I hope you weren't offended I wrote you a letter."

He felt hurt, not offense. Pastor Rose shifted in his seat. He was grieving, too. Since Lily left, he felt like he had lost a son; actually two since Kyle and Vaughn broke up. "Don't worry about my feelings. If you don't want to work on career week, it's OK. There is an event coming up in two weeks I'd like your help with. It will be our first Valentine's dinner."

Michael looked sideways at Pastor Rose. *Valentine's, cupid, love, couples, not something I am interested in.*

Unhindered by the lack of Michael's enthusiasm, he laid it out, "This is a youth event. We are honoring our youth to show them that we love them. It's more like an elegant ball." He smiled. He knew young people loved to put new clothes on.

Michael held his breath. *What do you need me for?* Firing up like he did on Sunday morning when he preached, Pastor Rose eagerly continued, "You really don't have much to do on this end, except invite some of the kids from the youth center where you volunteer. We are donating four thousand dollars. You can pick the children and provide them with money for clothes and a limo. Of course, I'll want you to chaperone the young people."

Carrying his message home, he picked up the pace. "I want the kids in this community to know we care and we want them to be a part of our church."

It was an exceptionally good idea, no, a wonderful idea. There were four kids that were working to help their parents while keeping their grades up. "I'll be more than happy to help."

Pastor Rose stood and extended a check made out to Michael for four thousand dollars. Stunned, Michael looked at it. "You already made the check out? How did you know if I would agree?"

Smiling, he replied, "It's like you said, you have a hard time turning me down."

Michael shyly agreed and handed him a list of names. Pastor Rose's brow wrinkled. "What's this?"

"It's a list of people who might be able to help with career week."

Pastor Rose accepted the list and shook his head. "Michael, you are one of a kind."

He knew Michael wasn't the only man in the world, but he was unique to say the least. He thought, *Lily, you made a mistake leaving, and Michael, you shouldn't have let her.*

Still Burning

Lily simmered from Rick's fiery kiss. Michael never kissed her hands. Not like that. She *was* learning something new everyday. Retrieving some water from the refrigerator, Lily didn't notice Vaughn sitting at the dining room table.

Vaughn watched her cousin do a little shimmy dance by the sink. *Something or someone sure made her happy tonight.* She knew exactly who that someone was. Mr. Rick had been watching her and Lily for months. She wasn't sure which one of them he would approach. She had her answer.

"So, how was dinner with Rick?"

Lily jumped, startled by Vaughn's voice. "Girl, you scared me."

Vaughn folded her arms across her chest. "Don't go changing the subject. You ain't over there dancing for nothing."

Lily kicked off her shoes and joined her. She heaved a sigh. "Rick and I had dinner tonight."

Vaughn groaned, "I know that. You ain't been nowhere in four months. I said how was it?"

She couldn't control her excitement. "It was sensuous," she blurted out.

"Sensuous? Well, I've never heard you use that word before."

Lily took a gulp of her water and realized, "I've never felt this before. I'm tingling all over. Can you believe I'm 25 years old, and still a virgin? I can't believe it sometimes." She flashed a mischievous smile. "I think that might change in due time. Rick could be the one."

Vaughn blinked several times, thinking, *Who is this woman sitting across from me with dreamy eyes?* It certainly wasn't her cousin Lily. Vaughn placed her hand firmly on the table. "Lily, I know how you feel. When my fiancé broke off our engagement, I felt rejected, too. I wanted some male attention."

Lily wasn't following Vaughn. "Girl, you always have more male attention than you can handle."

"Maybe so, but I felt rejected none-the-less."

"Your situation is totally different from mine. I waited eight years for Michael and he said pack your bags and go. You cheated on your man. He caught you in bed."

That stung. Getting upset, remembering the events of the past, Vaughn finished the last of Lily's water.

Lily further argued, "I would have left your butt, too! My situation is very different, extremely!"

"They are both the same Lily. You're looking for acceptance. You feel inadequate, like something is wrong with you. And I can certainly tell you, you're looking in all the wrong places."

Lily's eyes enlarged. "Vaughn, what have you been reading? The Bible?"

"Yes, I am reading the Bible, Isaiah 3:16. It's telling me about God's judgment against Judah. God's warning the women to be careful of their flirtatious and wondering eyes. If they ain't careful, He will strip them of their beauty and pass one mean judgment against them." Vaughn smiled, and pointed to the small book in front of her.

The message as well as the messenger annoyed Lily. *How can the Queen of Flirtation preach to me?* "What meaning could that possibly have for me? Vaughn, there *is* no comparison."

"Lily, it is plain as day. You better check yourself, before it's too late."

Lily moved toward the stairs. Tired, she headed for her room, and yelled, "Girl, stick to flirting. You're better at it than preaching."

Vaughn stood, placed her hand on her hip and leaned into it. *Oh, no she didn't!* She yelled back, "Take a cold shower!"

Vaughn walked to the sink and placed the empty glass. *"Lord, I tried to warn her. I've flirted in the past, but I don't want to end up like my mother battered, abused and desperate. Father, I am going to try to change my ways. I'll need your help along the way."*

A New Friend

Valentine's Day arrived. Lily and Vaughn were both without dates. As Lily flipped the last of the pancakes she exhaled, "Oh well, at least it's my first Saturday off."

Rick told her to take the weekend off. She had worked every weekend since she started. She wondered how Michael would spend his day.

The doorbell chimed and Lily shouted, "Vaughn, get the door!" She waited a beat as the bell chimed again. She called again, "Vaughn?" Silence. *Is that girl still in bed at eleven in the morning? Vaughn said she needed her beauty rest, but this is ridiculous.*

Racing for the door, she was out of breath when she opened it. "Can I help you?" A petite mocha complexioned woman stood smiling. Her crimped styled hair touched her shoulders. The young lady offered a hand. "Hello, I'm Mother Donita Stevens of Victory Assembly Church. I'm looking for Lily Rose?"

Lily wiped her hands on her low cut jeans, took the woman's hand and introduced herself, "I'm Lily Rose."

"Oh, uh, I'm sorry to drop in on you like this, but your mother said you could help us with the youth's career week. When she told me where you lived, I decided to stop by." She pointed down the street, added, "I only live a couple of blocks down."

I wish you would have called first. Lily was wearing one of Vaughn's white cut off shirts. Her firm belly was exposed. Uncomfortable that she was casually dressed in front of a first lady, she forgot her manners.

Donita frowned. "May I come in?"

"Oh, of course, please. I wasn't expecting you. Join me in the kitchen, I'm making breakfast."

"Ok. Oh, here, I baked you a pecan pie. Your mother said it's your favorite."

Lily smiled at Donita as she accepted the pie. "That was thoughtful of you. Would you care for some breakfast? It's just pancakes and coffee." Donita graciously declined.

Donita noticed Lily was staring at her. "You're wondering how old I am?"

"I'm sorry, most of the first ladies I call mother are much older."

"It's a long story. I think I'll have a cup of coffee after all."

Lily swiftly served her. She wanted to hear the story. "I'm thirty-five years old. I've always acted older than my age. My husband is a Pastor and he is fifty. He started calling me mother at church and it just caught on. Chile, please call me Nita. I hate being called mother."

Lily laughed at her accent. Donita had a strong southern drawl. Lily inquired, "Do you have children?"

"None together. I've lost three babies already. They just won't stay in me. Anyway, we've been married ten years. I do have a 13-year-old stepdaughter, Jessica. She's my heart." Lily felt for her. "I'm sorry to hear about your miscarriages."

Donita waved her hand. "Don't be, I'm not. We have Jessica. She's mine. It is not my fault that I didn't give birth to her." Donita was talking none stop. "See Stanley, that's my husband, his wife went off and left him and Jessica. Jessica was just a year old. He raised her with the help of the other ladies in the church, and his mama, until she died."

Whoa this lady can talk. Lily didn't discourage her, she enjoyed the company. "I met Stanley at the pediatric clinic. I'm a nurse. Now I work in the ER at the hospital. Anyway, Stanley invited me to his church. I loved it and just kept going." She winked. "I loved Stanley, too. One thing led to another, and he proposed. Then all hell broke loose when we got married. The ladies felt like he shouldn't be allowed to remarry with a wife running around. *We* didn't feel that way. We didn't know where she was, and had no way of contacting her. She never once tried to contact us." Donita paused, then asked, "Can I have a refill?"

Lily rushed over and just sat the pot before Donita. "To make a long story longer, the ladies in the church gave me some kind of a hard time. Didn't respect me at all. That's why Stanley made them all call me Mother Stevens. Many of the ladies left and took their families with them. At one point, we just had a hand full of members. Thinking back, I believe that's why I lost all them

93

babies. I was just plain ole stressed out. But not Stanley, he preached every sermon like it was his last. Now, we've got over four hundred members. Compared to your parent's church, I know that's small, but it's all we can handle. You know God won't put no more on you than you can bear."

Lily admired Donita. She was apparently strong-minded. Curious, Lily asked, "Donita, what happened to Stanley's first wife?"

"Oh yeah, I forgot that part. I try not to think about it. It was so hard on our Jessica. Suzy, that was Stanley's wife name. She was found dead in a hotel room; shot to death."

Lily put her hands to her mouth. "Nita, I'm sorry to hear that." Donita nodded. "It was a tough blow to all of us. At least finding out gave us closure. I guess I would have always wondered what happened to my husband's first wife. It hurt my heart knowing she died so violently without Christ."

Lily sighed. "That's tragic."

Donita suddenly remembered the purpose of her visit. One, to check up on Lily like she promised Mother Rose; two, to get the girls to join their church and, three, to ask for help with the career week.

"I'm going on and on about me and my family. Are you interested in helping us?"

Interested? Yes. Do I have the time? No. "Honestly Nita, I am so busy being a new attorney, but I will do my best to help." She needed to get the record straight that she wasn't going to do all the work. She couldn't. "I am going to need a team of at least five people. I pretty much know how to do this with my eyes closed, but I won't do it alone."

Donita was impressed. Lily was young and had a baby face, but she was direct and professional. Donita respected that. "Sure, I will put a team together this weekend."

Lily gave a friendly smile. She liked Donita. Other than Vaughn and her co-workers, she didn't know anyone in Atlanta. *Maybe we can become friends.*

Donita began to make her way to the door. "Thanks for your time. I know I barged in on you. I enjoyed our talk." Lily wanted to invite Donita to join her and Vaughn for their

Valentine's dinner, but she thought Donita probably had plans with her husband.

Donita could sense Lily wanted to say something. "Lily, why don't you and your cousin join us tonight?"

Lily could never conceal what she was thinking. *Lonely must have been painted on my forehead.* "I couldn't impose. Valentine's Day is a very romantic time."

"Not to us. We don't feed into the commercialism of the day. I'm just making dinner for my husband and daughter. I know he would be pleased to meet you. He met your father at a convention once. Come on over and have some collards and smoked turkey wings."

Lily's lips formed into a bright smile. "That sounds good. How can I say no? Besides, Vaughn loves turkey wings."

"I'll see y'all at seven."

Break Me Down Lord

Roosta sat in the most unusual place on this Valentine's Day - church. The ultimate player was without his wife, or any woman for that matter. He invited Flo to join him and she refused. She refused him every night. He hung his head in the sanctuary, listening to the speaker of the hour.

A Latin lady with creamy silk skin, rosy cheeks and a short-cropped brown hair proclaimed, "God is faithful and just to forgive us of our sins. Our sins are cast into the sea of forgetfulness, and God remembers them no more."

His pew partner chimed in, "Amen." She was a burly older lady in her sixties. Her *Amen*, alerted him to her long silver haired curls and a deep purple dress. She smiled. He didn't.

Why am I here? He could have just about any woman he wanted. Not because he was a handsome man, because he wasn't. However, most women in his care were treated like royalty. But he didn't want any woman. He wanted his wife, Floreece.

God forgave. He thought it easy for God to forgive. He didn't beat God with his fists. He didn't cheat on God constantly and break his vows to Him. No, he did it to his wife, the mother of his child.

The speaker made the appeal, "Tonight, if you need God to forgive you, come."

Roosta didn't need God to forgive him. He needed Flo to. He grabbed his Bible. This church thing wasn't working for him. The silver haired lady lightly tugged his arm. Her voice was quiet. "Son, go on up there, and give it to God"

"Give what to God?" Getting out of there, he whispered, "I already gave."

"Have you?"

"I gave my offering already."

She tugged his arm again. "You haven't forgiven yourself. Stop punishing yourself. Go on and give God your pain."

"My pain?" He frowned at her.

"He's waiting for you."

He didn't want to, but the lady persisted. *The sooner I go up there, the sooner I can leave.*

Roosta felt like all eyes were on him. He approached the tiny aisle, wondering, *Why did Pastor Rose recommend such a small church, when his church is so big?* The organ droned. *Come to Jesus, Come to Jesus, Just now, Just now.* The speaker asked his name. He answered softly, waiting for her to lay hands on him like Pastor Rose did. Instead, she placed her hands together and prayed, *"Oh most precious God. Your son is hurting. There is no sin too great for you to forgive. Let him know he is a new creature in you. Free his heart and lift his burdens."*

The small church glowed with power. He wasn't sure if it was the lighting, or his eyes. They began to water. He wasn't a crying man. Yet, he couldn't explain what was happening to him as his weak knees connected with the floor. He cried the only thing that would fall from his lips, "Oh God."

Come With Me

Rick's stomach did somersaults, feeling like a teenage boy on his first date. He'd chosen a tux, a red silk bow tie and matching cummerbund for Valentine's Day. All set, he rang the doorbell with a huge box of chocolates and two-dozen, long-stem pink and white roses in his hands.

Lily liked him. So he felt confident about where things were headed. Since their first date, they had shared dinner frequently in and out of the office. She told him about her Christian upbringing and the fact she was still a virgin. He told her that his late wife was also a Christian and just before they were married, he had given his life to Christ. But after her death, he had given up on God.

Rick wasn't sure if mixing business with pleasure was right. Finally, he decided it felt right. The instant attraction proved evident. Certainly two analytical, reasonable and responsible adults could share a meaningful physical relationship without interfering with their professional one. With those thoughts circling, Rick stared at the two-story home. It looked differently with all the renovations made to it. But it was the same home he briefly shared with his wife as a young attorney.

It seemed odd to him that he returned to that home to ask his protégé to be his Valentine. He shook his head at his unfair life. His wife and daughter had been stolen from him. Rick questioned if God really was a God of love. If so, how could He let something so tragic happen to his little girl, his baby?

The abyss in his heart could not be filled. Lily could not fill it. Nor would he attempt to allow her. Yet, something about Lily drew him. Rick marveled at the dark crystal sky and made a wish. If it came true, he would be holding Lily in his arms until sunrise.

She answered the doorbell with an adoring expression of curiosity on her face. Lily appreciated removing her big purple rollers, seeing Rick stand outside her door like a scared little boy. Putting on his cool, he winked at her. "You look nice, but I hoped to see you in formal attire."

She squinted as Rick glided into her living room like a *GQ* model. *Wow.* "Rick, you look handsome, but I'm not sure why you are here."

He gently brushed his lips against her cheek and presented her with the candy and flowers. "Happy Valentine's Day."

"I don't have anything for you," she admitted, slightly ashamed.

He realized the gift surprised her, causing her to laugh. Or, was it a cough? He couldn't tell. When he whispered in her ear and asked for the gift of her company for the evening, she offered the same coughed up laugh. He'd caught her completely off her guard. He liked seeing her that way - exposed and, yet, considerate.

"Rick, I would love to, except I've already accepted a dinner invitation."

Disappointment shot him down like a jet fighter. He tried not to show it, wanting to kick himself for assuming that she hadn't met any other men. It shouldn't have been a shock. Lily was a beautiful woman. "I should have called first," he apologized and turned to walk out.

Apparently he thought she had a date, she stopped him. "Please don't leave. I had plans to have dinner with friends of my parents. I can see that you went through a lot of trouble planning this. It's very sweet. I'm flattered." The wheels in her head began turning. *I wonder what else he has planned for me.* Her speech picked up as she suggested, "I could call and cancel, or I could ask Vaughn if she wouldn't mind going without me." Lily knew Vaughn wouldn't. She hadn't even met Donita, or her husband. *What to do? What to do?* She ran upstairs and yelled over her shoulder, "Have a seat and give me twenty minutes."

Rick heard Vaughn's rising voice at the top of the stairs. He couldn't make out the words, but it translated, she didn't like him very much. He didn't know why. *I am not pressuring Lily to do anything she doesn't want to.*

In less than fifteen minutes, Lily returned wearing Vaughn's engagement dress. It wasn't as filled out in the back like it was on Vaughn, but the look of her curvy bottom pleased Rick. His leg began to shake as she offered, "Mr. Parsons I am giving you the gift of my company this evening." *Maybe I won't be a virgin much longer.*

A white stretch limo, filled with red roses, took them into the country where he lived. It bared a lovely fragrance for the ride home. The secluded lush area resembled a scene in a murder flick. It was far from the suburbs, and very peaceful. She appreciated his large ranch house. It had a nice combination of warm elegance. The walls were lined in wood paneling. Rick settled in with a quick press of a remote, the fireplace lit and two male servers appeared out of nowhere.

Lily was happy she agreed to the amazing date. Rick once again gave her a new and enjoyable experience. He had prepared all the food himself. And really did go through a lot of trouble. She felt more than special. Her smile in the candlelight lured him. Riveted by it, Rick barely touched his food. He loved having this woman in his home. He smiled thinking his efforts were almost worth it. Giving her no indication of his thoughts, he raised his eyes from the veal. "I'm sorry if I ruined your plans with Vaughn tonight."

Sorry, too, she felt Vaughn overreacted. "Vaughn is like a mother hen these days. She'll be alright."

Rick sighed. "I hope so. I don't want her thinking I'm trying to push up on you."

It seemed to be the perfect time to ask Rick what *was* happening between them. They worked well together and they were physically attracted to one another. However, they were not a couple, per se. This was unlike any relationship she ever had. Michael was her only real relationship. She looked directly into his eyes, searching like an attorney examining the minds of jurors. She struggled to keep her voice steady, but she had to know if Rick was doing what Vaughn warned. *"'Out to steal her precious gift.'* "What *is* going on between us?"

She didn't have to wait long. "I'm not making any plans for the future," he answered immediately, "I can't even say if I am ready for a committed relationship."

Lily let a disappointed, "Oh," drip from her lips.

She's hurt. "Lily, I am not seeing anyone else, either. We enjoy one another's company, shouldn't that be enough?" He smiled and let his hands fall upon hers and continued, "And whatever happens, happens."

Lily looked up. "Whatever happens, happens? Are you referring to us having sex?"

She sounds like a little girl. It amused him, considering she gave him all the signs that she was not opposed to the idea of them being intimate. He smiled as to comfort her. "Lily, if that should happen, it would be because we both want it. I will be responsible when the time comes. OK?"

She thought about Michael, and knew her life had changed.

Rick waited for her reply, seeing her mind at work. After a minute, she nodded in agreement. He walked over and took her hand. "Shall we?" Their eyes locked. Rick escorted Lily near the fireplace. He removed his jacket. There were two large black faux throw pillows waiting for them to relax after a superb meal. He helped her sit and removed her shoes. He kissed her cheek. "Are you comfortable, darling?"

Rick had serious plans for them. Trying to conceal her nerves, she said, "I can't believe how much trouble you went to. It has been a fairytale evening."

Rick wanted to caress her face. Her skin was glowing with the reflection of the fire. "No trouble at all. I enjoy cooking. I know women don't think men can throw down in the kitchen, but we can."

Lily shook her head, and thanks to the wine, began feeling slightly dizzy. Her eyes looked lazily at Rick. "I know how well men can cook. My father is a better cook than my mother." She closed her eyes as she continued, "That's saying a lot because my mother can burn."

Rick admired the sleepy look on her face. His thoughts slipped out of his mouth. "I want you."

She trembled.

He went on, "I promise to make your first time, our first time; special." Inches from her lips, he lowered his voice. "I can see the wine is having an affect on you."

"It's you, not just the wine," she plainly stated.

They kissed long, slowly and steady. Tasting each other for what seemed like hours. Lily enjoyed the pace, but Rick struggled with his flesh to go in stages. Sweet sighs escaped her throat, enticed him. His hands went to her velvet back and down her waist with a questioning squeeze. "Now?"

Lost in the moment, she didn't hear him.

Without waiting for her reply, he knelt behind her and carefully pulled the dress from her shoulders, then kissed them. The tugging of her dress alerted Lily to the reality of the situation. Pulling the dress back over her shoulders, she panted, "Rick no, I can't."

He smiled. "You can. Don't be nervous."

"I'm not...it's just." She held her head down.

Frustrated, he sighed. "I won't rush you, but if we continue seeing one another, the inevitable will happen."

She began to rest on her knees. "Does it have to be, *inevitable*? I am saving myself for my husband."

A war raged within her; desire and curiosity against her spirit. Rick could see it, but no fight hindered him. Aggravated by her struggle, he tightly held her wrists with both hands. "Lily, if we can't have a physical relationship, let's stop seeing each other now. If we don't, in time, we will make love."

He waited, tried to discern the look on her face.   "Rick, take me home."

101

The Valentine's Ball

Michael once again concurred with Pastor Rose's idea for a Valentine's Ball for the youth of the church and beyond. He escorted four teens into the fellowship hall, strikingly handsome in his black tux.

They were in awe. Whoever was in charge of decorating did a splendid job. Red velvet hearts and roses lined the walls, tables and centerpieces. The lighting glowed in soft pink hues. The church band was at its best as they played contemporary gospel jazz. He wasn't sure if the kids liked the music, but he sure did. He let his head bop as he found their table.

Fourteen year old Trina looked jazzy in a red satin Cinderella gown. Her friend, Randi, wore an elegant turquoise dress that exposed skinny shoulders. She tried to soothe Trina as she fidgeted.

Michael observed the teens as the boys pulled the girls' chairs out just like he schooled them.

Randi whispered in her friend's ear and smelled the tons of hairspray that held Trina's stiff curls, "Girl, I know all you wear is jeans and sneakers, but you look good, so just chill."

Trina looked at Michael, ignored her friend. "They gone feed us right? Cuz, I didn't eat nuttin' but some salt and vinegar potato chips."

Michael chuckled. He knew they were trying to be cool. He lightly answered, "They have a wonderful menu. In the meantime, go to the buffet table and get some refreshments." He pointed behind them. He didn't have to ask twice, they were up and at it.

Michael called Trina, "Hey, Tre, wait!"

She walked back like her feet hurt. "Yes, Mike?"

"Listen to your friend. You look very pretty, so just chill."

She flashed her braces as she walked away.

Bittersweet, Michael saw his brother approaching in a red suit with Sapphire on his arm. He prayed that Kyle would come, and wished Sapphire would not. Disappointed, he attempted to smile. Unfortunately, his lips refused to cooperate. All the same, he would be a gentleman.

102

He stood, gave his brother a handshake, and kissed Sapphire's heavily painted cheek. She dropped her mink. Once again, daring in red, her cleavage spilled out of her evening gown. Michael thought, *The woman looks like she's got two puppies trying to escape.*

Michael turned to his brother, sadly admitted, "Kyle, that's some suit. You are hurting my eyes."

Sapphire smiled. "Michael, Kyle looks good in red."

Michael frowned and pointed, he asked, "Oh, so this was *your* idea?"

"It's my Valentine's gift to him." Sapphire leaned over and loudly kissed Kyle on the lips.

Kyle was flashy no doubt, but now he was wearing red suits to black tie affairs. He sat as he watched Kyle pull out Sapphire's chair, and then took his seat. He leaned over and massaged the back of Sapphire's neck. "Don't be jealous bro. I can't help it if I look better than you. You know I was never a tux man anyway."

That was more than true, but he was classier than that. To Michael, Kyle looked like a pimp. Without realizing it, he said, "Good God, you look like you need a hat and a cane."

Sapphire flaunted her pearly whites at Michael as she answered, "The hat and cane are in the car. I told him to bring them in, but he ain't listen to a Sister."

Michael leaned back. "You're serious? You got a cane and a pimp daddy hat?"

"My baby really hooked me up, didn't she?"

Michael shook his head, looked over at the kids. He found that they quickly made friends, and were sitting at another table.

Kyle followed Michael's eyes and spotted the buffet table. "Baby, you hungry?"

She looked over. "I sure am. Why don't you get me something?"

Kyle hesitated, he wasn't sure if he wanted to leave them alone together.

Michael turned his attention to the band and listened. Sapphire took Kyle's seat next to Michael. She flatly said, "I know you don't like me." She pointed her French-style manicured nails at him. "But you see that's your problem."

Michael didn't look at her and responded roughly, "I never said I didn't like you." He brought his face inches from hers. His voice was low and direct. "I don't appreciate you playin' my brother against an old friend of ours. I don't like how you're trying to change him, and make him a part of your world." He banged his finger on the table. "Sassy, Sapphire, I don't even know you. So to like you, or not, is neither here nor there."

Michael seemed to thrive on calm, but now his tone frightened her. She didn't let on. She kept her gaze level with his. "Look, you don't know nothin' about me or my world. Kyle is with me because he chooses to be. What happened between me and Ollie is over."

He snapped, "It didn't look like it was over at Lily's dinner party. I know he took you home and *I* know things got more intense in private than it did in public."

She rolled her neck, fiercely stated, "You don't know that."

"I know Ollie. *I* know his power over women. If he could get you hugged up and my brother was near by, then I know he got you at home." Michael pulled her card and Sapphire was spitting mad. That night she was angry with herself for being weak.

"Michael, you better get used to me, cuz I ain't goin' nowhere. As a matter of fact, in a few months, I could be your sister-in-law. So you better start respectin' me," she explained in her defense.

Michael laughed as Kyle approached with meatballs and broccoli and cheese casserole for them. He raised his eyebrows, asked, "What's so funny man?"

"Sapphire man, this one is a real piece of work." Michael stood and prepared to find another table. His brother met him squarely before he could walk away.

Kyle's tone was dangerous. "Don't disrespect my woman Michael." Michael looked at his brother in disgust. "I'll respect her when she starts respecting herself."

Let's Pray

Vaughn was out of character and glad about it. The old Vaughn would have never attended a dinner with people she hadn't even met before. Lily didn't believe her when she said she was tired of playing the field. It hurt that her best friend didn't trust her.

Sick and tired of the gossip at church, Atlanta was the perfect place for her to start again. She knew what everyone was calling her. People thought they knew her, because she flirted. They didn't. She still didn't know how or why she had sex with someone she didn't like. The event haunted her day and night. She never told anyone. She looked up from her dinner plate, and once again thanked the Stevens for their hospitality. The food and company was comforting. It reminded her of home with Mother and Pastor Rose.

When Pastor Stevens spoke, his soft voice soothed. Vaughn wondered how he preached with a voice like that, he said, "I remember you and Lily as little girls. You two were different as night and day. You always were very verbal and you sang in the choir. Lily was quiet and shy until it was time to speak about Jesus."

True enough, Vaughn smiled at the memory. "Thank you Pastor Stevens. I wouldn't trade growing up in the church for nothing in the world."

Donita chimed in, "Amen." Donita attended church the minute her mother brought her home from the hospital.

Something on Vaughn's mind made Donita wonder if she felt uncomfortable around her white husband and daughter. Although she was familiar with the looks, smirks and whispers, she hoped Vaughn would be different.

Already nine o' clock, Vaughn sat on the verge of politely excusing herself. She hoped for a chance to talk with Lily. Jessica, Donita's awestruck daughter, delayed her. "Oh, Mama, don't you think it's romantic that Lily's on a fantasy date - chocolates, roses and limo's, oh my!" She was cute with long brown hair that was pulled into a ponytail.

Donita wasn't sure what to think. Vaughn clearly made her exit move. Donita asked calmly, "Jessie, help your father clear the table." That was Pastor Stevens cue. Sometimes his bossy wife annoyed him. Tonight, it was OK. Vaughn was troubled. Donita had a way of helping people open up. Maybe it was her free personality. She didn't mind sharing herself with anyone.

Vaughn made a beeline for the door and put on a fake smile. "Thanks, again, everything was wonderful."

Donita rested a deep chocolate hand on Vaughn's yellow sweater. "Do you have a minute? I want to ask you a question."

Vaughn turned, answered, "Sure, you can ask me anything."

Donita led her to the red and gold plaid sofa. Vaughn particularly didn't like their taste in furniture. Somehow, the decor suited them. Donita wrinkled her forehead. "Does it bother you that we are an interracial family?"

Vaughn blinked thinking, *Where did that come from? I haven't given it a second thought.* She answered quickly, "Not at all. Hey, who you love is none of my business."

Donita leaned back. "I didn't mean to put you on the spot. I could tell during dinner you were…disturbed."

The old Vaughn would have walked away. The new Vaughn needed someone to talk to. Lily and Kyle were her best friends. She already lost Kyle. It seemed to her that Lily was on the way out.

"Nita, I'm worried about my cousin."

Donita lifted her shoulders. "Why?"

Without hesitation, she continued, "The man Lily is with tonight is her boss, more or less. I know he's trying to get my cousin into bed. I see the way he watches her."

Donita nodded. "Lily is a grown woman," she said. "Don't you think she's aware? Can she handle herself?"

Vaughn slowly shook her head. "Lily is grown, but also inexperienced. She's only had one boyfriend for eight years and, when he didn't propose, she decided to come here. I encouraged her to make this move, now I'm afraid she's about to get hurt."

106

Donita pretty much knew about Michael hearing the story from Mother Rose. It was also obvious to her that Vaughn felt guilty about the advice she had given her cousin. None of that mattered right now.

Donita pulled Vaughn with her to the floor. Vaughn jerked her arm away. "Woman, what are you doing?"

Donita's southern accent was stronger, she shouted, "Prayin' girl! It's time to pray. You say she's with this man now. Then we gotta pray right now!"

Before Vaughn could regain her composure, Donita was already calling on Jesus.

So Glad I'm Here

Listening to the silver haired lady at church had paid off for Roosta. He wasn't sure who she was. In retrospect, he wondered, *an angel*? She certainly was his. Roosta never felt so liberated in his life. To celebrate, he bought some roses and headed home. He prayed Flo would open her heart.

The sound of Flo's voice carried him to their bedroom. The woman loved pink. She dressed in a pink satin nightgown that was mesh on the top of it. She looked desirable. Her red hair grew longer. He wondered if she'd let it grow long like it was when they first met. Roosta wanted to walk into the room and drown Flo in kisses. It wasn't his room anymore. He had to knock, before entering; then he heard, "Vie, I wanna come up there again, this time for good. I want a divorce."

His hands grew cold as he listened. "What? What do you mean no?" Flo sucked her teeth and began pacing in her ankle length gown. "Vie, I ain't running and I know I've got a child to raise." Her voice picked up volume as she pulled the drapes back. "I do love him. I can't let him hurt me again. I thought you would be the first to understand. No, you don't. Fine, Vie. When I divorce Roosta, expect me." She hung up and placed her hands on her shapely hips.

She still loves me. She wanted a divorce, but she still loved him. Roosta didn't know how or why she did. He would never hurt her again. And, determined to prove it, as an unspoken promise to her, he left the roses in front of the doorway. He mimicked Pastor Rose as he walked to the guestroom, waving his hands. "Whew, Jesus!"

He Loves Me

Sapphire had to work. After midnight, Kyle watched Sassy dance her last number of the evening - not how he planned to spend the rest of his Valentine's. He was tired, sleepy and disgusted. His red suit was smoky; compliments of the club. Kyle ordered his seventh drink of the evening. Tossing the alcohol down his throat, he felt it burn with the bile that was rising in his chest. He didn't like men touching and drooling over his woman.

Kyle watched her, and it seemed none of it mattered. She was in rare form. She danced for herself, not for Kyle, not for the men sticking tens and twenties in her G-string. She blocked out the irritation, the shouts and screams from pounding in her head.

She worked at the club, Gems, for seven years. Maybe it was fate. Her birth name was Sapphire, and she stripped at a club called Gems. Her mother named her Sapphire because she said she was precious, special and priceless. She felt worthless. She believed her mother was wrong.

She loved to dance, but the groping and pulling on her body sickened her. She wasn't a commodity or, was she? Each time she walked onstage, she became, Sassy. She sold fantasies to anyone who paid - businessmen, fathers, husbands and pastors. It didn't matter who her customers were. She was a money-making professional.

That night, she offered no smiles, no playful interaction with the crowd. She didn't even stick around after her number to try to get some extra cash stuck in her G-string. She wanted to get dressed and go home.

A scrawny man, with short blond hair and a mouth full of gold teeth, met her backstage. It was Mac, the owner of the club. His sharp voice barked, "What was that? You didn't drop your top." He pushed her back against the narrow hallway, and she smelled the rum and coke on his breath. "Get back out there and give those customers what they came in here to see." He grabbed one of Sapphire's plump studded breasts.

She slapped his hand, pushed him away and spit the words in his face, "I'm tired." She fearlessly walked to her dressing room, knowing Mac wouldn't fire a good dancer. She made the club a ton of money and he recognized it.

Ollie dragged on a Cuban cigar as he waited in Sapphire's dressing room. The room was small, white and brightly lit. A floor length mirror, small couch and make-up chair were the only things that would fit in there. He turned in the direction of the door. He wanted her to see him the minute she entered. His smile was full and his heart was pumping fast. He needed Sapphire back. He missed her, and her money.

Sapphire closed the door and let the tears drop along her sparkled cheeks. She wasn't sure when the tears began.

"Sassy, what's wrong?"

Startled, she stepped back in her shiny silver stiletto heels. "Ollie?"

He walked to her and lifted her chin. "What happened? Did one of those guys get rough with you?"

She shook her head. "Ollie, why are you here?"

"Woman, you won't return my calls. I know what happened wasn't a one night stand."

She quickly pulled herself together. *I can't let him do this to me again.* Sapphire ignored him, sat in her make-up chair and grabbed the cold cream.

He continued to enjoy his cigar. He knew how to handle Sapphire. Patience was everything. "Sassy, I saw Kyle out front."

She continued to clean her face with a wet washcloth. Ollie leaned over her shoulder and kissed her neck, her spot. Her body jerked. *Be strong.*

"You really need to tell Kyle it ain't over between us. He's a friend. I don't want to see him hurt."

Sapphire looked for her jeans and shirt. She dressed quickly in front of him. Just about every man in the building saw her goods, now wasn't the time to be coy. She packed her costumes, make-up, robe and shoes. She didn't offer; *see you around* as she reached for the doorknob. Before she could pull it, Ollie had her in his arms. His lips warm and hungry; attacked her spot. She fought to be free, but only for a second. His familiar arms comforted, his kisses dominated and, once again, she surrendered.

Breathing heavily, he whispered in her ear, "Tell him, tell Kyle tonight. I still love you."

She tightly held onto Ollie then collapsed in his arms. She was exhausted with her life and the choices she made. "Ollie, Ollie, I can't do this anymore."

He caressed her back. "I know, Sassy. I'll take care of you. You gotta end this relationship with Kyle."

She looked into his eyes. "Ollie, you love me?" Her voice sounded pure.

"I want us to get married."

"Ollie, I don't believe you."

He kissed her deeply. She melted. *I believe you now.* She thought she was dreaming. She reached for Ollie. She wanted to hold him forever.

He stepped back. "You better go. I know Kyle is waiting for you. Talk to him and then come back here. I'm taking you out to celebrate."

She smiled, lifted by his proposal. Sapphire speedily pushed her way into the club. The moment was so unreal. They were going to get married. Kyle was waiting for her. *What am I going to say to Kyle?*

Kyle staggered his way out of the chair when he saw Sapphire approaching. He could barely stand as he squeezed Sapphire's bottom. His speech slurred, shouting, he declared, "This is my woman! This is my woman!"

Sapphire held him up with her weight. "Oh God, Kyle, you're drunk! You never drink."

He tried to kiss her. She quickly turned away.

"Nah, baby, I ain't drunk. I'm just more relaxed and ready for ya. Let's go home. I got something for ya." He tried to swerve his hips.

Sapphire looked back realizing that she had to drive Kyle home. She needed to get a message to Ollie, but she didn't want to leave Kyle alone. Drunks were easily robbed. She sighed. "Come on. Let's go home."

Ollie looked through the smoky room and saw Sapphire holding up a staggering Kyle.

You Say What?

Michael sat in his office and thought about Pastor Rose's message from Psalm 139. He meditated on the scripture. *"O Lord you have searched me and you know me. You know when I sit and when I rise, you perceive my thoughts from afar. You discern my going out and my lying down; you are familiar with all my ways. Before a word is on my tongue you know it completely, O Lord."*

The words brought some comfort. God knew that although Lily left four months ago, his heart still ached. He picked up the phone over a thousand times, but never completed the call. He hoped that distance and no communication would sever the tie bonding their love. He wasn't sure if that was working. It seemed that distance grew his heart fonder. He thought of her often and loved her more. He spent eight years loving her. It would take at least ten to release the love deep in his heart. The words escaped effortlessly, "Lord, you know my pain."

All he knew how to do was pray. He stood to close his office door at church and a familiar face met him in the doorway.

"Ollie!" he exclaimed, "Were you in church this morning?"

"I was." Ollie grinned at his old friend. "Believe it, or not, I enjoyed it."

"Man, how could you not? I can't begin to tell you how being in church lately has lifted me up. Being in God's presence and sharing in the joy of worship is food for the soul."

Ollie chuckled, but Michael's excitement annoyed him. He had mixed feelings about being in God's house after so many years. He hoped Michael wasn't going to preach him another sermon.

Michael studied Ollie. He looked well rested, healthy and doubtful. "So, what's up? You wanna grab some lunch?"

"Mike, I can't stay. I'm here to talk to my Uncle about something. I wanted to run it by you first."

"I'm curious."

They sat.

Ollie said, "I proposed last night."

Michael jumped back in his seat. "Proposed? To whom?"

Ollie leaned back in his chair and patted his pant leg for a cigarette. He remembered where he was and decided to wait until he was out of the building. "Before I answer that, let me tell you this. I saw your brother at the club last night."

Michael sighed as he rubbed his hand across his face. "Yeah, man, that's where he is these days."

"Mike, I know Kyle, and last night he wasn't himself."

"He's been out of character since he broke up with Vaughn."

Ollie folded his hands over his thin chest. "I don't understand what happened with those two. Kyle was crazy about my sister and, Vaughn flirted, but never slept around."

"It's confusing."

"Look man, uhma just say it. Yo' brother was wasted last night."

"What?" Michael rose from his seat.

"You heard me. Drunk, Sapphire had to carry him out of the club."

Michael wrinkled his forehead. "I don't believe it. We never put alcohol in our mouths. If he was drunk, it had to be the first time."

"Maybe." He paused, he wasn't sure if Michael wanted to hear the rest. "Mike, I proposed to Sassy last night. She said yes."

Michael slumped back in his seat. "You just said she carried Kyle out of the club last night."

"She did, after I proposed. I'm assuming she left with him to drive him home."

"Does Kyle know you're getting married to Sapphire…I mean Sassy?"

"I 'on't know. That's why I'm here. I love you and Kyle like brothers. Man, I don't want to hurt him. I know he's trippin' over Vaughn and this thing with Sassy, it's gonna mess wit 'em."

Michael took his car keys out of his pocket and grabbed his coat. "Ollie, thanks for stopping by."

Ollie stood and embraced Michael. Michael rushed for the door as Ollie called, "Mike, I hope you know I ain't here to start trouble."

He replied honestly, "I know, man. Look, leave your number on my desk. I want us to get together soon."

Having Michael's trust relieved him. He felt a sense of brotherhood with Michael; something he missed for far too long. *That went well, now off to my Uncle.*

Be Mine Sassy

The pounding in Kyle's head hurt too much. He quietly demanded the pain to stop. The sound of his own voice hurt him. "I can't take it." Sapphire tried to gently rub his forehead. He pushed her hand away. "Don't."

She had more than her share of hangovers and knew the pain. She spoke softly, "I'm only trying to help."

He looked up at her and his stomach began to stir up. "You've helped enough."

She rolled over to face him and stabbed her finger in his face. "I know you ain't blaming me because you got drunk. I don't know why you drank in the first place."

He sighed, exhaling a ruthless blend of alcohol, morning breath and vomit in her face. She sat straight up and felt her eyes water. *Good God Almighty.*

"Sapphire, if you don't know why I drank, then I guess you're stupid. I can't stand the way those men look at you and touch you. I ain't like Ollie," Kyle roughly stated.

She hadn't slept all night, thinking about Ollie's proposal. Lying in bed with one man, and technically engaged to another. Things were getting out of hand. She didn't think it was time to tell Kyle. She looked gloomy over it, leading Kyle to believe he'd hurt her feelings. He spun around quickly and dizziness overtook him. He slowly wrapped his body around Sapphire as she sat on the edge of the bed. "I'm sorry. It's not your fault. But Sapphire, I can't let you take off your clothes anymore. If we are going to be together, you gotta quit."

She tried to hold back the choking tears, but her body heaved. He squeezed her tighter. "Kyle, that's what I want to do. I want to quit," she whispered.

"Then marry me and let me take care of you."

Her prayers were answered. She nodded as the tears fell from her chin onto his strong arms. He kissed her cheek. "Oh, Kyle. Your breath!"

"It's pretty bad, huh?"

"God, it's nasty!"

"Ok, let me shower and brush my teeth."

She slid off the bed so he could get up.

"Start thinking of a wedding date!" he yelled on the way to the bathroom, "I want to do this soon. Last night ended your stripping career. I'm the only man you gonna take your clothes off for."

Two proposals, one from a man she knew she loved, the other, from a man she felt she needed.

Ebb and Flo

Roosta adored his wife. She slept peacefully as the morning sunshine bathed her. Glad that Lexi was at a sleepover, he didn't wake her for church. They would catch the evening service. Right now, he wanted to love his wife again. Unwrapping her from the covers, his eyes glided across her vibrant bare body. Her breasts had lost some of their luster, but they were full enough. He went to touch one with his hand. Her eyes popped open. Startled, she grabbed the covers back.

"Morning, Red."

Red? She could hear the smile in his voice. That was what he called her when they first met. She refused to tell him her name for over a month. Ignoring the memory, she asked, "Roosta, what time is it?"

"Noon."

"Aren't you going to church?"

His voice was a warm river. "I thought we could go together later." Once again, he peeled the covers back and stirred her breasts with his mouth. She shivered with enjoyment then slid across purple satin sheets.

"Roosta, no."

Confused, he reminded her, "No? Flo, you came into my bed last night. What happened between us was different. It's sad, but we made love for the first time."

With her back turned, she reminded him, "No, you made love for the first time. I always made love to you. You always wanted sex."

That was true. God had changed everything about him. He understood what he was supposed to feel as a man. He understood what he was supposed to be with his wife; and no other. Sex was not about triumph and orgasm. It was communication between husband and wife. It was a building up of appreciation for one another that created an intimate desire to please and to be pleased. *Give and take. Ebb and flow.*

He satisfied her in a variety of ways. And, after a while, she gave up counting, fell into the rhythm. And as she fell, she gave into him more and more. When she gave, he gave more, and it intoxicated them. Roosta wanted to feel her shudder with pleasure and relax again. He kissed her along her spine. "Red, you're right. Let me love you again. Please, this is new to me."

"Roosta, I made a mistake. I'm going to take a shower. I've got to get out of here." She swiped herself up from the bed, fearing she would love him again.

Roosta rushed behind her, the two stood naked before one another. He mistook the stone cold look on her face to be disgust. *Flo, please don't hate me.* Flo was ashamed. He wasn't. Roosta couldn't understand why her eyes roamed around the room, attempting to find a shield. "Red, please talk to me."

"Roosta, I can't." She walked out clothed in her hurt, doubt and shame. Flo went into her husband's bed for *sex*. She told herself that it would only be physical. So much more, she felt his love for her. *For the first time in seven years, he loved all of me.*

Let Him Work on You

Pastor Rose's chest heaved in thriving sighs at his favorite nephew sitting in his office. Examining the boy, he looked too skinny. Then again, he thought, *Ollie was always on the slim side.* Ollie, handsome with distinct features, had a slight mustache, and a daring smile that dusted his thin lips.

His sister-in-law had some good-looking children. Unfortunately, on the inside, he knew Ollie and Vaughn were out of sorts. Thinking about the children, he added Lily to the out of sorts list. Uncertain as to why Ollie was in his office, he seized the opportunity to counsel and pray with him. Pastor Rose shook Ollie's hand and gave him a firm pat on the back. "Son, you just don't know how happy I am to see you."

Ollie felt unclean just being in his Uncle's presence. He couldn't imagine how he would feel if standing before Jesus Christ. He remembered Psalm 139 preached by his Uncle that morning. *God knows my thoughts and deeds, that can't be good.*

Pastor Rose told him to have a sit down. He sat, fidgeted until he settled into a comfortable position, crossed his legs and said, "Uncle Desi, I am happy to see you, too."

Ollie nervously eyed the door. No time to back away from his plan, he blurted out, "I'm getting married. I'm hoping you would perform the ceremony."

Being a pastor for twenty-five years, couples usually requested his blessing. This one was no less special. It honored him. He warmly asked, "Who is the young lady?"

"Unc,' it's Sassy."

Confusion creased Pastor Rose's brow.

Ollie explained, "Sassy and I lived together for three years. Things weren't working, she moved out. It's been six months since she left. I can't stop thinking about her. I miss her."

Resting his face in his hands, his Uncle said, "I see. Have you prayed about choosing Sapphire as your lifetime partner?"

Prayed? He respected his Uncle too much to lie to him. "I haven't prayed in a long time," Ollie said.

"Alright, we can change that today," Pastor Rose said. "Do you have a job? Can you care for and support a wife?"

Job? What kind of questions are these? "I'm working as an overnight security guard at a department store." He hoped once they were married, he could quit. He thought he wasn't cut out for routine jobs. He was an artist.

"Are you in love with Sapphire?"

Love? What is real love? His late grandmother said she loved him. She raised him with such a firm biblical hand, her love, felt more like hate. His mother said she loved him, but she abandoned him. Sapphire said it, too, then, she left. But now, they were going to be married. Ollie would make sure she would never leave him again. He paused before answering. He wanted to be truthful. He stared behind Pastor Rose at the wedding portrait he painted of Pastor and Mother Rose. They stared intensely into each other's eyes. If there was real love, then they had it.

"I care deeply for Sapphire. I miss and I want her home. I want to do right by her, make her a wife, my wife." That sounded good to him, and the closest to the truth he could offer. He hoped Pastor Rose bought it.

I don't buy it, Ollie. "Ollie, do you mind if we pray about this, together?"

117

His voice rose, he said, "Now?" *I need a cigarette.* He believed the sooner they were married, the better, he sprang from the seat. "Sure Uncle, let's pray," Ollie said.

Pastor Rose walked around his freshly polished desk. Placing strong loving hands on his nephew's shoulders, he prayed, "*Dear Lord, we come to you thanking you for bringing Ollie home. Oh Father, I praise you and I worship you because you never cease to amaze me. Thank you, Lord Jesus. Your son has decided to take a helpmeet, a good thing. Lead him in your Godly counsel and speak to his heart. Remove the barriers that bind him and let him hear, know and obey your voice. Guide him to walk in your will and your purpose for his life. Make him, mold him and shape him. Oh God, you are the Potter we are the Clay. Do what you do, Lord. For Lord, you make all things new. In your Son's precious name we pray, Lord Jesus Christ. Amen.*"

The prayer choked out the reality of his past. Ollie's shoulders lifted and fell as the words pierced his heart. He swallowed hard, forced the emotions down. But they refused to be consumed. He stepped back, hoped Pastor Rose would release him; he didn't. God tapped at his heart, the same way He did when he was nine years old. Ollie promised God he would always be a good soldier, but he deserted the battlefield - never became the man he should have been. At that very moment, he heard the quiet voice of God call him to attention. It was quiet, but strong, pulling deep from within. Off balance, he leaned into his Uncle's hands.

Pastor Rose hugged his nephew. "If you are serious about this Son, bring Sapphire to my office tomorrow around three."

Ollie couldn't speak; he nodded.

Don't be Deceived

The unbearable pounding in his head decided for him, that would be the first and the last time he would drink. It grew louder and then he heard voices. He reached for sweats and a T-shirt, moved slowly to the living room.

Shaky legs and bloodshot eyes - Michael could see the sting of alcohol upon his brother.

Sapphire stood between the two.

"Bro, maybe you should sit down before you fall down." Kyle tried to be cool while recovering from a hangover. It wasn't pretty. He leaned onto the arm of the sofa and took a seat.

"Guys, I'm gonna buy some food." Sapphire asked harshly, "You stayin' for lunch, Michael?" It was an invitation for him to say no. She glared at him, remembering his tone with her at the Valentine's Ball. *Boy, aren't you gonna be shocked that Kyle proposed to me.* She didn't intend to accept, but she would enjoy having the satisfaction of sticking it to Michael. Her lips curved at the sentiment.

Michael didn't like the smile and wondered about it. "I'm spending the day with my brother. Bring enough lunch for all of us." He possessively tossed his coat and jacket across the room, lifted his pant legs and sat. Michael waited for Sapphire to leave while Kyle held his head in his hands.

"You look like you've been tossing 'em back," Michael said.

"I may have had a few."

"Looks like more than a few."

"You can leave, if you wanna start preachin.'"

Michael rested a long leg across his knee. He pondered on the brick walls of the studio to avoid the pitiful sight of Kyle. He let him know.

"Preaching, Kyle that's your department, remember?"

"My preachin' days are over."

"Really, from the looks of you, I could say that's true, but I know the real you, so does God. You are called to preach. I know you're hurting over Vaughn, but no alcohol, or Sapphire will take the pain away. Give it up, and stop acting defeated. You know the word," Michael said. He quoted a Bible verse telling him he was more than a conqueror through Christ Jesus.

Kyle put on a fake grin. The tiny facial curve hurt his head, but nothing hurt more than Michael's disappointing eyes. Disguising his pain, he said, "Oh, I ain't hardly defeated. You saw that fine woman that walked out of here? This morning, she agreed to be my wife."

Michael felt as if the chair had just been pulled from under him. He yelped, "You're lyin'!"

"Nope, so you see, we can't spend the day with you. We've got a wedding to plan."

"Kyle, Sapphire isn't going to marry you. She's going to marry Ollie!" he shouted.

His head was splitting in two. Kyle held it with both hands. "Get out Michael. You're miserable over Lily, and you wanna bring me down."

"Man, you bringin' yo' self down! Come to your senses. Ollie proposed to her last night and she *is* going to marry him. That woman is playin' you."

"I know Sapphire better than you and Ollie. She doesn't want to be a stripper anymore. Ollie can't take care of her the way I can. She wants to be with me. We are getting married! I'm sorry for Ollie, but that's how it's gon' be."

They stared each other down. Kyle added, "If you can't accept my future wife, we won't have a relationship. You should leave before she gets back."

Michael grabbed his coat and swung the front door open. It slammed against the wall. He had no intentions of closing it. Sapphire met him in the hall. The words came out muffled, "Congratulations, Sassy."

Her hands held their steamy Caribbean lunch. "Congratulations, on what?"

"Your upcoming wedding to Ollie, or is it Kyle?"

How does he know about Ollie? She wondered if Kyle knew. Sapphire hid her fear and smiled broadly. She felt Michael was always looking down on her. Sticking it to him, she announced to him, as well as to herself, "It's Kyle. What did you call me last night? Oh yeah, you said I was a real piece of work. Brother-in-law, I certainly know how to work your brother, don't I?"

He leaned over, whispered in her ear, "You agreed to marry two men at the same time. Sassy, you just proved my point."

She flinched uncomfortable with him in her personal space. His words cut her, and still she held on to the smile. *What is his problem with me?* Loving and kind, Michael was a good man.

He was active in church, deeply in love with the Lord and Lily, but she felt that he treated her like she was nothing. *Like everyone else, don't I have a soul that needs to be saved?*

The door slammed, Sapphire screamed and Kyle's head painfully vibrated.

"Kyle! You gotta do something about your brother!"

Gripping his throbbing head, Kyle whined, convinced it was about to roll off his shoulders. He explained through clenched teeth, "I already took care of that. Now can you keep it down?"

She dumped aluminum plates filled with ox tails on the counter. The juice spilled through the container. "You wanna eat?"

"I don't know if it's gonna stay down."

She fixed him a paper plate of white rice and handed it to him. He frowned at it. She shoved it to him, insisted, "Come on, the rice should stay down."

He twirled his fork around before putting any rice to his lips. If he threw up one more time, he thought he was going to die. It was ironic to him. *I thought I was consuming alcohol, but the alcohol is consuming me.*

It didn't take long for Sapphire to get to the food. She was loudly sucking all the juice and meat from the ox tails. Her poor table manners further nauseated him.

"Sapphire, do you have a wedding date in mind?"

Smacking her lips, she responded, "Kyle, you just asked me two minutes ago. Do you think you should propose to me when you have a hangover? Maybe you should wait until you're feeling better." Sapphire took a gulp of soda.

He gazed up from the plate, turned his head slowly. "I know what I want. I want to take care of you. I don't want a long engagement, like I had with...." He let the words trail off. Vaughn's face shined in his heart.

The idea of someone wanting to care for her sounded wonderful. Since she lost her mother, no one said those words to her. *Kyle is all I need.* Ollie had her heart. It wasn't enough to marry him. With Kyle, she'd never have to work again or even worry about hiding money from him. "Let's elope. We could go to

Jamaica or some romantic island? I could have my dress in a week."

Her voice, static in his ears, he wondered about Vaughn. *Why aren't we married?*

She repeated, "I said, let's elope on some romantic island in a couple weeks."

Finally, stuffing a small fork full of rice in his mouth, he said, "That soon, huh? OK. In two weeks, *you* will be Mrs. Kyle Carraway."

Do it Quickly

"Aren't you coming in?"

Lily parked the black Jaguar, but she didn't turn off the ignition. She gripped the wheel and shook her head. "Vaughn, I need to do something, and I need to get it over with today." She felt the message preached in church fueled her decision.

Vaughn knew where her cousin was headed. "You want me to go with you?"

"I can handle it alone. I won't be long," Lily said.

Pastor Stevens, unlike her father, was a calm teacher. But like her father, he spoke the truth, and taught directly from the word of God. His message, *Present your bodies holy and acceptable before God, which is your reasonable service.* She had heard the message before, but in her current conflicting state, she welcomed the review. Rick's intentions were clear. If she wanted the relationship to end, it would be up to her. She needed to set things right. She and Rick would end their flirting game. It was over.

Vaughn stood by the curb as Lily drove off. She thanked God that Lily had come to her senses, hoping Lily possessed the strength to do what needed to be done.

In the daylight, Lily found Rick's secluded country home with little difficulty. The nearest neighbor was five miles away. Lily didn't know why she reflected about life around her. She trusted Rick or, did she?

Pebbles crushed under the tires as she pulled into his driveway. She moved nervously from the car, leaving her purse in the passenger's seat. After ringing the doorbell twice, and not receiving a response, she blinked up at the sun peeking through the clouds. Rick's garage door was down. Unable to determine if he was home, she walked away.

It was noon. Rick just stepped out of the shower. Hearing the dong of the bell, he stopped drying off, reached for his monogrammed black terry cloth robe, and hopped downstairs. By the time he answered, Lily was halfway down the driveway and her curls were swaying behind her. She clutched her navy maxi coat around her. Seeing her steps were brisk, he called, "Lily?"

She ran back up the walkway, wanting to get the confrontation over with. Cold, she pushed past him. It wasn't the cold air that caused her to shiver. The smell of his freshly showered body awakened her senses. *Why does my body react like this?*

"Lily, you surprised me today. I was pretty sure things were over after you left last night." She didn't answer. "You wanna sit down?"

He directed her to join him on the sofa. She declined, averted her eyes and removed the thoughts of him being naked under his robe. "I'm not staying. I can see I caught you at a bad time."

"I'm happy you stopped by."

"I'm ending this. Last night you said having sex with you was inevitable. I can't let that happen."

He let her speak. She pulled her coat tighter around her as if she was freezing. She held her head down, stared at her black designer pumps. "We work well together and I hope it won't affect our professional relationship."

He nodded. Lily's lips were saying one thing, but her body language, another. She wanted him. He could feel it. If she really wanted to end the relationship, she could have called. He had her. He smiled within and pretended to listen to what he believed was a false argument.

"I'm sorry if I led you on. As a matter of fact, I did lead you on. I thought by being with you, I was getting over Michael. I am still very angry. I know me being with you, won't change that. I'll see you at work tomorrow."

He jumped up. "Lily, wait! I have something to say, too." He turned her slowly toward him. He knew this was his last chance. What he was about to do, he was going to do quickly.

Let It Go

Flo drove for hours heading nowhere. She didn't want to go home for fear she would succumb to her husband's touch. He abused her, cheated consistently and had other children running around. *How is it possible that I still love him? Is it love?*

When the car stopped, she found herself at a quaint little church in downtown Miami; Roosta's church. The one she refused to worship with him in, now here she was.

The four o'clock service would begin in half an hour. A knock at her window startled her. Flo looked up and wiped the salty tears from her cheeks with old tissues she found in her purse.

"Would you like to come in?"

Embarrassed, Flo quietly explained, "I was...uh, I was waiting until four o'clock."

She smiled softly. "You don't have to wait. The doors are open."

Flo drifted to the pleasant voice, joined the woman inside. "What is your name?"

"Floreece Jenkins, but most people call me Flo."

"I like that name. It kind of reminds me of that show years ago. Now what was it called? Oh, I can't remember."

Flo chuckled. It felt good. She hadn't done that since she returned from New York four months ago.

"Oh, forgive me for being rude. My name is Vivian Cruz. I'm the Pastor's wife. I haven't seen you before. Is this your first time visiting?"

Flo hadn't realized the lady had led her to an office and not the sanctuary. First Lady Cruz motioned for her to take a seat in the comfortable office. The chairs were old and black, but cushiony.

"My husband said he's been coming here."

First Lady Cruz ran her hand through her short-cropped cut. It was clear to Flo she was a woman of Latin descent. Flo detected a slight accent as she said, "Jenkins, I'm not sure I know him. What does he look like?"

125

Flo would bet for sure that the reason why she didn't know Roosta was because he probably lied about going to church. "Roosta, maybe you know him as Rochester. If he'd been coming here, you would know him. He's got dreadlocks all the way pass his backside."

"Wait a minute, yes, I know him."

"You do?" Flo didn't believe it.

First Lady Cruz removed her white sweater, hung it up on a coat rack next to the entrance. Wearing a simple black sleeveless dress, she sat next to Flo. "I sure do. I prayed for him last night." She raised both hands to the heavens. "It was a glorious moment. God took his pain away last night."

"I wish He'd take mine away." Flo mumbled the words unaware she spoke aloud.

First Lady Cruz squeezed Flo's hand. "Why don't you give it to Him?"

Tears begin to fall. "It's not that easy. I've suffered years of abuse from that man. The pain doesn't go away overnight." Concern was prevalent in the lady's eyes; Flo trusted her. She continued, "On the one hand, I love him. On the other, I hate him. I want a divorce, and then I don't."

"I've prayed and counseled many abused women and men. First and foremost, you've got to forgive Roosta."

Flo's head snapped up as the tears fell onto her skirt. "You mean I should stay married to the man?"

She answered calmly, "I didn't say that. That's a decision between you and God. Now if he is still abusing you, I say run to the holy hills." First Lady Cruz smiled while waiting for the answer.

"Roosta hasn't hit me in at least two years now."

"It's sad that husbands and wives go through such unnecessary changes." First Lady Cruz sighed. "You'll have to forgive him whether you stay with him or not."

She nodded even though she wasn't sure if she could forgive. "Flo, I can tell you last night Roosta forgave himself, and God has forgiven him. It's your turn. Do that, then pray about whether you can continue to be his wife." First Lady Cruz guided

Flo to her feet. "Service is starting. I believe God has a word for you. He led you here tonight."

Flo wanted to believe that with all her heart. She needed a special word from God. She stopped in her tracks when she saw Roosta sitting on the fifth pew. First Lady Cruz gently rested her hand on Flo's back. "Come on, open your heart and receive God's word."

Lord Please be With Her

Late in the evening Lily hadn't returned from Rick's. Vaughn's worry turned from staring out of the windows, to pacing the floors. *Lily, where are you?* She tried Lily's cell again. No answer, Vaughn remembered Lily had the phone tree of employees at the firm in her phone book and found Rick's number. No answer, Vaughn prayed for Lily.

Lily awoke and tried to decipher where she was. The sound of his steady breathing alerted her. She was in bed with Rick. Naked and exposed, he slept on top of the covers. Her clothes were thrown throughout the room. To gather her thoughts, she stared at the canopy, and then eased out of bed. Rick didn't stir. She quietly gathered her clothing, found her way to the master bath.

Lily didn't recognize herself in the mirror. *What just happened?* Her hair, tousled over her hand, her pelvic area, sore, and a blood stained bed-sheet called to her. She shuddered at her innocence soaking in the Jacuzzi tub. No way to reclaim it, she dressed quickly, and escaped to her car.

Vaughn exhaled when Lily returned home hours later. The sight of Lily frightened her. Her eyes were red and puffy. Her hair was in disarray. Vaughn yelled, "He raped you! Oh my God!"

Lily broke down in her cousin's arms as her body lost strength. She began falling. Vaughn couldn't support the weight. They plummeted to the floor, cried on their knees and embraced each other.

Lily softy croaked, "Rick didn't rape me."

"You're a mess, of course he raped you."

Again, Lily solemnly answered, "No. It wasn't rape. It happened so fast."

Vaughn held Lily's watery face in her unsteady hands. "Lily, what happened?"

"I was on my way out and he kissed me. Rick kissed me long and hard. I kissed him back. We were out of control and it was like I was somebody else. He kept whispering, *'I want you Lily. Let go. Stop being perfect, God will forgive you.'*"

She held her head in shame. "I just gave in. I wanted him, too. I didn't want to fight my flesh anymore. The need and desire was so strong. I followed him to his bedroom. He was all over me, ripping my clothes away. He moved so fast. His hands were fast."

Lily cried harder. She didn't think she could, but she did. She explained finally, "Before I knew it, we were in bed together and it was happening. I couldn't think straight with everything I was feeling."

Lily allowed her body to rest flat on the cool floor. "I gave in, then fell asleep. When I woke up, I realized what had happened. Oh God. Vaughn, how did I let this happen?"

Only Trust Him

Flo welcomed the benediction of the evening service. The parishioners gathered in small clusters hugging and greeting one another. It was a friendly group of people. But she didn't feel friendly. She avoided Roosta as she raced for the exit. He ran behind her. "Slow down, Flo."

"Roosta, I'm already an hour late picking Lexi up. That preacher wanted to talk and pray for folks all night." She was certain she'd done enough praying. So when Roosta invited her with him for prayer at the altar, she refused. Answers, she needed answers and wondered where was God when she needed him.

Roosta offered, hoping for some solace between them. "Do you want to leave your car here? We can pick up Lexi together. I'll send someone to get your car tomorrow."

Flo ignored Roosta's polite suggestion, needing more time with her soul searching questions. She fastened her seatbelt, started the engine of the Mercedes and speedily drove off. Roosta accepted the screeching take off as a no.

The preached word was sharp and it cut her to the core. Flo knew the word was for her. *Let this Mind be in you that was also in Christ Jesus. How I am going to do that?* Her mind was clouded with memories of Roosta's unfaithfulness and abuse. What really taunted her? She knew it was the shame and guilt for allowing him to do it to her. *How can I still love him?*

The sound of her voice filled the luxury car. "God, how can I have yo' mind when my mind is a mess? I can't even focus on the scriptures when I read them. I read them, and I forget what I read. Roosta was a monster. Lord, I just can't believe he's changed. I've been in and out of church for years. I don't even know if I'm gonna get it right this time. Roosta, the playboy, is a Christian now? It's hard to believe."

Her feet became confused as she turned a corner. Instead of pressing the brakes, she accelerated off the narrow road. Frantic, she fought with the wheel. Too late to regain control, the front end of the Mercedes became one with an enormous tree. As her head banged against the driver's window, the airbag filled, and everything grew black. For the first time in years, Flo rested in the stillness of her mind and body.

Flo, do you doubt me? She heard no words. The voice was distinct, coming from within. It scared her. *Do you doubt me?* The darkness that comforted, now frightened her. She didn't know where she was. *Am I dead or alive? Am I in Hell?* Maybe, it was so dark, and she always believed Heaven would be full of light.

"Help me, Lord." *Flo, do you doubt your God?* The question was pulling at her. That time, she answered, "I know my God can do all things." Darkness once again comforted her. She rested in it, feeling her body float peacefully.

It Can't Be Over

Rick awoke in an empty bed. He searched for Lily in the bathroom. Instead he found the symbol of innocence in the tub. He remembered stripping the bed after he stripped Lily of her purity. He broke the covenant that had been ordained by God; only to be given to her husband. It bought him to the night he made love to his bride on their wedding night. His virgin bride offered him a pure gift. He marveled at the thought that no other man knew his wife the way he did. Lily and her husband would never share that gift.

He walked downstairs for a drink of water. He felt as if he'd been asleep for hours. He wondered what time Lily left, scratching his brow. He saw her overcoat on the floor by the door where he had dropped it from her shoulders. Rick tried to shake the feeling of guilt that was enveloping his heart. He had to call her.

Lily's chirping phone brought worry. It was a bit after midnight. She hoped everything was OK in New York. Holding back her sobs, she answered, "Hello?"

"I need to know how you're doing," Rick said.

She trembled at the sound of his voice, pulled the comforter over her body as if Rick could see her. "Rick, don't call me anymore. You got what you wanted. It's over."

He spoke quickly afraid she'd hang up. "Lily, wait, it's not like that. I...I care about you. You're the first woman I've been with since my wife died." Her silence told him she didn't believe him.

He continued wanting to keep their connection. "Darling, please don't do this. We had a great time. You're beautiful in everyway. I had no idea..."

"Stop. I don't ever wanna talk about this again. When I see you in the office, it's business and business only."

He decided she needed time to digest their wild encounter. He didn't intend to go at it that eagerly. He knew how to love a lady. But she came to him, and he wouldn't let her walk away from something he craved just as much as she did. Considering her reaction to his touch, he wondered if she wanted it more than him. Her desire testified to what he believed. He'd back off for now.

"OK Lily, if that's the way you want it. But please, don't make this out to be one-sided. I know for a fact you enjoyed us being together." He hung up leaving the question of her pleasure lingering.

Did she enjoy her first sexual encounter? She couldn't believe the way her body violently trembled with him. At the height of pleasure like she never experienced before, she felt a break in her spirit; and a reality in her emotions. It was Michael's name she cried out in pleasure. The innermost parts of her being were off balance. She knew that God's hand would lead her back to peace. Guilt was causing her to hide her face from Him.

I'll Take What I Need

Kyle was feeling better when his alarm sang at five a.m. He tried to rapidly quiet it without waking his bride-to-be. She mumbled, "Baby, you going to work?"

"Of course, I gotta pay for our trip to Jamaica." He nuzzled her neck.

She rolled on her back to face him. "You're feeling better. I hope that teaches you a lesson not to drink."

"I won't." He kissed her chin. "From now on, I get all the private dances, OK?"

That part of her life was over. She grinned. "Husband, you can have anything you want, anyway you want it. I promise."

He crawled on top of her. "I like the sound of that. You gonna play around and make me late for work."

In one quick blow, she flipped him on his back. Her strength impressed him. "Oooo, I love a strong woman."

"You're the man I prayed for. I thank God for you."

She caressed his chest with her lips. His eyes expanded and the rising fire in him halted. He didn't want to think about God. Sapphire's generous bottom jiggled as Kyle spanked it. A smile washed over her voice. "I see you have some interesting ideas Mr. Carraway."

"I do, but you better let me up. I don't wanna be late for work."

He's pushing me away. Was it something I said?

Kyle raced to the shower, and hollered, "Drive me to work. Then you can take the car and pack up your things. It's time you move in with me. In two weeks, we'll be married."

She pulled her knees to her chest, not in the mood to force Kyle to tell her what bothered him. Sapphire also had other things on her mind, for one, talking to Ollie. They weren't getting married. She'd decided to marry Kyle. Moving in with him would be a great way to stay away from Ollie.

Serious Business

Exhausted, confused, ashamed, and overall determined, Lily made her way into the office. She was a professional. Lily agreed with Rick. Two professionals could have a physical relationship and not jeopardize their professional relationship. Shuffling through a book of financials covered with her numerous handwritten notes regarding the *Emerson and Davis merger*, she had her work cut out for her.

Projections and comparable reports were awaiting her compilation. Happy to oblige, she hit the floor running. Work helped her escape visions of her rolling around in Rick's bed. They haunted her all night. *Why did I enjoy him so much?* After all, she had sinned against her God and her flesh. The tender spot in her lower right pelvic area ached. She massaged it. *Why do I still hurt?* She perked up at the sound of her office door opening.

Mr. Peter smiled at Lily impressed to see her in the office at seven in the morning. She was proving to be the productive asset they hoped for. Lily forcefully returned his friendly smile.

"Good morning, you're in early." Lily observed Mr. Peter remove his Burberry coat as he sat before her.

She wasn't up for the unplanned meeting. "I have a lot of work regarding this merger."

He crossed his legs. "I'm glad you are taking it seriously. A merger of this size is nothing to laugh at."

Lily was afraid he was going to stay a while. She folded her hands on top of the financial reports, as she held his gaze, she added, "I couldn't agree with you more."

He was silent for a moment; it unnerved her. Lily remained eye level with him. "How are things going with Rick?"

He didn't mention he'd seen them leave together on numerous occasions after work. He hoped it was just friendly encounters and nothing more. An affair gone badly could have setbacks. Lily had potential and he wanted it to appreciate.

Broadening her smile to relieve his fears, and her own, she answered, "Things are working out well. He is a wonderful mentor." She hoped he would leave it at that.

His eyes drifted to his shoes and back to her. "That's good to hear. He's definitely one of our best." He gathered his Burberry and brief case. "Since you've come in early to work, I won't take up anymore of your time."

Air pressed to escape her lungs. She thought to hold it in until he was gone.

Before he turned, he added, "Lily, if you have any problems of any kind, please feel free to come to me. I will do everything in my power to make sure nothing interferes with the success of our firm."

Lily squeezed her folded fingers. *What does that mean?* She wouldn't let anything interfere with her success, or that of the firm. Revealing her teeth through her smile, she assured him. "I understand that it is in all of our interests to uphold the image of the firm."

He Holds Me Captive

Sapphire drove a black Porsche into her driveway. Ollie wondered how she could afford the sleek car, and then remembered it was parked outside of Lily's home the night of the dinner party. It belonged to Kyle. He leaped out of his old gray Sedan and approached the driver's side. She jumped when she saw Ollie waiting for her. *He keeps popping up everywhere these days.* She was glad about this time, since she had to get rid of him. She sang, "Good morning, handsome."

"Sassy, we gotta talk." Frustrated, he snatched the house keys out of her hand to let them in.

She followed him inside. Ollie took account of the place. *There was a place for everything, and everything was in its place.* Sapphire's furniture was old, but she kept everything clean. Ollie decided the little house was much better than his dump. That would be where they would live after the wedding. The last time he was there, they enjoyed a really good time. She wasn't as welcoming this time. She neglected to offer him a seat, or even consider him. Sapphire tossed her purse onto the kitchen counter, zeroed in on several lush plants and trees that adorned the living room and began promptly watering them.

He towered over her. "Sassy, you agreed to marry me. I understand Kyle was drunk and you took him home, but did you have to stay all night and the next day?"

She cut her eyes at him. He patted his pants pockets as jealousy fueled him on. Even with her back turned, she knew what he searched for and ordered, "Don't you smoke in *my home*."

Dumbfounded, he asked, "What? You gonna have to come again. We 'bout to be married."

Sapphire turned and sat comfortably on the loveseat. Secure with Kyle and her future, she would enjoy telling Ollie her good news. She scornfully roamed her eyes over him. Bad idea. Ollie's sex appeal oozed from his pores. It unnerved her. She tried to put some bite into her words.

"I thought a lot about your so-called proposal. I know you are not serious about marrying me. You want me to take care of you. I won't do that anymore, so you can hang it up."

You think you know me. Ollie prepared to pull out all the stops, got down on one knee and slid a diamond wedding band sheathed with sapphires on her finger. His eyes never left hers. "Sassy, I'm serious. Marry me. I've already been to church. I asked my Uncle to marry us. He wants to see us today at three o'clock for counseling and prayer."

Staring at the diamonds and sapphires, her hand trembled in awe. *He is serious.* She softly said, "Ollie, oh my God. I don't know what to say." Joy replaced the bite in her voice. He smiled, and covered her hands with his. "Say yes, Sassy."

"Ollie, I love you so much."

"I know, baby. Say, yes." He rose to kiss her. She stopped his lips with her hand. The diamonds sparkled before her. *I have to be sure.* "Ollie, I'm not stripping anymore. I quit. This time, things *will* be different. You are going to have to take care of me."

His eyes filled with tears. *Work? Take care of you?* It was a frightful thought. *I'll play along for now.* "Sassy, whatever you want." His lips brushed hers and released a sigh of pleasure. He whispered, "Sassy?"

Once again, strong within his hold, she surrendered. "Yes, baby?"

"Let's go to your bedroom," he simply requested.

"Follow me." And with ease, she led him into hours of blinding desire.

Husband and Father

"Dad, is Mom alright? I want to see her and I want to see her now," Lexi cried. "Dad, where's Mom?"

Roosta tried to smile at his little girl through the rearview mirror. "Lexi, Mom is fine. She's resting right now. I am taking you to school today."

She banged on the leather seats of the white Lexus. "Dad, no school, I wanna see Mom, now. Why didn't she pick me up yesterday?" She screamed and Roosta pulled the car over to the shoulder of the expressway.

Roosta spent more time making children than he did raising them. Lexi's hissy fit was trying his patience. Sitting next to her in the backseat, he realized soothing her would be no easy task. Calmly, he assured her, "Lexi, your mother is fine. I told you, she's resting." Lexi's watery eyes broke his heart. He watched as Lexi's jean shorts absorbed her tears. "Ok, I'll take you to your mother. But Lexi, listen to me good, OK?"

Smearing the salty tears with the backs of her hands, her voice steadied. "OK, Dad."

"After church last night, your Mom left to pick you up from Tasha's house. She had a minor car accident on the way. She hurt her head. Mom's in the hospital."

Lexi started to panic again. "Dad, is Mom going to die?"

"No! No!" His tone surprised him. He calmed, said, "She has a little head injury called a concussion, but she is *not* going to die. As a matter of fact, she's coming home today. The doctors wanted her to rest and watch her overnight. That's all. If you don't want to go to school today, that's fine. You can go to the hospital later when I pick her up. Ok?"

She wrapped her arms around her dad's neck and rubbed his dreadlocks. "OK, Dad. Dad?"

He continued to hold his little girl in his arms." "Yes, princess?"

"I love you."

Those three little words from his child melted all his doubts and fears away. They would be a family. He had three

137

other children he knew of to care for. With God's help, it would all work out. "Father God, I need you."

Lexi looked up and saw tears in her father's eyes. "Dad, are *you* praying?"

"Yes, I am going to be praying a lot these days."

Wanna Talk About It?

Vaughn's thigh flashed through an ankle-length black wrap-skirt as she walked into Lily's office. She looked down at her cousin who was diligently creating a spreadsheet.

Eyes on the monitor, she asked, "What's up?"

Vaughn sat and crossed her legs. "That's why I'm here. You tell me?"

Focusing on the numbers on the desk, she continued to type. "Vaughn, I got a lot of work to do."

"Yeah, so?"

"So, that's what's up."

Vaughn uncrossed her legs and leaned forward to rest her elbows on her lap. "Lily, I know you didn't sleep last night. You're probably feeling guilty about what happened. You know that drowning yourself in work is not going to help."

Lily snapped, "We will not discuss that in the office! What happened is personal. As for work, I do have a lot to do. Now, do you need anything?"

"Not at the moment."

Displeased Lily was closing her out, Vaughn stood and decided to continue the conversation at home.

"Vaughn?"

"Yeah?"

"Could you order me a corned beef sandwich and a tea?"

Vaughn frowned as Lily's office door opened.

"You're eating in today?" The ladies focused their attention to the door as Rick squeezed in. Vaughn sized him up through his blue and white striped-shirt. He was slick. She wanted to slap the smirk off his face.

"Lily, I'll order your lunch now." Loudly adding, "And I'll eat in with you." Sucking her teeth at Rick, she walked out.

Ignoring Vaughn, Rick continued to smile. Lily typed on. "Good afternoon, Lily."

Eyes on the monitor, she politely responded, "Good afternoon." He sat.

She sighed, wished he wouldn't stay.

"How are you feeling?"

He sounds genuinely concerned. With false cheer in her voice she answered, "I'm feeling fine. Really busy here."

"I can see that. I've put together some proposals. I thought I could go over them with you at lunch." He tried to catch her eye. It didn't work.

"As you've probably heard, I'm eating with Vaughn. How about later this afternoon?"

Bringing it back to the real reason for his interruption, he asked again, "Are you sure you're feeling OK?"

She finally looked at him. "Rick *am* I supposed to be feeling sick or something? Last night is history. I'd appreciate it if you would not bring it up again. This merger requires our full attention and that's what I intend to focus on."

His tone was hushed as if the walls had ears. "I agree. I was hoping things were not over. I would like to continue seeing you. Maybe things went too fast. I'll slow down."

She lowered her voice also. "Rick, there's no need for that. I like you, not *love* you. That's why last night was a mistake. I don't believe in casual relationships."

He raised his shoulders. "Neither do I, and it wasn't a mistake. We both wanted to be together and *I* have no regrets. Lily, it was beautiful. Don't make it out to be ugly, or wrong."

"Rick, it was a sin."

He frowned and mockingly stated, "You can't believe that."

The pain in her side was nagging at her as if it concurred with her statement. She continued slowly, "Rick, sex outside of marriage is not what I believe and neither does God. It's over. Let's focus on work and that's all."

139

Nodding, he got up. He directed sharply, "Meet me in my office at one thirty. We'll go over the proposals. Have *your* comparables and projections ready."

Relieved he left her office, she noticed the time on her computer, a quarter to one. She didn't have time to chat with Vaughn and complete the reports. No problem. She would wolf down a few bites of lunch and work faster. Determined to put the events of yesterday behind her, she turned the page and continued typing.

A Tie

A brutal wind flung ice and snow against the bedroom windows. Ollie wondered when it began to snow. Sapphire stirred. Sleep filled Ollie's voice, he asked, "Sassy, what time is it?"

She lifted her head and the bun in the center of it fell off. He chuckled as she said, "It's three thirty Ollie. What's so funny?"

"This." He threw the ball of hair at her.

She rolled onto her stomach. "Ollie, why you always gotta mess up my hair?"

He picked up the ball again. "Girl, this ain't hardly yo' hair."

Three thirty rang in his head. He bounced from the bed.

"What's the matter wit 'chu?" Sapphire looked up at him.

He fumbled for his cell phone in the pocket of his jeans. "We were supposed to meet my Uncle at three."

"Oh," is all she said. She didn't want to meet with Pastor Rose until she had a chance to talk to Kyle. Sapphire needed to get her men sorted out. Two days of on and off again decisions was making her hungry. Reaching for an oversized nightshirt, Ollie admired the silhouette of her insatiable body.

"Where you goin'?"

She scratched her short spiked hair. "To the kitchen, I'm hungry."

The purse on the counter was vibrating. She opened it and answered the cell.

He barked, "Sapphire, why aren't you answering your phone? I've been calling you all day."

"Kyle, I must have fallen asleep. My phone is on vibrate." She stretched as she yawned and searched the fridge for ham and cheese. "Is something wrong?"

"Aren't you picking me up from work? You know the market closes at four. You should be on your way."

Her body perked up from the fridge. She'd forgotten she had his car. "Oh, Kyle, I'm sorry. I ain't gonna make it by four. Is there anyway you could take the train?"

"The train?" His voice rose an angry octave.

She ducked into the bathroom near the kitchen for fear of Ollie overhearing. Adding a little sugar to her voice, she whined, "Oh, baby, don't be mad. Why were you calling me all day anyway?"

Huffing, he reminded her. "You said you wanted to get married in two weeks. I've been on the phone with the travel agent. I wanted to get your input. We leave two weeks from today." *Oh no, I didn't know you would book the trip today.*

Ollie knocked on the door. "Sassy, you in there?"

She flushed the toilet and pretended she didn't hear him and quickly said, "Kyle, I'll be over later tonight. We can talk about it then." Sapphire left the phone in the medicine cabinet.

Ollie was making a sandwich when she stepped out. "Is everything OK with your Uncle?" Sapphire asked while averting her eyes.

He chomped the sandwich in half. "Yeah, he invited us to dinner Saturday."

She nodded and slapped some ham on wheat. Saturday was good. She knew by then, things would be settled with Kyle. Ollie finished eating and gave her his sexy grin.

"Do you want more of me?"

Oh yes! His desire rose just at the sight of her. No need for foreplay, he pushed her into the fridge and leaned into her. She moaned. "Stop, Ollie. I'm hungry."

He pecked at her spot, knowing what she really wanted. She relaxed as he whispered, "Why don't you finish your sandwich in the bedroom?"

"I'll race you."

They took off laughing as they both tried to fit through the doorway. She squeezed through first and triumphed. "I win."

He pushed her onto the mangled sheets. Looking into her eyes, he declared, "It's a tie."

Lay Aside Every Weight

Flo spent three days in bed while Roosta waited on her hand and foot. He was *amazing*. And that really bothered her. It would be so easy to walk away from their marriage if he weren't. Weights had taken a hold of her mind. She remembered the message preached the evening she had the car accident. *Let this mind be in you, which was also in Christ Jesus.*

The words wouldn't depart her spirit. They compelled her to reflect on her entire life. Pastor Cruz told them, *"Death sometimes comes from self-destruction. Self-destruction is derived from weights of the mind. A weight could be bitterness, un-forgiveness, doubts, insecurities, hate, anger and jealousy."* She'd had her share of all of them. Un-forgiveness still harbored in her heart for Roosta.

Reading the scriptures softly, First Lady Cruz sat next to Flo. Flo's eyes were dark and swollen. Sleep consistently eluded her. Realizing Flo's mind was elsewhere, she asked, "Do you want to stop? We can finish Bible study another time. I don't want to overload you."

"You're not. I wanted to know if you could go over the message your husband preached on Sunday."

She clutched Flo's hand. "Oh, *Weights of the Mind,* that is a powerful message. What in particular do you want to know?"

Flo propped up on the pillows. "I want to know more about weights of self-destruction." "OK, mama."

First Lady Cruz' Latin accent was stronger. She seemed not to be a first lady, but a friend explaining the scriptures. Flo knew that sometimes pastors and their wives wore professional facades. She was happy she was dropping hers.

"Let me break it down to you. I am going to give you a Biblical reference to make it easier for you to understand, alright?" Flo nodded and was relieved the dizziness was mild.

"Let's look at Judas," Lady Cruz opened her Bible and continued. "Here you see because Judas could not deal with the guilt of betraying Jesus, therefore, he hung himself. The weight was guilt, and the result was suicide."

Flo understood. "Let's take a look at Genesis, Adam and Eve. They had a similar feeling of guilt because they were

143

disobedient. The weight of guilt, shame and disobedience led to the result of sin and death."

She flipped through her Bible for another reference. "Now, let's look at one more example, jealousy. Cain killed his bother Abel because he was jealous."

Flo quietly stated, "These three examples lead to death."

"Yes. Also, what's important to see is no one asked for forgiveness or forgave him or herself. Negative feelings that consume us, usually lead to death. Sometimes it is a physical death, or sometimes a spiritual death."

Flo rested her head back. Warm tears dripped down her chin, her voice barely understandable. "That's what I feel like, like I'm slowly dying. The more I hold onto the hurt from Roosta, the more I die."

First Lady Cruz left her chair, sat on the bed and dabbed Flo's cheeks with pink tissues. "Flo, you have to let the hurt go and forgive Roosta. Have you talked to him?"

She shook her head as the tears continued to drift.

"Do it tonight, don't delay."

Flo released her pain as sobs overtook her body.

Happy for her release, Lady Cruz encouraged her, "Let it go, mama."

Flo reached for her new friend. They embraced as First Lady Cruz caressed Flo's hair and sang.

I'm Not Going to Face Him

Donita frowned at Lily who was hunched over as she opened the door. Afraid of the tense look on Lily's face, she asked, "Are you alright?"

Lily lifted her head slowly. "I just have this annoying pain in my side. It started Sunday evening." The thought of sinning on Sunday was unbelievable to her. Lily straightened a bit as she made her way to the couch.

"You want me to take you to the doctor? It could be serious," Donita offered.

Lily declined, sat gently, feeling the pain radiated into her right leg. "I just took something. It should subside soon."

"Are you sure?"

She grunted, but said, "I'm sure. But I don't think I'm gonna be able to meet with the team for career week."

That disappointed Donita, but understood. "That's OK. Your health is more important."

Lily pointed to the table as she stretched out her right leg. "Those are some notes on how to get started. Vaughn agreed to meet with the team tonight. She's been to enough career weeks to know how it works."

Willing to accept Vaughn's unplanned assisternce, Donita sighed. "It's nice that she agreed to help us. I really like Vaughn."

Surprised, she asked, "You know her?"

Her voice was warm as she told her, "She came to dinner on Saturday. We enjoyed her company and we prayed for you."

"Me?"

"She told me about the man at your job."

Vaughn joined Donita and Lily. Lily smiled at her cousin and continued, "No need to worry. I've ended that relationship. I'm on the right path."

Vaughn *was* worried. She tried to get Lily to pray with her, but she turned away, explaining that she needed more time before she could face God. Vaughn reminded her that the scripture said that she could go boldly to the throne of grace, no matter what.

Donita asked, "Ready to go, Vaughn?"

Vaughn wondered about Lily. "Are you gonna be alright?"

Lily shooed them away. "Go, go. I'll be fine. The medicine should kick in soon, and then I can get some work done."

Vaughn pointed at her. "Don't over do it. I'll be back as soon as it's over."

When the door latched, Lily sprang up. She *was* in pain, but not as much as she led on. She couldn't face God or the church. Grabbing her reports off the coffee table, she pranced upstairs.

You Can't Tell Me Nothing!

Sapphire almost fell as she slipped in the snow. Kyle gripped her before she went down. "Whoa, it's slippery out here."

Kyle tried not to look into Sapphire's eyes. He knew it wasn't the snow that kept them apart for the past three days. She was avoiding him. There wouldn't be a wedding. "You got your balance?" He asked before letting her go.

She nodded. "I think so."

Kyle continued to dig his car out of her driveway as he let her know, "You don't have to help me. I can handle this. It's cold, go inside."

She didn't argue with him and had hot chocolate waiting for him when he finished. He sat and sipped it, not really knowing how it would end. "This is good."

"Um hum," Sapphire agreed and noticed the whip cream rested in Kyle's trimmed mustache. With a chuckle, she pointed to it. He grinned as he wiped it away.

Minutes of awkward silence hung in the air and then shock filled Kyle's eyes. "I just saw you three days ago, when did you get married?"

Sapphire wanted the hot chocolate to mellow the moment. It didn't. She responded nervously, "Married? Kyle I'm not married."

He pointed to the diamond and sapphire wedding band. "That's a nice ring."

"Oh this? This is a…"

Waiting for the lie and/or excuse she would offer him, he crossed his knee over his leg. Leaning back, he pushed. "It's a what Sassy?"

Uncertain of what to say, she walked toward the living room. "Kyle, please come over here so we can talk."

"No need. I'm comfortable right here." Kyle demanded. "*You* come back to the table and tell me the truth." She wavered. "I'm waiting Sassy." She said nothing, so he did. "Michael was right? You agreed to marry Ollie, and then you agreed to marry me."

146

"It's…it's not like that. I didn't want to hurt you."

"Spare me the pain, Sassy."

She flung the question at him. "Kyle, why are you callin' me by my stage name?"

Ollie used it as an endearment, Kyle, a curse.

"What else should I call you? You're, a performer."

"Kyle, what I do, and who I am, are two different things!" Her anger escalated. Although she knew she had no reason for it. Kyle just wanted the truth.

"Are you sleeping with Ollie?"

She didn't answer. "You were having sex with both of us." It was a statement as well as a question.

"Should I care? Men do it all the time."

"Not all men." The indifferent expression on her face explained she felt no penitence. Sapphire was out for self. They were done and, with nothing more to discuss, he neatly put on his bulky ski jacket and gloves. Approaching the closing door of their relationship, he looked at the woman he almost made Mrs. Kyle Carraway.

Beyond her store bought ponytail, inflated breasts and skin-deep beauty, he felt sorry for her soul. "Take care of yourself, Sapphire. I hope you know; Ollie can't save you. If you're looking for a Savior, look to Jesus."

Considering the hot times they shared, she doubted his advice. Disgusted with him, she looked him up and down. "You can't give nobody advice. You washed up, so called, Christian. Get the hell out of my house!"

I'm Free

Roosta helped Flo to Lexi's room so she could kiss her good night. She was almost asleep cuddled in her comforter. She smiled as her mother's lips grazed her cheek. "Nite, Mom," she whispered.

"Nite, baby."

Flo bent slowly adjusted the covers. Roosta helped Flo stand up straight, prevented dizziness from overtaking her. They took it slow to the next room. Roosta asked if she needed anything along the way. She didn't because he had made her very comfortable during her recovery.

There was one thing she desperately needed to give him. When she was settled, she patted the bed. Uneasy and unsure of what she wanted to talk about, he sat. "Roosta, I need to tell you some things. Things I was thinking about when my car ran into that tree. I should have been more focused on the road."

"Flo, don't blame yourself, accidents happen."

"I don't blame myself for the accident." Roosta hung his head. *Does she blame me?*

She took a couple of sips of water that he left by the bed for her. "Roosta, you've hurt me so bad over these years, inside and out. I've had bruises, bumps, black eyes and busted lips because of you. You cheated on me and gave Shay Lynn three babies."

He nodded feeling a lump in his throat. The memories were like old movies that played over and over again in his mind.

"I stayed with you for seven years and took the abuse. I thought if I watched what I said to you and gave you Lexi, the abuse would stop. It didn't."

Roosta held back the stinging tears as he listened to her heart. "I realize now that no matter what I did, you wouldn't stop. I'm not the problem."

He agreed. "I know. I'm sorry."

"I believe you, and I forgive you."

Their tears descended in harmony. "You do?"

"Yes Roosta, I want all the promises God has for me. I refuse to die."

He shook his head in agreement, told her, "I know how you feel." He stood, but not before telling her, "Thank you for forgiving me."

As he walked to the door, she called, "Roosta, I want to talk about the divorce."

Frozen, he stood in place. He didn't turn as he said, "Flo, please don't divorce me."

"Roosta, I don't know if I want one," she quietly admitted.

Exhilaration flooded his heart as he ran and knelt by her bedside. He buried his head in her stomach and his dreadlocks washed over her. She touched them and he declared, "Flo, I promise; I am going to be the husband God wants. I promise. I love you, Flo. I love you so much."

"Roosta, look at me."

Their faces were wet with tears when she said, "Roosta, I love you, too."

I Am My Sister's Keeper

March blew in a new season and Michael, decided to blow away his rule of no communication with Lily. He held his breath, hoping she would receive him with joy.

"Michael, I didn't know you had my work number."

Michael's voice, so uplifting, Lily turned from her computer and let it flood her spirit.

"I got the number from your father. I hope you don't mind."

"Of course not. It's been awhile. How are things?"

He doodled lilies and roses on his drawing board, told her, "Things are good. I'm glad it's Friday."

"Me, too. Although, I'll probably be working tomorrow."

"Yeah? Working hard, huh?"

"Too hard. How's the weather up there?"

"It's cold here."

"I bet. I don't miss New York's March wind."

"How's the weather in Atlanta?"

" It gets cool. We have some cold days, but nothing like New York. Ouch!" Lily shifted in her seat, and then, unzipped her skirt from behind. A month after the encounter with Rick, she still hurt.

"Lily, are you OK?"

Disguising the increasing pain in her voice, she said, "I'm fine, just a little pain in my side."

He didn't like hearing her having pain. Concerned, he stopped drawing. "Did you get it checked out?"

"Not yet. It usually feels better when I take something."

Her voice made him feel alive. He began pacing in his office, enjoying the sound of her voice. Just then, he received a call on his cell. It was Ollie. He decided to call him back and said, "Lily, go to the doctor today." He tried to put a chuckle in his voice. "Don't make me have to come to Atlanta and take you myself."

She laughed through the pain. "No need. I'll go. I promise."

"Good, happy to hear it. Does that mean… I don't get the opportunity to come see you?"

Her mouth dropped. "You want to see me?"

"I miss you."

"When do you want to come?"

He sat down again, asked, "You tell me when it's convenient, and I'll be there."

She checked her calendar. This weekend was the Career Week. She hadn't done any of the work, and she hadn't been to church in weeks. She was going to support Vaughn. Donita said Vaughn was doing an excellent job. She asked brightly, "How's next weekend?"

"Next weekend is perfect." He realized his voice was higher than usual. Bringing it down, he said, "See you then."

"I can't wait to see you. I've missed you too, Michael."

They ended the call with a few pleasantries and Lily called her cousin on the intercom.

Vaughn ran in. "Girl, what's up? You told me to get in here right away. Did I make a mistake or something?"

Lily leaped for joy as she hugged her. And forgetting the walls of the office were made of glass, she kept jumping until her skirt began to fall. *Uh, oh.* She caught it before she revealed too much information.

"Talk to a sister." Vaughn couldn't wait for Lily to spit it out.

Through squeals, Lily shouted, "Michael's coming to see me next weekend!"

Vaughn gasped. "He is? Lily, that's great!"

Vaughn thought Michael's visit might get her back on track with God. Vaughn pointed. "Hey, what's up with your skirt?"

Catching her breath, she brushed it off, "Oh nothing, my side was bothering me again."

Vaughn found Lily's purse and suit jacket, and pulled Lily by the arm. "That's it. We're going to the doctor, right now."

"Vaughn, I'm fine. Cut it out."

"Oh, no. I am my sister's keeper, and you are getting on my nerves with this pain. Let's go!"

Lily stood at the door with her hands on her waist.

"March girl, fo' I tare yo' hind parts up," Vaughn sternly ordered.

Lily thought Vaughn sounded just like her mother.

Welcome Home

"Do you have time for an old friend?" The tenor of Kyle's voice, so much like his own, drew Michael from his work.

Michael smoothly replied, "I always have time for you brother. Is the Market closed?"

"You know on Fridays, I'm out the door at four o' one," Kyle lightly joked. Bidding his time, he leaned over his brother's shoulder, wondering what it was he worked on. "Looks good."

"Thanks."

The artwork above Michael's desk captured Kyle's eyes. He studied it. "So, what is it?"

Michael answered, "That's a painting of rainbows. It's a reminder of hope. I sometimes forget God's promises to me."

"Me, too."

Kyle sighed. "But I was referring to the sketches."

"Oh, it's a design for an indoor children's playground. They're calling it *Bubbles*. It will be franchised throughout the Northeast." Michael chuckled.

Kyle sat in his brother's executive seat. Doubtfully, he inquired, "Have you given up on me?"

Michael turned away from the drawing board, faced his brother. "Never."

"Really? You stopped calling, stopped emailing me. I haven't seen you in over a month."

"That doesn't mean I've given up. I haven't stopped praying for you. It's only been a week since I last called you."

"It seems longer."

"You look tired, brother."

"Man, I am so tired. Tired of being out of my Father's will. I need the Lord back in my life. I need Him more than this air I'm breathing."

"Tell Him that."

Kyle stood and walked to face the wide windows of the office. "I spent the whole night in prayer, crying out to the Lord. I need to go back to church. I want you to go with me tonight."

Kyle's shoulders heaved. He shoved his hands into his jeans. Michael realized Kyle was crying. Within, Michael cried, too, tears of joy.

"Man, you don't know how happy I am to hear those words from you. You couldn't have picked a better night. Tonight is men's service." Michael joined his brother at the window. "I knew you'd be back. I just wasn't sure what it was going to take for you to realize it."

"I can't even explain it. From the time I caught Vaughn in bed, until the night Sapphire called me a washed out Christian, I felt like I was in a dream world. You know, underwater, drowning. I enjoyed Sapphire. Well, my flesh sure did, but my spirit, it was dying and I was ashamed. I wanted to let Sapphire go, and then I didn't. I thought if I married Sapphire, I could please God while holding a grudge against Vaughn. I was in sin trying to justify it anyway I could."

Michael let Kyle talk. He'd listen all night.

Is it a Bug?

Vaughn entered the sterile white examination room. Lily rested on her back covered by a blue sheet. Her size six feet was in stirrups.

Seeing the fear in Lily's eyes, Vaughn asked, "What'd the doctor say?"

"She said she felt a small cyst. They're bringing a sonogram machine down."

Vaughn smiled. "Cysts are very common among women. It's probably nothing." Warmly she inquired, "You wanna pray?"

Lily nodded.

"Heavenly Father, thank you for being there every time we call. We pray that if anything is wrong inside Lily's body, you will make it right. By your stripes, we are healed. Forgive us of our sins. We cast our cares upon you as you calm our fears. Our lives are in your hands. Amen."

The tears fell sideways out of Lily's eyes. Vaughn gripped her hand. It seemed like days before the technician set up the machine and the doctor trailed behind. "Who is this lovely lady, Lily?"

"Dr. Miles, this is my cousin, Vaughn. Can she stay while you do the sonogram?"

Dr. Miles could see Lily was frightened. She would bend the rules, this time. "Vaughn, you can stay as long as you remain in the corner. There's a seat, if you'd like to take it."

Vaughn was happy, even though, she preferred holding Lily's hand. For now, she'd take the corner.

The doctor explained, "Lily, this is what we call a vaginal or internal sonogram." She showed Lily a long white tube resembling a microphone. "It allows me to see what's going on inside of you. I can see everything on this screen."

Lily looked over and nodded.

She apologized before she got started. "Lily, I know it's uncomfortable. Try to think pleasant thoughts, OK?"

She nodded again, but couldn't stop the tears. She remembered Michael's phone call and that she would see him soon. That was a very pleasant thought.

"OK, Lily, I see the cyst. Most times they are not serious. These kinds of cyst usually develop when you ovulate. I'm assuming that's when you feel the pain?" Doctor Miles continued to focus on the mini screen oblivious to Lily's response.

Surprised, she asked, "Lily, why didn't you tell me that you're pregnant?"

Lily shouted, "Cuz I'm not. I haven't missed a period."

"Lily, you *are* pregnant. The embryo is about four weeks old. Look, that's your baby, right there." She highlighted the screen.

Vaughn raced over. Lily stared at the tiny baby in shock. To her, it didn't look like a baby at all. So tiny, it resembled a bug of some sort.

Date Night

Driving to meet her date, Flo decided she was going to give her new man a chance. The old man, she would have fed to the wolves. However, the new man was wonderful. She was never so much in love. A month passed since Flo forgave Roosta. She decided it was time to invite him back into their bedroom.

He'd given her a gift of pampering at the finest spa in Miami. Her day was spent being plucked, waxed, massaged, manicured, wrapped and released into a body of silky skin. She intended to let him feel his money's worth.

She chose a simple, yet elegant, navy knee length, sleeveless dress. Her red, shoulder-length hair was blown and flipped to perfection. The navy-matching mules she wore clicked against the pavement as she stepped out of her new white Mercedes. That was another gift from Roosta, since she crashed her old one.

Impressed she still had it, and only two months till her forty-sixth birthday, her pink lips sparkled into a smile. Flo's walk was dangerous when she put the umph in it. That day, she was putting all the umph in it she could muster up. Her thick bottom was swaying to and fro.

Russell, Paul's replacement, got a full view of the showstopper and immediately went to offer his assistance. "Miss, how can I help you today?"

"I'm on my way to see my husband."

Russell was looking at Flo as if she was his next meal and he hadn't eaten in weeks. "Does your husband work here?"

"I'm Roosta's wife, and you must be Russell." She extended a hand. He held it.

"Yes. Wow! Roosta is a lucky man."

Russell's attention was so engrossed on Flo, he didn't hear Roosta approach from behind. Roosta strongly informed him, "Blessed. I'm a blessed man." Realizing he was still holding Flo's hand, he let it go quickly.

"Excuse me. Roosta man, your wife, she's...very attractive."

"I know." Roosta planted a loud kiss on his wife's lips.

Pushing him aside, he instructed, "Russell, you can go help that father and daughter over there." He pointed to his left as he continued, "They're looking for a college car."

With his eyes still on Flo, he replied, "Sure, Boss. It was a pleasure to meet you, Mrs. Jenkins."

Softly and smoothly, Flo kissed her husband again. Roosta crowed, "This is a business. Let's take it in my office?"

Intertwining her fingers with his, she said, "Lead the way."

Roosta kissed her passionately, pressing her back against the door of his office. He was thankful he replaced the broken glass door with cherry oak wood.

Flo's voice was thick. "Babe, we're gonna be late for the movie."

"What time is the show?"

"Six thirty."

Massaging her hips in his hands, he said, "Ain't no show better than the one in this room. How 'bout a quickie?"

"Oh no! I really want to see the new *Tyler Perry* movie. Plus, tonight we are celebrating the new you, and the new me." She played with his dreads as she continued, "After the movie, we'll have dinner. Then I'm taking you home for a long night of heated lovemaking, in *our* bedroom."

After nibbling on her bottom lip, he said, "Thank you."

"Thank you for what?"

"Thank you for giving me this chance. Thank you for going to counseling with me this past month. After everything I've done to you, I know only God can and will make us complete. I love you."

"He will. Tonight, I want you to show me all the ways you love me."

All Have Fallen

Kyle entered the lobby of the mega-church and marveled at how many men were packing in. He wondered how he was able to stay away from the house where he'd spent most of his time. The doors of the sanctuary were open, but his feet almost wouldn't carry him in. He knew it wasn't true, but he felt he was going to bring the roof down when he entered.

Michael tapped him on his shoulders, interrupting the dreadful thoughts. "Hey, Kyle."

"Hey."

Michael looked around. "Man, Ollie said he was going to meet me here tonight. I don't see him anywhere."

Kyle wanted to think of Ollie as the man that stole his woman. The truth, Sapphire didn't belong to either one of them. He didn't know Ollie was coming to church, he asked, "When did you last speak with him?"

"Earlier, at work today. I'm gonna wait here. Save us a seat?"

Stalling, Kyle found his way to Pastor Rose's office. Pastor Rose was on the phone. "Sweetie, yes, service is about to start soon. You called the girls? Hum, I guess they're working late again. Wait up for me. I love you Vie."

Pastor Rose almost dropped the phone when he saw Kyle standing in his office. "Kyle! What a blessing it is to see you."

"Pastor."

Pastor Rose invited him to sit on the leather couch. "How are you doing Kyle?"

"Better now that I'm here...I think."

Pastor Rose discerned Kyle was consumed with painful emotions. Without thinking, the words of Romans 8:1 escaped him. *"Therefore there is now no condemnation for those who are in Christ Jesus."*

Kyle continued, *"...because through Christ Jesus the law of the Spirit of life set me from the law of sin and death."*

Pastor Rose smiled. "Don't you think that says it all?"

"I know God's word has the final say so, but I don't understand how I got so caught up with Sapphire."

Pastor Rose got up and closed the door of his office. He walked back with a story to tell. "Do you think you're the first man to get caught up with a desirable woman? Just read the Old Testament. There are plenty of men that fell short and some women, too."

"I know," Kyle somberly replied.

"Then you should know that it happened to me," Pastor Rose candidly stated.

Kyle looked at the man whom he loved like a father and squinted in question. "You?" He shockingly asked.

"Even me. I was intimate with a woman while married to Violet."

That was too heavy for Kyle to comprehend, so he just listened. Pastor Rose told the story like a tale he was no longer connected to. "When I say intimate, I'm not referring to sexual intercourse."

"So you weren't intimate?"

"I was very intimate. See you gotta be careful. The enemy is very cunning. I thought since there was no sex involved, I wasn't unfaithful. But if you're vulnerable, there's room for a fall."

Kyle wasn't following. Pastor Rose knew he needed to explain things quickly and head downstairs into the sanctuary. "I had a woman friend, the church secretary. I was spending more time at church than at home with Vie and the girls. They were about five and six and a handful.

Ministering was becoming very difficult. I spent more time talking about it to my woman friend, than I did my own wife. With each conversation, we got closer and closer. Then we started meeting for lunch and dinner outside of the church. We talked on the phone to catch up with one another. When an issue came up, I looked to her before Jesus, or Vie. Finally, we were both on a retreat and Vie didn't go. The woman considered me her man."

So glad it was long ago, Pastor Rose smiled at the thought. "The woman made it plain at the retreat. I came into my hotel room and, to my surprise, she was in bed, waiting for me. I told her I couldn't do what she wanted. She had a fit over it. She called my wife from the hotel room and told it all - we had held hands, kissed and shared secrets. It was all true."

Kyle couldn't believe Pastor Rose. "So, you see, we are all tempted. In my case, it wasn't as hot and heavy as things are today. But God forgave me, Vie forgave me and I forgave myself. The woman on the other hand hated me for a long time. Called me a fake and even warned some of the women not to come to our church. She reported that I played on their sympathies, using them. That hurt me deeply, because I value my relationship with Christ. I prayed earnestly for her soul. I didn't want what happened between us to cause her to lose faith. One day, she came back to church and she forgave me, too."

Kyle appreciated Pastor Rose for sharing such a personal testimony with him. Sapphire required his prayers. Most of all, he needed to forgive Vaughn. He hugged his Pastor before they made their way downstairs.

This Can't Be True

Nausea overtook Lily, not from the pregnancy, but from the thought of it. Vaughn descended into complete mother mode, nurturing her sister-cousin. "Here, take this."

Baffled, Lily asked, "For what?"

Holding out the fresh white towel, she said, "Girl, for a shower. I know you want to get the goop off of you that they used for the sonogram."

Lily accepted it and headed for the bathroom. Her head was spinning. *How will I take care of a baby? I can't take care of myself.* Throwing her business suit to the floor, she stood underneath the shower jets. The lavender shower gel that normally opened her senses, did nothing to sooth her. Massaging the bath mitt across her firm belly, it was difficult for her to believe a baby was growing inside her womb.

How will I tell my parents? How will this affect my father's image? A world-renowned pastor's unmarried daughter; pregnant? Sobs poured deeply from within. Even under the heated water, she quivered and went to her knees. She permitted the water to saturate her hair.

Lily cried more than she'd done in her entire life over the past five months - crying over Michael, crying because of Rick, and crying because of the unborn child that would change her life forever.

Vaughn quickly prepared a small dinner. It had been a long day and it was already nine in the evening. As she stirred the ground beef, she prayed for Lily. This was going to be hard for Lily. Vaughn knew she would be there for Lily no matter what. No need to look back now, she sighed. They would be strong, just like Mother Rose taught them to be.

She looked at the night sky that was full of clouds. Vaughn wondered if a storm was on the way. Lily found Vaughn gazing out the window. "Hey."

"I fixed you something to eat."

"I'm not hungry. I heard the phone ring. Who was it?"

"Auntie Vie."

Lily jumped. "You didn't tell my mother?"

Vaughn looked at Lily. She looked like she'd just been beaten. Her hair was dripping wet and she held a towel around her shoulders. "Girl, calm down. That's your department. But, you have to eat for the baby."

"I don't even want this baby."

The remark caused Vaughn to flinch. The coldness in Lily's voice saddened her. *Is that the way Flo felt about me? Maybe that's why she left.* Vaughn tucked the thoughts away, focused on Lily at the kitchen counter. Towel drying her hair, she frowned. "Are you saying you want an abortion?"

"I could never do that, but I still don't want this baby."

"That baby is yours and it needs you."

"What about what I need?" she snapped. "The last thing I need is a child."

"Lily, I know this is hard. But you *are* a pregnant mama." Vaughn pointed at her. "You are going to have a baby. Your *needs* are secondary now. When are you going to tell Rick?" she asked, lifting arched eyebrows.

Lily buried her face in her hands. Vaughn seemed to have a plan and checklist in order - eat for the baby, check, tell parents, check, tell Rick, double-check. She couldn't handle all the details.

"Vaughn, do we have to go over this now? I don't know what to do." She shook her head, and asked, "What about my father? And let's not forget Michael. My life is over." Vaughn bit her lip not knowing how to comfort her. Would Lily have to let Michael go forever?

She sobbed again. Vaughn held her. "Alright, you don't have to make any decisions tonight. Give yourself a couple of weeks to pray...think things through. The baby ain't going nowhere."

Finally, I'm Awake

Loud laughter; squeals and voices filled Ollie's head. He reached for the alarm clock - eleven-thirty at night. Ollie stumbled off the bed very drowsy from a deep sleep.

He and Sapphire had lived together for a month. After working two jobs, he was thankful that he was off from them both. Church was where he planned to be. But since Sapphire didn't wake him, he missed it. He sucked his teeth and let his eyes search the dark room. *What is all that noise?* Yet, he didn't want to turn on the light for fear it would hurt his eyes. Following the sounds, he called, "Sas- say!"

Sapphire giggled at her man in gray bikini briefs, rushed over to him and shoved him back into the bedroom. The guests filled the room with laughter. He rubbed the residue of sleep out of his eyes, and shot off the questions, "What is going on? Why are there at least twenty people packed out there? And who are they?"

"They're here for our wedding."

"Our wedding?" Ollie hit the light switch.

Sapphire was beautiful in a sleeveless off white chiffon gown.

"If we're getting married tonight, how come I'm the last to know?" Ollie said.

Sapphire headed to the closet and showed him a white linen suit. "I wanted to surprise you. Here, this is what you'll be wearing."

Ollie attempted to take it all in. He sat at the foot of the bed. Shoulder-to-shoulder, Sapphire sat next to him and tossed the expensive curly weave over her shoulders. Cheerfully, she asked, "Are you surprised?"

He flatly answered, "Sassy, I don't know what to say."

Reminding him of his words when he gave her the ring, she said, "Baby, say yes. I did all of this for you. I got a Justice of the Peace, ordered a cake, the girls from the club cooked and Opal's taking pictures."

"Opal? From the club?"

"Yeah, she's retired, too."

Ollie understood, but he wasn't happy. "Sassy, what about my family and friends? Did you invite any of them?"

"You've never been close with them before. Why should we include them now?" She shrugged, disregarding his request.

He waited a beat, then thought, *whatever*. Going along with his so called surprise, he told her, "Alright, let me shower and change. Keep the party going."

Ollie dressed quickly, checked the mirror and put his party face on. He walked out to cheers and applause. Women that he'd seen perform naked or half naked, flocked around him, offering their congratulations in the form of tight hugs and smooches. He spotted Sapphire. She seemed to be content, spending a lot of time around Mac, her former boss.

Ollie caught up to his bride-to-be and put a protective hand around her waist. He gave Mac a pound. "What up, man?"

Mac's gold teeth sparkled. Ollie thought he needed shades. "You tell me? You gonna marry one of my finest jewels."

Ollie believed he was at the club with all the flesh floating around. "Mac, who's dancin' tonight? Looks like all your jewels are in my living room."

"Enjoy the show, man. I got some hot, fresh, *young* talent at the club."

A small mocha faced man approached them. He grinned. "I see our groom is awake. You're a tough sleeper. We've been celebrating out here without you." That was apparent. The gentleman reeked of beer and cigarettes. *This wedding* didn't settle with Ollie. Somehow, he started to awaken from a sleep that went beyond his body. Too far gone to turn back, he listened as the man continued, "I'm Bill Baker. I'll be performing the ceremony. Are you ready to marry this beautiful Sapphire?"

Sapphire beamed at him. And not giving Ollie a chance to answer, she flaunted, "Do you see this ring he gave me? Let's get this show on the road." That was their cue, and with a wave of her hand, the girls dimmed the lights and Sapphire took her place. Nothing to do but fall in place, Ollie followed.

They were finally getting married. Ollie sighed with relief. Sapphire would go back to the club, and he could stop working so much. He was getting what he really wanted, or was he?

Career Week

"Lily, Lily?" Vaughn whispered.

"Hum." Lily opened her eyes.

"I gotta go. Career Week starts today."

Lily rolled over and saw Vaughn standing over her in a tailor-made deep brown pantsuit. "I'm sorry Vaughn. I'm not ready," she apologized.

"That's OK. Did you sleep last night?"

"Not much" Her voice was groggy.

"You need your rest. Try to get some sleep. The baby is growing. I left you some fresh oatmeal and muffins downstairs." Vaughn smiled as she rubbed Lily's forehead.

Lily rolled onto her side and felt the nagging discomfort of the cyst. Dr. Miles told her it should dissipate soon. It seemed Vaughn was happy about the baby. *Will I ever be happy about having this child?* She pulled the covers over her head, wishing Atlanta, Rick and the baby away.

Students packed the gymnasium of Roberson High to overflowing. They kept Vaughn buzzing and she loved every minute of it. She chatted briefly at each table. Doctors, nurses, veterinarians, judges and law enforcement represented each profession. Lily was supposed to be the representative for lawyers. That table was left empty.

Donita caught up with her new friend and drawled, "Vaughn, this place is jumping with young people. How did you get the word out? I know all these kids don't go to our church."

"I sent a press release to all the intermediate and high schools in the area. I even had it broadcasted on the local radio stations."

"It's wonderful, simply wonderful."

"Thanks Nita. It turned out better than I expected. The kids are talking to our professionals and getting an ear load of info. I can't believe it. I'm usually a behind-the-scenes person."

"Well, God is bringing you to the forefront. Hang on to yo' seat, you 'bout to take off." She jabbed a finger in Vaughn's shoulder as they laughed like old friends. "So, if these kids come everyday, on Friday they can gain free entry into the finale carnival?"

"Yep, sort of a reward."

Vaughn turned, feeling a tap on her shoulder. Donita observed the handsome gentleman. Vaughn lifted her brow at the unexpected visitor. "Great turnout," he complimented her.

"Rick, what are you doing here?" He raised his eyebrows, thinking, *She really can't stand me.*

Donita noted Vaughn's uneasiness and decided she'd get the scoop later. "Excuse me. I am going to mingle."

"OK, Nita." Donita walked off with a smile of curiosity.

"Whoa, that was cold. You didn't' even introduce me to your..."

"Again Rick, what are you doing here?"

"I saw the flyer on Lily's desk. I thought I'd come check it out."

She wasn't impressed with his support. "Why?"

"Because I think this is a great thing you're doing."

Vaughn did not have the patience for Rick. She knew she needed to get used to him as the father of Lily's child. "Well enjoy yourself, Rick. I've gotta make sure our guests are comfortable."

He pulled her by the hand. "Hey, where's Lily? I thought she was representing the legal table."

"Lily's got a cold," she lied. But it wasn't her place to tell him the truth. She knew just what to do to get him off her back. "Do you want to be a representative?" She was challenging him. He felt the sneer in her voice.

"I will be glad to help a sister out. What do I need to do?"

Her mouth fell open. "Uh…just stand at the legal table and be prepared to answer any questions they throw at you. There are brochures already on the table for you to give out." She pointed to his left indicating his position.

He raised an eyebrow and his lips into a smile. "You didn't think I'd do it?"

She gave him a flat, "No."

"If you would stop rollin' yo' eyes at me and suckin' yo' teeth, you'd see I'm really a good guy." He waited for something, anything; that said she could see his good nature.

She walked off.

Looking back, she said, "Have fun." *Will you be a good guy when you find out that you're a baby's daddy?*

That's Some Cold...

Wonderful, she had a cold. Rick thought things were looking up for him and Lily. Now he had the perfect time to show her that he really did care. His plan, convince Lily that their rendezvous was not just a one-night stand.

After the career event, he prepared a get-well bag. He bought an array of cold medicine, cough drops, juices, canned soups and crackers. If all went well, they could pick up where they left off. Lily was inexperienced, but she was passionate beyond words. Feeling his desires rise, he rang the bell.

Ruffling through the paper bag, Rick hoped he hadn't forgotten anything when Vaughn answered. She gave him a scolded look. Vaughn noticed he changed out of his suit into beige pants and a matching polo shirt. *He's smooth. I'll give him that.*

"I think today went well. I enjoyed helping you today."

She attempted to sound polite, but the sting remained in her hazel eyes. "I appreciated your help. What's in the bag? Are you here to celebrate?"

Vaughn didn't give him any indication he was invited so, he eased in. "This is for Lily's cold."

She looked sideways at him. "Her cold?"

Confused, he responded, "Didn't you tell me she had a cold? I'm guessing that's why she left work early yesterday."

"Oh yeah. Well, she's kind of out of it."

Persistent, he explained, "I won't stay long. I promise." He gave a dashing smile.

Charming, too, I can see how Lily was taken with you.

"Let me see if she'll come down."

He jumped at the opportunity. "I could go up." He tried to hide his enthusiasm. Clearing his throat, he added, "I mean, if she's not up to getting out of bed."

"Just stay here." She held up her hands, halting him.

Rick circled the living room and fastened his eyes upon the fireplace. Anytime he saw one, he thought of his deceased wife. She was always drawn to them. And finding them incredibly romantic, she ensured they made love in front of one often. His daughter was conceived right in front of their fireplace. He'd never forget the night or the glow upon his wife's face when she told him, "I know we made a baby, sweetheart."

The bittersweet memories of his past faded with the disturbing sight of Lily. Her hair was thick and untamed. It was the first time he'd seen her look so unruly. "That must be a terrible cold, you look awful."

She studied him, searching for the strength of the physical attraction that got her into the current situation. She felt nothing.

"Here, I bought you some things that might help you get over it."

Fumbling through the bag, she wondered what could cure pregnancy. Sure that nothing but nine months and a painful labor would, she cast the bag aside and took a seat. "Thanks."

"I could make you some soup?"

"No thanks."

"How about some tea?"

"Nope."

Wearily, he said, "I'm trying to help. I want you to know how I feel about you."

With a panged look, she inquired, "Rick, how do you feel about me?"

"I care about you."

Considering my circumstance, that's good to know.

"I saw you leave early yesterday." He asked, "Did you see a doctor?"

"Yes."

"Did he give you something?"

"Guess you could say that."

She hadn't planned to tell him so soon. She hadn't planned to sleep with him or have sex before marriage. All her plans were shattered, and finding no reason not to tell him, she said, "She gave me some unsettling news."

Fearful she was suddenly ill, he asked, "Are you sick?"

"If pregnancy is an illness, then I'm extremely sick."

He laughed. *She's joking.*

"Really, what did she tell you?"

Frustrated he wasn't taking her seriously, she yelled making it easier for Vaughn to hear them upstairs. "She said I am four weeks pregnant."

He felt his body collapse. The news hit like hail the size of bowling balls. Minutes departed before he spoke. "What are you going to do about it?"

The chill in his eyes stunned her. "Me? You were the one who promised if anything happened, *we* would be responsible. *You* could have worn a condom!"

"You caught me off guard. I wasn't expecting you."

"I caught you off guard? Rick, you practically devoured me."

With the tone of bitter truth he reminded her. "I did. It was beautiful. *You* enjoyed every second of it. Oh, by the way, my name is Rick, not Michael."

She winced at the truth. So he heard her call Michael's name when she reached her peak.

It was apparent he hurt her. "Make the arrangements. I'll go with you for the abortion."

"Abortion?" She shouted the question.

He responded candidly, "I don't want any children. You don't strike me as the single mother type. Think of the baby. Do you want it to grow up without a father?"

"I can't have an abortion."

With clenched fists, he raised his voice. "I can't be a father again." Rick's eyes burned as he stood to leave. "Lily, if you have this baby, you'll have to do it alone."

"I thought you said you cared about me. How can you walk away? I'm carrying your child."

He wanted to feel sorry for her, but his feelings were shielded by the resentment of his past. "Lily, we all have choices. You don't have to carry this child. I don't have to be a father."

She watched him walk out, leaving her to grieve for her unborn baby; sadly, rejected by its father.

Past Consequences

A week had passed since Flo and Roosta shared their celebration night. He did the butterfly dance in the middle of his bedroom shortly after hanging up the phone. The sight of him in white boxer briefs and nothing more created tears of laughter in Flo's eyes. He continued dancing as he sang, "Oh, yeah, oh, yeah, Fran is taking Lexi and Tasha to the movies. Oh, yeah."

"Aren't you working today? You usually go in on Saturdays."

Roosta slowed down and caught his breath. "Not today. Today, I want an instant replay of last Friday night."

Flo walked to him and tenderly stroked his hairy chest with her palms. "Me, too. You're getting good at this lovemaking stuff."

He grinned. "Practice makes perfect." Caressing Flo's neck with kisses, he directed, "Go slip into that nightie I gave you."

"Again? That's the third time this week. You like it, huh?"

Unbuttoning her pajama top, he said, "I regret not buying more than one. Your legs look so sexy in it."

"Yeah, right, not with these varicose veins in the back of my legs."

Roosta fell to his knees and gently teased the marks with his nose and lips while squeezing her thighs. "You have beautiful legs. I want to see them more often."

He stood and spanked her bottom. "Let's go."

"Roosta, go where? You got me all fired up."

"We're going to drop Lexi off and then hit the lingerie store to buy short nighties. We'll get one in every color. Then, you can give me a fashion show." He kissed the tip of her nose.

Flo stared at her new husband in awe.

"Why are you looking at me like that?"

"Man, I don't know who you are, but I am so in love with you."

Massaging her bareback beneath the opened top, he proudly explained, "I'm a new man in Christ that is very much in love with his wife." *Married life is proving to be wonderful.*

Flo dropped her pajama top and Roosta loved her with all his heart.

Roosta sang, "Oh, yeah!" as he bounced downstairs. He found Lexi slurping the last of the fruity milk created from a second bowl of *Fruit Loops*. Roosta smiled, seeing the milk drizzling down her chin.

"Good?"

"Yes. Dad, where's Mom? I need some breakfast."

He cleaned her chin and milk mustache with a flowery printed napkin. "She's taking a shower. Want some bacon and eggs?"

Lexi slipped out the oversized kitchen chair in a sunflower nightgown. "You gonna cook?" Shocked, her already youthful voice pitched higher.

"Don't sound so surprised."

"But you never cook."

He winked at her. "Don't you think it's time I start?"

"Uncle Desi cooks. Mom says better than Auntie Vie, but I'm not supposed to tell her that."

Roosta looked into the side-by-side refrigerator as if he was staring into space. Lexi squeezed in front of him and found the bacon. "Here, Dad."

"Thanks."

"Dad, can I go to the movies with Tasha?"

"Yes, her mother already called."

"Can I have some money?"

"Yes."

"Here, Dad." She passed him the eggs.

"Thanks."

"Dad, can I sleep over, too?"

Roosta continued to stare into space wondering what else he needed. "Now Lexi, you stayed over last weekend."

"I know Dad, but Tasha has a new bedroom. It is painted in purple sparkles."

He closed the fridge and scratched his head. "We'll see what your mother says."

"Dad, you don't know how to cook, do you?"

He grinned. "I guess not."

"I'll teach you. I've seen Mom make bacon and eggs millions of times."

Roosta chuckled at his daughter's wit.

"Lesson number one..."

"What's that?"

"Wash your hands."

He obeyed his six year old.

The phone rang. Lexi answered, "Jenkins' residence." A casual female voice answered, "This must be Lexi Jenkins?"

"That's right. Who are you?"

The woman smiled through the receiver. "My name is Shay Lynn, is your Dad home?"

Rinsing suds off his hands, he wondered. "Who is it Lexi?"

"Some lady named Shay Lynn."

Roosta stumbled in his bare feet, reached for the phone and dried his hands on his jeans. Fearful, he whispered, "Shay Lynn, why are you calling me on my house phone?"

"Because, I miss you Roosta, and so does your children."

It was the longest time Roosta ever stayed away from Shay Lynn. She could always count on him to come back, even after he married Flo. Now, she was starting to worry.

"Are you getting the checks?"

"Of course. When are you coming to see us?"

Hoping Flo was taking her usual long shower, he answered, "I was planning on scheduling a visit."

"Roosta, are you crazy? You pay the rent and have a key. You don't have to schedule anything."

Playing with Roosta's dreads, Lexi stayed close to her father. Curious, she listened intently. "Roosta, I've never tried to interfere with your marriage."

"Now is not the time Shay Lynn."

Every time he was with Shay Lynn, she was interfering with his marriage. It was amazing to him how things seemed differently to him with God in his life.

"I need five hundred dollars."

"I'll bring a check by tomorrow."

"I need it early Roosta. I'm transferring Lena into a private school. I need it in the morning."

"Alright, I'll see you at seven." Without a bye, see you around, or later, he hung up. Hoping Flo didn't hear the phone conversation, Roosta froze when he caught a glimpse of her in jeans and a white T-shirt with a big red heart on the front of it.

A Sweet Set-Up

On time, and as promised, Michael arrived in Atlanta, Georgia. It was a grueling week for Lily. Rick became cruel, relentless and downright nasty. In his eyes, she went from being a quick study and sharp attorney, to a know nothing, loser.

Lily and Michael embraced at the airport as if he'd just arrived from the war in Iraq. Lifting her off her feet, he breathed. "Baby, oh Baby, I've missed you so much."

When he called her baby, it felt as if nothing had changed between them. The months of separation floated away. She broke down in his arms.

"Baby, don't cry. Come on, let's find your car."

Lily grabbed a fist full of tissues and wiped her face. "I'm sorry. I didn't mean to. I'm just so happy to see you."

Lily drove the black Jaguar in silence. "You look good." He noted, "You're glowing."

"Stop it, Michael."

"It's true, you are glowing," he said again with conviction.

She wanted to believe the glow was from seeing him. *The glow is from this baby growing inside of me.* She changed the subject. "I prepared lunch for you at home. I hope you don't mind. We can have dinner tonight and go sightseeing."

"Whatever you wanna do is fine with me." Michael gazed out of the window and commented, "Atlanta is pretty. It's got a country like setting, yet it's citified with all the tall buildings and traffic."

She nodded with her eyes on the red light. This was supposed to be a pleasure trip for him. She wanted to scream that she was pregnant and beg him to marry her. It was not his child, nor his responsibility, and not likely.

"Lily, Lily?"

Dazed, she looked at him. "Huh?"

"It's green, baby."

The honking SUV behind them blew her into drive. "Sorry."

"Are you OK?"

"I guess I'm a little tired." She gave a pleasant smile.

"You don't look tired. You're a sight for sore eyes." Pondering on the words, he glanced at the sky, and repeated, "Sight for sore eyes. My mother used to say that all the time."

Lily parked in the garage when they reached home. She asked, "You still miss your mother?"

He found his bag in the backseat and responded wholeheartedly, "Ain't nobody like your mother."

Michael followed Lily's long trench as it floated backward against the wind.

"Whoa, it's breezy today," she stated as she opened the door.

"If you think this is breezy, you should be in New York." She wished that she was.

Michael was impressed with the bright and inviting sunshine walls of the home. Lily took his bag from him and set it in the hall closet. She casually asked, "Would you like a tour?"

"In a minute." And before she could say OK, he hugged her again. When he released her, she looked at him with tearful eyes. How could she tell him the truth?

Loaded down with groceries, Vaughn believed Kyle was standing in her house. Michael looked so much like his fraternal twin. He gave a toothy grin, happy to see her. "Hey, Vaughn."

Vaughn dumped her packages. "Don't hey Vaughn me. You betta come over here and give me some love."

He hugged her tightly. "Girl, you look good."

"Don't I?"

Michael laughed. "You still a mess, too."

"Why bother with perfection?" She gave a spin, showing off her flair. "Now help me get these bags into the kitchen."

173

Michael happily followed. "What's all this?"

"I'm cooking with a friend tonight. She's the first lady of our church. You know, you and Lily are invited to Sunday dinner at her house."

"No, I didn't, but that sounds good."

Lily looked up at Vaughn. The word no, was painted all over her face. She wasn't feeling up to being around a lot of people. Vaughn recognized Lily's staggered expression. Using her eyes, she screamed, yes. Lily needed to stop hiding and ducking.

The phone rang and Vaughn chided, "Lily, get that." Afraid to leave the room, she hesitated. Vaughn pretended not to notice Lily was apprehensive. She continued to chat with Michael. "I ain't taking all this food to Nita's house. Some is for us, sisters." She winked at him. "And you can have some, too."

Vaughn tiptoed to the doorway and peered around the corner. Lily was on the phone. Vaughn rushed back and whispered in Michael's ear, "Lily has been very depressed lately. She's been working too hard and not seeking God like she should."

Michael wrinkled his forehead. Vaughn sped up. "I need you to get her back into prayer mode. I don't even know what to tell you to say to her."

"What's the problem?" Michael asked.

Vaughn knew she couldn't reveal the truth. "She's stepping into new territory. She's afraid."

"That's it? Is it health-related, work-related? What?"

She heard Lily's footsteps. "That's all I can tell you. Trust me, in time she's going to tell you herself." She thought, *In time, she won't have to say a word. Her rising belly will tell it all.*

Packing plastic grocery bags away, Vaughn smiled and innocently asked as Lily walked into the kitchen, "Who was on the phone?"

Lily knew Vaughn was up to something. She frowned and told her, "It was Nita. She wanted to make sure you bought the collard greens."

She waved the bushel. "I got 'em right here. Thanks for reminding me. I thought I left everything in the car that I am taking to Nita's house."

Lily was set-up by Nita and Vaughn. She wanted to be angry with them, but they were only trying to help.

Vaughn pranced in her boots. "Well, I'm off."

Michael called, "Aren't you eating lunch with us?"

"No, I'm meeting Nita and her daughter, Jessica. We're going shopping and then back to her place to start on Sunday dinner." She swiped the greens off the spacious blue tile counter. "I don't want to forget these. Lily, I'll be home late. Michael, I'll see you in church tomorrow."

Church? Lily didn't realize that she *was* going to church. It was a given, Michael would expect them to.

My Heart Belongs To You

Michael smiled at Vaughn's heart and concern for Lily. He was pleased she looked good, too. Michael hoped Vaughn would go on with her life after Kyle. Then again, he knew first hand, you could go on with your life, and still not get over someone for a long time. The smell of freshly baked lasagna shifted him to the kitchen counter. "When did you bake this?"

Lily licked leftover sauce from her thumb as she gave Michael his plate. "I got up at six this morning. I couldn't sleep."

Michael dug into the cheese-filled saucy layers. "I didn't sleep much last night. But, I did sleep on the plane."

She joined him and forgot about the elegant table she'd set for them in the dining room, finding being close to him at the counter comforting.

Michael walked to the refrigerator and Lily melted at his smooth walk. He thoughtfully filled glasses with ice for each of them, and poured soda. "I'm sorry, Michael. I don't know where my head is. I forgot your drink."

"No problem, I can do it." He did, sat next to her and took a bite. "Lily, this lasagna is good. I'm gonna need seconds."

"You haven't finished your firsts."

"So counselor, what does that have to do with wanting seconds?"

For the moment, she felt like they were back in New York, she wasn't pregnant and she was his soon-to-be fiancé. Lily played along. "Well, after you finish firsts, you may be too full for seconds."

"I beg to differ. Having seconds is not always based on if you're full or not. Sometimes you can't help yourself, cause, it's plain ole good." A long string of cheese

extended from Lily's fork to her lips. Michael pulled it away slowly and deposited it in his mouth. "Baby, your cheese tastes better than mine." They silently held one another's gaze for several seconds.

After lasagna and several unspoken words expressed by smiles, Michael asked Lily to rest in his arms on the sofa. It was obvious something was weighing on her mind. Lily settled into his strong arms and allowed the familiar scent of him to surround her. She rested and alleviated feelings of fear and sadness. Once he knew about the baby, it would be over, with no hope of return to the love and mutual respect for each other.

Comfortable, Michael's head reclined against the sofa. He felt her body fall and rise within his. Lily lifted both legs to the sofa, crossed them at the ankles. Within minutes, her breathing slowed. He only heard soft sighs drift away into the calmness of the afternoon.

Holding her was so natural, as natural as creating any sketch or design. It was part of what he was meant to do. *To have and to hold.*

Instinctively, he realized what he knew for the past eight years. Lily would be his wife. Whispering not to wake her, he talked to the Father, "Abba, Daddy, This is my wife. I promise you I'll never let her go again. Let your blessings be upon us now and always."

Still Not Satisfied

Sapphire spent her Saturday the same way she'd done for the past month, alone. She wanted Ollie to love and support her. He was doing that, driving a taxi during the day and being a security guard overnight.

Having sprayed too much bleach into the toilet, she lifted the small bathroom window and took a deep breath. Her eyes watered. Fresh air blew into them bringing the tears coolly down her cheeks. "I'm 'bout to kill myself with this stuff." She hadn't realized she spoke aloud, until she heard her voice.

Her attention shifted to the next-door neighbors. A father and son tossed a football in the cold air. It didn't seem to bother the cinnamon faced little boy at all. Joy radiated through him. He yelled, "Dad, go long."

She craved for that same relationship she shared with her mother long ago. Her mother, her only companion and best friend, was struck down by a hit and run when she was eighteen.

Pleased to have some communication with the outside world, she rushed to the singing phone. "Whoa."

"Sassy?"

"Ollie, I just waxed the floors and slipped into the end table."

He chuckled. "You're the only person I know that can clean a house and make it dangerous."

Rubbing her leg through black leggings, she knew it bruised.

"I'm on my way home. Sassy, let's go to church tonight. There's a concert." She realized he sounded hopeful, but she had no idea why he should be.

"Church? The same church that Michael and Kyle go to?"

"Michael is out of town."

"Ollie, church on your night off is not what I want to do," she complained.

"Sassy, we can go to church and still come home and get our groove on."

Ollie could hear the resentment in Sapphire's voice. He was trying to connect with his past. He couldn't understand her irritation.

"Ollie, how you gonna remain friends with Kyle?"

"I grew up with Michael and Kyle."

She snarled. "I grew up in the projects, but you don't see me trying to go back there."

"Sassy don't start, you didn't even invite my family to the wedding. My mother doesn't know I'm married, yet."

"Like you care about that woman. You told me she ain't never been a mother to you. I can't believe you're still complaining about that. Is that why you're hangin' out with Kyle, to get back at me?"

"Sassy, you're nuts. This has nothing to do with you."

"You, Kyle, and yo' mama are all a bunch of hypocrites. Doing whatever you wanna do, and then running back to the church for forgiveness," she criticized them.

Knowing he wouldn't give her what she wanted from him, he relented, "Bye, Sassy. I'll be home after the concert."

"Don't look for me when you get here." She slammed the phone down and stewed over his reluctance to obey her.

I Wanna Know

Vaughn met Donita and Jessica in front of the mall. Jessica gave her a big hug. Vaughn held on to the teenager's shoulder. "Thanks Jessie. Are you ready to spend yo' mama's money?"

Laughing, Donita agreed, "I know that's right. This girl loves to save her money and spend everybody else's."

"Jessie, you're my kind of girl." Vaughn patted her shoulder.

Casually looking to and fro over the display of designer clothes, Donita asked, "So, how is Michael?"

Vaughn smiled. "Fine as ever and still in love with Lily."

"Mama, look at this black leather jacket!" Jessica exclaimed pulling it from the rack. She gave it a good sniff enjoying the new leather smell.

Donita took if off the hanger for her and said, "It's cute. It's a leather vest with sweater sleeves. Try it on." Never missing a beat, Donita responded to Vaughn, "I think that's great. What I want to know is, what's up with that Rick guy? He was fine, too."

Vaughn pulled off her brown suede jacket and found the same jacket Jessica was trying on in her size. Raising her eyebrows, she didn't answer Donita. Donita drawled, "Girl, come on now. I know something is up. Also, let me not forget, I saw y'all at the hospital last week."

"Nita, how do you think this jacket looks on me?" Vaughn held out her arms, found a full-length mirror and admired herself from front to back.

Donita snapped, "So that's it? You gonna ignore me? I thought we were friends."

Vaughn crossed her arms over her midsize breast. "Nita you are a busybody. Jessie ain't yo' Mama busy?"

"Sometimes, Dad says she is," Jessie honestly admitted.

Donita's reflection in the mirror revealed an oily face and crinkled forehead. She found her compact in her hefty purse and patted lightly. Defending herself against Jessica's honesty, and the fact she wasn't getting anywhere with Vaughn, she whined, "I'm not a busybody. I'm your friend. I'm concerned about you girls. Mother Rose, asked me to keep an eye on you."

Vaughn sang, "Oh, I'm getting this jacket. I look good in it."

Donita stomped her foot a little too hard, and felt pain tingle up to her knee. "Vaughn!" she shouted.

"Alright, I'm messing wit-cha, but you gotta ask Lily. It's not my business to tell. However, I do appreciate you calling when you did. It gave me a minute alone with Michael."

"First chance I get, I will ask Lily *myself*," Donita stated.

"I know you will," Vaughn laughed.

"Oh, so you think I'm funny? Since you don't want to talk about Lily, then maybe you'll tell me what really happened with you and Kyle."

"You just don't quit, do you?"

"Nope, ask my husband. I love a good mystery book. That's what you are, a good mystery book. I'm gonna keep flipping the pages until I figure it out."

A firm grip held onto Vaughn's heart. She didn't want to be figured out. She didn't want to think about what really happened between her and Kyle. In Atlanta, she wanted to be free of that. *Why is Donita pressing the issue? Would I ever be able to escape the truth?*

Relentless Truth

"Nita, I ain't never cut up this many greens in my life. Well, not at one time anyway." Elbow deep, peeling white potatoes, Donita looked under the island counter for a bigger bowl. "I wanted to make sure we have enough. There's me, you, Lily, Stanley, Jessie and Mr. Fine Michael; who I can't wait to meet."

Vaughn leafed through, folded and chopped away Donita's plan of action. She dodged. "What else is on the menu?"

Accepting the brief intermission, Donita politely replied, "Baked ham, fried fish, candied yams, green beans, macaroni and cheese, corn bread dressing, chocolate cake and banana pudding."

Just thinking about it made the ladies drool a little. "I guess we gone be up cookin' all night. It's a good thing you have a big kitchen," Vaughn estimated.

"Between the two of us, it shouldn't take long. Do you think Michael will like the menu?"

Back to the drawing board, Vaughn needed to cut her down quickly. "Nita, I told you whatever you want to know about Lily and Michael has to come from Lily and Michael."

Delayed, but not defeated. Actually, the conversation was going directly where she intended it. "So, let's hear about you and Kyle."

Annoyed at Donita's persistence, she attempted to hide it from her voice. "Why is it important to you?"

"Because it's important to you." The annoyance was slipping out. It couldn't be helped. "Nita it's not. I'm over Kyle."

Donita was going to get Vaughn to admit she couldn't be over something she was running away from. Donita found two honey buns in the pantry. Shifting to the refrigerator, she gathered a couple of drinks and a half block of cheddar cheese.

Neatly setting cloth blue and white place mats, she motioned for Vaughn to join her. "Let's take a break. Our Chinese lunch is wearing off."

"Nita, why do you push? Girl, why can't you let this be?"

She gave her a honey bun lesson before answering. "Here open your bun and place some cheese on top, it's good like that."

She obeyed awaiting Donita's reasoning. Donita wasn't as old as Mother Rose, but she had that look in her eye. The look when a mother could see past the smiles and know her child was hurting.

"Mum, it is good," Vaughn agreed and enjoyed the honey bun and cheese snack.

Donita took a swig of her soda and said, "Told you. Now, you need to talk about you and Kyle."

Vaughn frowned. "Why?"

"Because you shoot down every brother at church that comes your way. It's like you are angry with men."

"See Nita, you don't know what you're talking about. Kyle and I broke up over a year ago. Right after the break-up, I dated a lot of men." She stressed the words, "The dating game can wear you out."

"There's your problem. With you it's feast or famine; a lot of men, or none at all. You need balance." She laid a chocolate hand on Vaughn's beige one. "Just talk about it. Was Kyle abusive? Did he hurt you?"

Vaughn shook her head and her voice shook. "Kyle was wonderful. The Carraway brothers love deep and strong. Once they take you under their wing, they're faithful, protective and loving."

Donita smiled inside and out. "Sounds like my Stanley."

The thought warmed Vaughn. She calmed and told the story with fluid ease. "Do you know he took me to a theme park with an engagement ring burning a hole in his pocket? I wanted to ride the water rides first. He insisted we ride the fiercest roller coaster. When it took off, he started yelling, 'Life is full of ups and downs.'"

Vaughn laughed aloud. "I kept yelling, what? I couldn't hear him over the ride and the screams. When it stopped, he yelled, 'Life is full of ups and downs, but with Christ as the rails, we'll glide along well. Vaughn, marry me.'"

Supporting her face with her fist, it seemed like yesterday. "He slipped a ring on my finger and we had the best amusement trip of our lives."

"He sounds fun and adventurous."

"He is."

"Why didn't you get married then?" Donita finished the last of her bun and started polishing off the rest of the cheese.

"I think…I cheated on him."

Donita raised her brows over the paring knife and the cheese stopped just before her lips. "You think?"

"I can only remember bits and pieces of it."

"What *do* you remember?"

The passionate light in Vaughn's eyes went out. "I remember coming into our building. Kyle bought a condo for us. I lived there until the wedding. He moved in with his Dad. I knew he loved me, because he and his Dad, they are like fire and ice."

Donita was getting anxious, she urged, "Don't sidetrack. What happened when you came into the building?"

"I saw Courtney, an old high school mate. I wouldn't even say friend, cause I didn't know him very well. We shared homeroom, and I think a math class. Anyway, he spotted me right away and gave me an innocent hug. He said he was visiting his sister who lived in the building. An hour later, he came knocking on my door."

Her eyes became distant as if she was back in the condo far from Donita. "Thinking back, I felt uncomfortable letting him in. He asked if he could use the phone. His cell was out and his sister wasn't home. I let him in. Without a word he looked around, and then my phone rang. I went to answer it in the bedroom. When I came back, he asked for something to drink. I poured us some juice and we chatted a bit. He told me he was teaching at a high school. I think it was history. My phone rang a second time, but by the time I answered, there was no one on the line. So, I went back to the living room, and he was gone. A little later, I finished my juice and started to feel... I don't know, it's hard to explain, but I felt spaced out."

Downing the rest of her soda, Donita said, "I ain't heard nothin' about you cheating yet."

Vaughn felt a chill and looked over her shoulder. "You alright?" Donita touched her hand.

"Yeah, I'm ok. I don't remember when he came back. I do remember Courtney undressing me, touching me and kissing me, and then nothing. The next morning when Kyle came in, he had a hard time waking me. Then he lost control. There was an opened condom next to the bed, unused." Silent tears slid down her cheeks. "He kicked me out. It was over."

"Sounds like date rape to me." The ladies looked around at the sound of Jessica reaching into the apple shaped cookie jar.

Her mother barked, "Jessie, what I tell you about being in grown folks business?"

"Sorry Mama. I just wanted a cookie."

"Get yo' cookie and go Jessie." Donita soothed her tone. "Vaughn I'm sorry. That may be why you can't remember anything. He could have put something in your drink when you went into the bedroom. Maybe he even hid in a closet, or something. He waited for you to pass out."

The truth was coming into her consciousness. Donita drew out what Vaughn tried to suppress. No one knew about it. Not Kyle, not even Lily. She didn't want to be a victim of rape of any kind.

When In Doubt, Pray

Michael hadn't realized he'd fallen asleep until he felt coolness against his chest. Lily had gotten up. He saw his precious Lily walk back dressed in a shimmering royal blue blouse and black velvet pants. "You changed. You look nice."

"Thanks, and thanks for the nap. I needed it. Are you ready to go sightseeing now?"

He reached for her. "Baby, not yet. Come sit down. I wanna talk to you." She wanted to talk to him too, unsure of when the right time would be; she sat. Caressing her face with a smooth hand, he began. "You're so beautiful." Ashamed he thought so, she looked down. "Vaughn told me you seem off track. I've noticed it too. Are you sick? What did the doctor say?" *The doctor said I'm pregnant and we'll never be together.* Those were her most frightening thoughts.

Her lips parted with no words escaping. "Baby I promise what ever it is, I'm gonna be there for you. I still love you, more now than when you left. I don't have a plan mapped out. I guess it's something we can work out later. I may move here. Atlanta's a good place for an Architect."

Oh God, he's going to propose. "Michael, things haven't changed in my heart for you either. If I ever doubted your love, I know now I was deaf, dumb and blind."

"We acted without God. I jumped to conclusions. I'm sorry. Let's not do that again."

He knelt at the sofa. Her blood grew cold. He wanted them to pray to the God she sinned against. "Michael, I can't pray. I can't talk to God."

Completely bewildered by her response, it scared him. Lily was a prayer warrior. Something was terribly wrong. Her soul was in trouble.

184

"Lily, there is nothing you can't talk to God about. Remember, that's what you always told me?"

Crying, she quoted a familiar scripture, "Michael those that worship God, must worship Him in Spirit and in Truth." She added, "Michael, I am a liar, a fake."

He gripped her hands. "Baby, what are you talking about? You are the example that kept so many people seeking God."

She wailed. "I'm sinful Michael. I'm pregnant."

"Pregnant?" He said the word, but no sound echoed.

"Michael, I'm pregnant with my mentor's baby. I'm pregnant and nothing in my life will ever be the same."

Angry, hurt, and confused Michael remained on his knees. *Should I pray? Should I grab my bag and leave?*

Lily sobbed and waited for Michael to run. Now he knew the truth. Lily pulled her hands from his and curled into a ball of misery. Lily listened and waited for him to go. Nevertheless, she heard, "Our Father Who Art in Heaven. Hollowed be thy name...."

Michael continued the prayer and tugged Lily's arm. Looking into his face, she saw such hurt. She came to her knees for the first time in five months. The words came through her sobs. Still, they came. "And forgive us of our trespasses..."

Michael remembered his earlier prayer. He would never leave her again. *How can I stay? Who is the father? Does the father want Lily and the child?* In a voice that rocked Michael and Lily, he urgently called, "Father, help me! What am I supposed to do?" His silent tears forcefully fell. She clung to him and prayed not for herself, but for those she hurt -- Michael, her unborn child and her parents who she still hadn't confronted.

The Things I Would Not Do

The familiar sights and sounds of *Gems* clogged Sapphires pores. She lit a cigarette from her bag and immediately inhaled like it was her last. Savoring the taste with strong drags, she wondered why she quit.

Opting against joining her husband at church, she knew there were so many other places she could have gone. Dinner, the movies, or call her friend Opal. *Why does Ollie have to remain friends with Michael and Kyle?* Unsure of how to destroy their friendship, she came to the place she vowed she would never step foot in again. The real reason she went was because Mac told her at her wedding, he was moving into new territory.

She sat in the back. She wanted time to gather her thoughts, and enjoy the cigarette. The girl dancing on stage was young. Younger than any of the girls she'd known to work at *Gems*. Tons of blue eye shadow and ruby red lipstick combined with a long curly wig didn't conceal the child's age. If Sapphire had her guess, she would say the girl was sixteen. Mac was getting dangerous hiring minors. Mashing the hot ash into an already overfilled ashtray, it was time to go.

He caught her at the door and gave her cheek a smooch. "Sassy, don't leave. You just got here." Rum and coke was fresh on his breath. His face only inches from hers caused his dusty blond hair to brush against her forehead.

"Hey Mac, I just stopped in to see the new talent. It's kind of young, don't you think?"

 Flapping his gums through a mouth of gold teeth, he grinned. "These girls are hot. You see this crowd? Young is in baby."

"If you say so."

Mac could see she was ready to go. He slipped his arm around her waist and rubbed the soft chestnut brown mink. "Come to the back with me. I wanna tell you about my new business."

She said cynically, "I'm not sure if I want to hear about it."

Confident that she did, he added, "This is something just perfect for you. Come on."

Curiosity traveled through Sapphire's mind at the speed of the Concord. *What could Mac have that was perfect for me?* Following behind him in the narrow dimly lit hallway, she believed it could be nothing good. *Here I am. I'll hear him out.*

Being the gentleman he rarely was, he assisted her. "Let me help you out of your coat. It's warm in here." Mac's eyes twinkled at the slinky formfitting black pantsuit. It was more like a cat suit without the leopard spots. "Nice."

Sapphire hesitantly sat in the dusty office. The old desk was peeling wood, covered in ashes and water spots. "Wanna drink?" Observing the half empty rum bottle, she shook her head. *Yes you do Sassy.* He poured two shot glasses. "Sassy, have a drink, loosen up. You've worked for me how many years?"

"Nine years Mac."

"And have I ever steered you wrong?"

Flatly, she answered, "No."

The rum burned his esophagus as he snapped his neck back. He let it tumble down his throat. "Then have your shot." She did, and felt the warmth within her stomach.

"Are you going to tell me or not?" She asked impatiently.

"Baby, this scene was getting tired. I knew it, and I'm glad you quit. You're too big for this small stage stuff. I'm setting up a private business."

"A private business?"

He poured two more shots. They tossed them back in unison. "That's right, upscale private dancing." He opened his arms. "Big time. I'm talking politicians, doctors, and judges that want professional performers. That's what you are, a professional."

"You mean, all I gotta do is dance?"

He gave her the golden grin. "That's all. Plus, you ain't gotta work but once or twice a week; depending on business. I'll pay you five hundred a night. What do you think?" She slouched down and her body softened. "I think I'm married and I shouldn't be dancin' no more."

"Ollie can't buy you a new fur every year."

"I'm ok with the furs I got."

He chucked, poured two more shots, and offered her a cigar. Frowning upon it, she looked to the door. He let her know, "Sassy, this is Big Mac. I know you better than Ollie and that choirboy you was playing with. You change furs like you change your thongs. You like a good cigar from time to time, and you are a professional. An extra thousand a week will be nice."

Sapphire accepted the cigar, closed her eyes and gave it a sniff. Mac quickly flicked a match lighting hers, then his. Inhaling nice and slow, the taste was mellow. Easily releasing the smoke through her mouth, she said, "It's a good one." Mac elevated his glass. "Can I count on my best jewel?" Their glasses clicked in acceptance of their new venture. She threw back her third shot of rum. "An extra thousand a week will be real nice."

The dollar signs in their eyes twinkled between them.

The Morning After

Michael followed the smell of pancakes, sausages, and eggs into the kitchen. "I see you're up early cooking again." Lily turned in a long silk emerald robe. He looked as bad as she felt. Except for his jacket, he was fully dressed for church.

She avoided his eyes. "I'll fix your plate. I assume you're going to church with Vaughn." He grabbed his own plate and piled it high. "I'm going to church with you, and Vaughn. Why aren't you dressed?"

"Michael I..."

"Lily, I know you're going through a lot right now. But if you wanna get through it, God's the only way. Go get dressed." It was an order.

Lily passed Vaughn on the stairs without a word. Vaughn was exhausted toiling with the reality of a possible date rape all night. Dark circles surrounded her eyes. Lily didn't notice. Vaughn asked, "Going to church?" Lily nodded. So did Vaughn.

She thought a speeding train hit Michael, or Lily broke the news. "She told you?"

"Do I look that bad?"

"Yep."

Michael sliced through a stack of buttermilk pancakes. "Vaughn, who's the father?"

Vaughn gathered her breakfast and a small saucer of cantaloupe. Joining Michael, she asked, "She didn't tell you?"

"We didn't get that far. All we could do was pray."

With a mouth full of cantaloupe, she hollered, "She prayed? Thank God!"

"Yeah, we prayed."

"Michael, you're amazing! I hate to say it, but if it were Kyle, he would have been back in New York."

"Amazing, that's why the woman I love, is having another man's baby."

She laid a hand on his shoulder. "You really do love her. That's why you're still here."

Frustration raising his blood pressure, he asked a second time, "Who's the father?"

"Her mentor, Rick Parsons."

"Are they in love?"

She pushed her lips to the side. "Come on, what do you think?"

"You mean to tell me Lily's having unprotected causal sex?"

"What Lily had was a moment of insanity. I believe Rick was on a mission the minute he laid eyes on her."

Michael inhaled his sausage, and snapped, "Apparently, mission accomplished."

"Yes and no. Did he want to get her in bed? Yes. Did he want a baby? No. He told her he wanted no parts of the baby. Rick's turned into a monster. He can't seem to stand the sight of Lily."

His fists and jaw clenched. "Vaughn, I'm angry that Lily did this. And this Rick guy, I wanna kill him."

Vaughn placed her hand on his shoulder. In all the years Vaughn knew Michael, she never saw him act violently. She didn't recognize the look in his eye. Her brows creased. *He might just kill Rick.*

"Vaughn, if he loved her and wanted the baby, I would be hurt. The fact that he doesn't, I'm angry." She offered a comforting smile. Her voice was polite. "It's ok to be angry. I hope if nothing else, you can be Lily's friend. She needs us."

He nodded. "I'll always be her friend. I won't let her lose her soul over this." She embraced him.

Changing the subject, he put a bug in Vaughn's ear. "Give my brother a call. He'll love to hear from you."

Say What?

"I could have picked you up from the airport." Kyle figured Michael's visit didn't go as well as he hoped. He looked beaten. His eyes were red and shoulders slumped.

Michael handed his brother a cola in the can and told him, "I had Ollie pick me up and take me straight to the office."

"I'm sure he appreciated the fare."

Kyle turned the can in his hand. "No ice?"

"You know where the ice is."

Kyle pressed crushed on the automatic icemaker and filled his cup. Dividing the ice into two cups, he poured some for himself and his brother. "Here."

Michael drank his soda in one heaping gulp. Pressing his palm to his forehead, he sat. "Ouch, brain-freeze." Kyle felt it too. It was times like these; he believed they were identical twins. Michael had experienced similar moments. He dreaded discussing his recent Atlanta trip with him, instead he asked, "How was the concert? Ollie told me you two went together."

Kyle finished his drink, loosened his tie and pulled off his shoes and admitted with a sigh, "It was awkward, to say the least."

"You had sex with his wife."

"She wasn't his wife at the time. I didn't know about Ollie until Lily's going away dinner."

"You know how it is. He might feel like Sapphire's comparing you with him."

Kyle knew it, but that was their problem. "I can't change what happened. If I could, I would."

"Don't we all wish we could go back and change the events of the past?"

"Speaking of the past, you'll never guess who Ollie and I saw at the concert."

"Who?"

"Your old flame, Rebecca Stokes," Kyle threw out in excitement.

Michael mimicked his brother, removed his tie and shoes. "Get out of here."

"I can't. It's true. She even gave us her business card. She owns a restaurant. It's Spanish cuisine up in Harlem. We should go check it out."

Wondering what became of Becky, Michael thought, *Maybe.*

Kyle brought up Atlanta. "You gonna tell me about your visit?" Michael opened his mouth and Kyle's phone chirped, he said, "Hold that thought."

His voice raced through her like electricity. She stumbled on, "Hell...Hello."

"Vaughn?" She sat unsure if her legs would hold up. But Kyle, stood and paced. "Are you ok?"

No, I'm not. Her fear led her to say. "Great. I know this may seem unreasonable after all this time, but I never said I'm sorry."

"I never gave you the chance."

"Considering the circumstance, I understand. Kyle, you are a good man. I never meant to hurt you."

Silence. Vaughn waited for a response. Taken aback by the phone call, Kyle remained quiet. He prayed for this moment. And now, his only regret, it was happening by telephone.

"Take care, Kyle," Vaughn ended the call.

"Vaughn?"

Michael saw his brother's bewilderment. He patted his back. "Everything alright?"

"That's it? She hung up?" He zeroed in on Michael with a strained look. "Man, she didn't give me a chance to respond."

Kyle and Michael stared at one another as Kyle thought about Vaughn; and Michael, Lily. It was going to be a long night and a good night for Chinese. Michael ordered and dispatched Lily's news to Kyle over sweet and sour chicken.

Vaughn shut down her computer, turned off the desk lamp and headed to Lily's office. She thought along the way. *I did just as Michael suggested. Kyle certainly didn't sound happy to hear from me. Michael was playing matchmaker. It's obvious to me Kyle is done, and so am I.*

Old Tricks?

The electronic thermometer beeped normal with the rising sun. Lexi was going to school, even though, she whined, complaining that she still didn't feel well. Flo refreshed Lexi's memory, "You weren't sick when you were playin' video games last night. I let you stay home yesterday. Come on, get up." Flo yanked the comforter back and lifted Lexi out of bed. "Oh girl, you're getting heavy. You definitely have the Foster butt."

"What's the Foster butt?"

Getting Lexi settled into the bathroom, she answered, "Foster is our family name. That was Auntie Vie's and my last name before we got married. We all have big bottoms, me Auntie and Vaughn. But I think yours is growing faster than ours. You're only six. Wash up good now. I'm going to start breakfast."

"Mom, can we go visit Vaughn again?" Lexi stalled. "I like my sister."

"We'll see. Go on, get ready." Flo closed the door, and leaned against it. *I like Vaughn too. She doesn't like me.*

Roosta found his wife in deep thought. "I hope you're thinking 'bout me." He kissed her full on the lips.

"I was thinking about Vaughn."

"I know it's hard for you. Why don't you talk about it in counseling today?"

"Roosta, it is marriage counseling."

He shrugged. "Whatever is affecting you, affects our marriage. Bring it up, and then later, schedule something alone with just you and Pastor Cruz, or Mother Cruz. I don't know; whoever would handle it."

She smiled at her husband. Roosta folded his arms around her waist, pulled Flo close. "I love you." And she loved him back. They kissed with the fierceness of the promise. Roosta saw tears in his wife's eyes. "What's wrong? Morning breath?" he asked.

"I've never been this happy before," she proclaimed, wiping her tears.

He kissed her again, possessively. It would hurt, but he would tell Flo about Shay Lynn and his future plans. He swallowed the growing lump in his throat. "I'll see you in counseling, afterwards we'll have lunch."

"Thanks for helping the class today."

"You're welcome, Ms. Jones. I like being a part of the class. You know I always wanted to be a teacher."

"It's never too late." Ms. Jones was round in shape, very pleasant and fifty-five years old. No one would know it with all the energy she illuminated. Flo thought she was perfect for Lexi's first grade teacher. Even at almost forty-six, Flo still remembered hers. Maybe that's why she wanted to be one. She sighed at the so many maybes in her life. But now she was finally content with God, Roosta and Lexi.

She watched her little girl curl up on the red alphabet carpet for story-time. She wanted to stay and listen too, but she'd be late for counseling. "Ms. Jones, I better get going. I have an appointment."

Ms. Jones smiled, picked up the storybook of the morning. "Remember," she told Flo, "if you still want to be a teacher, I can help you get started."

Flo flashed a smile thinking Ms. Jones must be crazy. Then the smile dropped. Shay Lynn bolted in the classroom. Ms. Jones sang, "Oh here's our new student, Lena, Lena Jenkins."

Flo couldn't move. Shay Lynn marched in giving a mischievous smile. "I'm sorry we're late. I had car trouble. My husband is going to get me a new car. You know he's a used car salesman."

Ms. Jones eyes swayed to Flo, still standing in the middle of the classroom. "Mrs. Jenkins, and Mrs. Jenkins. Are you two related?"

"We're not." Flo's answer was fire. "And her last name is not Jenkins, it is Ling."

Shay Lynn gloated. "I always use Roosta's name. Flo, you know that."

No, I didn't know that. Apparently, seeing Lena in Lexi's class, there was a lot she didn't know. Shay Lynn kissed her little girl and sent her to join the others on the carpet. Lexi said hello to the new student.

Flo jerked Shay Lynn's arm and handled her in the hall. "We better go outside and talk."

Ms. Jones slanted her head in wonder.

Refusing to budge outside of the school, Shay Lynn regained control of her arm. "Why do you seem so upset? Didn't Roosta tell you I was transferring Lena?" Tall, slender, young and attractive, Shay Lynn Ling was half Asian, half African American. Her copper skin was flawless and velvet smooth. Her midnight black hair was thick and forever swept up in a glamorous do.

Shay Lynn taunted Flo, gathering she had no knowledge of the prior phone call or, that Roosta and Shay Lynn had a meeting the day before. "I called your house just, let me see, when was that? – Oh yes, Saturday. I spoke with Lexi. She's very polite."

"You're a liar," Flo spat.

"A liar, I am not. You should ask Lexi. I also saw Roosta yesterday. He stopped by and bought me money for the school. You sure you keeping that man satisfied? He was mighty hungry when I saw him."

Shay Lynn pouted her thin shaped lips, thinking Roosta loved her mouth. She started to tell Flo that just to anger her a little more, but Flo would have decked her. However, she shared the reality of her relationship with Roosta, "Flo, Roosta and I go way back, before you, during you, and he'll be with me after you. No religious fling is gonna change that."

Shay Lynn's cell beeped. "I'm on my way. I had car trouble." Hanging up, she glanced at Flo, a teasing smile upon her lips. "I tell you, owning your own hair salon can be a trip. You know Roosta's my silent partner. I couldn't have gotten started without him. He's more of a husband to me than you. We're not legally married, but for what we have, we don't need papers."

Rage filled Flo's spirit.

She didn't believe Roosta gave into temptation with Shay Lynn, then again, she wasn't sure. Shay Lynn smoothed her hand across her white slacks, enjoying the red color in Flo's cheeks.

"Flo, give Roosta a message for me; tell him I need a new car. I want a BMW 525 I."

She stepped so close to Shay Lynn, she smelled her mouthwash. "Shay Lynn, you better be thanking God my little girl is here and we are in a school. Cuz the next time you try to play me again, I'll be wiping the floor with you."

Flo walked briskly, leaving a hint of fear in Shay Lynn. When she sat behind the wheel, she counted to ten, and prayed for strength. It was going to take God's strength to keep her from killing Roosta in a church.

Counseling was going to take on a new meaning when she got there. *Roosta, if you think I am going to tolerate your mess while you're lying about being faithful, you got another thing coming.*

I Was Prepared

Flustered, Lily looked through a pile of reports unaware of where the updated financials she prepared were. Mr. Connelly, a handsome older gentleman, waited patiently for the young associate to order herself. And Rick did nothing to assist her. He let her sweat, holding the required report in his hand while swerving in the black leather chair.

Mr. Ramsey wasn't as patient as his partner. He'd chosen Williams, Wright and Wilson for his merger because he was told they were the best. Apparent to him that the female attorney was incompetent, it unnerved him. He considered the amount of legal fees they were paying and tapped his thick fingers against the table. "Ms. Rose, surely you prepared for this meeting."

Lily felt perspiration dripping down the back of her silk white blouse. "Of course, Mr. Ramsey. I'm sorry I seemed to have left those reports on my desk. Please give me a minute to retrieve them."

Lily raced to her office, passed Vaughn on her left. Vaughn lifted her arms in question. With no time to answer, Lily waved her off. She searched the Excel files on her hard drive and couldn't find the report. There was no trace of it in the outbox either. Certain she emailed a copy to Rick, she questioned, "How can that be?" The thought of returning to the meeting without it was terrifying.

Throwing up into her waste pail underneath her desk bought no relief. She held her head down, planning her next move. It would take all afternoon to recreate the report. Confident Mr. Ramsey wouldn't be pleased with that, she sprinted to the ladies room, splashed cool water on her face and rinsed out her mouth.

Her reflection was disturbing. Lily patted dry her face with a stiff paper towel. Within seconds, tiny beads of sweat fled her pores again. She held onto the sink, drew in two deep breaths and let them out slowly through her mouth. Head held high, she pretended to be in control and walked back to the conference room. To her dismay, it was empty.

"Burney, can I have a word with you?"
Mr. Peter smiled when he saw Rick standing in his office. He meant to find out how things were going with the merger, and Lily. "Sure Rick."

Rick usually enjoyed the infrequent visits in Mr. Peter's extravagant office. Today, he needed a verdict. No time for deliberations. He began his closing argument, "It's Lily."

He let out a huge breath. "I was afraid of that. I do have to ask, is it business or personal?"

"It's both. Lily is a very unstable woman."

"My impression of her was she is a very intelligent woman."

Rick jumped on that before his boss sang her praises. "Mine too, at first. I thought two professionals could have a good time. Lily had other plans. I believe she wanted to trap me into marrying her, since her last boyfriend didn't. She's a smart enough woman to know how to protect herself from pregnancy."

Mr. Peter's voice rose an octave. "She's pregnant? Rick, how could you?"

Rick exploded, "Burney, she set me up! She said she was responsible. I told her we could take care of this mishap, but she won't hear of it. Lily is trying to corner me into being a father." He paused, reeling him in as he stared into his eyes and slowly added, "Burney, it's affecting her work. Today she walked into a merger meeting unprepared."

His fears manifested, he nodded. "I see."

"I can handle the merger without Lily."

"Rick, I know you can. See that you do. I'll handle Lily."

The verdict was in. Grinning victoriously, Rick headed to his office.

Mr. Peter folded his hands. He would surely arrest the situation before things got ugly. He wondered if all was true. Mr. Peter had caught the glare in Rick's eyes when Lily first arrived.

He picked up his phone, dialed Lily's secretary and requested her immediate presence. He would at least hear Lily's side before he made a decision. It would be easy to assign her another mentor, but the baby made things very complicated.

"Mr. Peter, you wanted to see me?" Lily sat across from Mr. Peter in a gray suit. Grateful that the jacket hid the circle of perspiration in the back of her blouse, she crossed her legs and lifted her chin.

"Lily, I've heard some disturbing news."

"Oh?" Feeling her stomach roll over again, she decided to let him do the talking.

"You attended an important meeting without preparation."

"I was prepared."

"That's not what I heard."

"What I meant was; I did prepare for the meeting. I think someone deleted the files from my computer."

"Your computer is password protected. Only someone in the IT Department can enter your computer."

She cleared her throat. "Mr. Peter, I know. However, I also emailed a copy of my reports to Rick. He never said a word in the meeting. I think he purposely tried to make me look bad."

Rick's words came into focus in Mr. Peter's mind. *Lily is unstable.* His voice was patronizing. "Lily, why would he do that? He's your mentor. If you look bad, so does Rick. There's no way *he* would jeopardize a merger for personal reasons. I've known him far too long. I also know about your personal situation with him."

197

Shifting in her seat, she felt apprehensive about hearing her situation from her employer.

"Lily, we've invested a lot in you being here. We expect better."

Mr. Peter might as well have been speaking Russian to Lily. She might have had a better chance of following him. She wanted to shout that Rick was the unprofessional one. She knew Mr. Peter wouldn't believe her.

He continued, "I think you need to take some time off from work. Get some professional counseling and reevaluate if Williams, Wright and Wilson is where you want to be."

She blinked repeatedly. "Excuse me? Time off? How long?"

"Take a few weeks, more if you need to."

She couldn't believe that *she* was being dismissed from the firm. Solemnly, she inquired, "What about my secretary?"

Mr. Peter gently answered, "I'll call Human Resources, see about getting her on as a floater. I'm sorry Lily, your unpaid leave is effective, immediately."

A New Meaning

Roosta didn't know what hit him. One minute he was talking to Pastor and Mother Cruz, the next, his head was flying violently to the right. Flo slapped Roosta so hard that him, and his chair, hit the floor.

"You lyin' cheatin' son of a ..."

"Flo!" Pastor Cruz screamed, "Flo, you're in a church!"

The instant knockout had Pastor Cruz' tanned complexion heating up. He ran a hand through the soft black hair flickered with silver flecks. Mother Cruz put a hand around Flo's waist. "Calm down Mama, please. We can't let you beat up your husband."

Flo's voice was labored and choppy. "He's not my husband. He's a h..."

"Flo, please calm down." Pastor Cruz requested a second time.

Unsteady, Roosta stood. Flo's voice still off balance, she spouted, "Roosta, how could you let Shay Lynn put Lena in Lexi's school? They're in the same class. Lexi don't even know about her sisters and brother."

Confused, everyone turned towards Roosta for an explanation. He asked, "Flo, what are you talking about?"

"Oh, you gone lie about it?"

Embarrassed and completely baffled, he offered as defense, "I don't know what you're talking about. Shay Lynn called and said she was changing Lena's school. She never said which school."

Flo fought the urge to hit him again, yelling, "Why didn't you tell me she called our home?"

"I was going to tell you today in our session. Ask Pastor Cruz, I talked to him about it." He looked to the pastors for assistance. *Please tell her.*

They came quickly to Roosta's defense. "It's true, Flo. He was going to tell you. Unfortunately, Ms. Shay Lynn got to you first. Can we all please sit down and talk this out?"

They sat, all eyes on Flo waiting for her to say something. She boxed her arms around her. Her temper was still flaring, she requested, "Forgive me. I thought you were up to your old tricks."

Pastor Cruz advised, "You should tell Flo what you planned to." Through water filled eyes Flo looked at Roosta. He leaned forward on his legs, and stared into them. He didn't speak right away, so she did. "Roosta, I feel like we have no privacy at home. We don't share anything special. All that I know about you; so does Shay Lynn. You share children and every bond that goes with it. I don't have anything secure or sacred with you Roosta. You don't belong completely to me, and you never will."

He wanted to take her hand and make her know that wasn't true. He was afraid to touch her. "Flo, I'm yours, all of me. I haven't seen my kids in months. I was afraid of how you would take it. We're still trying to build our marriage. I didn't know if you were ready to be a part of my kid's lives. I didn't want to see Shay Lynn or the kids without you knowing."

That was news to Flo. His oldest child nine, the second eight, Lexi was just a few months away from Lena. His former mistress was a kept woman, and she was threatened by his renewed marriage. Flo understood, but she wanted to know more. "Do you love Shay Lynn?"

He didn't hesitate. "No. Shay Lynn and I had a convenient relationship. She was convenient. I know that sounds horrible. It's no secret how I used women." He shook his head. "It isn't love."

She wrinkled her eyebrows. "What makes me so special? Why did you marry me?"

He smiled, telling her, "In the beginning, it was because you challenged me. You weren't easy. You didn't give it up, or give in easily."

The Cruz' smiled, hearing Flo held up a standard. The rhythm between Flo and Roosta synchronized. More relaxed, Roosta continued, "You challenged me to take over my father's business, to be a man and to accept the Lord."

"I didn't do that?"

"When we were in New York, you seemed...content. You were at peace with Christ and without me. I wanted Him and I wanted you." Roosta pulled her hand out of the protective box and stroked it. "Flo, I promise never to break my vows to you again, but I want to see my kids."

"Roosta, you stayed away from Shay Lynn and the kids because of me?" His eyes said, yes. She shook her head. "I don't want you to do that. I don't want you to do what I did to Ollie and Vaughn. We'll fix this. We are going to have to have a long talk with Ms. Shay Lynn Ling."

He intertwined his fingers in hers as a sign of solidarity. Shay Lynn would see their love and commitment whether she wanted to or not.

Reality

Lily told Vaughn she had an appointment outside of the office. She instructed her to finish whatever she was working on, give it to Rick and take the rest of the day off. Vaughn had a mouth full of questions. Lily couldn't stand to be in the office any longer to explain. She would tell all when Vaughn got home.

Twenty minutes later, Lily sat in the garage, wondering what was going on with her life - Michael, Rick, the unwanted child and the unpaid leave. She closed her eyes. Her mind floated away with the racing thoughts. Then suddenly, it anchored when she felt warm fluid invading her underwear. Grabbing a hold of her briefcase, she ran into the house thinking she was losing control of her bladder, like everything else in her life.

Eyeing the stairs, she decided if she needed to go, it was better to go downstairs. She stormed into the mint green powder room, lifted her skirt, and tugged down her underwear. The white lace was blood soaked. Dr. Miles warned her that bleeding in the first trimester could be a sign of miscarriage. On instinct, she said, "Jesus! Help me, Lord. Please help me and my baby."

Leaving the underwear, she ran barefoot upstairs. She wanted to change and head for the hospital. But, still bleeding, she forgot about changing.

Securing a sanitary napkin and fresh underwear, she slipped them on, found a pair of white tennis shoes and ran back to her car. Donita was parking when she recognized Lily's passing car. Trying to get her attention, she honked. No response. She called Lily's cell phone. No answer. *Where is Lily racing to driving sixty-five in a forty-five mile zone?*

Curious to find out, she followed her to the entrance of the emergency room. By the time Donita parked and caught up to her, Lily was wobbly, in a cold sweat and the neat bun in her hair had loosely fallen.

Donita didn't ask, but took her hand, leading Lily past reception, and directly to the triage center.

Tonya the head nurse slid in front of Donita as if she were on ice skates. "Nita, you know the procedure. Your friend here has to register."

"I'll register her. You get her settled," Donita rattled off the order.

Donita didn't leave triage and Tonya rolled her eyes at her.

Lily sat, so Tonya took her temperature, pulse and then blood pressure. "What's the problem Miss?"

"I'm five weeks pregnant and I just noticed I'm bleeding." Lily's hand tenderly clutched her womb as if she could hold onto the child with it. Tonya started going down the list. "Any cramping, clots, severe pain..."

Donita retorted, "You heard the girl. She's pregnant. See if Dr. Miles is working. Now, Tonya!" Nurse Tonya unwillingly obeyed. She touched Lily's shoulder. "I wish you would have told me you were pregnant."

Lily blinked through a flood of hot tears, not ready to have the explanatory discussion. All she wanted was her baby to live - regardless if Rick wanted it or Michael wanted her. Nothing mattered except the life that was growing within her. She now understood the physical and spiritual heritage that was connected to her child. She held onto her womb and prayed.

Remembering the fear and pain of losing a child, Donita squeezed her hand in silent prayer.

Slipping Away

She wore stilettos. Not sure if she could still do it, she gave it her complete concentration. Sapphire balanced herself; then lifted her right leg up over her head. She held it high for several seconds, and let it down with a sigh of relief.

Ollie stood quietly in the distance, watched the silent routine - no music, just Sapphire and her moves. She was a work of art in skimpy dungaree shorts and a dancer's bra. Sapphire gyrated at the waist then stumbled when she turned and spotted Ollie.

"Oh baby! Don't stop. This is what you do while I'm out busting my chops? Missing the night life?"

Preparing for her first professional performance, she reached for her towel, patted her face dry and sucked her teeth.

"You still not talking to me? Still mad at me for being friends with Kyle and Michael?"

She rolled her eyes and swung her butt towards the kitchen for some water.

Hungry, Ollie decided to have lunch and get back to his cab. "What did you make me for lunch?"

"Why didn't you have Kyle and Michael make you lunch?"

Clearly realizing she didn't make him anything, he hunched down into the refrigerator. "Sassy, I ain't gonna argue with you. You're my wife, not my boss. They're my friends and that's all there is to it."

"Good, I'm glad. I'd like to see you have sex with Michael and Kyle."

In a Tupperware dish, he found left over spaghetti and nuked it in the microwave. "Oh, you wanna play the no sex game?"

Sassy looked into Ollie's eyes and he saw resentment in hers. "This is not a game. I am your wife, Ollie. That means my feelings should count for something. But they don't. Not to you."

He yelled, "My feelings don't count to you! You planned our wedding without even telling me, or my family."

203

There was a stack of paper plates on the counter, he took one and poured warm spaghetti in it.

"Ollie, I don't understand you. We were together three years and you never once brought up your family or friends to me. Now all of a sudden they're a big part of your life. I used to be your life. I took care of your rusty butt for three years Ollie. I quit school because of you, stripped to support you. You remember that? Or has holiness given you amnesia?"

Ollie picked up his fork and then dropped it. "I do remember, Sassy. I remember I was a man who would never have a woman take care of me. I remember I was a man of God once. I remember I had a family that loved me. It's true that when I met you I wanted to forget all of that. I grew up in church. My grandmother had me in church all the time. I wanted out. I wanted to see what the world had to offer. I found you, and you were good to me, maybe too good."

Sapphire didn't know who Ollie was, or the man she married. She listened with her eyes, but her heart remained hard.

Ollie continued, "Being around Kyle, Michael and my Uncle is reminding me Sassy, that God didn't intend for me to be that way. I hid from God and everything connected to Him for three years. I don't wanna hide no more. I wanna be what God wants."

Sapphire snapped, "Where does that leave me? You're telling me the man I knew and loved was a coward? So who's the real Ollie?"

"I hope he's a better man than the one before. I thought you would be happy. I'm doing what you asked me to do."

"Ollie, I want things the way they used to be, just you and me."

"Sassy, if being in the presence of Godly men is helping me do right by you, you should support me."

Sapphire walked close to Ollie, her lips almost touching his. It would have been tempting if it were not for the snare in her voice. "You are disgusting to call Kyle a Godly man. Do you know Kyle? Do you know the things we did in bed together? Do you know how he touched me, Ollie? Where he touched me? You don't know Kyle the way I do. How can you be friends with a man that's been with your wife? You're sick, Ollie. All of you! Is that what church is all about? Forgive and Forget? If you can honestly look me in the eye and tell me that you hold no hard feelings for the relationship Kyle and I had, I'll go with you to church tonight, and throw myself on the altar."

Ollie put his head down. It was a struggle for him and Kyle, but he was trying to get back to the essence of himself, his past, his brotherhood, his kinship, his God.

She took his silence as his answer. "You've proved my point. There ain't' no way you can truly forgive and forget. You're fooling yourself. In a way, I can understand you wanting to go back to the good ole days. You can't. Relationships end, people die and you go on. End this relationship; I'm your wife, Ollie. I'm your future."

She left him alone in the kitchen to ponder her words as they rang in her head also. *You can't go back.* Yet, she was preparing for her first professional performance that very night - going back to a profession she promised she wouldn't.

A Change Is Coming

"The bleeding is normal Lily." Dr. Miles smiled at Lily, thankful the baby was doing fine. She peeled off the latex gloves, lifted the wastebasket with her white clogs and tossed them.

Lily picked herself up out of the stirrups and covered herself. She exposed more of herself than ever, first to Rick and now the doctor. Being a non-virgin wasn't something she found enjoyable.

"Normal, I don't understand. I shouldn't be bleeding."

Dr. Miles washed her hands and spoke to Lily with her back turned. "When I say normal, I mean right now, I don't see any signs of a miscarriage. Some women do bleed in their first trimester. I've had women bleed throughout the entire pregnancy."

Dr. Miles dried her hands, dumped the paper towel and walked over placing a soothing hand on Lily's shoulder. "Lily, I'm putting you on bed rest for a week as a precautionary measure. No work."

That certainly would not be a problem, considering she was on unpaid leave. Lily thought, *It's funny how things are working out.*

"Do you think you can get the time off from work?"

"Very sure."

"Good. You have the number to my office, call to set up an appointment one week from today. Now if the bleeding gets heavier any clots or cramping, you come back right away, ok?"

"I will. Thank you Dr. Miles." "You're welcome. I'll leave so you can get dressed."

Donita looked in just as Dr. Miles was leaving. "Hey, Dr. Miles."

To alleviate worry, she said quickly, "Nita, Lily and baby are fine. I'll see you later."

Clutching the blue sheet around her waist, Lily looked up with relief. Donita embraced her. "Oh girl, I'm so happy to hear you're alright."

Just for the need to release, Lily cried in her arms. "Oh, Nita, I was so scared. I thought I didn't want my baby, but I do. I do."

"I know you do. Is Rick the father?"

Donita didn't let her go because she still cried. "He is, oh God, he is." "That explains the long faces at Sunday dinner. I could see Michael was in turmoil."

"I'm in love with Michael. I wish this was his baby."

"So does he. It's all over him. He's in love with you too. I'll turn around so you can get dressed."

Donita patted Lily's back and rubbed it as if she was burping her, then turned and chatted while Lily slipped off the table. "I called Vaughn. She was worried sick when she saw your underwear in the bathroom. She tried your cell, but you left it at home with your purse, wallet and money. Girl, you must have lost it. It's a wonder you were able to drive yourself. God got you here safely. So, Dr. Miles put you on bed rest?"

Lily fastened her skirt in the back. "How do you know?"

"I'm a nurse remember? I've lost quite a few babies in my past."

Lily touched her shoulder. "Nita, I'm sorry."

Donita turned. "I told you before, don't be. It wasn't meant to be, but this baby is. It's gonna stick. And it's gonna be beautiful, just like it's mama."

Jamming her feet into her shoes, she asked, "How do you know?"

She smiled. "Cuz, I know. Now come on, I'll drive you home. Vaughn's got dinner waiting."

Lily slipped her hand around Donita's waist and rested her head on her shoulder. "Nita, I don't know what I would have done without you and Vaughn these past five months. I love you."

"I love you too, girl. Now let's go home. You know we've got to figure out how we're going to tell your mother all of this."

Lily jumped. "My mother?"

"Yes yo' mama is going to be a grandmother. Let's go home, eat, pray and talk it over. Then Vaughn's got something to tell you."

"Me?" Lily lifted her brows.

"Uh huh, Vaughn has been strong for you and she needs the same from you. She may hate me now, but she'll thank me later."

Nurse Tonya watched Lily and Donita walk out of the triage center arm in arm. She rolled her eyes. Donita noticed and sang, "Thanks for your prompt assistance. Have a good night."

Together We Stand

Flo and Roosta laid silently in bed for over an hour. Roosta lifted his head, looked at the clock. Already ten thirty, he exhaled, "I should call Shay Lynn. I know we agreed to wait till morning to give ourselves some time to cool down, but I can't sleep."

Flo rolled over and rested her head against his hairy chest. "Call her then. I can't sleep either. Make sure you ask her not to say anything about Lena about Lexi being sisters, until we have a chance to talk to Lexi."

Roosta rose up and made the call. Shay Lynn answered on the first ring. Through caller ID, she knew who it was. "Hi honey." His back stiffened when she called him honey. He knew Flo could hear Shay Lynn through the receiver. "We need to talk."

"I know we do. I miss you. Come over tonight. Please, honey."

Flo wanted to snatch the phone and tell her Roosta wasn't her honey. But this was Roosta's chance to prove to her who he really was. She gave him the freedom to handle it.

"No, Shay Lynn."

"Then tomorrow, tomorrow afternoon. I'll push my appointments around so we can spend some time together."

Roosta struggled; he didn't want to hurt Shay Lynn. She hadn't accepted the reality of his marriage to Flo. It took him seven years to accept it. Roosta knew it wouldn't be easy to convince Shay Lynn. "There's no need to rearrange your schedule."

"Roosta, I'll be here at noon."

"Ok Shay Lynn, tomorrow at noon," he agreed and pleaded, "Shay Lynn, please don't say anything about Lena and Lexi being sisters."

"I wasn't planning to. I think as her parents, we need to do it together. Don't you agree, honey?"

"Shay Lynn, I'll see you tomorrow." He hung up.

Flo tried to steady her breathing. Roosta slid back under the covers and reached for Flo's hand. Willingly, she gave it to him. "We're going to see Shay Lynn tomorrow at noon."

"We?"

"*We* need to do this as one. Shay Lynn needs to understand; I'm your husband. I'm not cheating on you. I'm not leaving you. I want visitation rights. I want her to know you're going to be a part of that."

"Roosta, this is going to be hard on her."

"Are you worried about Shay Lynn?"

"Aren't you? I can't believe you feel no compassion for her."

He regretfully confessed, "I do."

"That's what I thought, considering your history together."

"I've created a mess. This is hard on you accepting my children. What is Lexi going to think?"

Flo rested on top of Roosta and listened to his heartbeat. "It's a mess alright. That's for sure. Still, ain't no mess too big that God can't help us clean up."

Roosta felt the softness of Flo's hair as he stroked it. He stared at the ceiling and wondered if Flo's words were true. God was new in his life. *Can He help me clean up the situation?*

Trailing kisses up and down his chest and stomach, she made love to her husband. Not because she wanted to, but because he needed her to.

New Territory

"Welcome. Seeing you're the only women here, I assume you're the entertainment for the evening."

Mac grinned at the dimpled man in the navy suit. His eyes were shades of blue and green. Proud of the service he was offering, he bragged, "You gentlemen are in for a show like you've never seen before. These are my best jewels."

The host looked past Mac and locked in on Sapphire. "I'm intrigued." He replaced his drink in his left hand and took Sapphire's. His diamond and gold wedding band sparkled. Sapphire noticed it, realizing she wore her wedding rings. "Hello, I'm Dr. Kline."

"Sassy, and this is Opal."

"It's a pleasure to meet you."

Mac grabbed hold of Dr. Kline's hand, giving a clear indication that he was the man in charge. "Dr. Kline, the ladies need a private space to get ready."

He led them to the through the penthouse suite towards the bedroom. It was a combination of festive sophistication. The ladies walked in and Mac behind them wearing an orange and navy plaid suit. Sapphire told him he looked ridiculous, but in his new line of business, he was convinced this was the style for him.

The men seemed harmless standing around in expensive suits, chatting and sipping on chardonnay and champagne. It seemed like a typical evening for a group of doctors.

Opal, tawny brown, all of four foot nine with a cropped haircut, squeezed Sapphire's arm. "Girl, you can smell the money in here."

Mac greedily agreed, "That's right ladies, so I want you to give these men a show they'll never forget."

Sapphire observed someone at the bar and halted. He looked very familiar. The gentlemen smiled, raised his glass and nodded. Sapphire returned the greeting and tried to place where she'd seen him before.

Secrets Exposed

If it were not for all the tears, the ladies looked like they were having a slumber party. Lily spread across the sofa, Vaughn curled up in the loveseat and Donita sprawled in the Lazy Boy. It was eleven at night and they were beyond exhausted.

Lily wiped away tears as her heart flooded with compassion. She sniffled. "Vaughn, I feel so selfish. All these months I've been crying over Michael and Rick and you've been hurting. So wrapped up in my problems, I didn't even see your pain."

"Lily, I didn't want anyone to know. That's why you didn't." Vaughn squinted at Donita with a disgusted eye.

Lily asked, "Kyle has no clue?"

"I want to keep it that way."

"Vaughn! The man thinks…" Lily cut the words knowing what they all thought was a horrible lie.

"I know what he thinks. I'm not going back to change it. I called him today. Kyle's going on with his life."

Donita's head lifted. "You did?"

"Yeah, he really didn't have much to say to me."

Lily stated, "I find that hard to believe. Maybe you caught him at a bad time."

"Whatever the time, it doesn't matter. It's over."

Donita voiced, "Vaughn it's over because you didn't tell the truth." Silence.

"I'm going to bed," Lily announced through a yawn.

"You should have been in bed the minute we got home," Donita explained.

Lily yawned again. "I've been lying on the couch since we got back from the hospital. You and Vaughn wouldn't let me pee in peace."

Donita stood and stretched, she said, "That's right. I'll be by with your breakfast in the morning." She gave Lily a hug and continued, "Vaughn thanks for dinner. You make a mean pork chop. I better get home before my husband and child divorce me."

Vaughn eased up. "Nita, I'll walk you out."

Donita sensed Vaughn had a few choice words for her. She stalled, fished for her car keys in her suitcase size purse as they stood in the driveway.

"Nita, I don't appreciate you putting me on the spot tonight. I didn't want Lily to know about the date rape."

Donita held in a yawn. "I know you didn't." "Vaughn," she illuminated, "you've been carrying this burden around for a year. God has blessed you with a good family. Learn to lean on them."

"I've been doing ok." She held her chin up in defiance.

"Are you going to live in denial forever? Do you want to go to your grave knowing the real reason you didn't marry the man you loved was because another man violated you? Don't you think Kyle has a right to know?"

A pause. Donita leaned forward, waited for anything Vaughn offered as acceptance of her reality. Silence. Receiving nothing, she strongly urged, "Think about how much he's suffered believing a lie. He has a right to know the truth. If you don't tell him, then you've let the enemy rob you both. Not only has he taken your virtue, he's stolen your future."

Looking up at the half moon, Vaughn fought back tears. A cool night, Vaughn wrapped her arms around herself for warmth.

Now she had a question for Donita. "I've thought about that. Even if Kyle knew the truth, do you think he would marry me? That's a heavy burden for him to carry, knowing his wife was raped."

"It's all heavy if you ask me. He believes you betrayed him, that you slept with another man."

Vaughn sighed. "Nita, I appreciate what you're trying to do. The bottom line is; I did sleep with another man, even if it was involuntarily. You know what's so bad about it? I can't remember it. Who knows what Courtney did to me?" The tears arrived coolly down Vaughn's cheeks. "I'm afraid if Kyle touches me, or any man, it will all come rushing back. That's why I stopped dating. Donita, I'm afraid I will remember."

Donita grabbed her wrist and shook her arms. "Oh Vaughn, you've got to expose this fear. You've got to pray, tell your family and Kyle. Talk to a professional and once you expose the fear, it will leave you. The harder you try to run from it, the more it will hold you captive. Lily knows and that's a start. Ask God to give you the strength to get free of this."

She smiled into Vaughn's hazel eyes. Vaughn nodded, hoping she could do just that.

Let's Have Lunch

Sapphire's leg lift was the showstopper as her body parts oozed out, over and around the costume. The room full of previously calm doctors; now vibrated with hoots and hollers. And Mr. Familiar's grin, formed into an opened mouth laugh. Sapphire was sure he had a cavity in his left molar. On impulse, she decided to make the routine a little more physical.

After letting her leg down, she motioned with her finger for Mr. Familiar to join her in the center of the floor. Surprised and delighted, he handed his drink to his colleague and danced onto the floor.

Jokingly, he asked, "Do I have to take off something?" He had good moves. Sapphire shushed him with a finger to his lips and danced around him. Forgetting she was married, she allowed her body to brush up against his. The man touched his chest, breathed into her ear, "You might wanna take it easy on me. I have a weak heart."

"I think we might be able to find you a heart specialist in here." She winked at him.

They both grinned and he swayed with her and the music.

The men clapped and cheered for more. When the music stopped, he shook her hand and politely thanked her for the dance. She said nothing, smiled and then with much attitude, flashed her curly weave over her shoulders and jiggled away.

"Sounds like you wowed them," Opal realized. She was up next to assist the doctors get their fantasy freak on.

Sapphire slid into her plain clothes. "They're easy to please."

"Well, that's good. I'm tired. It's going to be mid-night soon. Where's Mac?"

Sapphire smoothed cold cream on as she wiped the sparkles off her face. She went into the bathroom for a warm washcloth. "He's out there getting drunk."

Opal chuckled. "Rum and coke right?"

"You know it."

"Hey, since you're dressed, come and watch me dance. I put together a new routine."

Sassy rinsed her face, dried it with a white posh towel. "I was about to put some make-up on."

"You're a natural beauty. You don't need make-up. Come watch me. I'm scared." Opal pulled her arm, pleading with her.

Sapphire backed up in disbelief. "Scared? Girl, you've been strippin' longer than me."

"This is different. We're dancin' in the middle of the floor, no stage, no bouncers."

"Mac's out there."

Opal sucked her teeth. "Drunken Mac can't protect me."

"Well, I can't."

"At least, you're sober. You can do better than Mac."

Since she wasn't giving up, Sapphire looked in the mirror, fluffed her hair, slipped on black stilettos and followed Opal out.

Opal motioned for Mac to start her music. Astoundingly, he wasn't so drunk that he couldn't understand. She gestured for

Sapphire to come closer." Sapphire denied Opal's appeal, stood near the bedroom against the wall. "This is close enough. I can see from here. Go on, do yo' thang." She waved her hand.

Wanting another opportunity to get near the flexible beauty, he was pleased she emerged out of the bedroom. He trotted to the bar and ordered two glasses of red wine, found her gazing at her wedding rings when he eased over. "I thought you might be thirsty. You sure made me thirsty."

Sapphire accepted the glass, guzzled and handed him the empty glass. "Whoa, you were thirsty. Here you want mine?" he offered.

Smiling, she said, "Do I know you?"

"Of course you know me," he asserted.

Curious, her forehead creased. "From where?"

"From my dreams. You're what every man dreams of."

Hearing that tired line before, she frowned. Suddenly, she lifted a sideways fist to her lips. "Wait a minute, you're Marcel Reid. We were in dental school together."

He backed away and studied her. "Hold up. I remember you too. You look different." He felt her tresses. "It's your hair. Didn't it used to be shorter?"

"Much shorter, this is a weave. You're lying, you don't remember me."

"Nah, I do. Give me a minute. I'm bad with names."

Marcel was boyishly cute, about five feet, eight inches tall, and had butternut brown skin. He had a thin mustache, and his hair was cut close to his head. But not so close, that she couldn't see his natural wave pattern.

"Marcel, you don't remember me. You don't have to pretend." She let him know, he did not need to flatter her with lies.

He really did remember her. She was the smartest in their class. He remembered he was jealous that she grasped concepts faster than him. So they we're former friends, proving it, he fumbled, "Your name was something like Crystal, no Ruby, no Emerald."

She laughed. "Sapphire, my name is Sapphire."

He grinned. "See I told you. I remembered."

"You didn't."

"I came close."

"You did."

She took the other glass of wine out of his hand and drank it down.

"Whoa, you can toss 'em back."

"I am thirsty. So, you're a dentist?"

"Yes, and you?"

"If I were a dentist, would I be here doing leg lifts?"

He tilted his head to the side. "It could be a hobby of yours. You're very good at it. What does your husband think?"

"My husband?" She blinked.

"Nice rings," he pointed at her hand.

"Oh, well, my husband has no idea where I am right now."

"Foolish man, if you were my wife, there's no way I would let you out of my sight."

She wrinkled her nose. "Oh Marcel, please. While we're on the subject, where's your wife?"

"Home, with our two year old," he shot out prideful.

She nodded, impressed with the truth. Still holding the empty wine glass, she folded her arms. "Well, at least you didn't lie."

"I never lie about my family."

"And you shouldn't. But, how does she feel about you being here watching strippers?"

He laughed. "She knows I'm here. She doesn't know I'm watching strippers."

"I didn't think so."

"She'd be pretty upset that I danced with you. I'm sure your husband wouldn't like it either."

"That's exactly why I ain't gonna tell 'em."

Opal walked up and stood between them. The energy radiating from the married doctor had danger screaming in all directions. She hoped Sapphire could hear it, she asked, "What did you think of the routine?"

Sapphire said, "I liked it."

Opal knew she lied to her. Sapphire never saw a second of it. "You ready, Sassy?"

"Go change, I'll be ready in a minute," Sapphire acknowledged.

"So, you gotta go?" His voice was glum. He gave her the puppy dog eyes.

"Uh huh, it was good seeing you, Marcel."

He jumped at the chance. "I'd like to you see again. Here's my card. Maybe I can take you to lunch, or something." His eyes raced over her lush body, and then locked in on her eyes. He liked what he saw in them.

"Uh, Marcel, we're married."

He stuffed a hand in his pocket. "Did I say something wrong? All I said was lunch."

"Were you thinking only lunch?"

"You can't fault a man for his thoughts. Besides, after that dance, you've given me a lot to think about. I'll leave it to you. Here's my number. Don't give me yours. If you want to have lunch, call. Good night, Sapphire."

Sapphire watched Marcel slither away like he had achieved something. He left it up to her. *He's tricky.* She smiled, thinking they had something in common. It wasn't just the fact that they were both bound by holy matrimony - a little danger in their life intrigued them.

My Answer

Kyle was inserting his cell and wallet into his suit jacket when the doorbell rang. The bell made him jump. He answered, thinking it might be Michael. They were back into their habit of riding into the city together. Opening the door, he squinted at the two unknown figures. "May I help you?"

The male spoke first. "Kyle Carraway?"

"Depends on who's asking."

They both flashed their badges. "I'm Detective Kris St. Laurent, and this is my partner, Detective Dee Spelling."

"Is there a problem?"

"May we come in?"

Very uncertain as to why two detectives would be at his door at seven am, on a Wednesday morning, he stepped back.

216

They walked in and pulled out their police pads, pens and a photo. Kris asked, "Mr. Carraway, do you know her?"

The adrenaline started pumping. Kyle's hands grew cold. Not really answering, but shocked at the situation, he said, "It's Vaughn."

Kris continued, "Do you know where I can find her?"

Kyle wanted answers, and he wanted them fast. "Vaughn is my former fiancé. I'm not giving you any information until you tell me what this is about."

Kyle's cell chirped. He barked, "What?"

Annoyed, Michael snapped, "I'm waiting for you downstairs. What's the hold up?"

"Michael, you better come up. I've got two detectives in my living room with a year book photo of Vaughn."

Kris started up and Kyle said, "Wait, my brother's on his way up. I want him to hear whatever you have to say."

Michael was upstairs in less than a minute. Kyle already had the door unlocked for him, and out of breath, Michael rushed in asking, "What's the problem?"

Kris explained, "We have reason to believe Vaughn Sparrow is a possible date rape victim."

He might as well have said *Vaughn had a sex change*. That he could have comprehended. Both Kyle and Michael shouted, "What? When?"

Dee took over. "Mr. Carraway. We've had three women come forward about date rape. We got a search warrant for the suspect's home. There was a wall of photos of the three women, along with a number of other women. One was of Ms. Sparrow. All the women's pictures were taken out of the high school yearbook."

Kyle held his head, feeling a violent migraine attacking. Michael added, "We know Vaughn very well. If she'd been raped, we would know."

Dee explained, "Ms. Sparrows' case is unique. The suspect has a system. The women that he has allegedly raped are placed on a board with a thank you note attached. But Ms. Sparrow had a knife, stabbed into her picture."

Exasperated, Kyle requested, "Please, just tell us in comprehensible terms what you're saying."

Kris made it plain. "We don't think the suspect finished what he started to do. He's angry. We believe if he does catch up with her again, he'll finish, and then kill her. He had this address on the back of the photo. Does she live here?"

In disbelief, Kyle and Michael stared at one another. Kris pleaded, "If you know where she is, we need to know. She can give us some idea about what happened to her."

Kyle couldn't get it all clear in his mind. "This bastard, may be roaming around looking for Vaughn?"

Dee replied, "That's right."

Michael explained, "Vaughn is in Atlanta. She moved there about five months ago."

"It may be safe for her to be there, that's if the suspect has no idea she's left town," The male detective noted.

This all frustrated Kyle, he asked, "You two don't know where 'the suspect' is? That means he may be in Atlanta, or here. Is that what you're saying?"

Dee warned, "It's highly unlikely that's he's in Atlanta. His latest victim came forward just days ago. But he may be looking, asking her neighbors, friends, and co-workers. He got this address. Unfortunately, he's pretty clever."

Feeling helpless, Kyle demanded, "What are you going to do?"

"Since we know she's in Atlanta, we need the exact address and contact information. We'll contact the Atlanta police and get someone out there to talk to her."

"What about protecting her?" Kyle questioned.

Kris assured him, "We'll do our best, but it will be difficult until we know for sure where this guy is."

Michael pulled a pen from his suit jacket and asked for a piece of paper. Dee handed it to him. His hands were shaky but he wrote down the address and phone number for the detectives.

Dee smiled. "Thank you. Please pray for her and the other women on his list."

Kyle's head shot up. "Do you believe in prayer?"

Dee said, "Yes. We believe Courtney didn't accomplish what he set out to do. God protected Vaughn and the enemy's angry. If God protected her once, He'll do it again."

Michael asked, "Are you a believer?"

"We are. We're praying for guidance that God will reveal to us where Courtney is."

That was the second time, she said Courtney, and not, 'the suspect.' Kyle vaguely remembered Courtney from school. Kris and Dee thanked Michael and Kyle for their assisternce and left their phone number.

Michael rested a hand on Kyle's shoulder; then squeezed, he asked the obvious, "What flight do you want to be on?"

"The earliest one you can get me. I'll call the office and pack."

"I'll take you to the airport. Let me call my office too."

Ties Broken

Flo and Roosta walked hand in hand down the concrete walkway of Shay Lynn Ling's home. It was pleasant and not what Flo expected from the "other woman." Actually, she didn't know what to expect. It was a small white house, with a flourishing lawn. The red, white and pink rose bushes in the front of the house were beautiful in the spring.

At that very moment, it all glistened under the high noon sun. It was a lovely home. Odd to her that her husband's former mistress, lived in a nice home, owned and ran her own business and a mother of three. She was a woman like herself - a woman that shared her husband.

Roosta shook her hand slightly, causing the mind-boggling thoughts to escape. "You ready for this?"

"Let's get it over with."

Out of habit, he pulled the keys to the front door out of his pocket. Flo flinched at the reality. *Roosta has keys. Easy access whenever he wants Shay Lynn.* At the very intricate moment, Roosta's face dropped. "I'm sorry. It's just…"

"Please don't say it. I know what it is. Just ring the bell."

Shay Lynn floated to the front door in a sheer short black negligee, revealing all. Disgusted, Flo observed her youthful body and Shay Lynn's heart broke. She slammed the door.

Flo let out a deep breath. "I guess she was expecting more than an afternoon chat."

"Flo, I…"

"Roosta, we're here. Let's do what we came to do. Use the darn key."

Roosta never stumbled or stuttered around women in all his life. However, at that moment, he wanted to hide under a rock. What man brought his wife into the home of his former mistress? This was more than what he had bargained for when he begged Flo's forgiveness. Yet, his issues needed to be settled with Shay Lynn.

Unlocking the door, he stood in place and searched for Shay Lynn with his eyes. Astonished, at what she saw, Flo stood behind her husband and made a face at the eye-catching home. It was clean, decorated in Asian and African Culture. The motif was expressed in the red and cream oriental carpet, matching drapes with touches of artwork and statues throughout the room.

Roosta called, "Shay Lynn, we need to talk to you."

She yelled, "I agreed to talk to you, not the old bag."

Roosta could tell by the sound of her voice she was in the bedroom. "Who you…"

Roosta said quickly, "We are not here to argue. Shay Lynn you started this by putting Lena in Lexi's school."

Shay Lynn stomped out of the bedroom in a fire red robe. "Oh, you think Lena's not good enough to go to that fancy school? She's your blood too."

"Shay Lynn that ain't got nothin' to do with what you did."

Shay Lynn was wounded, seeing Flo at Roosta's side. She folded her arms across her chest. "Shay Lynn my intention is not to hurt you, but I want you to understand Flo's my wife, my place is with her."

Shay Lynn's hands fell and then she shoved Roosta, causing him to step off balance. Emphasizing every word with an unsteady voice, she said, "You got nerve to stand in this house and tell me Flo's your wife. She's been your wife for seven years, but that never stopped you from sharing my bed. I gave you ten years of my life Roosta. How dare you bring her into my house and tell me this." She started to cry.

He reached for her and Flo knew it was too much to take. "Shay Lynn, I didn't come here to hurt you. You've got to understand, I'm committed to my wife. What we did was wrong. We got three children together. I plan to take care of my kids." Her ability to speak was impaired with pain.

Finally, she asked, "What are you saying? You want my kids?"

"I want to see them. Maybe have 'em for weekends. I would never take the children away from you."

Anger struck her again. "You expect me to believe Flo is going to be a step-mother to your mistress' children?"

It was Flo's turn to speak. She watched, listened and understood. Nevertheless, now was the time she would make things clear. "Shay Lynn, I feel for you. I really do. Cuz I don't believe you could have had all these years with Roosta and not love him, but don't make yourself out to be a victim here. You willingly participated in this so-called arrangement. You were available when he wanted and I guess in return you got some kind of companionship. But, you ain't nobody's victim. I'll be the first to admit, I was stupid. I knew if Roosta wasn't in our bed, he was in yours, or some other woman's."

Shay Lynn brushed tears away and studied Roosta with surprise. Flo expressed, "I know you don't think you were his only convenience."

Shay Lynn said, "I suspected."

"That's what I thought."

"If you knew all this Flo, why are you with him now?"

Sweating bullets soaked Roosta's silk gray shirt. Flo slid her hand down his dreads. "Roosta is a different man now. I'll honestly tell you, there ain't no way I'd be with him if he wasn't."

Roosta smiled at Flo and Shay Lynn saw the love he had for his wife. Tears fell afresh. "Roosta, what about me? I've got three children. What man is going to want me now?"

"Shay Lynn, I'm sorry. I want to do what's right. When can I see the kids?"

Uncertain if she would let him see the children, she answered, "Let me think about it. I've got a lot to deal with. Leave now."

She held out her hand. "My keys, Roosta. Since you're so committed to your wife, you won't be needing them."

Separating the keys from the ring, he sincerely apologized, "Shay Lynn, I am sorry. I never meant to hurt you. I'll be praying for you."

She slapped him and Flo grabbed Shay Lynn's red nail polished hand. She jerked her arm from Flo's grip. "Praying for me? You're sorry? You never meant to hurt me? Well it's too late for that, because I'm hurt. I've been with you ten years Roosta, and that's the best you can do."

Flo retorted, "You can't do no better than prayer Shay Lynn. Roosta, please give her the keys. We're going to talk to Lexi tonight about her siblings. When do you plan to talk to your children?"

"I don't know. Get out."

Roosta gently laid a hand on Flo's waist as they walked out, then he turned under the threshold. He saw an anguished Shay Lynn. "I'll be waiting for your call about the children. If you want, we can tell them about Lexi together."

She shoved him out the door. "Get out Roosta. Don't do me any favors."

Roosta continued to hold Flo's waist, with the other hand, he touched his stinging cheek. "If another woman hits me..."

Flo smiled. "I'm sorry for hitting you yesterday. I promise to keep my hands to myself, even when I'm angry."

Roosta opened the car door for his wife, and then he slid in the driver's seat. "I hope so, because you women hit hard."

"Other than the tears and the slap, I think it went well. Shay Lynn got the message."

Roosta sounded disappointed. "Yeah, but I don't think she's gonna let me see my kids."

"Maybe not right away. In time, she'll see that the kids need their father."

Roosta hoped and prayed that would be the case.

Shay Lynn peeked out the window and considered the tenderness and respect Roosta had for Flo. *I don't care what you say Roosta, it's not over.* She watched them drive away, believing with all her heart, Roosta would come back. *You always come back to me.*

That's When it Happened...

It's interesting how things are happening, Vaughn thought as she typed. Sometimes she felt life wasn't fair. Lily was on unpaid leave and she was working for Rick. As timing would have it, his secretary was out with the flu. In any event, Rick wasn't talking to her, unless it pertained to work. She was fine with that. In a way, they were related. Rick's blood ran through her unborn cousin. It didn't mean a thing to him. Rick sabotaged Lily's job, the mother of his child.

Vaughn glared up at him as he lightly touched the elbow of a Cadence Pelham, a partner at the firm. He announced, "Cadence and I are going to lunch. Please take messages and let people know I'm out. *Do not* transfer them to my line."

Through clenched teeth, she said, "Certainly." Underneath her breath, she said, "Heartless jerk."

Her private line rang. She grabbed it while watching Rick whisper in Cadence's ear.

"Vaughn Sparrow."

"Ms. Sparrow, this is security. I have Kyle Carraway here to see you."

She gasped, "Kyle's in New York."

"I'm looking at his driver's license. It *is* a New York license."

Kyle asked to speak to her. "Vaughn, it's me."

She almost fell out of her chair. "Tell him to let you up, or maybe I should come down?"

Excited and confused, Vaughn didn't know what to do.

Kyle asked, "Can you have lunch now?"

"You came all the way to Atlanta for lunch?"

"I came to talk to you."

"I'll be right down. Wait, I can't leave. The attorney is out. I have to answer his phone. Let me speak to the security guard."

The receptionist escorted Kyle to Vaughn's desk and the office ladies admired the tall handsome gentlemen. Vaughn spotted the carry on bag; it awed her.

"Kyle, I didn't know you were coming."

"I just found out myself. Is there some place we can talk, privately?" He didn't seem happy. Worried was more like it.

"Let's go into Rick's office." Sitting at the round glass table, Vaughn wanted to squeeze and smell Kyle. Instead, she asked, "What's wrong? Is it my family?"

"Have the police been by to speak with you?"

"The police?" Ok, enough with the questions, she shouted, "Kyle, you're scaring me!"

"Vaughn, two detectives came by my apartment looking for you this morning. They said you might be a victim of a possible date rape."

Her chest tightened and deep breathing took over. *Is she hyperventilating?* Kyle couldn't tell. He took her arm. "Sweetie, take it easy." He looked over his shoulder, found a bottle of water on a server table. Handing it to her, he said, "Here, drink it slow." She sipped.

"Vaughn, what happened between you and Courtney?"

Trying to pull herself together, she whimpered, "I don't know. Out of the blue he shows up, asked to come in to use the phone and then disappears. That's all I can recall." She didn't want to repeat how he undressed her without her consent, but admitted, "I think he drugged me."

"How?"

"He asked for something to drink. I poured some juice for the both of us and then went to answer the phone. Maybe he put something in it. I remembered the next day when you woke me and found the condom," she rattled off the only details she had.

In disbelief, Kyle stood and backed up. The muscles in his face tightened. "So that's when it happened." The events of that heart breaking morning came flooding back to him. He was livid. He called her a slut, threw her out. His voice was hard. "All this time - why didn't you tell me?"

"Kyle, you thought something that I couldn't prove otherwise. I can't remember what happened." He tried to calm himself. She needed to hear the rest. "Vaughn, the police believe Courtney is a serial rapist. You were one of the victims on his list. He didn't get what he wanted. Maybe that's why the condom wasn't used. He could be looking for you."

"What?" The blood in her hands and feet grew cold. "They think he's going to try again, and then..." Kyle shook his head. He couldn't repeat it.

Vaughn saw primal fear upon him. "Oh my God, Kyle!"

"They don't know if he knows where you are. As long as he's out there, I'm staying with you."

Rick's phone rang. She answered and took the message. It would be a wonder if Rick could read it. She was shaking and her attention never left Kyle. When she hung up, she asked, "Kyle, what about your job? You can't just stay with me."

Kyle emptied the space between them. His breath was warm against her ear. "I'm staying sweetie. I love you. I never stopped loving you."

"Kyle, I …" She wrapped her arms around him. "Kyle, I love you too. I'm sorry."

"Not as sorry as I am for treating you the way I did, and not as sorry as Courtney's gonna be."

Shaking, they held tightly on to each other.

Driving Me Crazy

Ollie waited for Sapphire to come home. It was after two in the afternoon. He took the morning off and now it was afternoon. Lighting a cigarette, he inhaled, and prayed, "God, uhma give these up, but I don't know what I got myself into with Sassy."

He decided to call his Uncle. *Yes, Uncle Desi would know what to do.* Too upset to call, he chose to call Opal a third time. Before anyone answered, the front door unlocked. Focused on Sapphire, Ollie replaced the receiver in the cradle.

Still wearing her jeans and white shirt from the night before, she asked, "Shouldn't you be at work?"

Full of thanks and turmoil, he snatched her arms, causing her bags to fall. "Where have you been?"

Struggling to free herself from his strong grip, she said, "Ollie, you're my husband, not my boss. Let me go!"

"I asked you a question. Where were you?"

"I spent the night with Opal"

"That I know, but she said you left early. Where did you go?" He pulled her tighter.

"Oh, you're hurtin' me."

"I'm not letting you go until you tell me."

"I went shopping. I got my hair done. I said, let me go!"

Her hair was different. He saw a straight long ponytail and bangs replaced the curly weave. Shopping bags were at his feet. He loosened his grip, and then kissed her fiercely. When he let her up for air, he apologized. "Sassy, you're making me crazy. I don't know what to do anymore."

Kneading her arms, she proclaimed, "I already told you what to do." She stooped down to collect the bags and he helped her.

"You want me to turn my back on my family and friends," he said.

"I want you to consider me."

"Sassy, I do."

She touched her lips slightly against his. It wasn't really a kiss, just contact to lure him.

He closed in, taking in her scent, begged, "Please, tell me what you want from me?"

"Ollie, I want to be your whole world. I want to know that nothing else and nobody matters. Just me Ollie, I want you to want me."

He whispered before he took his wife in front of the shopping bags, "Ok, whatever you want. We haven't done it in two weeks. I want my wife."

She had played the game perfectly, withholding sex and staying out all night. Ollie loved her back. Sapphire wondered when he started. *Was it when I left you? Was it the night you proposed at Gems? Or was it our wedding night?*

She set him up, flipped the script, and arranged the wedding on the down low. She had him working for her. Everything worked in her favor. She had Ollie right where she wanted him. And yet, contentment was still so far away from her soul. She peeled off her clothes; urgently wanting Ollie's touch to satisfy her longing soul.

My Name is Kyle

Rick returned from his lunch with Cadence at four o'clock. Famished, Vaughn ordered sandwiches for her and Kyle. They were finishing up when Rick walked into his office.

"Vaughn, why are you having your lunch in my office?"

Kyle got to his feet before she could answer. Extending a hand, he introduced himself, "Kyle Carraway, you must be Rick."

Without taking Kyle's hand, he answered, "I must, this is my office."

Kyle couldn't believe Lily let this arrogant anus get her pregnant.

"Vaughn, could you clean up this mess and give me that proposal I asked for? I have a conference call in twenty minutes."

Kyle was liking Mr. Parsons less, and less, he volunteered, "Vaughn, I'll clean up. You get the proposal, so Rick and I can talk."

"Craig."

"It's Kyle."

"Whatever, I don't have time."

Not being dissuaded Kyle assured him, "You'll have your conference call in twenty."

Kyle prayed Lily's child wouldn't be like the man he was looking at. He jabbed the question at him. "What's your plan with Lily?"

Rick appeared to be distracted as he read the messages on his desk. "Kevin, excuse me?"

"Kyle. You get a woman pregnant. What is your plan?"

"It might be my seed, but Lily got herself pregnant. She came to me. Lily could have said no. She didn't. I don't want a child. Lily knows that. It's not my responsibility. You done?" Impatient that a complete stranger was badgering him about something he disconnected himself from, he asked, "Man, who are you? What's it to you?"

Kyle sat. "Lily's like a sister to me. I care about her."

"There you go. You take care of the baby."

"Lily has rights. You will pay."

Rick smugly smiled. "Let me worry about that."

"You don't think your child will ever come looking for you?"

He affirmed, "It's not my child. Please leave my office. I have a call to make."

Lily was such a gentle soul; it was like she had entangled herself with a fiend. Kyle realized while he was in town he was going to take care of Vaughn and Lily.

Pure Hearted

Lexi pondered the information around in her six-year old mind. Her friend Tasha had a little sister that didn't live with them. Tasha said her Dad did sex with another lady and that's why she had a sister. So, at six, that was a disturbing thought. That meant her father did sex with another lady, too. Even though she really didn't know what doing sex was; she knew it had something to do with kissing. Daddies were only supposed to kiss the mommies. With the same directness she inherited from her mother, she asked, "Dad, does that mean you did sex with Lena's mother?"

Flo blinked profusely. Roosta opened his mouth, not sure how to answer the question.

Lexi's big brown eyes were completely innocent. In all the years he spent with Shay Lynn, he didn't feel like he was doing anything wrong. As a man, he thought he did what he was supposed to. Roosta provided for his family. And, what he did with Shay Lynn, or anyone else, was about him.

He was aware that was no longer true. Roosta hurt them all, Lexi, Flo, Shay Lynn and his other children. God had forgiven him and he saw the purity of God in his child's face. God amazed him. He had forgiven him for so much, giving him a chance to build a strong marriage with Flo after the abuse. Now the power of God was upon him and he felt His presence. He needed Him. Confessing his sins to his child was harder on him than everything he'd been through.

Roosta placed his hand on his heart and cried. Yet, he tried to speak. "Lexi, do you know what sex is?"

She answered honestly, telling her parents what she knew about sex at six, "It's when you kiss a lot."

Flo dabbed a tissue at her eyes and listened. Roosta needed to take his place as the spiritual leader of the family. It was a relief to know she had a leader. "Lexi, that's not exactly sex."

"Then what is it?"

"Sex is something that mommies and daddies do in private."

"Mom, you had another husband before Dad, that's why you have Vaughn and Ollie right?"

"Yes, but their Dad died when they were little."

"Dad, you said I have two sisters and a brother, does that mean you did something bad three times?"

It was killing him. He nodded. Stroking a hand across his face, he said, "Lexi, I am sorry."

"That's OK Dad. Mom says when you do something bad, you're supposed to say you're sorry and not do it anymore. Dad, will you do it again?"

"No, honey. I'll never do it again."

Flo spoke softly. "Lexi, how do you feel about this?"

"OK."

"Just OK?"

"Yes, Mom. I like Lena; she's nice. Do I get to see my other sister and brother? How old are they?"

Lexi forgave easily. Roosta wished for the same faith of a child. It was simple, taken at a single word and then believed.

Choked up, he couldn't answer. Flo explained, "Your other sister's name is Tia, she's nine. Your brother's name is Tyrone; he's eight. We don't know when you'll get to meet them. Their mother will call when it's ok."

Lexi hugged her Dad. He was still good in her eyes. "Dad, don't cry. I'm not mad." He couldn't stop crying.

He thanked her and his heavenly father.

Flo knew it was time to give it a rest. "Lexi, you have school in the morning, let's pray."

"It's my turn to pray, Mom," she proudly announced.

They knelt around Lexi's bed. "*Thank you for the world so sweet, thank you for the food we eat. Bless us now in Jesus Name. God, thank you for my sisters Vaughn, Lena and Tia, my brothers Ollie and Tyrone. I pray their mom will let them play with me. Amen. Oh God, thank you for my Mom and Dad. My Dad is sad, please make him happy again, Amen.*"

Roosta couldn't take it anymore. He kissed Lexi and found solace in the guestroom. It became his prayer closet and the place he prayed so often for God to heal him and his marriage. He knelt down and thanked God over and over for being with him.

This Belongs To You

It was nine in the evening when they finished dinner. Vaughn began clearing the table and Lily watched Kyle, watch Vaughn. He didn't want to let her out of his sight. The love was still there. She was happy for them.

Life for Lily was finally coming into perspective. The veracity set in. She sinned, asked for forgiveness and she was with child. It was; what it was. She was ready for motherhood. The passion in her life was returning. She put a hand on Kyle's. "Do you really think Courtney is going to hurt Vaughn?"

He sipped his coffee and sighed. "Nope. I ain't gonna let him near her," he said fervently. Lily began playing with the belt on her robe and then caught Kyle's eye. Being home, away from the office, helped her spend the day reading her Bible and praying.

Her hope was restored, and she said with conviction, "I know someone who isn't gonna let him near her."

Puzzled, he asked, "Who?"

"You know 'em. God, our protector."

"I know but..."

"No buts. Kyle, look at us. Look where we let our anger and emotions lead us. I'm a pastor's kid; you're a future minister. We got set-up and we fell for it. I got involved with Rick, and you, Sapphire. Ollie married her. I'm praying for that situation. Anyway, I've learned to be angry and sin not."

Kyle rubbed his eyes with the palms of his hands as an attempt to wipe out the exhaustion. He was guilt ridden. "Lily, I threw her out, when she was violated. She needed me and I wasn't there. She suffered rumors and gossip in her own church. Vaughn didn't do anything wrong, except trust an old acquaintance."

"Kyle, I felt the same way when she told me last night. But, you know what else I've learned? Vaughn is strong. She's still standing. We know the truth now, and we *can* be there for her. You're here Kyle. It means the world to her."

He gave a weak smile. "Thanks. You're going to make a wonderful mother."

"I'm looking forward to it, even if, it was a major surprise. I better get back to bed."

"Vaughn told me about the situation."

"It's getting better," she reported. "Did Vaughn show you your room?"

"Not yet."

"I'll show you, since I'm on my way up."

"That's ok. I'll wait for Vaughn."

Lily gave him a stop-worrying look.

"I wanna talk to her before I turn in. Goodnight, Lily," he quickly justified his delay for rest.

She kissed his cheek and squeezed his hand. "Goodnight, Kyle. Thank you for coming."

The humming dishwasher led Kyle into the kitchen. Vaughn was vigorously wiping down the counters. He stuffed his hands into his pockets, waited for the right words to pop into his head and out of his mouth. They didn't. He just watched her.

She didn't look like a victim of a possible date rape, or frightened that a madman had her marked for death. She looked magnificent in navy slacks and an ice blue sleeveless sweater.

Finally, he spoke as she rinsed the sponge clean, "You must be tired. Is there anything I can do to help?"

"I got it covered."

"I know you do. Lily's right."

"About what?" She looked at him.

"You. You're a strong woman - perfect for a minister's wife."

He walked over to the sink, stood next to her and gently stroked her face.

She flinched.

"I'm sorry. I didn't mean to startle you."

Expose your fear. Donita's advice came to mind. "It's not you Kyle, it's me. When you touched me, it was Courtney's hand that I saw."

He knew vengeance belonged to the Lord, but even if Courtney didn't finish the task, he'd left bruises on Vaughn's

232

spirit. He wanted some time alone in a locked room with Courtney. He held out his hands. "Vaughn, look at my hands."

She closed her eyes, and then opened.

"Look at them. Do they look like Courtney's?"

"That's not it. When you touch me, I feel unclean."

"Ok Sweetie, Courtney is not going to win. We are. I know you may not be ready, for any type of intimacy, and that's fine by me. When the Lord heals you, I'm gonna be right here, waiting. I have something that belongs to you."

"Oh yeah? Did I leave something at your apartment?"

He knelt down on one knee. Vaughn's engagement ring sparkled before their eyes. Tears flooded Kyle's voice. "Vaughn, sweetie, I was so wrong. Please be my wife. Please Vaughn."

"Kyle, you wanna marry me, considering I may not be able to be with you?"

"I'll take you any way I can get you," he avowed. "I love you. We're going to heal together. Will you marry me?"

She held out her perfect fingers. "Kyle, I want to be your wife."

He slipped the ring on her finger and kissed her hand. "I love you. I love you."

"Get up man, so I can kiss you."

Amazed, he asked, "Are you sure? You just said..."

"We just got engaged again. I *want* to kiss you."

He got up slowly, careful not to frighten her. She wrapped her arms around his neck; he tilted his head and kissed her lightly. She started to close her eyes. He whispered, "Open your eyes. I want you to see me. Only me." Closing his eyes, Kyle gently kissed her again, again, and again. It was the most precious kiss she ever gave him.

The next morning, Kyle was showered, dressed and sipping fresh coffee as he read the paper. It was a rainy morning. For Kyle, the rain was a sign that God's blessings were showering down.

Vaughn admired her handsome man in jeans and a t-shirt.

"Good morning, Mrs. Kyle Carraway."

Vaughn giggled. "Not yet."

"Soon," Kyle affirmed. He saw no reason to prolong the inevitable.

She shared the sentiment. "I like the sound of that, soon."

"Looks like all of us have a lot of planning to do." He looked upstairs. "Is Lily going back to the law firm?"

Vaughn grabbed a blue and green coffee mug and filled it with a lot of cream, a little coffee, and no sugar. She sipped, closed her eyes and enjoyed the moment. "I don't think she's made that decision yet. What are you doing about work?"

"I called my sales manager this morning and explained the situation. He understands and he will personally handle my clients."

Vaughn joined him at the table, peering over the mug she inquired, "Did you tell him how long you'd be away?"

"I told him three weeks to start. If it's going to be longer than that then, I'll decide what kind of job I'll do out here. I can always work as an accountant."

"Kyle, you would give up your whole life for me?"

He leaned back in his seat. "What, a job? That's not my whole life. *You* are my priority. Woman, you're my future wife and mother of my unborn children."

"Man, since you put it that way; drive me to work."

He jumped up, happy to oblige. "Let's go. I'll swing by with your lunch later."

"I'm taking you to lunch today. I know a really good rib place."

"It's a date."

"It's our life baby. I love you, Kyle."

"I love you too, Sweetie."

I'm Bored

Sapphire rose early to make her husband breakfast before he left for work. Ollie certainly was a different man. She was so frustrated a year ago when she moved out of his apartment. She couldn't get him to do anything. Now, he was up at the crack of dawn in prayer, then off to work. They had a wonderful night and morning, and still, she was unhappy. She couldn't understand what her problem was.

Ollie finished chomping on his toast and swallowed his orange juice in one gulp. "You keep cookin' like this Sassy, and I'll work three jobs."

Smiling, she pretended to be amused. "Then you won't have anytime to eat the food."

"I guess that's true, Sassy. Let me go."

She walked him to the door in a short yellow terry cloth robe. He kissed her quick, opened the door and then closed it back. He whispered, "Give me a juicy one." She kissed him longer and slower. He smiled, leaving his eyes closed. "Mumm...Delicious...I don't want to leave." As he opened his eyes, she witnessed pure joy.

"Sassy, remember that day I came home for lunch and you were doing leg lifts?"

"Yeah."

"Why were you doing that?"

Sapphire didn't tell him about her private dancing or the fact she was making some money on the side. She still didn't completely trust Ollie. If he found out she was making extra money, he might quit working. Sapphire didn't want to risk it, so she lied, "I was just exercising. I want to stay in shape."

"I want you to stay in shape too. Will you do it for me when I come home for lunch today?"

"What? The leg-lift?"

"Yeah, and wear one of your costumes."

She frowned. "Ok? What time will you be home?"

"About one thirty."

"I'll be ready."

The leg-lift, it was amazing the response that one little gesture got her. Ollie loved it and so did another man, a married-man. A man that was honest about his wife and child. Marcel made it clear he wanted to see her again. Sapphire was smart enough to know, a man like Marcel Reid would never leave his wife. He was out for a good time.

Kyle wanted commitment and so did Ollie, but Marcel wanted fun. *I need some excitement. This could be fun, a sexy hard working husband, and a risk taking sexy playmate.* She did the cha, cha dance on the way to the bedroom, found his number in the jeans she wore the other night and dialed. A very professional receptionist answered. "Marcel Reid, please."

"May I ask who's calling?"

"Sapphire Sparrow."

"Please hold."

Marcel sounded very pleasantly pleased. "I wasn't sure if I was going to hear from you."

"I wasn't sure if I was going to call."

He smiled through the receiver. "I'm glad you did. Can you do lunch today?"

"I'm having lunch with my husband today."

Disappointed, he said, "Lucky man."

"I'm working tonight. How about a late dinner?"

"Sorry, that won't work. I'm having dinner with my in-laws tonight. Let's try tomorrow?"

"Dinner or lunch?"

"I would love to have both with you. Let's make it lunch. Say around two."

"Ok Marcel, two tomorrow. Where should we meet?"

"Uh, do you know the diner on Fifty First and Park?"

"In the city? I know it."

"I'll see you then. I'm looking forward to seeing you."

"So am I Marcel. So am I."

Full Speed Ahead

Ollie took the elevator and greeted Clara, "Hello, beautiful, I'm here to see Michael Carraway." Clara was impressed with the light skinned slim brother. He reminded her of *Prince* and she was a BIG fan. "You must be Oliver."

"I prefer Ollie."

"I see, handsome. I'll show you to Michael's office."

Stunned by the posh office, Ollie followed. *Why am I driving a cab and working as a security guard? I graduated with a degree in Art History. I have extraordinary artistic talent. Something is wrong, very wrong.* He would talk to Michael about it.

Ollie laughed when Michael stood up from the drawing board. He was wearing suspenders. "When did you start wearing these?" Ollie pulled one and it snapped back.

Michael slid his thumbs under the suspenders showing off the burgundy and blue stripes. "Man, these are cool. You don't know it cause you like to dress for the ladies exposing your chest." They laughed. Michael was glad Ollie was back.

"Shut up, man."

"Can I get you something, Ollie?"

"Like what?"

"Soda, juice, coffee?"

"Nah, I'm cool. Sassy made me a big breakfast."

"Really? So, things are getting better?"

"That woman put a hurtin' on me last night, but she don't know I'm here. I had to agree to cut you off so she'd be with me."

Michael laughed. "You lied to your wife so she'd hook you up?"

"I got needs."

"You crazy man. Have a seat."

Michael directed Ollie to the leather sofa in the back of his office. He wasn't sure how Ollie was going to take the news. Kyle wanted Ollie to know. He wanted Vaughn's Uncle and Aunt to know too, but he'd let her tell them.

Michael grew very serious. He rubbed his hands along his pants as if he was trying to dry his palms. "What's up Mike?"

"Your sister, man."

"What's wrong with Vaughn." Michael laid out all the grueling details for Ollie.

"Someone wants to kill Vaughn? Is that what you're sayin'?"

"That's what the police believe."

"Do they know why the guy didn't rape her?"

"No. For whatever reason, he didn't. It really pissed him off. He's crazy."

"I don't believe this. How could something like this happen?"

"I don't know."

Ollie got up abruptly. "Mike, I gotta go to Atlanta."

"Kyle and I thought you would. Kyle's there now."

"Uncle Desi and Aunt Vie, do they know?"

"Kyle said, Vaughn wanted to tell them."

He huffed, thinking, "I should call my mother. I know Vaughn won't."

Michael stood too. "I know how Vaughn feels about your mother. I agree; you should call her. When are you leaving?"

"I don't know. I'll have to take a train. I don't have money to fly."

"Of course you have money. Tell me when you wanna leave, and I'll take care of the arrangements. Do you think Sassy will go with you?"

"You would pay for Sassy?"

"Of course, she's your wife and now Vaughn's sister-in-law."

"I'll go home now and talk to her."

Michael gave Ollie a brotherly hug. "Thanks Mike, for everything." Ollie caught the artwork on the walls. "Great painting."

"Kyle likes that rainbow too."

"Mike, when I get back, I need to talk to you about selling some of my artwork. You think your firm would be interested?"

Michael felt a light bulb go off in his head. "Not only will the office buy some, I will too. Hey, we could have a showing at the church."

Ollie was glad he didn't listen to his wife about cutting off his family and friends. He needed them. "Mike, I'd appreciate it. I'll call you later about Sassy."

My Baby

Roosta rushed home. He couldn't understand what his wife said over the phone. She kept saying her baby was in danger. *What was wrong with Lexi?*

He did ninety on the expressway and thanked God he didn't get a ticket. He took the stairs two by two. Flo was throwing clothes into a suitcase. He held onto her shoulders. "Red, slow down, talk to me. What's going on?"

She fell apart and he caught her in his arms. "What's wrong?"

"A man tried to rape Vaughn. The police said he didn't succeed, but now he's looking to kill her."

Roosta couldn't comprehend the words. She repeated it again then, sobbed in his arms. "Ok, sit down." She did.

He knelt in front of her. "Where did you get this information?"

"Ollie called. Michael was at Kyle's house when the police came looking for Vaughn."

"Did you book a flight yet?"

"I just called you and started packing."

Roosta looked around trying to put a plan into motion. "I'll get us on the first flight out, and see if Tasha's mom can take care of Lexi."

Panicked, she clutched his arm. Flo didn't want to be separated from any of her children. "Roosta, Lexi *has* to go with us."

"Red, Lexi's not the one in danger. If Vaughn's in danger, maybe we should keep Lexi here."

She knew he had a point, but she was afraid. They just dropped a bomb on Lexi about her siblings, and now they were leaving without notice. "Roosta, you're right, but I want her with us. I want to take her."

He steadied his breath. "OK, we'll take her."

Flo touched her forehead, hoping it would help her think. "Oh Roosta, what are we going to tell Lexi about her sister?"

"Nothing. We're going for a visit. That's all. OK?"

She held onto his neck. "I'm glad you're here."

"Me, too. Can you handle the packing while I call the airport?"

"Go ahead, I'm calming down."

My Family

Michael called Kyle to tell him Vaughn's family was on the way. Kyle was preparing lunch for Lily when he got the call. Not one to spend a lot of time in the kitchen, he prepared her a monster sandwich, ham, turkey, cheese, lettuce, tomato, black olives and honey mustard. He was just wiping on the honey mustard. "What's up Bro?"

"You 'bout to have a house full - Ollie, Flo, Roosta and Lexi, are on the way."

"Whoa, I was going to meet Vaughn for lunch but I better go food shopping. I'm making Lily's lunch and it ain't much food here."

"Lily's lunch? What is she doing home? Is she sick?"

Kyle realized that with everything that was going on with Vaughn, Michael had no idea about Lily. He explained the set-up at work, the unpaid leave, and Lily's scare.

"Man. Kyle, how's Lily?"

"Surprisingly, she's doing great. She's staying in bed, praying and reading her Bible. But, Vaughn's got to work, and Lily's got to stay in bed. So I guess I'll be playing host."

"I wish I could be there to help you. You sure Lily's ok?"

"She's fine."

"Kyle if you need any help, you can ask Nita. She's the first lady of their church and an awesome cook."

Kyle poured grape juice for Lily, found a bag of chips and put everything on a tray. "I'll ask Lily about her. Hey Michael,

240

Vaughn and I got engaged last night." Kyle's voice was flooded with joy.

"That's wonderful, man."

"It's your turn now."

Silence. Kyle knew Lily was pregnant with Rick's baby, but it was obvious there was no love between them. Maybe Michael wasn't ready to accept the fact that he could love another man's child. Kyle knew his brother's heart. If any man could do it, it would be Michael. "You still there?"

"I'm here."

"I know you and Lily had big plans and high hopes, but you still love Lily. She made a mistake."

"Kyle, could you marry Vaughn if she was pregnant with another man's child?"

"A year ago, I would have said no. To tell the truth, considering the mistakes I've made, if I were a woman, I might be pregnant. Don't make the same mistake I made with Vaughn - letting her go and I was in love with her. What we have, and what you and Lily have is special. I learned that when I was with Sapphire. It goes deeper than the flesh man; it gets down in our spirit. There ain't nothing Lily wouldn't do for you, and you wouldn't do for her. Her child needs a father. I met Rick yesterday and he made it clear that he doesn't want this child."

Lily called from the top of the stairs, "Kyle, my baby is hungry."

He chuckled. "I gotta go, the mother-to-be is hungry."

"You better go feed her then. Thank you for taking care of her."

"It's my pleasure. You remember how Lily used to hold prayer meetings in her dorm room in college?" That was a thought from the past. But Michael remembered. "It was those prayers that kept all of us on course and in this spiritual walk. I believe it was those same prayers and yours of course, that got us back in the race. So yeah, I'll feed her, and be a good Uncle to the baby. I'll call you later Michael."

Michael looked at his phone. Just a few months ago Michael was ministering to Kyle, and now, Kyle to Michael. Lily needed a husband, her baby; a father. He knew he loved Lily with all his heart. He still didn't know if he could love a baby that wasn't his.

Fun Begun?

Sapphire hugged Ollie goodbye at the airport and told him she'd say a prayer for Vaughn. She waved to him until he was out of sight and then raced back to the car. Juggling around in her purse, she found her cell. Marcel's number was still in her phone. The timing of Vaughn's drama couldn't be more perfect. Sapphire wanted to test the waters to see if time alone with Marcel would bring a little excitement into her life. She grinned remembering the dangerous yet, sheepish look on Marcel's face.

Breathlessly, she demanded, "Marcel Reid. It's Sapphire Sparrow." This time she had to wait. The receptionist informed her that he was finishing up with a patient, but he asked if she could hold. She did and looked at her fresh powder blue manicure.

After several heart-pounding minutes, she heard, "I hope you're not calling to cancel on me tomorrow."

She smiled. "Actually, I was hoping we could do it today. My husband had to cancel on me."

She could tell it was good news to him. He gave an elated laugh. "This must be my lucky day. Can you meet me at the diner in an hour?"

"I'm on my way home, how about I make us lunch?"

Marcel couldn't believe his ears. "What about your husband?"

"He's out of town."

Lifting his eyebrows, he said, "I see. Where do you live?"

"Jersey City."

"That's not that far. Give me the address."

She did; then raced home in Ollie's cab. She needed time to prepare the grilled steaks and salads, shower and change.

Marcel arrived exactly two hours later. He brought her yellow tulips. In a beige suit, he was just as attractive as the night she saw him at the Doctor's party. She changed into black pants and a nylon pinstriped top that generously showed off her cleavage. Captivated, Marcel's eyes widened.

He walked in hesitantly and looked around. "Nice place. I see you have a love for plants. So does my wife."

Sapphire led him into the kitchen. "How is *the wife*?"

"She's great," he commented. "She should be at her step-class right now."

"Is she in shape?"

"Very good shape." He said it with a grand smile.

The table was nicely set with blue and white fine China; a wedding gift from her mother-in-law. She served Marcel. "I assume you're ready to eat."

"Oh yes, it smells wonderful."

Taking her place at the table she studied him. He was a lot more confident now then she remembered in school. She guessed the degree made the difference. Marcel ate a mouthful, never taking his eyes from Sapphire.

"It's delicious."

"Thanks. Is your wife a good cook?" "Sapphire, why do you keep bringing up my wife?"

She drank a little of her wine. "I just want to know why you're here. Are you happy with her?"

Surprised, he stated, "I could be asking you the same question. I'm in your husband's home."

"Marcel, to be honest, I don't know what I'm doing."

"I thought we were having lunch. Do you want more than that?"

He was letting her take the lead. If anything other than lunch happened, Sapphire would have to initiate it. He had a way of making her want to take the plunge. The whole act of innocence was enticing. "You're right. We're having lunch. Thank you for coming."

"Thank you for calling. So, why aren't you a dentist now?"

She sighed. "It's a long story."

"Give me the short version."

"Do you really want to know?"

"That's the only reason why I asked."

"Ok. My boyfriend, now husband refused to work. I had to quit school and strip full time."

"Sorry to hear that. I remember you being one of the brightest in class. Do you think you can go back?"

"I would love to and stop dancing all together, but I've got a lot of loans to pay back. My husband doesn't make enough to keep me happy and pay my bills."

Marcel held his chest. "Ouch. If my wife said that about me, it would really bruise my ego. What does your husband do?" Silence.

She changed the subject. "Marcel, what do you do for fun?"

Careful not to press the issue, and happy she asked, he replied, "Watching you dance was really fun."

Offering a mischievous grin, she said, "I guess I'll have to dance for you again."

That's exactly what I am hoping for.

After lunch, Marcel sat in the living room while Sapphire cleared the table. When she finished, she found Marcel admiring her wedding photo. He smiled when she walked in. "You two make a handsome couple. You're a vision in that gown."

Uncomfortable silence lingered. Marcel suggested, "I should be getting back to the office. I hope we can do this again sometime."

"Me too, Marcel. I like talking to you."

She walked him to the door. He turned to kiss her cheek, but instead leaned in closer and inhaled her perfume. His nose brushed her neck, her spot. "What are you wearing?"

"*Sexy.*"

"And so you are."

He stayed close to her, his nose drifted on her skin, and down her shoulder. "Sapphire, I asked you earlier, is there something more that you want. Is there?"

The physical tension between them was building. It began with their seductive dance the night before. Annoyed that he left it up to her, she struggled to hold her ground. Sapphire ached to the bone, hoping he would be the aggressor. "Marcel, lunch was enough."

He let the warmth of his breath touch her neck. "Really? Then why are you trembling?"

"Marcel you're teasing me."

He breathed on her again. "Am I?"

"You know what you're doing."

He moved his lips to the tip of her earlobe. Careful not to make contact, he breathed again. "Why is it so hard for you to tell me what you want?"

Marcel whispered, taunting her, "Say it Sapphire. Say you want me to touch you. Say it."

"Marcel please, do what you came here to do."

"Sapphire say, I want you to touch me. I won't until you say it."

"I've never met anyone like you before."

"I know. The choice is yours. This is the last time I'm going to ask you. Do you want me to touch you?"

You have no idea. Her lust for him was unparallel to anything she ever felt. It was raw, primal and feral. At the sound of his voice, she panted. "Marcel, I want you to touch me. The desire is driving me mad."

He waited a beat, admired her breast rise and fall in anticipation of his touch.

Sapphire knew what she wanted from Marcel was wrong. However, the more wrong it was, the more she wanted him. He stared at her. She trembled.

"Take off your clothes," he ordered. She obeyed. When she got to her underwear, he demanded, "Stop." She did, becoming more aroused by the directness of his voice and the danger in his eyes as he tore the lace away from her. She gasped.

He grabbed her wrists, pinned her against the door. Their eyes locked. The danger in her eyes matched his. "You're not afraid?" It was more of a statement than a question.

"If I were, you wouldn't be here. You're just what I want."

He let her go. She watched, waited and smiled as he slowly undressed. Forcefully, he pushed back against the door again. She laughed.

Startlingly, Marcel's ringing cell phone brought the forbidden dance to a frustrating halt. He noticed the number. It was his wife.

Sapphire was clawing at Marcel. He fiercely demanded, "Hold up! Hold up! This is my wife."

He answered cheerfully, "Hi, sweetheart."

Sapphire listened. She hoped the *Mrs.* would make it quick.

"Really, the step-teacher wants you to help with the class, that's wonderful. What? Can't Ms. Nelson pick up the baby from your mother's? No, it's fine. I'll pick her up. OK, honey. I love you too."

They weren't going to finish. She could tell by the aggravated expression on his face. "Sapphire, I have to pick up my baby. I'm really sorry. I mean *really* sorry."

"So am I. We could try again tomorrow."

"Hey, you said you're working tonight, right?"

"Yeah, but I thought you were having dinner with your in-laws."

"I was, but now, I don't think I'll be able to sleep tonight until we finish this. I'll cancel. What time should I come back?"

"I don't have to leave until eight to meet Opal and Mac. Can you come back around six?"

"I'll be here."

I can't wait Marcel.

God of Wonders

Ollie parked the rental in the driveway. Lily waited at the door. She knew God had a way of working all situations out for the good - even in a bad one, the family was coming together. Ollie hugged Lily and kissed her cheek. He called her by her childhood nickname, "Cookie, what are you doing here? I thought Kyle was gonna meet me."

Lily led him into the family room. He couldn't believe the company home they were living in, from the marble floors, to the elaborate furnishings. "This is how you living?"

She purposely avoided answering why she was home. Her parents didn't know about the baby and she didn't want to tell Ollie. Lily didn't want the family to think she was sick either so she traded her robe for a pair of jeans, and a purple and lavender Jersey.

"Kyle went to pick Vaughn up from work. What took you so long? I was expecting you over an hour ago."

"I got lost," he admitted.

"I'm sorry. You hungry?"

Ollie really hadn't thought about hunger until Lily mentioned it. His stomach was full with fear. Therefore, he didn't eat on the plane. Now he wished he had. "What do you have?"

"Not much. A friend is picking up groceries and bringing some prepared food by later. I could make you a sandwich."

"A sandwich would hit the spot." Ollie followed Lily into the kitchen. He noticed something was different about her, but he couldn't put his finger on it. He sat at the counter while Lily gathered cold cuts and all the trimmings. "Ham or Turkey?"

"Turkey."

He folded his arms across the counter and gave Lily a glance over. "Lily, Atlanta must agree with you. You look good girl. Look at you. You got your hair all down."

"I just washed it and blew it out. You want black olives?"

"Girl, the works. A brother is hungry."

Lily quickly assembled Ollie's sandwich, got him a soda, joined him at the counter and started nibbling on Turkey. After two oversized bites depleting the sandwich in half Ollie asked, "What's the story with this date rape?"

Lily huffed. "We're speculating. But it seems that Courtney attempted to rape Vaughn. He had been watching her, waiting. Only God knows why he didn't."

Ollie repeated, "God only knows. I thank God that he didn't. I haven't prayed yet. I will pray that the police find him, because, it will be hard to rest knowing he's still out there."

"Then we'll pray." She held her hand out and through a full mouth, Ollie asked, "Now?"

"Why not?"

He took her hand. "You mind if I lead," Ollie requested. He finished chewing and washed it down with soda. Lily thought he just said they won the Million Dollar Lottery. It was music to her ears. Ollie was coming home to his spiritual father. "Not at all. Ollie, pray."

"Father, where have I been? How can I have turned my back from you for three years? - A God so kind, compassionate and full of grace and mercy. You're better to us, than we've been to ourselves. Forgive me for my abandonment. We need your Divine Protection for Vaughn, Lord. Lord, we pray for Courtney, wherever he is whatever he's doing, that he'll turn away from this. We thank you for our family. We pray for you to bring peace between my mother and Vaughn. You're a God of Wonders. We trust you and believe in you. Amen."

Vaughn and Kyle entered the kitchen, overhearing Ollie's prayer. Kyle said Amen and Vaughn wondered if there could be peace between Flo and her.

Waiting for Fun

On the first ring Sapphire said, "Hello." It was seven in the evening and Marcel hadn't come back. She prepared for his return, wearing a skimpy white piece of short, short, short lingerie. She plopped down on the bed disappointed it was Ollie. She never gave Marcel her number. She remembered that Marcel had no way of calling her.

"Sassy what's wrong?"

She tried to kick the irritation out of her voice. "Nothing. How's Vaughn? Your Mother get there yet?"

"Vaughn's fine. My mother's flight was delayed. She's not here yet. I wish you were though, I miss you."

It wasn't like Ollie to get sentimental unless he wanted something. She didn't reply.

"Sassy, while I'm away, if you have any problems, you can call Michael."

Hearing Michael's name disgusted her. She sucked her teeth. "Why would I do that? Michael don't even like me and I thought you weren't hangin' with him anymore."

He wasn't going to argue with her. When he returned home, he would make her understand why it was good to have other people in their lives besides each other. "Sassy, I love you. Look at what happened to Vaughn, things happen."

The doorbell rang. Her body vibrated in anticipation. Marcel was an hour late, but he was back. Dumping Ollie off the phone, she said, "Ollie I love you too. When do you think you'll be home?"

"Maybe in a couple of days. Kyle is going to stay with Vaughn."

The doorbell chimed again.

"I'll understand if you need to stay longer. Bye Ollie." Sapphire hung up before she heard Ollie say bye.

She ran to the door, took a deep breath, made sure her bosom was well exposed, and then opened the door. To her surprise, it was her next-door neighbor's kid, selling candy for the school fundraiser. The child's mother shielded her son's eyes. Sapphire transparent outfit was not for a seven year old. She slammed the door and screamed.

Sapphire tried Marcel's office. The evening service refused to give her his cell phone number. No way of contacting Marcel, she paced wondering where he was. He promised he'd come back.

A Mother's Love

Roosta, Flo and Lexi arrived ten minutes after eight. Lexi was asleep in Roosta's arms when Lily opened the door. Flo had the look of a distraught mother. Lily wondered would she have that look for her child. Considering the scare she received, she knew a mother and child bond formed before birth. She could clearly see that bond in Flo's weary eyes. Lily prayed Vaughn would see it too.

"Auntie, come in." Flo decided not to become too emotional too soon. She pretended to be herself. The trio walked in and Flo smiled. "Come give yo' Auntie some sugar." Lily hugged her aunt and suddenly felt a tugging at her own heart for her mother.

"Ooo let me look at you. Girl, you are as pretty as me. Good Lord."

"Thanks Auntie. Hey Roosta, I see Lexi is knocked out."

Roosta's arms ached. "This little bundle of joy is heavy."

"Come on, I'll show you to your room."

Flo glanced around for Vaughn. If she was home, she knew; she wouldn't come out right away to greet her. Nevertheless, Flo was there for her baby and would be, unless Vaughn told her to leave. She followed Lily upstairs and prayed that wouldn't be the case.

Roosta rested Lexi on the bed and she didn't stir. He removed his sports jacket and sat down. "It has been a long day."

There was a tap at the door. "Come in," Flo answered. It was Ollie. He smiled at his mother.

The tears fell. Flo couldn't help it. Ollie squeezed his mother. "Ollie, my baby." She pulled back and held his face in her palms. "My handsome boy is a married man. Where's Sapphire?"

"She's at home. She's not really into family."

Flo was not particularly pleased at Ollie's choice for a wife, but it was too late. They were married. All she said was, "Too bad, cause we're a good bunch of people."

Roosta walked over and shook Ollie's hand. "What's up Roosta?"

"Tired man. Tired."

Ollie was drained as well. "I know. Y'all wanna eat? Some woman named Nita brought food."

Flo perked up. She was hungry. She asked, "Is the food good? What does the woman look like? Is she clean? I don't eat everybody's cooking."

Roosta added, "That's right, not even mine."

Ollie laughed. "The food is good and the woman is very clean and nice."

"I'm coming down." She turned to her husband. "Roosta, you wanna eat?"

He shook his head no. "I'm beat. Save me a plate."

Ollie took his mother by the hand and led her downstairs. It puzzled Flo that Ollie's heart was more pliable than Vaughn's. Flo was grateful for Ollie's warmth.

Open Your Heart

"It's open," Vaughn yelled as Kyle knocked on her bedroom door. He found she changed into pink terrycloth jogging pants and a matching tee. Her thick wavy hair was pinned up with a large black clip. "Aren't you pretty in pink?"

She looked up, but didn't smile. "My mother's here right?"

He sighed sitting next to her. "Just got here a few minutes ago. She's in the kitchen. You going down?"

"I know I should." She pondered the thought and continued, "Kyle, why is she trying to be my mother now? I'm twenty-six. It's a bit too late."

Taking Vaughn's hand, Kyle admired her soft French manicure. He especially liked the fact she was wearing his ring again. "She's here the same reason why Ollie and I are, she loves you, Vaughn."

"It's guilt. She feels guilty for leaving Ollie and me. She wants to make-up for it." She hurled the words out, "She can't Kyle, and she can't make up for all those years I wanted her around."

He nodded, kissed her fingertips. "Sweetie, you're right, she can't. I can't make up for the way I treated you. I want to, but I can't."

She saw his pain. "Kyle, that's different. You thought I cheated on you. She just left us, her own flesh and blood."

"You're right, she did. Does that mean there's no room in your heart to forgive her?"

Staring at the white vanity table in the corner, she didn't answer.

Let's Do This

Marcel banged on the glass of the Cadillac. Opal asked, "Hey, isn't that the guy from the doctor's party?"

Mac said, "I don't know. There was a lot of money, I mean men, at that party."

Sapphire was fuming when she saw him. "Mac, let me out."

"Sassy, you gotta dance in thirty minutes. You ain't got time for groupies."

"Give me five minutes."

Mac unlocked the doors and Sapphire leaped from the backseat. Marcel was still wearing his suit from earlier in the day. "Sapphire, I'm sorry. I couldn't get out of dinner. My Father-in-law is persistent."

Careful not to show any signs of anger, she smiled. "Marcel, you don't owe me any explanations."

"I'm a man that keeps his promises. I had every intention of coming back."

She raised her eyebrows underneath her bangs. "A man that keep his promises." She gave a cackling laugh.

"What's so funny?"

"Us, we are *married*. We're trying to arrange to break our vows. It's not working out, is it?"

He paused for a minute, and then asked, "Have you changed your mind?"

She hadn't and wondered if they still had a chance. "Marcel, how'd you know where to find me?"

"Your manager told me that he owned *Gems*. I took a shot and came out here. As I was pulling up, I saw you getting into the car. Do you still want to do this?"

She leaned into him and sniffed his neck. "Do you want me to touch you Marcel? Cause I won't unless you say it." She teased, offering his words back to him.

He didn't hesitate. "I really, *really* want you to touch me."

She held her head down and smiled. Things were working out. She was going to have an exciting night after all.

She looked up. "Come to my gig. You can drive me home afterwards. Tonight Marcel, I am going to touch you."

"Alright, y'all lead, I'll follow."

He raced back to his red Mustang. Sapphire jumped into the car and said, "Mac let's get this show on the road. I have plans tonight. Big plans."

I know You Can Do It

"Vaughn, baby, why didn't you tell us? I can't believe this happened over a year ago." Still not ready yet to face her mother; Vaughn sat in the garage in her blue *Beetle*. She wanted to speak to her Aunt. Mother Rose raised her, not Flo. Before she sat down and talked to Flo, she wanted to talk to her real mother.

"Auntie Vie, I'm sorry I didn't tell you. I thought whatever happened that night was over. I didn't want to think about it or deal with it."

"I'm sure it was dealing with you."

Vaughn understood her aunt. Since she wouldn't face the situation head on, it kept haunting her. It kept creeping into her mind, preventing her from living life as a whole person. The truth was in focus. That was the reason she never attempted to tell Kyle. She didn't want to face it. It was easier to bury it.

"Your Uncle Desi is not back from Bible class tonight."

"Oh, you didn't go?"

"I had a headache. We'll try to get to Atlanta tomorrow."

Vaughn reclined the driver's seat a little and rattled off the guest list, "Kyle, Ollie, Flo, Roosta and Lexi are here."

"What, Vaughn? That's wonderful. I'm really happy to hear you and your mother are trying."

"Now Auntie, I ain't say all that, but she's here."

"You know that's because she loves you."

Vaughn sighed, hearing it again. "That's what Kyle said."

"It's true. Vaughn, when your mother lied to your grandmother and me, she asked us to keep you for a little while. It was three months before we heard from her again. We didn't know what to tell you. I was very upset with your mama. What she did was wrong. Anyway you slice it, it was wrong. Nevertheless, Flo didn't abandon you."

Vaughn closed her eyes and said, "She did Auntie."

"No baby, leaving you with us was the best thing she could have done for you and Ollie. Your mother was in a bad state. I mean bad. After your father died, she took it hard, drinking, running around with all kind of men. That was no life for you. The best thing she could have done was leave you with people she knew loved you and would take good care of you."

Vaughn knew her mother's history, but she never realized she was a good mother for putting her and Ollie in better hands. "Auntie, why didn't she come back for us when she got it together?"

Mother Rose refreshed Vaughn's memory. "By the time she pulled herself together, you were thirteen and Ollie sixteen. You didn't want to leave New York and go to Florida, and you were very harsh towards her. She wasn't going to force you, and neither was I. Do you remember that?"

"I do. I guess I didn't want to give her a chance back then."

"God has given you an opportunity to forgive. Don't let it pass you by again, Vaughn."

Through choking sobs, she said, "It's hard Auntie, it's so hard."

"Oh baby, I know it is, but you can do it. I know you can. I raised you. You're strong. If you have the will, then God's already strengthened you with His love and power."

"I do, Auntie. I do want to forgive her."

"Listen to me, Vaughn you don't have to say a word. The words will come later. You march up to yo' mama and wrap your arms around her. That's all. Ok?"

She whimpered, "Ok Auntie, I love you."

"I love you, too. I'm going to go down in prayer for you right now. We'll be out there as soon as we can."

"Thanks Auntie."

Vaughn closed her phone and searched the glove compartment for tissues and blew loud and hard. A beaming flashlight alerted her up from the glove compartment. She saw the gun and the hands, and knew it was Courtney.

A Private Dance

Sapphire danced for Marcel. There was no one else at the party she would dance for, or with. She was angry with Mac. He promised she would be dancing for professionals. The only professionals she saw were professional drinking college students. They were in the penthouse of a hotel. It was obvious the kids had money. Yet, being among the untamed crowd made her sick. Sapphire remembered why she quit stripping.

She told Mac she was cutting the routine in half. He told her if she did, he'd cut her pay in half. So she danced, enticing, taunting and teasing Marcel with every gyrating, butt rotating, move. Sapphire saw his cavity again and the thought of taking him home with her was delightful.

One brown haired guy staggered close enough to Sapphire and stuffed a twenty-dollar bill down her bra. It annoyed her, but she didn't let on. Instead, she gave him a winning smile. The kid searched his pockets for more money. He dropped three quarters down her top. His breath smelled of vodka. "I love the way you move."

Sapphire gave the kid her back, and Marcel, the show-stopping leg-lift. He applauded and she blew him a kiss. She whispered in his ear on her way back to change, "I'll be ready in five."

"I don't think I can wait that long."

They both grinned as she jogged off.

Opal looked up and asked, "Sassy, you're happy tonight. What's up with you and that doctor?"

She shrugged, reaching for her black wrap dress. "Nothing. I know him from dental school."

Opal grabbed Sapphire's arm. "Don't nothing me. You're going to get busy with that man."

Sapphire waved her off and lifted her bag. "Opal please, so what if I am? It's my business."

"It's Ollie's business."

"Opal, you *don't* understand. Ollie's out working all the time. I'm getting bored. Marcel's married too. He don't mean nothing. We're just gonna have a little fun."

"Sassy, I thought you loved your husband."

Sapphire wiggled her wedding rings and snapped, "I do love my husband. And Marcel loves his wife. This is just physical. Nobody's gonna get hurt, because Ollie is out of town. He won't even know."

Mac banged on the door and called, "Opal, get out here, these kids are gettin' rowdy."

Sapphire and Opal heard the crowd. "Opal, what I'm gonna do with Marcel is the same thing I do on the dance floor. It's all fantasy. Ollie's my husband, he's real."

Sorrowfully, Opal shook her head. "Sapphire, it seems you've changed over the years. Ollie used to mean the world to you. I feel bad for Ollie, he don't know what he married." Opal walked off.

Who is Opal to judge? Sapphire stood for a moment twirling her wedding rings. Going through with her plan, she stepped forward. The drunken kid met her at the door.

He grinned. "I've got fifty dollars here. I want a private dance?"

She walked passed him. "Sorry kid, I don't have the time."

He grabbed her elbow. "You can spare a few minutes." He tried to kiss her.

She jerked her arm away. "Boy, get off me! You better go get a young chick."

He grabbed both her arms. "I said, I got fifty dollars and I want a private dance."

"And I said, no. Let me go!"

Sapphire didn't see it coming. The kid punched her in the face and she fell to the floor. She tried to slide back on her hands and get up, but the kid landed on her before she could. She scratched his face and found enough balance to slap him. "Get off me!" Sapphire screamed for Mac, but he couldn't hear her over the crowd's cheers at Opal's dancing.

He spit on her. "Shut up! Dance for me!"

She shouted, "Get off me! Get off me!"

He punched and pounded her face until she felt her cheekbone crack. Warm blood flowed from her eyes, nose and mouth.

Angry that she teased him on the dance floor, he punched her again. Sapphire fell unconscious. The kid threw the money in her face. On his way out, he startled at the sight of Marcel standing in the doorway. The kid ran.

Marcel froze, she was bloody and beaten to the point he wouldn't recognize her. He did, after he looked at her dress and hair. Sapphire's face was monstrous. The wrap dress was undone, and her bare body, exposed.

If the police were involved, he didn't want to be on the scene. Marcel got away as fast as he could, without knowing if Sapphire was dead or alive.

Long Time Coming

Hauled from the car before the doors locked, Vaughn's screams stifled in her throat. The world around her became ominous. She prayed in her heart for help. Haggard and unstable, she could plainly see that Courtney crossed the threshold of destruction. His beard was full and he wore a black jogging suit and baseball cap.

Smiling, he pressed Vaughn against the car and leaned into her for a kiss. Nauseated, she turned her cheek. "Later you'll relax and let me kiss you. I promise."

She couldn't decipher what Courtney was saying to her. His voice dragged five speeds slower as he whispered in her ear, "Atlanta's real nice, Vaughn. You know the girls at your church are so friendly. They were nice enough to tell me where you were."

Coming down the garage stairs, Flo rattled the keys before she pressed the remote of the rental to retrieve her overnight case from the trunk. The sound caused Courtney to panic.

In the distance, he fired twice. Vaughn screamed. Flo went down. The scream and shots were heard inside. Kyle yelled, "Vaughn? Where's Vaughn?"

In a matter of seconds, Roosta bolted downstairs in his socks. Lily, Donita, Kyle and Ollie quickly assembled from the kitchen and met him in the living room. In short sharp breaths, Roosta said, "It sounded like it came from the garage."

Kyle jetted for the backdoor. Roosta held him back. "You can't just run out there like that. Go around out front. I'll go out back." He added, "Lily, keep an eye on Lexi." Donita quickly dialed nine-one-one.

Disconcerted, Courtney wanted to hurry and get Vaughn to the curb and into his car. He rested the gun at the base of her skull. "Who was that?"

Vaughn whimpered, "My mother, you shot my mother."

"Bad timing." He chuckled. "She shouldn't have gotten in the way. Now, *you* are going to walk fast to that silver car out front, quietly, unless you want me to shoot somebody else in your family."

Kyle's protective instinct went ballistic at the sight of a gun to Vaughn's head. Ollie, right by his side, Kyle spewed, "Courtney, it is over. Let her go."

Courtney grinned. "Kyle Carraway. *Mr. GQ,* from high school. You thought you were the man back then. You had all the girls liking you. Vaughn you flirted, but you wouldn't go out with me. You wouldn't give me the time of day. It's time you get what you deserve. Last time we were together, I didn't have you like I wanted. I heard you come in, Kyle. But know this; I'm going to enjoy her tonight." The gun glided to Vaughn's neck. Courtney massaged her cheek with his lips, and then he took a bite. "Yum. She tastes good, Kyle. Of course, you know that already."

Vaughn jerked her red face away. Courtney laughed as he held a firm arm around Vaughn's midsection. "Don't worry baby, you'll like it later."

Ollie's fists balled. "Courtney, somebody's going to die. Let my sister go."

"You're her brother?" Courtney, sincerely surprised, continued, "Didn't know she had one. I bet you didn't get the brains in the family. I got the gun. Who do you think is going to die?"

Roosta tipped toed down the garage steps. Flo grabbed his ankle. He jolted and looked at the concrete. She held a finger to her lips; then mouthed, "Help Vaughn." He nodded and whispered, "Are you shot?"

"He missed, go Roosta."

As quietly as Roosta could walk, he eased up behind Courtney who was at the front of the house.

Kyle and Ollie kept him talking. Roosta thought that would give him the perfect opportunity to rush him. From behind, Kyle caught Roosta's eye. Unfortunately, so did Courtney, he twisted in a split second.

It was all the time Ollie needed to grab the gun. It fired into the night sky.

You Got Insurance?

"Insurance?"

"Uh, I don't know. Can you find out for me how Sassy is doing?"

The clerk huffed annoyed Mac wasn't giving her the data she needed. "Sir, who?"

"I mean Sapphire."

Sapphire was still unconscious when the ambulance took her from the penthouse. She had a seizure on the way to the hospital. Mac didn't need a degree to know; Sapphire was in bad shape.

"Sir, the doctor will be out as soon as he can," the clerk carelessly mentioned.

He staggered away shaking his head.

"Sir, I haven't finished yet."

Opal held up her hands. It was a signal for time out from the police questioning. Mac was heading for the exit. Regretting she still wore her red studded bra and thong costume under a floor length black sweater, she power walked towards Mac in matching stilettos.

His baby blues were blood shot and his hands were shaking. "Mac, where you goin'?"

"Car. Drink." Formulating complete sentences was a chore.

"Mac, don't leave. The police want to ask you some questions."

"Not now." His eyes were angry, not with her, but with the reality of where they were, and why. Opal probed, while holding Mac's hand and helped him calm down. "Go talk to them and then have your drink. I'm going to go outside to get a signal on Sassy's phone. Hopefully, we can reach Ollie."

Mac swore and then started for the uniformed police officers. They met halfway in the lobby.

Opal stood outside and watched a husband escort his very pregnant wife into the emergency room. The soon mother-to-be breathed heavily holding her womb. "There's no time. This baby's coming right now, I can feel the head." The father yelled for immediate help.

Opal's eyes clouded. She wondered as one life was coming into the world, was another one leaving. Clutching Sapphire's designer bag, Opal rummage around for Sapphire's cell. She scrolled through the phone book and found Ollie's cell number. Dialing, she prayed he would answer. Praying wasn't something she did often, but if anybody could help Sapphire now, it had to be God.

No answer. She left a message that Sapphire had been hurt and was in the hospital.

A Long Walk

Yanking Vaughn forcefully away from Courtney, Kyle shouted, "Run!" And as she did, he sweetly decked Courtney in the jaw. He fell backwards, giving Ollie the advantage and the gun. That wasn't enough. Roosta wanted Courtney off his feet. He sideswiped Courtney and he staggered. With a piercing blow to the chin, Kyle hit him again. Courtney was out for the count.

Vaughn ran and stooped next to her mother. "Mama, are you ok? Are you shot?"

Flo's knees were badly bruised and bloody. When Courtney fired, instinct pulled her to the concrete with an unbearable crush to her knees. The excruciating pain was replaced with unspeakable joy. Vaughn called her, *Mama*.

"I'm fine baby. I just fell down the stairs." Relieved, Vaughn embraced Flo. Their hearts were pounding from fear and elation.

Vaughn shifted her weight, raising Flo. She leaned on Vaughn and asked, "Are *you* OK? Did he hurt you?"

"I'm OK. Can you walk up the stairs?"

"I don't think so. I can't bend my knees. Can you walk me around to the front of the house?"

Vaughn sniffled in tears and laughed. "Of course." She was at peace leaning into her mother. It was a long walk. They took baby steps, neither one of them wanted it to end.

Roosta smiled within as Flo and Vaughn held onto each other. The smile turned downward, Flo's face was masked with pain. Roosta pounded the pavement, gathering at her side. "Flo, what's wrong?"

"My knees, I'll be fine."

Roosta saw the knees of Flo's pink linen pants were ripped, blood seeping through. He wished he'd sucker punched Courtney twice, one for each of Flo's legs. Giving her balance, Roosta took Flo's right side as they continued their trek.

At the front of the house, Vaughn retreated, seeing Courtney passed out on the ground. The memory of a gun pointed to her head poured tears down her face. It inundated her mind.

On impulse, Kyle discerned her thoughts, demanded, "Don't look at him, Vaughn. Just go inside." It was taking all the control Kyle had to not fire Courtney's gun and finish him off before the police showed up. *I could say it was done in self-defense.*

Lily and Nita held hands, prayed and listened for more gunshots. It seemed like an eternity before anyone returned inside. Finally, they breathed a sigh of relief seeing them fall back in.

Observing Flo, Lily's voice became unsteady. She trembled when she asked, "Auntie, are you shot?"

Roosta answered hurriedly. He didn't even want those words spoken. "No. Courtney's down. Ollie and Kyle are staying watch."

Nita informed them, "The police are on the way. Flo, do you need an ambulance?"

She grunted. "I'm fine. Is Lexi still asleep?"

"Thank God all the commotion didn't wake her," Lily answered.

Roosta and Vaughn guided Flo to the sofa, sitting her down gingerly, Roosta kissed her lips. "Red, you almost gave me a heart attack when I saw you on the ground."

She kissed him back. "Oh God, I'm just glad I came outside when I did."

Vaughn agreed and the events once again overcame her. Hysterically, she cried. Flo folded her arms around her and she cradled her head against her mother's breast and let it all go.

Things Don't Look Good

"Sir, do you have any idea who attacked Sapphire Sparrow?"

Mac shook his head and wished for Rum and Coke. "There was a lot of drinking going on at the party. It could have been anybody."

The officer read his notepad. "Ms. Opal Brown said there was a young dentist by the name of Marcel, hanging around Mrs. Sparrow from the night before? Do you have any idea where I might find him?"

Mac thought for a minute and found his wallet in his back pocket. Flipping through his cards, he found Dr. Kline's number - the host of the doctor's party. He handed it to the officer. He thought, so much for business. Dr. Kline probably would never call on him again. That didn't matter at the moment. Mac wanted whoever hurt Sapphire to pay. He grunted. "That guy might know who he is."

Disappointed, Opal didn't reach Ollie; she walked back to Mac and the Officer. The Officer thanked Opal and Mac and gave his card in case they remembered anything else.

"Opal, I really need a drink."

"Wait, hold up Mac. The doctor's coming."

"I'm Dr. Raison. You're both here with Mrs. Sparrow, correct?" They both nodded swiftly.

"Doctor, is Sassy going to be ok?" Opal managed to ask.

"There has been extensive damage to Sapphire's head. There is also internal bleeding. It doesn't look good. Mrs. Sparrow has slipped into a coma."

Opal quietly repeated, "A coma. Is she going to come out of it?"

"Like I said, things don't look good. Are you her next of kin?"

"Her husband is. He's out of town."

Dr. Raison looked solemn. He responded, "I suggest you try to get him here as soon as possible. We'll need to know what to do if her brain dies? I'm sorry."

Opal lost her balance and Mac caught her. She couldn't believe Sapphire may die.

Holy Spirit

Kyle walked Donita to her car after the police left. He was feeling drained from the day's events. "Nita, thank you for everything. Vaughn says you've been a wonderful friend."

"No need to thank me. Vaughn's a very special lady."

Kyle smiled, and then suddenly, felt the cracked knuckles on his right hand. Squeezing it, he grimaced.

"Your hand hurts?"

"I'm just feeling it now."

Donita held his hand and examined it. "It's starting to swell. I'm sorry I didn't think to tell you to put ice on it."

"I will now. I want to thank you."

Smiling, she reminded him, "You said that already."

"I know but I believe God led you to help Vaughn face her pain. I hope you'll come to the wedding."

"Of course I will. I'll sing too."

Kyle held his head sideways and thinking, *Vaughn was right*. Donita was pushy, but in a sweet sort of way. He didn't care who sang at the wedding. He just wanted Vaughn to be his wife. "We'll be happy to have you sing."

Saddened, Donita asked, "Is Vaughn going back to New York with you?"

"We haven't had a chance to discuss it. I'm sure she won't want to leave while Lily's pregnant. Pray for us?"

Donita smiled. "I already am. Go wrap your hand in ice. And you should have a Doctor look at Flo's knees."

He kissed her cheek. "I'll tell her. Good night."

Kyle walked back to the house and stopped to marvel at the star filled sky. "Thank you, Jesus." When he looked ahead, he saw Vaughn, waiting for him at the door. She ran out to him and hugged him. Sweeping her off the ground, he whispered, "Are you sure you're OK?"

"You've asked me twenty times already. He didn't hurt me."

Her voice was shaky, but she smiled. Kyle knew she would need time to get over the horrible memories. "Let's go in."

She held his hand. He attempted, and failed to hold in a grunt. "Kyle, you're hand. You really decked him."

"I wanted to beat 'em to a pulp."

"I know you did. I wanted you to do it, too, but I'm glad you didn't. I don't want my husband in jail."

He kissed her forehead. "I need some ice."

The living room cleared out. Everyone was exhausted and on the way to bed. "I see everybody has the right idea. I'm beat."

"Rest, I'll get the ice."

Kyle reclined on the sofa with one foot on the sofa and one on the floor. He recalled Courtney mentioned something about the reason why he didn't rape Vaughn, was because he heard someone come in.

Vaughn came back and Kyle scooted over. She sat next to him and wrapped his hand in an ice cloth.

Eyes closed and breathing the words into a tired yawn, Kyle asked her, "Do you know who came into the house that night? Courtney said he heard someone."

She cocked her head and thought. "Kyle, I don't remember everything about that night."

He pointed out, "Nobody else had keys to the condo but you and me." He yawned again. "The detectives that came to see me in New York were right. They said you were *divinely* protected. The Holy Spirit walked in and scared Courtney off."

Vaughn put her hands to her face. That was something to ponder, but most of all, she was thankful.

For Love

Ollie and Roosta carried Flo upstairs. Flo hugged her son and he whispered in her ear, "Goodnight, Mama." He kissed her forehead.

After Ollie left, Roosta unbuckled Flo's pants and helped her slip out of them. She painfully groaned as she lifted her leg. Flo shifted her weight against her husband, while she took baby steps to the bed.

Roosta laid her down and looked at the bloody sight. "Red, I'm gonna clean those up for you."

She smiled. "Look at Lexi, the girl is still out." Lexi was sprawled across the air mattress next to the bed.

"I'm glad I don't sleep that hard. When I heard the shots, and Vaughn screamed, I didn't know what to think."

Flo chuckled. "I did. I thought, girl, you betta duck fo' you get shot." He wanted to laugh but the thought of Flo getting shot wasn't funny. Roosta walked away and returned with two warm washcloths, cotton balls and peroxide. "I found these in the bathroom. It's going to sting."

"Go ahead. I'm a big girl." After gently applying the washcloths he dabbed peroxide filled cotton balls to her bruised knees. She bit down, careful not to wake Lexi. He gave her his hand. "Squeeze it." She did.

When she let go, he said, "I guess we're going to have to spend a couple days here until you can walk a little better."

"That's fine. I'd like to spend time with the kids."

He helped her get out of her shirt. "Where's your nightgown?"

"That's what I was going to get, my overnight bag. It's still in the car."

"We'll just sleep in the nude," he joked.

Flo laughed. "Not in front of Lexi. I'll sleep in your shirt. You can sleep in your boxers."

Roosta undressed and gave Flo his shirt. When he slipped under the covers, Flo gave him a mind boggling kiss."

Disappointed Lexi was sharing the room, he asked, "What was that for? Wow."

She simply said, "Love. Let's pray and give thanks to God for His love and protection."

"I am not thinking about praying now."

She grinned as they bowed their heads. He led them in prayer.

On The Way

Ollie was calling home when Kyle walked in Vaughn's bedroom. Vaughn was sharing Lily's room. Ollie called home to check on Sapphire and tell her the news. No answer. He wanted to swear. *Where are you Sapphire?*

Lately, she couldn't stay home. Kyle sensed Ollie frustration, undressing, he asked, "What's wrong?"

"Kyle, just be happy you didn't marry Sassy."

Kyle was, but he wasn't going to admit it to a ticked off husband. "Sapphire's not home?"

"No. Let me check my messages." Before he could, his cell rang. He recognized it was Sapphire's number. "Where are you?" He heard sniffling. "Sassy?"

Opal swallowed the sobs. "Ollie, this is Opal. Sapphire's in the hospital."

Ollie wanted to get up from the bed he made out of comforters on the floor. He couldn't, his legs lost their strength. "What happened?"

"She was beaten at a gig tonight."

"A gig? Is Sassy dancin' again?"

"None of that matters right now. Sassy is in bad shape. She's in a coma. She's bleeding in her head. The doctor said it looks bad. Ollie, they need you here to sign forms."

Ollie just shook his head. Kyle saw the desperation. "Ollie, did you hear me? You need to get to New York now! We're at St. Vincent's in the city."

"I...I heard you. I'm coming."

He let his phone fall. Kyle asked, "What?"

"Sassy is in the hospital. She may be dying."

All Kyle could say was, "Ollie."

Ollie somehow regained control of his legs and found his bag. He started for the door. "Kyle, tell the family I gotta go."

Kyle jumped in front of him. "Ollie, wait, you shouldn't be driving. I'll drive you to the airport. Give me the keys to your rental." Kyle wanted to stop and tell Vaughn that Ollie was leaving. He wasn't sure if Ollie would wait. Ollie handed the keys over.

Kyle tapped on Lily's door on the way downstairs. Vaughn answered wearing a pair of Lily's gray satin pajamas.

He pulled her into the hallway. "What's wrong?"

He sighed. "Ollie's gotta go back to New York, tonight. I don't know the whole story. Sapphire was badly beaten at a gig. She's in a coma. I'm gonna drive Ollie to the airport. Can you call Michael and tell him to head over to St. Vincent's Hospital? Somebody needs to be with her and pray."

In shock, Vaughn held a hand to her mouth.

"Vaughn?"

It was a second before she said, "Kyle, Oh my God. Where's Ollie?"

"He's downstairs."

Barefoot, Vaughn ran to her brother and reached for him. She could tell he, too, was in shock. They both stared at each other unable to believe the night they were having. Putting his handsome face between her hands, she told him, "Ollie, I'm praying for Sapphire. She's going to make it. I'll stay with everyone here tonight. Tomorrow, I'm flying out, too."

He nodded not sure if anything was going to be all right. Sapphire told him she didn't want to strip anymore. She was lying to him, and doing only God knows what. Beyond angry, he asked "Kyle, you ready?"

True Friendship

Michael rolled over, sleep clogging his voice, he answered, "Vaughn? Is everything OK?"

"Sapphire's been badly hurt. She's in St. Vincent's. It's bad, Michael. Can you be with her? Ollie's on his way."

He tried to understand and rub the sleep from his eyes. The red numbers on his clock read eleven at night. He sat up, hung his legs over the bed. "Sure, Vaughn. How's everyone else?"

She knew he was concerned about everyone. His main concern was Lily. "We're all fine, and Lily, too. She's sleeping and I didn't want to wake her. We had a long day."

"Did something happen?"

"Yes, we'll talk about it later."

"I'm on my way."

Michael changed into jeans and a black T-shirt. Concerned and confused, he didn't know what happened to Sapphire.

Ollie was in Atlanta and he was in New York. Sapphire needed someone.

Michael met Opal and Mac in the waiting room. They explained, only family was allowed to see Sapphire.

Michael heard them, but he still beseeched the nurse. She repeated, "You're not family. You can't be in the ICU."

The little nurse with the long red ponytail stood firm. So did Michael. "Mrs. Sparrow's husband had a family emergency. He had to go to Atlanta. He just found out about his wife. He's on his way back. From what I hear, Sapphire could be dying. Would you want your spouse to die alone and you had a friend who could be with them?"

It was a reasonable argument. "I guess not. Come with me, sir."

Opal and Mac watched the nurse walk Michael away. They wondered; *what did he have, that they didn't?*

Michael cried when he saw her - eyes blacken, face swollen and bruised and her jaw wired. She was a horrific sight. The nurse laid a compassionate hand on his back. "I'm sorry, sir."

"How long do you think she has?"

"I really can't say. If the bleeding stops and the swelling goes down, maybe she'll have a fighting chance." She noticed he was shaky. "Why don't you have a seat?"

Unsteady, he sat. "Thank you." The nurse left him. It grieved Michael to see her like that, and to think, Ollie would have to also. It was no secret he and Sapphire butted heads. At that moment, he didn't really care if she liked him or not. He loved her soul.

Michael took her hands in his. "Sapphire, it's me, Michael. I know you're a strong woman. You can't die now, not without salvation. Ollie's on the way but, until he gets here, I'm going to pray and talk to you."

He squeezed her hand. No response.

Not far from death, Sapphire laid in a state deeper than sleep. She felt weightless, like she was in a field of flowers. There was a full bright sun and it warmed her. The field was bright and overflowing with yellow flowers. All was yellow except the green petals. She felt warm, not only with heat, but also within.

She looked down and saw she wore a yellow gown. Her feet were bare. The softness of the earth caressed her feet as she walked through the field. She saw Michael walk in the field.

He didn't say a word. Neither did she. He just stood and watched her. Then he walked toward the sun. Michael and the sun had a conversation. She could only see Michael's back. She couldn't hear what he was saying, but she could see he continually talked. Then he lifted his hands and waved them. She wanted to go ask him who he was talking to. She was too intrigued by the field. She began to pick flowers. Occasionally, she would look to Michael.

She felt a ball of fur graze her feet. It was a kitten covered in tiger stripes. She wanted to ignore him, but he kept purring against her feet. She lifted him. The minute she held him in her hands, the kitten grew larger and larger. He became a full size cat and then the size of a cub. She put him back into the field. However, the cat continued to grow. He became the size of a grown man. He stood on all fours, then two, and his fur disappeared. He became flesh. The face glared at Sapphire. It was Marcel. He offered her his hand. She reached to give him hers, and then, she heard Ollie's voice.

Ollie stood with Michael and they both talked in loud voices to the sun. Marcel still extended his hand. His hand was beautiful and golden

270

and she longed to touch it. She held it. The warmth of the sun left her. Her flesh grew cold, dry and began to wither. She turned to see Michael and Ollie were gone. Marcel disappeared. Alone now, the sun remained bright, but she could no longer feel its warmth.

All My Love

Drinking coffee never warded off worry. Not for Roosta. He wished Flo wasn't so adamant about flying to New York that next morning. He understood about loving your children and being there for them no matter what. And that was the very reason why he was in Atlanta. Now Ollie's wife was in bad shape. Flo wanted to be there for him. Roosta *would* fly to New York, but he was concerned about Flo.

She had a fitful sleep. Her knees stiffened and inflamed overnight. Now, she could barely bend them, and getting downstairs was going to be painful for her. Flo was convinced she didn't need a doctor, just an icepack. Roosta told her the best thing to do was stay in bed, and pray for Ollie and Sapphire.

Flo wouldn't hear of it. She was upstairs, struggling getting Lexi ready for their morning flight.

"Roosta, you look as good as I feel. I didn't get back from the airport until one this morning," Kyle said chewing on a blueberry muffin.

Roosta sipped his cold coffee. He had been thinking and staring off into space thinking about Flo's stubbornness for some time. "Flo didn't sleep well."

"I guess neither did you? Believe it or not, but I'm looking forward to sharing my bed, even on the nights Vaughn can't sleep."

Roosta gave a half smile. "You may regret saying that one day."

Kyle raised an eyebrow. "Do you?"

Roosta closed his eyes and rubbed the back of his neck, pressing the kinks away. "Nah, I don't think Flo should make this trip to New York. I don't see how she is going to be able to sit with her knees bent for two hours."

"It will be hard on her. She won't be any good for Ollie if she's in pain."

"She won't listen to me. Maybe you or Vaughn can talk some sense into her."

"Vaughn, talk some sense into whom?" Vaughn entered the kitchen and grabbed a carrot muffin, took Kyle's half glass of orange juice and sipped. She kissed Kyle's neck. "Morning, my Love, I just got off the phone with Michael. No change for Sapphire."

Roosta shook his head. He was praying Sapphire would be better. "Vaughn, do you think you can talk your mother into staying here? She's still in a lot of pain from the fall."

Vaughn stopped the glass from reaching her lips a second time. "I didn't know she was going."

Roosta added, "She's determined to be there for Ollie."

It was clear to Vaughn her mother would do anything for her children. They hadn't had a moment alone since she arrived. Time for a talk, she hugged Kyle. Uncertain what the hug was for, he squeezed her back. "What's wrong?"

She whispered in Kyle's ear, "I think I am about to have my first daughter and mother talk."

Kissing her cheek and inhaling her sweet scent, he said, "Go to it, baby."

Waiting For My Change

Ollie arrived at Sapphire's hospital room at seven in the morning. Afraid to walk in, he stood by the door for ten minutes, listening to Michael pray. In his heart, he prayed silently with him. Unsure of what he would encounter, he prayed for strength and then walked in. Seeing her, Ollie shouted, "No! No! No! That's not Sapphire! It's not her!"

Michael stood.

"Oh my God, Michael, her face... Tell me that is not Sassy!"

Michael wanted to tell him that. He couldn't. He said nothing. Ollie lifted her hands and saw her wedding rings. He kissed them then held them to his face. Michael gave Ollie his chair. Unshaven and un-showered, Ollie could pass for a derelict. Michael didn't look much better from a night of broken sleep and prayer. Michael gave the latest report. "There's been no change. At one point, I thought she was coming out of it. She mumbled something, like Ma."

Ollie nodded. "I guess she's calling for her mother. Michael, I don't want her to die like this." "Me, neither. Keep praying. Read the scriptures to her. I know; she knows we're here. Have you eaten?"

Ollie shook his head. Once again, he forgot to eat.

"I'll get you some breakfast. What do you want?"

"It doesn't matter." Ollie's somber response, translated; Ollie needed to eat just to be alert for Sapphire. He pulled the little black Bible from the bed and searched for a scripture to read.

At the door entrance, Michael connected with his Pastor and First Lady. "Pastor Rose?"

Pastor Rose shook Michael's hand. Michael kissed Mother Rose softly on the cheek. Pastor Rose asked while removing a baseball cap from his salt and pepper hair, "Is Ollie here yet?"

"He got here a little while ago. I'm on my way to get him some breakfast."

"Get you some too, Son. Vaughn told me you've been here since last night."

Michael nodded and walked away to the nurse's station to get directions to the cafeteria.

Pastor Rose and Mother Rose heard Ollie reading *Psalms 27* when they came into the room. He turned, began to stand to greet his aunt and uncle. Pastor Rose stopped him, saying, "Keep reading, she can hear you."

Sapphire found herself still in the deep sleep, weakened and lying in the field. She saw Pastor Rose and Mother Rose enter the field. They walked to the sun and began speaking with it.

It Comes to Light

Marcel sat on his patio in the Sheepshead Bay area of Brooklyn. He enjoyed a second cup of hazelnut coffee, listening to his wife play with their two-year-old daughter. He smiled at the sound of it. It was more like his daughter playing with his wife. The curly-head baby flung scrambled eggs across the kitchen floor. It was her daily game.

The doorbell rang and his wife yelled, "I'll get it! Marcel, come keep an eye on the baby."

Marcel picked his baby up out of the highchair and asked the familiar question, "Why do you give your mother a hard time?"

The baby mimicked him. "Ma, Ma, hard time."

He chuckled. "Yeah, hard time."

"Mrs. Reid?"

The pretty petite woman with large almond shaped eyes, wearing a black jogging suit squinted curiously at the detectives. "Yes."

They flashed their badges.

"Hello, I'm Detective Kris St. Laurent and this is Detective Dee Spelling. Is your husband home?"

Marcel walked to the front door, carrying his baby in his arms. He said, "I'm Dr. Reid."

Kris got straight to the point. This was the second Sparrow woman that came across his desk; first, Vaughn, then Sapphire. Kris took a special interest, wondering if they were related. "Dr. Reid, may we have a word with you alone?"

Dee wanted not to give him a word alone. She thought his wife would want to know where her husband was last night.

Mrs. Reid spoke for herself. "You may not speak to my husband alone. What is this all about?"

Convinced his wife wouldn't be put off, Marcel said, "You may speak freely, detectives."

Dee began. "You were identified as being at a frat party last night on, 72nd street and Fordham Road. A woman was brutally attacked, Sapphire Sparrow. She's an exotic dancer. Do you know her?"

Marcel wanted to lie, but he knew they already knew most of the truth. "We were in dental school together."

"You were seen running from the crime scene. Do you deny being at the party?"

Mrs. Reid waited for an answer, afraid of what the truth might be.

"I was there visiting an old friend. He's a grad student," Marcel lied.

"So your connection to the party had nothing to do with Mrs. Sparrow?"

"Detectives, am I under arrest?" he asked, defensively.

Dee answered, "Not at the moment."

"Then, we're finished."

Kris cleared the air. "We are not finished. You were at the crime scene. You know Mrs. Sparrow. We need you to come down to the station and give a statement. Oh, you might want to call your lawyer. Mrs. Sparrow's friend said she saw you leaving the bedroom just before she found Mrs. Sparrow beaten and unconscious."

Mrs. Reid felt sick to her stomach. She took the baby from Marcel and watched him walk away with the detectives.

Our Time Has Come

"Where's Lexi?"

"In with Lily, she's combing her hair for me."

Flo struggled on her feet as she flipped the ends of her red hair with a curling iron. She smiled at Vaughn's reflection in the mirror.

"Girl, you look so much like your father. He was a beautiful man."

"Even though I only had him a short time, I still remember him," Vaughn said. "He was a good man."

"That he was," Flo said. "We had Ollie when we were seventeen and too young to marry. A year after he was born, we got married. Girl, if I knew then what I know now."

Unable to turn around, Flo spoke to Vaughn via the mirror. "We had a tough time living with his mother and paying the bills. We were saving to move out. Then two years later, I found out you were on the way. I was afraid to tell your father I was pregnant. But he was excited to hear the news. He was proud and loved you the minute I told him I was carrying."

Vaughn sat on the bed and watched her mother struggle as she shifted her weight. Just like her, she tried to appear strong in the midst of the pain.

"You still miss him?" Vaughn asked.

"I do, but every time I see you, I see him."

"Is that why you left me with Auntie Vie? Was it too painful for you to see me?" Vaughn hadn't expected those words to be so easily spoken. She leveled her eyes on Flo, and waited for the answer.

The heat of Flo's tears burned her eyes and Vaughn's heart. "Vaughn, I loved your father too much. I lost myself in him. I made him my whole world, my god. When he died, you were only three and Ollie five. I didn't think my life was worth living. He was the first man I let love me after being abused by my stepfather. After his death, I couldn't take care of you. I wanted another man to love me like Samuel did. Samuel left me all his love, you and Ollie. I ran away from it, looking for love. I was a stupid woman."

"Auntie said your leaving wasn't abandonment. You did your best as a parent, by leaving your children with someone that could love and care for them. Did you ever want us?"

Flo wanted to hold Vaughn, but her legs wouldn't let her. Containing the moans, she struggled and stood. "I wanted you. I prayed for you. I just couldn't take care of you. Mentally, I was a mess. Emotionally, I was crippled. I didn't love myself. Even when I met a man that was good to me, I did something crazy to end the relationship, afraid he would leave me. Oh Vaughn, we make some terrible mistakes in life."

As painful as it was to hear, Flo's words offered peace. Vaughn accepted it.

Flo continued, "Seeing you now, I know I didn't make a mistake leaving you with Vie and Desi. You're smart, beautiful, strong and saved. They did a better job than I ever could. I owe them so much. I can't make-up for all the yesterdays, but I can be here today. I plan to be, until the day I die, if you'll let me."

Vaughn pushed herself up, walked over to Flo and wrapped her arms around her. "I love you, Mama."

"Thank you. I love you and Ollie so very much."

Vaughn let Flo go, looked her squarely in the eyes. Flo frowned. She needed a painkiller of some sort.

Vaughn deciphered the painful expression, helped Flo lie down on the bed. It took a minute for her to get comfortable. Vaughn mounted pillows underneath her pink manicured toenails.

"We have the same feet." Flo smiled. "Ain't that something? All those hours of labor, and all you get from me is my feet. At least they're pretty." They both laughed.

Vaughn asked, "Do me a favor? Ollie knows that you love him. He would not want you to make the trip, knowing how much pain you're in. Stay here with Lily."

"Lily's not going to New York?"

Vaughn still couldn't spill the beans about Lily. She couldn't wait until the family learned that a new member was on the way. "She's got some issues with work." That was true. Lily had some real issues with work. However, considering the bleeding, although it had stopped, Lily didn't want to fly.

Flo gave in. "I'll stay and spend some time with my niece. I forgot to ask, when's the wedding?"

Vaughn's face glowed with excitement. "We haven't set a date. But, to be honest with you, I hope as early as June."

"June! That's only two months away. How you gonna plan a wedding in two months?"

"It won't be easy. I don't want anything big. I just hope…"

Flo wondered what the problem was. This really was a mother and daughter talk. Vaughn hesitated not sure how to talk about sex with Flo. After several seconds, she said, "I just hope I can be with him on our wedding night. After what happened between me and Courtney, I don't know what to expect from myself."

Flo held her hand. "That's natural. I told you, my stepfather abused me. I let your father love me, because I knew he loved me. What Courtney did, or did not do, was about control. He took control over you. Now you are going to *give* yourself to your husband. Keep the lights on. Let it only be you two in the room. No one else belongs there."

Roosta tapped on the door. Flo called for him to come in. He asked, "Are we going?"

"Roosta, we'll stay," Flo said. Relieved, he sighed. "Vaughn, Kyle's ready."

"Thanks Roosta. Can you tell him I'll be right down?"

He nodded giving the ladies a few more minutes.

Vaughn kissed and hugged her mother again. "Thank you."

Flo explained, "No, thank you. I've prayed for this day. Oh, and Vaughn, one more thing, God intended for sex to be beautiful. Pray for Him to heal you so that it will be. I'll be praying, too."

Vaughn blushed and Flo noticed the rosy color in her cheeks. "Oh girl, don't be shamed. Sex is a major part of a good marriage. You'll want to start it off with a bang."

Vaughn laughed and waved. "I'll call you when we land."

Unanswered Questions

Michael didn't get into the office until three o'clock Friday afternoon. He didn't think he was going to get much work done. Spending the night at Sapphire's bedside exhausted him. He was relieved to see Kyle and Vaughn walk into the hospital hand-in-hand - engaged to be husband and wife. That was the highlight of his day.

Looking up from his drawing board, he reflected on the painting; he, Kyle and Ollie admired - the rainbow. Michael's earliest childhood memory was his mother, telling him and Kyle the story of Noah's Ark - the warning, the design, the construction, the flood, and destruction and, lastly, the new beginning.

The thought of a new beginning led him to ponder on Lily. Michael knew that he could have a new beginning without Lily. Lily would go on, have her child and be a good mother. He would one day love again and create a family of his own.

He believed with every cell of his being he could live fully and completely without Lily. What he certainly was not sure of was, could he find that special love that went beyond the flesh and into his spirit. It was a love that required no words and, yet, it soothed his mind. He wanted that love for a lifetime. Michael had a rare find in Lily. But there were questions; he needed answers to. Until he had them, he would never be free for a new beginning.

My Warmth I Give To You

There was still no change with Sapphire. Ollie took that as a good sign. The very fact that she was still alive was a positive. Even near death, she still had a chance to come to know Christ. He believed that.

The doctors asked Ollie if he wanted her resuscitated and placed on life support in the event she became brain dead. Ollie cuddled in Vaughn's arms and asked the doctors to give him more time. It wasn't a decision he was prepared to make.

Mother Rose wasn't giving up. It would break her heart if Sapphire were to die without Christ in her life. She was still breathing and she was certain Sapphire was aware of the love, support and prayers that surrounded her.

Brushing Sapphire's bangs aside with her fingertips, she leaned down and ever so lightly kissed her forehead. It was the one part of her face that was not bruised or swollen. She lifted her hand and quietly spoke into Sapphire's ears, "Baby, we're here. Your family is here. We love you, Sapphire. God loves you. Can you see Him? Can you see his Son? He sacrificed His life for you. He wants you to live. Listen to me. You've got to reach out to Him. He's going to bring you back to us. Press your way Sapphire to the Son."

Mother Rose held onto Sapphire's hand. She thought she saw Sapphire eyelids flutter.

Sapphire remained in the field and she looked to the Sun. She could see Kyle, Vaughn, Ollie, Mother and Pastor Rose standing in front of the Sun. She heard a quiet gentle voice. It came out of the Sun. She heard the words, "Sapphire, I love you. I want to share my warmth with you. My comfort and my peace I give to you. I want to be your Father and you my Daughter. I offer you a touch that brings fulfillment; contentment and you will need no other. I offer my hand to you."

Weakened in the field, she stretched her hand. She wanted that touch that would end the longing in her spirit, bringing peace to her restless soul.

Rays of sunlight floated through the air and covered her body from the crown of her head to the soles of her feet. Her body glowed in soft hues of gold. She received strength in her legs. She rose from the field. Smiling, she said, "Thank you."

Sapphire opened her swollen eyes.

To Leave, or Not To Leave

Saturday morning, and six weeks pregnant, Lily felt good. She heard the news the night before. Vaughn called and told her Sapphire opened her eyes. And several difficult hours later, Sapphire asked for paper and pen and wrote, "The Son healed me."

Ollie asked, "Jesus?" She painfully nodded and wrote, "I don't want Him to leave me."

"He never will. He'll always be with you," Ollie said.

That news was enough to make Lily wanna dance.

Now surrounded at the breakfast table with Lexi, Donita, her husband, Stanley, and their daughter, Jessica, Lily ate eagerly.

Roosta entered the kitchen with an empty plate and Nita looked up from a crisp piece of bacon. "Whoa, you finished already? You don't play wit the food, do ya?"

Roosta laughed and his dreads fell back. Today was a better day for everyone. Physically, they all felt revived and refreshed. Roosta explained, "Nah, not me. That wife of mine can eat." He laid the plate on the counter and walked over to Lexi, kissed her cheek. "How are you doing, sweetie?"

Lily inspected Roosta in awe. God was a miracle worker. She never thought him to be an attractive man, but Roosta was actually, charming, sensitive and loving. For what Lily overheard as she passed their bedroom the night before, he was passionate, too. She didn't know how they made love with Flo's injuries. Somehow, they had. Lily heard the muffled cries of ecstasy pour out from both of them. She was thankful Lexi shared her room and apparently, so were they.

Lexi happily announced, "Jessie asked if she could take me to the mall and the movies. Is it OK, Dad?"

Roosta looked at the small teenager with the long brown ponytail falling over her shoulders. Jessica added, "My Mom will be taking us. Is it OK?"

Donita chided in, "Don't worry I'll take good care of your baby. Maybe you can help Flo downstairs and take her for a stroll. She needs the exercise."

It was a good idea and a beautiful day. If Flo had another good day, they would go home tomorrow. The sun warmly illuminated the family size kitchen. Roosta appreciated the patio view, as he answered, "I'll do that."

Stanley had the same brown hair as his daughter. His was starting to gray. He pushed his silver frames up on his nose. He chuckled. "That's smart of you to just go with the flow. Nita is a relentless woman."

"That's why you've been happily married all these years." Smiling, Donita said, and reached for his hand. Stanley held it and brought his attention to Lily. After taking a sip of his coffee, he questioned, "Lily would it be OK for us to take a walk together? I have something I'd like to discuss with you."

Everyone turned to Lily who was biting into a jelly biscuit.

Having not the faintest idea what Stanley wanted to talk about, she gave a coughed up response, "Uh...sure Stanley."

Everyone left the house, leaving Roosta to clean the kitchen. Donita asked for the fifth time, "Roosta, you sure you can handle it?"

"I'm happy to do it."

Donita waved bye. "We may be gone a while. I left my cell number on the counter, if you want to get up with Lexi."

Lily watched Lexi and Jessica pile into the backseat of Donita's minivan. The girls giggled as if they were the same age even though there was six years between them.

Stanley interrupted her thoughts with a small touch to her elbow. "You ready?"

She gave a frown and Stanley reassured her, "Don't worry. I won't keep you long."

The two-block walk to Stanley and Donita's home seemed like an eternity. Lily's curiosity was so peaked she wanted to blurt out, *what is this all about.*

Donita knew for sure. Lily wished she had a heads up. That was just like Donita. She would spring things on them without giving them a chance to react or contemplate - especially if she felt it was for their own good. Lily knew Donita would never do anything to hurt her. She let her shoulders relax as she entered their quaint home.

It wasn't quite Lily's taste, but she enjoyed the red and gold plaid furniture, and the red throws across the chairs. "Can I get you anything?"

Lily took note of Stanley's crisp white shirt; she was sure Donita starched it. She didn't know where Donita found the time to be a wife, mother, part-time nurse, First Lady and cook for her this past week. Donita was a remarkable person. Lily shook her head no.

Stanley held out his hand. "I hope you don't mind us meeting in my office?"

"Sounds OK."

Understanding it was business related, since they were meeting in his office, Lily softened her steps as she glided into the old-fashioned office.

He held out her chair. She sat, thanked him, crossed her legs and wondered what it was she could do for him. Without prolonging their business, Stanley opened a leather bound notebook. "Lily, have you decided if you are going to go back to Williams, Wright and Wilson?"

"Actually, no." She couldn't offer more than that because she just wasn't sure.

He nodded and believed it was a fair answer. "I've been praying about something for quite some time. I know you're well aware as a pastor's daughter we come across a lot of information everyday. It has become clear to me over the years that we as Christians don't always take care of our legal matters. Attorneys are needed for church matters. I have a very good firm that I work with, but I'd be happy to give that business to you. Additionally, I'm concerned about our members, regarding small legal matters and advice, for example, purchasing a home, starting a business, creating a will, or small claims regarding accidents and things of that nature."

Stanley occasionally read his notes, and then regained eye contact with Lily. She leaned into the armrest of the chair, tilted her head and brought a finger to the side of her face. Stanley could see she was intensely listening.

He continued, "I have a proposition for you. Victory Assembly would like to hire you as our chief attorney and legal consultant."

Not sure how to answer, Lily squinted her eyes. The opportunity to use her law degree in ministry was an awesome request. She never felt more at home than when she put her hands in God's service.

"Stanley, this is a great honor. I don't have very much experience, yet."

Grateful that she was delighted, he smiled. "Nita and I think a lot of you. If you do stay in Atlanta, this may be perfect for you. Although, we can't offer you as much as you're currently making." Finding a white sticky on his desk that said Victory Assembly he wrote down a figure, folded the paper and handed it to her.

Thirty-five thousand a year. That would cut her salary nearly in half. She would have to move out of the company house, support herself and child.

A lot to consider, he said, "I don't need an answer today. I want you to pray about this before you say anything."

Standing, she followed and they shook hands. "Thank you for the offer. I promise you, I will pray about it and get back to you as soon as I can."

"Great. I'll walk you out."

A Question for Baby

Lily walked the two blocks from Nita's house, thinking about Stanley's proposal. When Stanley said the words, it was like she heard them before. She had held out and waited for the right job offer. When Williams, Wright and Wilson offered, it seemed too good to be true. It sounded right; however, it never felt right.

Coming to Atlanta gave her a child. She didn't regret it, but it would change her life forever. She didn't know if she could afford to support herself and her child on the salary Stanley's church offered.

She knew if this was God's will for her to use her law degree to serve Him and His people, He would provide the way. She needed to call her parents. Lily decided, as soon as her aunt was well enough to leave, she was taking a trip home. There was so much to tell them - the baby, the job and now maybe working in a legal ministry.

Still in deep thought, it surprised her when she saw the red rose and letter at her doorstep. Lily lifted the rose and letter and went inside.

In Michael's handwriting, *Lily* was written on the small envelope. Anxious to read it, she didn't sit down, but placed the rose on the coffee table and ripped the envelope. But it was not written to her. It read:

Dear Baby,

We haven't met yet. I hope to soon. I've known your mother for quite some time. She's a wonderful person. You're very blessed to have her as your mother.

I love her very much. She has a heart of gold and the strength of a warrior. She's very precious to me. I let her go once. I thought that was the best thing to do. My main concern is for your mother to be happy. You see, your mother is a brilliant woman. She has a strong, keen, analytical mind. She worked very hard in school. I want her to fulfill her every dream.

I hope she knows that's why I wanted her to go. However, there was a question that I wanted to ask her. I neglected to do that before she left. I hope it's not too late.

I think I have to ask you a question first. If it's OK with you, then I have a question for your mother.

I'm a little nervous. Please be patient with me. I've never done this before.

OK, here it goes, is it OK for me to be your Dad? I promise to love, guide, protect and provide for you. If your answer is yes, tell your mother to go into the kitchen. I have a present for you.

Lovingly,

Michael

Lily was balling by the time she'd gotten to the end of Michael's letter. She knew he was somewhere in the house.

Following the instructions of the letter, she found a three-foot teddy bear on the floor and a beautiful three-tier, pink and blue cake on the counter.

Her hands were shaking as she dropped the letter on the counter.

Her engagement ring sat in the center of the cake. Written on top of the cake in pink letters were, *Lily, will you marry me?*

She brought her shaking hands to her face. Through tear filled eyes, she searched for Michael. He came from behind her. "I'm guessing the baby said yes?"

At a lost for words, she nodded. Michael took the ring from the cake and tasted the icing on it. He knelt before her. Lily couldn't stop crying.

Michael held her hand, slipped on the ring and kissed it.

Finally, when Lily found her voice, she looked at him as tears fell from her chin. "Michael, you would be a father to my child?"

His voice was cracking. "I'll be a father to our child. He or she has to be mine."

"Michael, it will be. It will be. Oh, Michael, I can't believe this. I love you."

"I love you too, baby."

Lily knelt down with Michael and wandered into his eyes. His were full, too. He kissed her deeply, passionately and lovingly. She returned his every gesture, caressing his neck, shoulders and back.

Involuntarily moans and peaceful sighs released from deep within them both. Michael didn't want to stop, but he had to. He pulled away just inches from Lily, looked down, slowly lifted her shirt, and eased his broad hand onto her bare belly. He smoothly rubbed it, connecting with his unborn child.

Michael's face was so serious. Lily placed her hand on top of his. Simultaneously, their tears fell silently. He kissed the corners of her mouth. Taking possession, as well as responsibility, he said, "Lily, this is my baby."

"Michael, it is yours. I am yours."

"I paid Rick a visit."

Her voice hushed and surprised. "You did?"

"I got into Atlanta late last night, drove out to see him. He wants to relinquish his parental rights."

That wasn't news to Lily. Rick sent Lily an e-mail, telling her just that. She nodded and held her head down.

Forgetting those things that were behind, Lily held her head up and smiled at her fiancé.

Not wanting to stop touching Lily, he held her shirt up then slid both hands to her back.

Sighing, Michael leaned into her full curls and basked in the silkiness of her bare back. He drew closer. She rested her face in the crook of his neck. And she barely spoke, but he heard her say, "I love you."

"Are we gonna get a taste of your engagement cake, or what?"

Michael and Lily looked over at Flo as she leaned against Roosta. It wasn't easy, but Roosta eased Flo downstairs, so she could eavesdrop on the engagement. It took her so long to make it downstairs, all she heard Michael say was, "Rights."

Well, she knew that meant Lily said yes. Why else would they be on their knees hugging and kissing so much?

It was time to celebrate. Roosta said in his defense, "I'm sorry, Flo made me do it."

Flo held onto Roosta and kissed him. Michael laughed as he helped Lily to her feet. He found a handkerchief in his pocket and dried Lily's tears, then his own.

Lily smiled. "Michael, this is one eavesdropping family. Are you ready to be a part of it?"

"Ready, baby. I am ready. Let's cut this cake."

New York
A Year Later - Christmas Day

Lily rested in bed as baby Nicholas rested in her arms. "He's beautiful." Lily smiled down at her son, amazed at how sweet he was.

Mother Rose kissed her daughter's forehead. "Just like his mother." Mother Rose's voice trembled as she wiped the fallen tears on her cheeks. She continued, "I am so proud of you, Lily."

Also, fighting tears, Lily glanced up as the baby held a firm grip on his mother's finger. "Mom, I thought I let you down."

"Lily, you've never let us down. You're a wonderful daughter. You were a straight A student and strong Christian for the most part of your life. Conceiving baby Nicholas was the sin, but how can I be disappointed? I have the perfect grandson."

Lily ran her nose against the baby's forehead. "He is precious, and we're not saying that because he's ours."

"Yes we are!" Mother Rose laughed loudly.

"How's my boy?" Pastor Rose's voice roared as he and Michael walked into the bedroom.

"He's perfect, Dad."

Pastor Rose reached for the baby and cradled him gently in his arms. "I just wanted to hold him one last time before we go home."

Lily thought her father was going to burst. The baby was having a joyous effect on all of them. "I can't believe how much he's changed in just a month. Y'all gonna have to bring this baby over more often."

Michael chuckled. "Dad, we bring him over almost every weekend."

Everyone laughed.

"We better get going."

"So soon, Desi?" Mother Rose pouted.

"You'll have another baby to go crazy over," he predicted.

Lily asked, "Who's pregnant?"

Pastor Rose raised his eyebrows. "Not yet, but it won't be long. Didn't you see how fast Kyle and Vaughn went home? I

289

think y'all done started something. Ollie and Sapphire rushed out of here. Even Flo and Roosta had that look in their eyes."

Lily held her hand out. Michael leaned down and showered her with a kiss.

Pastor Rose stated, "I guess that's our cue." He handed Nicholas to Michael. "We'll make sure we lock the door behind us. Good night, kids." Pastor Rose turned just before he crossed the threshold and directed his focus on Lily, he said, "Chief attorney, there's a basket on the dining room table from the legal ministry. You're doing a wonderful job at our church."

Lily proclaimed from the depths of her soul, "It's a pleasure serving God and His people."

Mother and Pastor Rose walked out at peace with Lily and Michael's family.

Smiling down at his son in his arms, Michael expressed, "This is the first time that I held him today."

"It's amazing; he's not fussy with all the attention he received. I'm glad we had his baby dedication on Christmas Day; Nicholas Michael Carraway."

Michael smiled at the sound of it. "He's got a great name."

"Oh yes, he does. And, he's got a great father, too. Come to bed, husband."

Michael smiled. "You don't have to ask me twice."

Michael kissed his son's forehead, placed him softly in his bassinet and joined his wife.

Dear Reader,

Thank you for reading my first novel. This story is fictional. However, it is connected to biblical principles.

The character's situations represent real life. Maybe you can relate to one. Specifically, is it Lily, Vaughn, Sapphire, Flo, Michael, Kyle, Ollie or Roosta?

Where are you headed in your life journey? Are you missing your mark, while focusing on past mistakes?

If you are, it's not too late. Return to the source of every good and perfect gift. I know that Christ is waiting for you. I am excited and waiting to hear your success stories.

Email me at brooklynndorcent@gmail.com. Find me on Facebook, or www.brooklynndorcent.com.

Loving you. Remember, victory is waiting for you. Have yours today!

Love, Grace and Peace

Brook Lynn Dorcent

Discussion Questions

1.   Michael sought and followed the advice of his natural father. As a result, he told Lily to take the job offer in Atlanta. If she did not, then she might regret it and possibly resent him one day for turning it down. Do you believe this advice was sound? Why, or why not?

2.   Vaughn ended up going with Lily to Atlanta. Was this a shock to you? Why do you think she decided to go along? Do you believe this was a sudden decision for Vaughn?

3.   Should Ollie be held responsible for Sapphire becoming a full-time exotic dancer and dropping out of dental school? What was Sapphire really seeking in life? Was it marriage and motherhood, or something more?

4.   Sapphire begins to resent Ollie. She finds fault in him for rebuilding relationships with his Christian family and friends. She believes Kyle and Ollie are hypocrites because of the intimate relationship she has shared with them and refused to listen to their witness or testimony in Christ. Additionally, she added Ollie's mother, Flo, to the list of hypocrites. Is Sapphire correct in calling them hypocrites? Why, or why not? In your walk in Christ, have you experienced a fall, and when you returned to Christ, how did those closest to you respond?

5.   In the intimate chapter with Sapphire and Marcel, Marcel plays the innocent role. He does not take the lead, and chooses not to bluntly confess his ultimate goal to Sapphire. Why does Marcel take this route? Is it effective? Who does Marcel represent in the spiritual realm of seduction?

6.   Roosta, like Sapphire, had no upbringing as a Christian. He makes a shift and dramatic change in his life. So much so, that Flo, his wife, cannot accept it to be sincere. Can a man with Roosta's background make a firm decision to serve Christ, and do it victoriously? Why do you think Roosta was successful in his decision? Do you agree with Flo's decision to forgive Roosta and continue their marriage?

7.   For eight years, Michael made a conscious decision and respected and honored Lily's virginal right. Is this typical of today's Christian man? Can God create a man like Michael? Does Michael represent the love of God in our life?

Take a look at the sequel...

Pressing Toward the Mark   Available Now

Love My Enemy? – Chapter 1

"**I** wondered how long it would be before you'd ask this question." Three years later, Michael had his answer.

Rick smiled, waiting a second, before he confessed, "I didn't think I ever *would*. I see now that I wasn't in a good frame of mind to make such a vital decision."

Michael leaned back in his seat and thought about his reply, he admitted, "Your frame of mind wasn't important. It isn't now. The answer is the same as the one I sent you in your emails. Nicholas Michael Carraway is my son, and you will not be a part of his life -- ever."

Rick spread his lips into a thin icy grin. "And Lily, she feels the same way?"

"Lily and I are in complete agreement." Michael warned, "Do not involve my wife."

Until now, Rick had respected Michael's request. He wouldn't any longer. His only choice required force. "I will see *my* son."

Michael stood up from his desk. Fighting for composure, he stuffed his hands into his slacks. He relied on two deep breaths for calmness, and then, slowly educated his opponent. "Don't battle with me, Rick. You'll lose."

Rick stood up as contentment reflected in his eyes. He could read the anger flashing in Michael's. "I know that you'll always hate me."

Michael scoffed, "I don't hate you."

Rick laughed. "I did what you weren't man enough to do. Not only did I receive Lily's virginity, I gave her my son. And that's something you'll live with for the rest of your life."

Disgusted, Michael shook his head. "Rick, your negotiation skills are lacking."

"What I lack is a sense of judgment about your character. I considered you to be reasonable. It took a lot for you years ago to come to my home, ask me what my intentions were for Lily and our child. I admired that you came to me -- as a man. Can't you see; I'm doing the same here?"

Michael did not answer.

Rick had finally regretted his decision and wanted a second chance. With one final shot, using humility, Rick explained, "I know I made a major mistake signing away my parental rights, but, I pray and hope that we could reach a solution. Michael, understand; I was wrong."

With another shake of his head, Michael agreed with Rick. He was wrong to think he'd honor his request. "This is *my* family that *you* want to be a part of."

"I am the reason you have a *family*." Rick stabbed his finger at him. "Don't you think if *I* would have accepted Lily and the baby, she would be my wife today, not yours?"

Michael noticed Rick's trembling hand as he spoke. He wondered what that was about. Brushing the curiosity aside, he pointed out, "Lily never loved you."

A tap at the door brought the literary duel to a halt. Clara, Michael's office assistant stepped in, reminding Michael that his boss awaited him in the executive conference room.

He had almost forgotten his meeting. Rick's interruption ran much longer than he had planned for. He had to end this and move on. He asked Clara to let his boss know he'd be there soon. He slid his strained shoulders into his jacket while gazing at Rick.

He wanted more than anything, for Rick Parsons to no longer exist in his life. "I advise you to go on."

"You'll be hearing from me."

Rick calmly left Michael's office, but not his mind.

The attractive men walked in opposite directions. Their appealing faces, made most women stop and stare. Michael's skin radiated a glorious golden bronze tone. Rick's deep skin tone against his pearly whites struck and awed the ladies.

Michael muddled over what Rick had said before he stepped into the conference room. His wife had her first sexual experience with Rick, which led to him being the biological father of their child. The unpleasant reality deeply ingrained the fibers of his mind.

Consequently, the question of hating Rick persistently shadowed his sub-consciousness. Was resentment coming to collect its fee, and could Michael afford to pay up?

Have Your Cake At Home – Chapter 2

Daily prayer ended at Victory Ministries' church. Few participants stayed behind, some crying out to God for help. Lily Carraway was one of them. She remained, unable to gather enough strength to get up and off her knees.

Her mother stood nearby watching her weep. And she had watched Lily do this for months now, becoming increasingly difficult for her not to say anything. Lily and Michael, married almost four years, had serious problems. They almost did a good job of pretending that all was well. But Mother Violet Rose, pastor's wife, first lady and Lily's mother, had much wisdom. She counted the signs.

For one, it seemed that Lily and Michael communicated only when necessary. Their affection dwindled. They rarely shared easy loving touches, or exchanged secret smiles that interpreted their longing for one another. And finally, she saw the disappearance of joy in their laughter.

What was apparent? - their cry for help. The pain seeped from their hearts into their eyes. And she saw the difference in their call for help. Lily's resulted in prayer, but Michael ignored the issues.

Today, Mother Rose would break her promise and interfere – not only for their benefit, but hers as well. She would not stand by and see her children suffer.

The prayer room cleared, Lily thought she wept alone. Mother Rose quietly knelt down next to Lily. "What's wrong?"

Lily didn't open her eyes, but asked, "Mom?"

"Yes, it's me, mom. Lily, you've been crying like this for months now."

Lily rocked on her knees, pressing her fingertips to her forehead, she sighed. "I want to tell you. Michael doesn't want me to discuss it with anyone. I promised him I wouldn't."

Mother Rose offered, "I'll have your father talk to Michael."

Lily opened her eyes. "Mom, don't."

"Don't, what? Let you go on in pain?" She gently touched Lily's shoulder.

"I'm praying about it. God will work it out."

"Praying, yes, you're doing plenty of that. But faith without works is dead. You and Michael need to *work* on this. Your father and I may be able to help."

Lily propped her elbows on the chair in front of her where she knelt. "Trust me. You can't help with this."

"Does this have to do with sex?" Mother Rose asked with a matter-of-fact expression.

Lily's mouth fell open as heat flushed her skin.

Mother Rose said softly, "I know a little bit about sex. How do you think you got here?"

"Mom, we shouldn't discuss this in church."

"Well, how do you think the church members got here? Lily, sex is a big part of life, and a major part of married life."

Starting to feel her knees ache, Lily stood, then sat in a chair. Mother Rose did the same. Lily explained, "It's not what you think. Our sex life is great; whenever we had sex."

Lifting her brows, she nodded. "Oh, I see. It's not enough for you."

"No. Yes. Wait." Lily blinked, feeling confused, she added, "I mean the sex we're having is not making a baby. I want us to keep trying and Michael, he's...." The cat sauntered out of the bag before Lily realized it.

Understanding clearly, Mother Rose finished Lily's sentence, "He's feeling incompetent. He has shut down the sexual part of your marriage."

Feeling a weight lift, she exhaled. "It's so weird. It's been six months and it's like he's forgotten about that part of our life. Mom, he used to be so drawn to me. But now, he pretends like life without sex is OK. I can't even entice him into it."

Lily held her hands out in question. "Is something wrong with me?"

Mother Rose bit her bottom lip as she thought about it. Realizing someone else might be better at getting through to Michael, she said, "Kyle."

"Huh?"

"Kyle should be the one to talk to Michael, not your father. Since they're brothers and both newlyweds, it should be Kyle."

Lily stood and Mother Rose observed Lily under the dim lighting. Her daughter was simply beautiful. She had a heart shaped face, big bright eyes, long lashes, perfect shaped lips against dark chocolate skin. Her figure was shapely, and keeping up with the family genes, she had a full round bottom.

Lily broke her mother's observation with some information. "Mom, Kyle doesn't know. If he talks to Michael about this, Michael is going to know I broke my promise."

"No, he won't. Kyle knows his brother. I'm sure he's seen a difference in him. I have, and so has Vaughn."

"Vaughn?" Lily thought about her sister/cousin. They grew up together, lived in the same house after Vaughn's mother left her when she was only four years old. They were more like sisters than cousins, and ironically, their husbands were twin brothers.

Thinking it through, Lily knew her mother made valid points. Vaughn constantly asked Lily what was wrong. Lily wondered, "Do you think Kyle has asked Michael about our problems?"

"He probably has. You see, it won't be out of place if Kyle brings it up, again. Once he has these details, he'll know how to steer the conversation."

Lily gave a half smile and shook her head. "I never knew how sneaky you are, Mom."

"Smart." Mother Rose stood and put her arm around Lily's waist. "Let's fill Vaughn in, so she'll know how to approach her husband."

Lifting her brows, Lily asked, "Now? You're on a mission."

"I am not going to stand by and let your marriage fall apart."

As Lily and her mother stepped into the halls of the church, she said, "It's not that serious. We're fine."

"Just because Michael is not having his cake at home, doesn't mean he don't like cake."

Lily frowned. "Mom, Michael would never cheat."

"Never say never." She wagged her finger at her for emphasis. "Your husband is feeling incompetent; maybe blaming you for it. And those women out there can sense a man in need of sweets. Michael is not out looking for something to eat, but he's hungry nevertheless."

Feeling defensive, Lily blurted, "It's not because *I'm* denying him."

Mother Rose knocked and then stepped into Vaughn's empty office. "True, but when he's with you, he's feeling less than. Don't think for a second that his needs have changed. Yours haven't."

Lily didn't answer, but it was true. Her needs hadn't changed. She considered herself a conservative woman by nature. And yet, she was not hindered by the passion she owned as a sexual being. As a Christian, she had a clear two-fold understanding of herself. Lily was the professional attorney that lived by the Bible, and the law of the land. But within the bedroom, she loved her body, and her husband's. Ultimately, she had a healthy appetite toward desire and enjoyed what God created to be a physical and divine experience for the husband and wife.

It was not until now; since her mother mentioned it, she questioned if Michael would break his vows.

"Lily, I am telling you this, because I don't want you to be naive. I never thought your father would even look at another woman. He did, and it almost ruined our marriage." Shocked, Lily asked, "Dad cheated on you?"

"You could say that."

"Uncle Desi did what?"

Lily looked up as Vaughn entered her office. Vaughn wasn't sure if she caught what her Aunt said just right - Pastor Desmond Rose, cheating?

Her Aunt and Uncle raised her, and that made them her parents. The thorn that pricked her mind screamed, *Did seasoned Christians like Pastor and Mother Rose, allow infidelity's ugly head to sour their marriage?* Vaughn needed to hear more.

"You're late Madame Secretary," Lily joked.

Vaughn smiled and then blushed. She had a sexy runway model appeal about her. Her creamy beige skin created a nice balance with her hazel eyes, pretty pink lips and thick black wavy hair. She explained, "My husband got in late last night from the leadership conference. We were uh…catchin' up."

Mother Rose added, "That's why we're here. If I'm not mistaken, Michael got in around the same time as his brother. And Lily, wasn't, uh…catchin' anything."

Vaughn's cheeks turned beet red.

Mother Rose could clearly discern the difference between Lily and Vaughn.

Vaughn was in complete contentment with her mate. And now, she knew that Lily wasn't, she shouted, "I knew it! Lily, why didn't you tell me?"

Lily shook her head and tried to think of an excuse to get out of the room.

Mother Rose directed, "Let's sit down."

Vaughn quickly plopped down while Mother Rose watched Lily hesitate as they took their seats around the small table.

Vaughn ordered, waving Lily over, "Come on, Ms. Conservative." Giving Lily a head to toe look, she pointed her finger at her. "Pitiful, you in that grey turtleneck, those black wool pants and, black penny loafers - got the nerve to have a penny in 'em. Lift your pant leg?"

Lily did and Vaughn gasped. "And those polka-dot socks! Girl, the first thing we need to do is work on your wardrobe."

Vaughn turned to Mother Rose. "And Auntie, what's this about Uncle Desi cheating on you? Oh yeah, I heard you talking when I walked in." She couldn't picture her Pastor Rose breaking any vow.

Mother Rose let out a deep breath. A long morning ahead, she ordered tea and croissants and got to work on *Operation: Make Sho' You Eat Yo' Cake at Home!*

Keep It Simple - Chapter 3

Michael returned to his office after his meeting. Clara was there making him a fresh pot of coffee. "You don't need to do that. I just had lunch," he explained.

"It's my job, Michael." Clara smiled.

Michael removed his jacket. Clara snatched it out of his hands. "Here, I'll hang this up for you."

"Clara, it's not your job to do that."

She winked at him. "This one is on the house."

Michael forced a smile as he walked to his drawing board.

"I heard you're the head man in charge of the Condos we're building in Brooklyn. That account is huge," Clara commented as she observed him.

Michael rolled up his sleeves. "It's a lot of responsibility."

"I know you'll handle it fine. Trent has been here ten years and he's never received an assignment this big."

That, Michael knew. He also knew that his co-worker wasn't too happy about his recent success.

Michael began sketching rapidly on the white-laced paper. He wanted to get the ideas down from the morning's meeting. He didn't realize Clara hadn't left until he saw her rest a black coffee mug next to him.

She studied his drawings, standing over his shoulder. "You're good. And fast. That looks great."

He gave a grunt.

She lingered, watched him sketch. Impressed, she mumbled, "Precise, detailed, inventive."

He didn't look up. "Uh, thanks. I'm sorry. I really want to get this down."

Clara stepped back and gave a half smile. "I just…. Michael, can I get a few minutes of your time?"

Slightly aggravated, he agreed, and laid down his pencil. "What's up?"

She didn't sit, but stood next to him. "That guy that was here earlier, Rick Parsons, he seemed to really upset you. Lately, you're different. I know that you got this project, and then you and Trent aren't speaking."

"Clara..."

Clara held up her hand. "Wait, let me get this out. I just want you to know; I'm here. For *whatever* you need. Last year, when Trent and I broke up, you did so much for me. You invited me to your church, dinner with your family and you even got my son involved with the youth center. And I couldn't believe that when my car was stolen, you and your wife helped me get another one. I really appreciate everything."

Michael looked at Clara. She had changed over the few years he knew her. Her cute mocha face and body were fuller. After her last break up, she put on about ten pounds. There was something in her eyes. He wondered if she were sincere. "I gotta work on this assignment, *now*."

She knew Michael had given the hint for her to exit. And still unable to resist, she walked behind him, laid her hands on his broad shoulders and massaged them.

He tensed up. She lowered her voice. "I don't bite. Relax and look at the picture over there."

Michael focused on the smiling faces of his wife and son.

Feeling the knots in his shoulders, she said, "Um, it's worse than I thought." She deepened the massage, and finally he relaxed some. "Anytime you want to talk, just call."

She walked her thumbs up and down the back of his neck, tilted his head forward. He closed his eyes and she heard him sigh. Her warm lips brushed his earlobe. "That's it," she whispered.

Michael smelled of cologne and sheer masculinity. She tasted his neck. "There, doesn't this feel good?"

Aroused, his belly flickered. Ashamed, he shouted, "Clara, stop!"

She stepped back. "I just..."

He stood up and away from Clara. "I got a lot going on; almost too much. I appreciate the concern, but..." He saw his rejection in her eyes.

"Michael, I was just..."

"Clara, I'm a straight and narrow guy, not stupid."

"You want me to be real?"

"Please," he said honestly.

Clara folded her arms across her chest, looked around the elaborate office as if she were looking to see if they were alone. "OK.

You're a good man. And I'd say for the past few months or so, you haven't been yourself," she shrugged and continued, "so, if you're not happy at home, I could make you happy, here, and right now. Real enough?"

Michael whistled, shoved his hands in his pockets.

Clara nodded, waiting for his acceptance.

"All I have to do is say the word. No questions asked?"

"No strings attached." She licked her lips.

Feeling his temples throb, he couldn't believe the day he was having. "Clara, I'm going to be simple with you."

She smiled. "Michael, that's what I was hoping for."

"I don't think you were. You see, *sex* is a string. There's always an attachment. The man I met with today, he's a string. I'm really tired of strings."

Clara frowned. *Is Michael gay?*

"Simply speaking Clara, I'm not interested."

Furious, Clara let her hand conveniently tip over the coffee mug. His rough sketches were destroyed. "Oops, I'm simply sorry."

Wearing an evil grin, Clara stormed to her desk.

Enough ain't Enough – Chapter 4

$\mathbf{V}$aughn rushed home; her husband had already arrived first. They had more *catching up* to do. Anticipating her entrance, Minister Kyle Carraway, had just enough time to trade his business suit for jeans and a navy sweater, grab some sparkling cider and slide in a smooth jazz CD.

It didn't matter to Vaughn what he wore. He looked good, smelled good and felt good. She took off her coat and threw it on the chair. His eyes twinkled, as he approached his bride. He greeted her with a generous kiss, tender embrace and a sigh of release. His baby was in his arms.

He handed her a drink. "I could get use to this."

"That's the plan. How was your day?"

She thought for a second as he took her empty hand and followed him to the sofa. "Informative. It's true that you learn something new everyday."

Kyle knelt down and removed her black high heel boots. When he finished, he sat next to her. "What did you learn today?"

Vaughn rested her glass on the glass table, hiked up her pencil skirt and straddled her husband. "This."

The quick fluid move knocked the wind out of him. His startled eyes drew out her laughter. Catching her breath, she asked, "Did I frighten you?

He grinned. "A little."

Leaning in, he quickly caught on and nibbled on her neck. "Who taught you this?"

"My Auntie."

"See, I always liked Mother Rose."

Vaughn chuckled.

Kyle tasted the other side of her neck. Vaughn let her head fall back, bidding him complete access. He ran his hands along her sides and eased the long sleeve baby blue tee over her head.

His peaceful touches produced her enthusiastic responses. She took pleasure as he carefully disrobed her, experiencing his tenderness and self-control. She breathed in his ear, "Honey, don't hold back. I won't break."

As time slipped away, their loving became more fervent and when they were complete, they held onto each other, listening to the rushing sound of their rapid heartbeats. They loved it, considered it applause and praise of their union.

304

Vaughn rested her face in the crook of his neck, letting Kyle trail his fingertips over her bareback. Aftershocks and little tremors traveled through her. "Hum, I take it you enjoyed yourself?"

"Enjoy, that doesn't come close to describing this." He let out a deep breath. "If you keep taking lessons from your Aunt, we gonna have a house full of kids."

Vaughn smiled at the thought. "I hope so. I can't wait to have your babies."

Gently, Kyle lifted her chin, admired her radiance from the afterglow of their lovemaking. "I love you so much. Is there another word, other than love, to describe what I feel for you?"

"Kyle..." Her eyes filled with tears.

"Sweetie?"

"No...I'm happy. When we broke off our engagement, I never thought we'd get back together. And now..." Her bottom lip trembled.

He kissed it. "You're my heart, Vaughn."

"And you're mine."

He held her as he felt the tears fall from her cheeks and onto his shoulders. When he felt her stop, he asked, "Hungry?"

"I'm a little thirsty."

"Hold on, I'll get you something cold."

Vaughn rolled onto her back and covered up with the throw. She smiled as Kyle jumped into his jeans. "Yummy."

He lifted his brow. "Ready for round number two?"

"After we talk. I need water."

"Back in a flash." And he was.

She took the glass from him. He sat on the sofa and pulled Vaughn onto his lap. "What do you wanna talk about?"

"Lily and Michael."

Distracted, he said, "I see." He lifted one of her breasts in the palm of his hand, loved the weight, feel and texture of it.

Vaughn pulled the covers up. "Luv, listen."

"That's difficult to do when I'm holding my naked bride."

"I'll get dressed," she suggested.

"Nooooo. Talk fast."

Vaughn smirked. "Alright, alright." Vaughn lifted her arched brow. "Well, what we're doing, Lily and Michael haven't done in six months."

Kyle's eyes widened. He thought for a minute. "They haven't done this, in six months? One hundred and eighty days?" Kyle furrowed his brows. "Whew. That's... that's... what is that?"

"Unhealthy."

"Yeah, that's what that is. Why? What's wrong with Lily?"

Vaughn's voice pitched higher. "Why something gotta be wrong with Lily? It's your brother. Why it always gotta be the woman? Like we don't like sex."

"I just assumed…"

Vaughn rolled her eyes. "You need to talk to your brother. If he ain't eatin' at home, he may be eatin' elsewhere."

Kyle twisted his lips. "You know Michael."

"Do you? Would you have guessed he wasn't taking care of business for *six months*?"

Kyle admitted, "Nah, if I had to look at your fine butt everyday and not touch it, something would be seriously wrong."

"You'll talk to him?"

Kyle thought for a moment and admitted, "We knew something was up, but I don't know where to start with this."

"Call him. Ask him out for lunch tomorrow."

"Now?"

Vaughn let the throw fall away from her. His eyes danced.

"The faster you make the call, the faster you can get back to me."

Kyle leaped up. "Where's my phone?"

"Check your suit jacket."

He ran into their bedroom, yelled, "Ain't nothing gonna be fast about me getting to you!"

Vaughn laughed, but she really did love his skills. Kyle took ample time when they made love to ensure she was completely satisfied, and she did the same.

The couple couldn't seem to get enough of each other. And she didn't want enough, she just wanted more. Vaughn sympathized as she prayed for Lily and Michael.

Your Needs First – Chapter 5

Lily's husband walked into their bedroom at seven-thirty. The daily pattern started to get stale. She'd get home at five, prepare dinner, feed their two-year old, eat, bathe, read him a story and put him to bed. She couldn't remember the last time Michael put Nicholas to bed.

Michael watched Lily read at her desk. She felt him standing there, so she let him say, "Hey," first. She then looked up and observed him tugging at his tie. He looked beat.

"Long day?" she asked, while looking back at her desk.

"Too long."

"Hungry?"

"I ate at work."

"I figured."

"Nicky asleep?"

"Yep."

Michael realized, she spoke with him, but barely looked at him. She traded her usual sleepwear for really short shorts and a T-strap top.

His wife, a firm, shapely size six, was most attractive. Looking at her, he wondered, where the heat was that he felt when Clara touched. Disgusted with himself, he headed for the shower.

He didn't comment on what she wore. It infuriated her. She slammed her hands against the desk, waited for him to shower, and walk back in. Before he slipped into bed, she said, "No more. I can't live like this."

"Lily, not tonight. I can't..."

"You can't? I can't. Just tell me, do you want a divorce?" she shouted, then regretted, hoping she didn't wake their son.

Michael frowned. "Where is this coming from?"

"You haven't touched me in months." She lowered her voice. "Are you having an affair?"

He raised his voice. "Oh God, no! I love you. You know that."

"I do not. You don't want me."

Drained, Michael wanted to tell her everything. She started crying. That was something Michael couldn't stomach. His heart broke when she cried.

He sat on the bed and took a deep breath. "I'm not a machine, Lily."

She whimpered, "What?"

"When we were trying to conceive you wanted sex all the time."

"I *want* a baby with you."

"But you aren't getting pregnant..."

"And?" she asked, impatiently.

"Lily, I'm tired. Don't make me spell it out."

"Since I'm not pregnant, you don't want to have sex?"

"I can't *get* you pregnant." His voice was strained.

"Michael, that's ridiculous. We've been through the tests."

"I don't care what the tests say. I know it's me. Rick didn't have any problem getting you pregnant."

Lily reached over and put her arm around him. He pulled away. "Michael, what can I do?"

He wanted to tell her about Rick, he couldn't. He kept all his recent communication with Rick from Lily. The thought of Rick coming into their life made him sick. Michael pleaded, "Lily, don't leave me."

She blinked as tears fell onto her legs. "I don't want to leave. I'm frustrated. I have…"

He gave a tired laugh, and finished her sentence. "Needs."

Insecure, she looked away. He pulled her face towards him. The gentle touch made her cry harder. Michael stared at her. "Michael, don't you want me?" She lowered her lashes and admitted, "I need you."

He leaned in, and she kissed her lover. The gentle kiss barely started a blaze in Michael, yet, it scorched Lily. She zealously wiggled out of her clothes. Michael whispered, "Baby…wait."

Michael stared into her eyes. Her hunger for him commanded fulfillment. Silently praying for strength, Michael rested Lily onto the bed, hoping he could answer her needs.

Brothers United – Chapter 6

Kyle and Michael checked their coats at the restaurant, and followed the hostess, she told them, "Kara, your server, will be out in a minute. "

Kyle thanked the hostess and took his seat. He saw Michael make a face.

Kyle frowned. "Hey bro, problem?"

"Did she just say, Clara?" he asked, sitting down.

"Kara, I think. Why?"

Shaking his head, Michael said, "No reason." He didn't want to tell his brother how Clara hit on him or how it got his blood flowing. He redirected his thoughts. "How's it going?"

Kyle studied his brother. He was tense. *Poor guy.*

Michael asked, "Well?"

"What?"

"I asked you, how's it going?"

"My mind drifted for a minute. It's going great. Really great!" Kyle lifted his brow and gave a mischievous grin.

Feeling jealous that he hadn't smiled like that in months, Michael said, "I get you."

Yeah, are you getting Lily? Kyle thought.

"Good afternoon, gentlemen. Welcome to Armstead's."

"Good afternoon," The men replied in unison at Kara, their server. Kara, an exotic beauty gave the men her winning smile. She was not the Clara; Michael had in mind. He wouldn't admit it to most, but Kyle knew. Michael was drawn to Latin women. At 16, Michael's first love, Rebecca, was 18, a very experienced Puerto Rican beauty.

Like Rebecca, Kara had that fresh girlish look, pouting red lips and long wavy black hair. Kyle saw the tiny gleam in his brother's eyes. *I oughta punch you in the face.*

Kara said, "I hope you two don't mind me saying, but you both look a lot a like."

"We're twins, fraternal," Michael replied before Kyle could open his mouth.

Kara blurted out, "No! You have to be identical." Eyeing the brothers, she commented, "God, you're both so handsome. I can't tell you apart."

Kyle knew she was laying it on too thick. They did look a lot alike, but not *that* much.

Michael's grin, wide with flattery, explained, "We get that a lot."

Kara nodded, wondering, *What else can I give you other than compliments?* She liked his style. From the cut of his suit, she could see that he had class and money. And since he smiled back as much as she did, she disregarded his wedding band.

Kyle pursed his lips and retorted, "Kara, what are the specials today?"

Focusing most of her attention on Michael, she recited the list, "Salmon in a butter cream sauce, lemon chicken and the crab cakes are really good."

"I bet they are," Michael commented.

"Want to try it? I believe you'll enjoy *them*."

There was a strong undertone in her statement if Kyle ever heard one.

"I'd love to," Michael charmingly agreed.

Kara turned to Kyle. "Sir, how about you? What would you like?"

"I'm a plain ole steak and potatoes man. I take mine well done."

"No red meat for you, huh?"

"None."

Kara folded and retrieved their menus. "It'll be out in a few. Oh, what would you like to drink?"

Kyle answered before Michael could fix his lips, 'We'll have two iced teas with lemon. Thanks, Kara."

Michael's eyes zeroed in on Kara's narrow hips as she twisted away.

"I oughta punch you dead in yo' face," Kyle threatened with clinched lips.

Michael blinked.

Kyle lowered his voice. "You flirtin' with that *girl*, like you ain't got a wife."

Appalled, Michael defended himself, "Please. I was being nice. You know we get that all the time." He tilted his head, waiting for him to concur.

He didn't, but pointed his finger at him. "You tryin' to hit *that*."

Michael leaned back. "Watch it, Kyle."

Pacing himself, Kyle took a sip of his water. If he pushed too hard, he wouldn't get Michael to talk. He backed off, until Kara returned with their drinks.

They thanked her and Kyle watched Michael deliberately keep his eyes downward, away from Kara's booty. *Brother, you're close to the edge.*

"Things OK between you and Lily?"

Michael drank a little of his tea and lied, "Fine."

"You looked at that woman like you used to look at Lily."

Michael didn't comment, believing that was ridiculous. Kyle folded his hands together on top of the table, pleaded with his brother, "Remember when we first got married? We promised that we'd always be straight with one another. I got your back and you have mine."

Michael sighed. "I remember."

"Talk to me." Kyle opened his hands at the invitation.

Michael looked up at the ceiling lights. "I don't know where to start."

"*When* did things start?"

It took some time to pinpoint the origin. Finally Michael answered, "A year ago. Lily stopped taking the pill and we went into baby making mode overdrive." He laid a hand on his chest, feeling a ton of bricks on it, confessed, "And I can't get my wife pregnant..."

Frustration crawled out of Michael. Kyle was thankful for the release. "Go on, Michael."

"We went for all kinds of testing. The doctor said there is no medical reason why we shouldn't be able to get pregnant, but still, no baby. We kept trying though, until about six months ago. That's when I first heard from him."

Kyle looked from side to side, lowered his voice and asked, "Who?"

"Rick."

"Cold blooded, Rick?"

"That's the one. He wants to see Nicholas. Says he's a changed man. That he was grieving when he signed over his parental rights."

"You flicked him off, right?"

Michael laughed. "I'm glad you're on my side."

"And you know that." Kyle looked protectively at his brother.

"He came to see me. Yesterday, he came to my office."

"Son of a biscuit eater."

Michael laughed.

"Remember, Mom used to say that." Kyle looked up as Kara approached the table with their plates. Naturally, she bent a little closer to Michael when she sat his down.

"Can I get you anything else?"

He caught a whiff off her pungent, seducing scent. He knew he shouldn't have, but sweet to him, he inhaled it. "We'll let you know," he replied.

Kyle couldn't believe she had the nerve to bat her long lashes as she told them, "Enjoy," and eased away.

Kyle repeated to Michael, *"We'll let you know?"*

"I meant, if we needed anything." Michael's voice was raised.

"Uh huh." Kyle let out a snort. "Back to Lily. What did she say when you told her about Rick?"

"I haven't."

Annoyed with the responses he had heard from Michael, he demanded, "Bless the food." Michael did, and Kyle lifted his fork and knife. He dug in with hopes of helping Michael fix whatever had broken in him.

Michael lifted his brows with a full mouth. "Um, the crab cakes are good."

Kyle warned; slicing through the tender steak, "You better be careful before you get crabs."

"Funny."

"I'm just sayin' - Mr. *'We'll let you know.'*"

Grateful to talk it out, the frustrated crawl became an easy skip. Michael went on, "When Lily was pregnant with Nicholas; she had these terrible nightmares of Rick taking our baby. She couldn't understand how someone could walk away from a child. I don't know how she's going to take it when I tell her."

"If you want, Vaughn and I can be there."

Michael thought for a moment. "I may ask you to. I think I need someone to be there for me."

Those words touched Kyle. "You got it, man."

Michael shoved more food in his mouth. "This is really good. How's yours?"

"Great. I think you should be the one eating red meat. Maybe your iron is low."

Michael wrinkled his forehead.

Kyle perceived, "You need to get your blood pumping. You know, so you can handle your business."

His blood started pumping real fast. "She didn't."

"Women talk. And you know what my woman is sayin' about me? I'm a real stallion. Yours' is sayin' she can't get you out of the stable."

Huffing, Michael threw his fork down. "This ain't no competition."

"That's a good thing, cuz you'd lose. What's the problem? You got a honey on the side?"

Michael lowered his voice and leaned in. "No!"

"Six months -- no action." Kyle shrugged, thinking, *Come on with it*. Maybe he had pushed too hard. Michael pressed his hands to the table in preparation to stand. "Don't get up Michael." Empathic, he eased his tone. "I'm not making fun of you, but Lily's young, healthy and unhappy."

"I took care of her last night."

Kyle looked him over and blurted out, "You don't look like it. You look, *frustrated*."

Michael slowly repeated, "I said, I took care of her."

Shocked and amazed, Kyle understood and expressed, "This is serious."

Michael put his head down and rubbed his hand over his face. "I don't want to talk about it, Kyle."

"You need to see a doctor," Kyle realized, "you're too young for this." He would not allow Michael to tiptoe around the issue.

"It's not me. I'm just not feeling it with my *wife*."

Holding onto his utensils, Kyle said, "Oh crap! You love her, don't you?"

"With all my heart."

"Then you'll fix this, and fast."

Michael nodded and picked up his fork again.

They sat in silence and finished their meal.

Still Missing – Chapter 7

Vaughn walked in her Aunt's office at church, refreshed from another evening of catching up with her husband.

Mother Rose told Vaughn to meet her there, but she found her brother, Ollie, instead. She lifted her voice. "I didn't know you were here! Give me a hug."

Squeezing his sister tightly, he gave her a bear hug.

"You're crushin' me."

He laughed and let her go.

Vaughn eyed him. His handsome structured face showed off large hazel eyes, full lips and a crooked smile. Growing up, she teased him often, telling him that he looked like the artist, Prince. As he got into his teens, he took it as a compliment as the young ladies began flocking to him. Now she teased him about something else. "As skinny as you are, it's amazing you're so strong."

His deep raspy voice, playful, he joked, "And you're putting on weight. Sign of a content married ole lady." He poked her in the side.

Vaughn dipped a hip to the left and with a hand on her waist, she pointed out, "I haven't gained one pound."

"I'm just teasing. But you do look happy. Sassy looks that way everyday."

Thrilled with her life, Vaughn asked about Ollie's questionable marriage, "How are you and Sassy?"

"You know Sassy."

Vaughn did know her sister-in-law, who also happened to be Kyle's ex-girlfriend. Although the retired exotic dancer was a Christian now, she was still, Sassy.

Ollie and Sassy didn't frequently attend Sunday dinners. Vaughn wondered if it had anything to do with the fact that Kyle and Sassy dated briefly.

Vaughn and Kyle accepted they couldn't change the past and welcomed Sassy into the family. Vaughn had a feeling it was Sassy, not Ollie, that decided to keep distant.

She took the seat in front of her Aunt's desk and Ollie sat in the chair next to her. "So, what cha doin' here?" Vaughn asked.

"Aunt Vie called. She asked me and Sassy to stop by. Sassy's busiest day is Tuesday. She couldn't make it."

"The dance studio is that busy?"

"It's goin' real good. She likes it."

Since they were there, Vaughn seized the moment. "We haven't seen you and Sassy much. Why?"

"We'll be at Sunday dinner."

She nodded then looked behind her when she saw her aunt, uncle and *husband,* walk in. "What's all this?"

Kyle gave her a blank look. He didn't know. He got the call, just as he and Michael were finishing their lunch.

Vaughn asked Kyle, "Lily and Michael alright?"

Pastor Rose spoke, "They're fine. We thought we should talk to you and Ollie first." He looked around and asked, "Where's your wife, Ollie?"

"She couldn't leave work."

"Didn't you tell her I said it was important?" Mother Rose snapped.

Vaughn felt panicked, she shouted, "You didn't tell me it was important! What's the matter?"

Pastor Rose positioned some more chairs around the desk. Kyle sat next to Vaughn. Pastor and Mother Rose remained standing.

Mother Rose took Ollie and Vaughn's hands. "Your mother found out this morning, she has cancer."

Vaughn felt a punch in her belly. Her blood went cold. Kyle took her other hand, squeezed it. Vaughn quietly asked, "Cancer? What kind?"

"Breast cancer. She has more testing scheduled on Friday. After that, we'll know more," Mother Rose answered.

Ollie asked quickly, "She doesn't know how bad it is?"

Mother Rose shook her head no.

Pastor Rose said, "Let's pray." They stayed in their places and he led them, *"Father, God, we need you. Our beloved Flo needs you. Right now God, we know your grace is sufficient for us. Give us a peace that surpasses our understanding. We thank you for this close knit family, our church family and the doctors. We trust you to heal Flo. For by your stripes, we are healed. In Jesus' name we pray, Amen."*

Vaughn's stinging tears fell onto her face. Ollie reached around and held his sister.

Mother Rose knelt in front of them. "I'm leaving Thursday to be with your mother. Do you two want to go?"

Vaughn released Ollie and whimpered, "Yes, of course."

Ollie added, "Yeah, I'm there."

"I'll take care of everything. Vaughn, you can take the rest of the day off, the week if you need it," Mother Rose explained.

"No, no. I don't want to be alone at home. I need to be here," Vaughn realized.

"Sweetie, let's go home. Just for today." Kyle lifted her up out of her chair, guided her.

Vaughn had the expression of a lost little girl. She turned to her aunt and uncle, searching for confirmation.

"Vaughn, it's OK. We'll take care of things here. Someone is already at your desk filling in. Don't worry."

Ollie stood, too. Kyle hugged Ollie and immediately felt a daunting pain in his heart. Kyle lost his mother to breast cancer. It was an awful way to watch his mother die.

Vaughn asked, "You need a ride home, Ollie?" He answered, "I'll be OK. Call me when everything is set."

Feeling the need for air, Ollie rushed for the door.

As she watched her brother walk out, Vaughn angrily lashed out, "Sassy should have been here!"

Out of Place – Chapter 8

Sapphire "Sassy" Sparrow could win an award for the loudest lover. Sassy, her former stage name; was a woman that thrived on playing with fire.

Marcel Reid, her playmate, supplied all the fuel she could burn. He ignited her engine for the second time that afternoon.

The fleshly fire consumed her. In the midst of the flames, she screamed. She screamed for more, and at the same time, for deliverance, knowing she was adultery's most faithful slave. She couldn't stop this. Adultery gripped her flesh with a tightly closed fist. It would not let her go and she could not fight it - not without divine help.

Now deep within the pit, Sapphire screamed again, releasing the smoke from her lungs. With Marcel, she became something she couldn't put a label on. She pushed beyond her limits, feeling the life choke out of her. But fear of death didn't stop her from going back, again and again. She clawed and panted at the height of their time together. "I can't…breath…Oh God!"

Allowing the thrashing flames and smoke to engulf him as well, Marcel drove them to the point of an exhausting demise. When he reached his climatic death, he collapsed onto Sapphire, crushing her with the weight of his body. His broken breath, hot in her ears, repeated familiar praise, "You are so animated. I love making you scream. It is a good thing these walls are soundproof."

The vigorous workout covered them with a sodden perspiration. She held onto his slick back. Her eyes searched the ceiling in hopes that her blurred vision would soon return. She managed to say, "Oh, God. Oh-my-God."

What they did, she could not and would not, call love-making or sex. She dared not use vulgarity to describe it. She considered herself a lady, not a whore.

But whatever it was, it convinced her that their encounters would one day be the end of them. Nothing in her life had ever felt so good. Sapphire risked everything she once believed in to experience it.

Two minutes later, after contemplating their affair, Marcel rolled over and she turned onto her side.

He grinned, nudging her. "Get me a drink, will ya?"

She groaned, "I can't move."

Marcel rolled onto his belly and hugged the pillow. "Come on. I've got to get back to work."

Thirsty too, Sapphire dragged herself across the expansive condo without a garment for cover. The windows were ceiling to floor. There were no window treatments, and being on the forty-nine floor, she doubted there were any peeping Tom's.

She loved the condo. It was their *cave*, as she liked to call it. Marcel bought it a year ago as a way to show her how serious he was about their relationship. It was strategically located between his dentist office and her dance studio.

She downed two glasses of wine before walking back to her lover. She heard him let out a little snore. Sapphire tilted her head and the glass. A few drops of the wine dripped onto his back.

He bolted up, shouted, "What the!"

"Your drink, my lord," she interrupted.

Marcel sat up and snatched the glass out of her hand. The red wine spilled on the white silk sheets. "Look at what you did."

She giggled. "You did that."

Sapphire stood over him and watched him guzzle the cold liquid. When he finished, he confessed, "I love what you're wearing."

She gyrated for him in her birthday suit. "Sassy, we gotta stop. I gotta get back to work."

She kept her groove swaying clearly, captivating him. It pleased her when his eyes glazed over, halfway closed under her seducing charm. He watched Sapphire gently lift her arms and twirl her wrists, making sensual circles using hands and fingers.

316

It was nothing like having a former stripper with a body that made men like him rollover and beg. Marcel had more than his share of one-night stands. Occasionally, he'd return to the scene of the crime a second time, but never a third. However, when he saw the sexy dancer's moves, he knew; he wanted her on a regular basis.

Sapphire had all his favorites, big breasts implants, a round firm backside, thick thighs, connected to shapely sexy legs. Watching her move now, Marcel wanted nothing more than to spend another three hours with her.

She whispered, "Let's take a shower."

Practically drooling, he admitted, "If I shower with you, I'll never make it back to work." And remembering his four o'clock oral surgery, he sighed, stood up, and shoved the empty glass in her hand. "Step aside, woman."

Sapphire obeyed, and opened her arms with a bow. "Your majesty."

Marcel began walking toward the shower, without looking back, he demanded, "Get your Sassy self in here."

Sapphire giggled again, running after him.

They were both late for work by the time they got out of the shower and started dressing.

Sapphire glared at her vibrating cell phone on the nightstand. Marcel said, "He's blowing up your phone. If it's important, you need to call him back. You don't, he'll get suspicious."

She blew him a kiss and slipped into her underwear. "Marcel, I know how to handle my husband. You're not the only cheatin' spouse here."

Marcel buttoned up his shirt. "We've been doing this a year now, and my wife has no clue. You, on the other hand, have come close to getting caught. I'm not trying to break up my happy home."

Sapphire sat at the beautiful gold and white vanity table Marcel had custom built for her. She started applying her make-up and laughed. "Happy. Yeah right. That's why we're here at least once a week."

He rolled his eyes then gave her the finger.

She hated when he was vulgar, and then, she loved it. She let him know; "Oh yeah, and last week when I cancelled, I thought I heard you crying."

Marcel sucked his teeth.

"Admit it, Marcel, you love me, even though you left me for dead."

Marcel thought back to the night when they began their relationship three years ago. She was brutally beaten at a gig she was working. Lily-livered, Marcel panicked and left her to die.

After her recovery, Marcel chased Sapphire for two years. It took a lot of pleading and lavish gifts, but, he finally wrestled her into bed, and away, from her newly formed relationship with Christ.

Now he admired her as she expertly applied make-up to her already seducing eyes and stunningly high cheekbones, while wearing nothing but the new lace underwear he bought her. But loved her? Certain he did not, he put it bluntly; "You know what I love about you."

"I know. I know," she whispered as she moved onto her hair, fluffed out her weave. But Sapphire understood he was just as much a slave to their relationship as she was.

She turned to look at him, saw him completely dressed – impeccably, in his designer suit. He had butternut brown skin and a young looking face, innocent dark eyes – almost boyish. But there was nothing boyish about his body. He wasn't overly built, or extremely tall, but chiseled lean muscle lingered under the suit.

"Don't worry about the sheets. The cleaning service will take care of it. See you next week?" he said, starting for the door.

He never kissed her goodbye, or called her endearing names - their experiences, raw. Yes, he bought her gifts, but then, he also dictated his desires, directing what he wanted, and how he wanted it. And she pleased him.

Again, the question of being a whore pricked at her.

"Maybe, maybe not," she answered her thoughts, rather than his invitation to see him next week. *Maybe I've become something that I had no respect for.*

He knew she belonged to him. Marcel shouted over his shoulder, "You'll be here."

She watched the doorway until she heard the front door slam. Sapphire looked at her wedding rings, and thought about the oath she made to her husband and her God years ago. She groaned as she picked up her cell phone and called Ollie back.

Yes, she knew; next week Tuesday, when adultery knocked, she'd answer the call - with pleasure. Marcel Reid wasn't the only one getting what he wanted.